*To L
Keep climb.!
Howard*

Climbing the Rain

a novel

Howard Cincotta

Copyright © 2015 Howard Cincotta
www.howardcincotta.com

Auto-da-Fe Press

All rights reserved.

ISBN-13:978-1516961832
ISBN-10: 1516961838

For Debby, of course

CLIMBING THE RAIN

CONTENTS

LIST OF CHARACTERS vii

PROLOGUE: EËLIOS 1

PART I: FALLING 2
   1 THE DROP 2
   2 MR TIRUN PAYS A VISIT 7
   3 TUNDRA 17
   4 LIZARD PEOPLE 22
   5 FOG 27
   6 MUSGRAVE'S DANCE 32
   7 MISSION STATEMENT 36

PART II: FLOATING 44
   8 RUNNING THE WHITEBONE 44
   9 CAUGHT IN THE KEEPER 49
   10 PORTAGES 54
   11 THE DRONES 60
   12 CHAEBOLS AND TRIADS 70
   13 FISHING FOR CYCLOPS 81
   14 THE ABYSS 87
   15 KYTE'S FLIGHT 92
   16 THE MOUTH OF KRONOS 96

PART III: CLIMBING 102
   17 BLACKBONE SWAMP 102
   18 LARGE CHARISMATIC FAUNA 107
   19 BLUE BOY 112
   20 WOMAN IN GREEN 118
   21 SPEAKING IN TONGUES 123
   22 ANCHORWOOD 130
   23 LIGHT GAPS 138

PART IV: BALANCING 147
   24 NAUSICCA'S FEAST 147

   25 GUELPH AND GHIBELLINE 154
   26 FREELANCING 161
   27 JKH2 169
   28 THROUGH THE LOOKING GLASS... 176
   29 SYLLA'S CHANT 182
   30 WILD BAMBOO 189
   31 HOSTAGES 196
   32 OSSUARY 201
PART V: BURNING 207
   33 GHIBELLINE GAMBIT 207
   34 THE GINN'S SECRET 217
   35 THE NEGOTIATOR 227
   36 RONIN PLANET 234
   37 BURNING BRIDGES 240
   38 SPINNERETS 247
   39 IN THE HEART OF THE WOOD 253
   40 LEYDEN'S CHOICE 263
   41 EËLIAN EYES 271
   42 DRAGONMASTER 277
   43 CASUALTY COUNT 287
   44 ARAMANTHIAN WINE 293
   45 TEA FOR THREE 301
EPILOGUE: RETURN 308

LIST OF CHARACTERS

Eëlios Biological Mission
    Leyden – negotiator
    Hawkwood – Illium League officer
    Tirun – mission leader
    Trans-Illium representatives – Verlaine, Mkeki
    An San Kee – exobiologist
    Planetary bioteam – Modrescu, Ka-Sung, Carpentier, Cabenza, Bois
    Mercenaries – Chácon, Suslov, Tranner, Ehrenburg, Zia, Holmes
    Biochemists – Chapandagura, Bertelsmann
    al-Saqua – physician

Eëlians
    Sylla – healer and guide
    Nausicca – Sylla's cousin
    Cleanth – Guelph leader
    Nouvé – Cleanth's chief of staff
    Shinsato – Ghibelline leader
    Ulam – Illium traveler

Braga – rival mercenary

PROLOGUE: EËLIOS

Scattered and solitary, the Eëlios grew at a remarkable height, where the sheltering canopy of the rainforest finally broke open to the sky and the light of two suns.

The Eëlios only germinated among the branches of certain lianas, attaching itself to their coarse bark, digging its rootlets into the fragmentary humus carried aloft by the planet's air currents. The Eëlios possessed large quadrilateral leaves that served as excellent collectors of rain. Small white flowers bloomed regularly, and the the plant relied on the wind — not seed-eating glowbirds nor the planet's varied insect species — to distribute its pollen.

Nevertheless, the Eëlios's rarity, together with its identification as the planet's highest flowering plant, had transformed it into an object of veneration for generations. So each year, despite the danger, the peoples of the Eëlian rainforest suspended their animosities for the ceremonial climb to search out the upper reaches of the canopy and harvest the Eëlios.

This rite culminated in the ritual grinding of the leaves into an aromatic tea, each cup garnished with a single pale, floating blossom, and drunk while the old songs were sung again, accompanied by traditional lyres and drums.

Not surprisingly, then, the Eëlios gave its name to the entire planet.

Now, however, the sky would open once more, and off-worlders would descend again, eager to explore the planet's surfeit of green life. And to possess its most precious secret — isolated and remote — blowing in the high wet winds of the planet Eëlios.

PART I: FALLING

1 THE DROP

The pod skipped into the atmosphere like a flat stone thrown over still water, and layers of ceramic-alloy skin blackened and sloughed off in ragged gouts of flame.

Inside, held in an envelope of fire, Leyden could only grip the anchor posts of his gravity couch. A sudden burst of heat caused him to wheeze and fumble for the venting switch on his carapace. With the entire pod swallowed in the ruin of burning alloy, the view panel displayed a bank of gray-black smoke, punctuated by pieces of incandescent pod skin ripping off and disappearing. The sound was like a wildfire chewing through bone-dry timber.

As the entry pressures squeezed his chest, Leyden momentarily wondered if anyone on his home planet of Toranga would recognize him now, with years of exile and months of prison etched in a face once characteristically smiling and confident. He had long since cut short his mane of pale brown hair, although his dark eyes remained unchanged. Folded uncomfortably into the pod, he felt overweight and out of shape, a fact reinforced by the restraint harness cutting into his stomach.

Leyden coughed and cursed. Illium warriors and mercenaries — the young, the restless, the stupid — dropped in flaming pods onto unknown worlds, not him. He belonged on the lightship *FS Balliol*, waiting for the burn through the portal back to the Illium Core Worlds, where fusion shuttles or sky hooks handled civilized planet falls. Instead, he faced the risk of burning to death in the thick atmosphere of a planet that, until three months ago, had been seen as nothing more than an abandoned outpost.

The pod jolted again. For a moment, Leyden saw himself descending in a flaming chrysalis, emerging not as a butterfly, but as some kind of scarred horror show. He counted at least seven layers that had already burned off in the atmosphere; the pod had a total of twelve. Ironically, these layers constituted the pod's most elaborate and expensive feature, especially in these second-hand models.

Cheap and expendable, space-planet transition pods like these had no real instrumentation to speak of: the designers assumed that in a hard planetary drop, most occupants had little pilot's training and needed to focus on other matters. The builders claimed that they could be reused: pour new ceramic layers over the football-shaped skeleton, reinstall the retractable wings, and the pod could be dropped again. But increasingly, few missions bothered to haul them back — one less thing to gather up in planetary withdrawals.

As a result, salvagers collected pods from a dozen worlds and dominated the market with cheap refurbished models. One industrial-grade chip to handle basic readouts and communications, crude instrumentation for altitude and speed, a simple control stick, and a perfunctory gravity couch to absorb the atmospheric shock.

Leyden wished he had a combat pod with skins that burned down to a layer of armor — a vehicle invulnerable to almost any explosive smaller than a Dragon-class railgun. But those features made them tremendously expensive and out of the question for any except military or large chaebol-run missions.

Disoriented, still trying to count the skins as they burned away, Leyden could feel the heat filling the capsule and jamming the NavCom with static. Under his helmet, his eyes stung from the salt of his sweat.

Leyden blinked at the console displays of speed, altitude, and temperature; they held little significance for him, so he activated the Voice Supplemental, a phlegmatic computer voice known universally as The Tongue.

"Altitude eight thousand klicks," said The Tongue. "Optimal descent. Thirty-five percent shield use." *Good.* That sounded about right. Leyden had avoided many of the sessions on pod operations aboard the *Balliol*. Neither mercenary nor mission specialist, he had not involved himself in the interminable round of shipboard briefings. Only the reading materials and VR simulations of Eëlios had held his fitful attention. Let Tirun, the mission leader, and Hawkwood, head of security forces, worry about the technicalities.

By five kilometers above the surface, the heat and buffeting began to ease, replaced by the thin whistle of the upper reaches of the atmosphere. Leyden tried to wipe some of the interior moisture from the inside of the view panel. A pale wall seemed to be turning over his head, and it took a minute to understand that he was seeing the planet's upper cloud layer as his pod revolved slowly end over end.

The NavCom on his chest snapped to life. "All personnel, acknowledge." Tirun sounded uncharacteristically curt. Leyden thumbed his chest unit and sent back a short buzz identifying himself. Tirun had made it clear that he wanted no conversation whatsoever during the drop unless someone was in serious trouble.

"Stand by," came the clipped response.

Leyden watched the sky float languidly over his head, unable to see anything of the planet's surface, only the indigo demarcation between the upper atmosphere and a lower-altitude bank of featureless clouds. As he watched, at least two other pods swam into view, also spinning, blackened, and trailing plumes of gray smoke before veering out of sight.

Tirun's voice emerged from the NavCom. "Prepare to deploy wings and activate LZ beacon. On my mark."

At least this phase had seemed clear enough in the simulations. The screen, a rudimentary grid of the horizon and planet surface, displayed a glide path to the landing zone already marked by an earlier probe. "Don't steer out of the window," Tirun had lectured mission amateurs like Leyden. "Use the control stick to follow the glide path. Like a kid's virtual reality game, only dumber and duller."

"Mark," came the command. "Release wings. LZ on."

Leyden hit the release, and the pod's twin stubby wings slammed into position. He felt the pod's motion stabilize and tested the feel and resistance of the control stick. The pod was at least moving in something resembling a glide and not simply tumbling downward.

He flipped the LZ indicator, and the screen glowed with lines displaying surface, horizon, and relative position. But no glide path. Frowning, Leyden flicked the screen off and on again. Nothing. They had rehearsed several emergency scenarios through which Leyden had basically sleepwalked. If they got into serious trouble during the drop, he figured he would simply die. Leyden saw no reason to learn techniques for surviving in a pod that actually tore open, nor to figure out how to navigate planetfall with dead instruments.

That was then; this was now. Death was no longer abstract, but a screen display without a glide path. Leyden hit The Tongue. "Altitude is 2.3 klicks. Maintain glide path." Leyden squinted again at the meaningless console displays and hit the select button, trying to remember exactly what information Tirun had said you could squeeze out of the pods. "Glide path not achieved," said The Tongue noncommittally. "Confirm your altitude and relative position."

With a traditional curse suggesting that The Tongue's tongue should rot from syphilitic disease and fall out, Leyden hit the button again for the landing site. "LZ not acquired. Establish course now, using glide path indicator."

They should be virtually on top of the landing zone. If the instrumentation malfunctioned, he should be seeing warning lights from the display panel and hearing more from The Tongue. Leyden started to thumb the NavCom when the channels filled with queries to Tirun from at least three other pods. One he recognized as Bertelsmann, mission biochemist; the other two voices belonged to mercenaries, Zia and Chácon. A second wave of communications crowded onto the channel from other pods. He wasn't alone; Leyden felt a bubble of momentarily relief.

A new voice cut in on override: flat, precise. Hawkwood. "Cut the chatter. It does appear we have been dropped out of beacon range. Either that or we have a probe malfunction."

Unlikely. They had had confirmation of a successful probe landing before they dropped, along with deployment of a mapsat with hundreds of sensors enveloping the planet in geosynchronous orbit. All standard procedure. Even Leyden knew that. A static-filled interval while Hawkwood and Tirun undoubtedly talked on a secure channel.

Hawkwood returned. "Set your screen headings for one-zero-eight degrees, your control sticks in the shallow dive position. Stand by for further instructions."

They're lost too, Leyden thought; his bubble of relief evaporated. He looked at his console, wondering where to punch in the heading.

Then the wind hit. As the pod flipped in the blast, Leyden slammed against his harness restraints, the wings useless. The pod rolled a hundred eighty degrees and he caught a glimpse of a cluster of lights hanging in the black curtain of space, but he had no time to decide whether he had glimpsed neighborhood stars or the departing shuttle vehicle.

Grunting with effort, he pulled back hard on the control stick, but to no effect. The pod rolled another half circle and he was again looking at the onrushing cloud bank. He began to tumble once more.

The NavCom channels burst into life with voices full of curses and the first edges of panic. Despite the necessity of deploying pods for a planet without landing facilities, Tirun and Verlaine had repeatedly assured Leyden and the other mission civilians that the drop would be routine and uneventful.

Tirun apparently hit some kind of override, cutting off the chorus. "Hold course one-zero-eight as best you can. One-zero-eight. Landing area is a north quadrant plain along riv. . ." His voice abruptly ceased. Leyden hit the NavCom several times futilely; again he could hear anxious queries from other pods, rising and then fading amid the wind gusts and bursts of electrical activity.

North? The drop zone was near the equator and the rainforest. What the hell were they doing north?

Leyden pulled the stick back hard with both hands to the position for level flight. His trumbling slowed, but the sky still flickered through the view panel like a video on fast forward.

Somewhere below he glimpsed the flash of an electrical storm, presumably over the northern plain. Leyden had no idea how far they were from their intended landing. An intense wave of nausea gripped him; he flipped up his helmet and vomited on his feet.

The pod descended into a thick gray cloud and Leyden heard the sudden high-velocity spatter of rain against the smoking exterior. The air grew denser, the wind lessened, and the control stick began responding to the increased air resistance, the wings again functioning. He pulled back and the tumbling slowly stopped. He centered the stick on shallow dive and checked the screen for his position.

The rain battered the pod; he could see nothing. The console still held no glide path, but he watched the blip of his pod drop toward the spreading virtual grid that represented the planet's surface.

Final phase, he managed to remember, pull up to allow the wings maximum drag. A light blinked on. Deploy chutes.

Leyden felt the satisfying lurch of the parachutes pulling free, then a ripping sound. After a frozen nauseated moment, he knew that the powerful northern wind had ripped the lightweight chutes into useless ribbons. The pod tipped wildly out of control again, and Leyden flailed with the stick.

The clouds tore open, and Leyden had a momentary vision of a flat dark landscape braided with pale streams, rushing up hard and fast to meet him.

2 MR TIRUN PAYS A VISIT

Seven months before the launch of the Eëlios Biological Mission, Leyden passed his days in prison.

The Freehold Reform Facility on Rigel Prime represented a triumph of efficiency and utilitarianism. Above ground, a complex of square-jawed buildings, faced in Rigel's ubiquitous gray-green granite, clung to the mountain ridges; below, a winding series of stone-walled cells occupying what once had been some of the earliest mines on the planet.

A thousand cybermoles still chewed out the rich veins of ore that had first brought it prosperity, but Rigel Prime's true wealth resided in its easy access to the core planets of the Illium Archipelago, a fact that Rigelians had shrewdly exploited to become its principal financial hub. Their financial acumen allowed Rigelians to underwrite activities legal and otherwise and to amass the wealth sufficient to construct the Illium's most renowned leisure world, the orbiting ocean resort known as Poseidon.

For Leyden and the other prisoners in Rigel Prime's eastern quadrant, Poseidon existed only as a blurry, blue-green sphere hovering just above the horizon. On most days, the winds blasted the mountainside prison with bits of granular rock that bit into their faces and arms, often drawing blood, and the prisoners remained below ground to contemplate their granite-lined futures. But in the evenings, the wind subsided, and the prisoners emerged, blinking in the fading light. At those times, Leyden could watch for Poseidon and scan the alien star clusters, pretending he could see the unimaginable distances to his home on Toranga and to the Illium worlds he had traveled to reach this ignominious conclusion.

◆

In his distracted, painfully distant childhood on Toranga, Leyden, like virtually every sentient human of his time, had learned the tales of the Illium — of its discovery, the First Illium War, and its exploration by the legendary Anton Kirov.

When Earth astronomers first detected a singularity within an outer area of their solar system known as the Oort Cloud, they quickly realized that they had discovered a remarkably small region where the rules of space-time physics did not seem to apply — a window into the uncoiling of multidimensional superstrings whose existence had only been theorized, never witnessed. But probes and even an early space station — conducted by an ad hoc organization with the clumsy name of International League for the Investigation of Unknown Space-Time Matters — ILIUSTM — brought only frustration; one scientist compared studying the singularity to tracking a water molecule inside a hurricane.

The first breakthrough came with development of a nanotech technology that permitted construction of a massively parallel computer network using advanced ceramic materials. The network, unconstrained by gravity, expanded into a sprawling hemisphere around the singularity, whose vast energy fluxes and massive data flows interacted with the nanotech structure and caused it to proliferate wildly. As it grew, the network became increasingly autonomous, fusing in obscure ways with the singularity itself. Whether you called the new object that emerged a machine or something else, scientists and cult worshipers alike gave it the same name: the Illium.

When Earth authorities attempted to cut funding for what they regarded as a dangerously out-of-control enterprise, the newly formed Illium League found private corporate backing and declared its independence. The League not only defeated a military expedition from Earth and seized full control of the singularity, but also produced the Illium's first great figure, Anton Kirov.

Kirov's later exploits constituted the great founding myth of the Illium. In a series of pioneering voyages, he discerned how to navigate the Illium's enigmatic data streams, establishing that the singularity could function, however unpredictably, as a portal to a steadily increasing number of inhabitable worlds, each linked to other Illium worlds, each with its own portal, although the cycle times among planets could range from days to decades. In the era that followed, this collection of inhabited worlds, connected by their own singularities, now known simply as portals, evolved into the Illium Archipelago.

Most worlds acquiesced to the Illium League's control over the portals; a few such as Toranga, did not. Leyden, like many of his generation, embraced the cause of Toranguin freedom — or more precisely, Toranga's claim to control its own access to the Illium. But the revolt failed, and Leyden escaped with his life and little else.

With the help of a few friends, he bribed his way aboard an Ozumian freighter traveling to the arctic world of Umlivik Four, then to the sea-island planet of Arishima. Several Illium-standard months later, he talked his way aboard a Betelgeuse lightship that burned through to the Illium frontier planet of Delium-Ghahan, which had a cycle of roughly five standard years to the major core worlds of the Illium, like Rigel Prime.

With its relative isolation, Delium-Ghahan knew little and cared less about conflicts in the core. Undisturbed and unquestioned, Leyden spent the cycle recovering from the physical and psychic dislocations of multiple burns through the Illium. He also met several business acquaintances and casual lovers — often both — who were intrigued by his checkered past and his ideas for making outsized profits in Illium trade.

At the opening of its next cycle, Leyden, traveling under an alias, left Delium-Ghahan with licenses for trading monopolies in some of its potentially most saleable products: pottery from a distinctive marbled clay, frozen embryos of several species of native birds and feral cats with potential to become the latest in fashionable pets, and a mining concession for an enormous reserve of titanium sands.

But the jewel in the crown was wine. Delium-Ghahan possessed a large region of temperate, rolling foothills where small vintners produced boutique wines that caused connoisseurs to melt into puddles of rapture: complex, full-bodied reds suffused with alien smoke and woods, fruits and soils; crystalline whites, dry yet laced with delicate berry undertones. Unfortunately, the lightships from Delium-Ghahan transported only a few hundred cases, and their scarcity triggered intense speculation and soaring prices. When he left, Leyden held export permits for three of the planet's largest and most popular wine labels.

Leyden's ship burned through the portal to Illium League Center, a complex of wheeling artificial worlds and spaceports in the Ozumian system, its principal recruiting ground. There, Leyden, in his guise as a Delium-Ghahan merchant, bought a landing permit and spent the last of his credits to buy passage aboard the Rigelian lightship *Illium Anvil*.

Once on Rigel Prime, Leyden found himself in a race between his dwindling supply of money and efforts to register and finance DG Futures Unlimited. Predictably, Delium-Ghahan's marbled pottery and exotic animals drew only mild interest. The titanium concession held huge potential for enterprises with vast fleets of robot freighters, but would require formidable up-front investments.

The wine, however, proved to be a sensation. DG Future's initial stock offering soared and kept climbing, accelerated by a substantial advertising outlay and a lavish series of receptions and parties where Leyden served virtually all the remaining wine stock he had brought with him.

Living in a fashionable section of Rigel Prime's capital, Freehold, Leyden joined the party circuit and invested in high-yield securities and complex derivatives. He soon accumulated enough capital to finance the ultimate vacation: Poseidon, where he met Irina-Nakamoro on a wall dive down a spectacular coral reef. On their next descent together, they floated into a dim underwater grotto, twenty meters below the surface, enclosed in the vivid colors of coral species from ten worlds. Leyden stripped away her translucent bathing suit as they twisted slowly in a curtain of bubbles. Later, on a vast bed in one of Poseidon's most select resorts, the two of them continued their lovemaking by using the virtual wall panels to simulate the colors of the reef's lower depths.

Irina-Nakamoro, the daughter of one of Rigel Prime's most successful investment bankers and divorced from another, offered Leyden entry into some of most rarified circles on the planet. Within a month, they announced plans to be married.

Leyden then simply waited for his ship to come in. Life become one vast, golden bubble, which burst when the cycle to Delium Ghahan opened and the first lightship expeditions returned. They indeed brought out huge consignments of wine; but by then the authorities had revoked Leyden's exclusive licenses, and opened the dealerships for competitive bidding. Stock in DG Futures crashed, and Leyden found himself cash-poor, with most of his money locked into highly speculative financial instruments without any ready buyers. DG Futures disintegrated in a welter of stock-owner suits, bankruptcy filings, and finally criminal proceedings, charging fraud and violation of Rigelian securities laws.

But none of these unpleasant matters placed Leyden in prison: Irina-Nakamoro saw to that.

◆

Leyden had been reviewing yet another legal brief, this one suing a consortium of Delium-Ghahan wineries, listening to the muffled yowl and thump of the wind, when the guard appeared to announce a visitor. He didn't recognize the name — probably someone else eager to carve off a chunk from the DG Future's still-warm carcass.

CLIMBING THE RAIN

The man in the interview room filled the doorway, with a torso like a tree trunk, and an untended red beard, heavily streaked with gray, and cold blue eyes.

"Leyden," he said in an emphatic tone. extending a hand with fingers as thick and coarse as Arashimian sea rope. "My name is Tirun and I'm here to discuss your future."

Leyden blinked. "I'm sorry?"

"I'm here to save your ass and offer you a future far away from here."

The two of them stared at each other. Finally, Leyden said, "I think I need my lawyer here before we go any further."

Tirun laughed. "The *last* person you need is your lawyer."

Leyden contemplated Tirun for a moment, then gestured for him to sit.

"I have been hired by a firm called Trans-Illium to lead an expedition to a planet in the Selucid Swarm," Tirun said. "Eëlios. Way the hell from the major clusters, which means extra slowtime travel. Main reason it hasn't had a lot of attention. Quite remarkable rainforest. . . perhaps you have heard of it?"

Leyden shook his head no. But as he talked, Leyden realized that he had heard of Tirun himself.

"No matter," Tirun continued. "Point is, Trans-Illium has the League license for the upcoming cycle. So we've put together an expedition — researchers, specialists, some company flunkies, security team. We'll drop to the surface, conduct surveys, collect samples, and return. All with the cooperation of the Eëlian population, I might add."

Security team, licensed mercenaries. . . Tirun, Leyden thought. Of course. The Viking, they called him, veteran of more than twenty planetary drops, one of an elite group of mercenaries hired to lead expeditions to new or remote sectors of the Illium. He had achieved this status by bringing most of his people out alive, and making the companies that hired him very rich.

On one level, little that Tirun said surprised Leyden. Armies of licensed mercenaries were ubiquitous on most of the larger Illium planets. To travel through the Illium portals, nevertheless, required daunting resources, even for relatively wealthy worlds such as Rigel Prime, Arishima, The Cold Moons, and, before its revolt, Toranga. The Illium League collected fees and tolls to maintain and protect the portal Matrices that enclosed the singularities at their center.

But the League took no responsibility for interstellar commerce or law and order within any planetary system. After an early period of anarchy and outright piracy, Illium worlds began issuing letters of marque to the chaebols — corporate conglomerates with the resources and economic motivation to launch high-risk expeditions and maintain regular travel throughout the Illium. These authorization letters, once approved by the Illium League, permitted chaebol expeditions to arm their ships and hire mercenary forces to protect their interests and investment, a mandate that sometimes extended to assaults against the assets of other corporations — provided they were selective and did not threaten any assets of the Illium League itself.

"I appreciate the offer," Leyden said carefully, "but my immediate future seems to be right here, at least until I get a hearing."

Tirun glanced at a crumpled printout from his pocket and grunted to himself. "Illegal diversion of funds, three counts. Embezzlement, two counts. Perjury, two counts."

"Lies, fabrications, bullshit. . . false evidence," Leyden said. "All those counts. Not a single action there that Rigelian companies don't engage in every day."

"And the perjury?"

"I simply didn't remember how the accounts had been structured. I wasn't the damn accountant."

Tirun shook his head. "Then there are the civil suits and bankruptcy claims and counter-suits. Almost too numerous to mention."

Leyden felt his voice rising in spite of himself. "Look, are you from a reenactment service or something? Maybe you should talk with my solicitor. I'll be happy to give you his address. The simple fact is that an Illium investment went sour. There are always big risks, big returns. . . that's what built this place. Besides, I have strong claims against the Delium-Ghahan vineyards, and when those are settled. . ."

"A planet whose cycle closed a while back and won't reopen for another standard year," Tirun said. "At which time, the plaintiffs will file their responses and counter-claims. And you get to wait out another cycle before you're even on the docket for a second hearing. What do you figure, four, five cycles before you even get into a real courtroom?"

"My solicitor is a little more optimistic than that," said Leyden. "Besides, I wasn't aware that I had much choice in the matter."

"You do now!" Tirun roared. "You do now! You can rot in this mineshaft they call a prison, or you can join me in exploring a chunk of the universe!"

Leyden was taken aback. The frontier days of the Illium Archipelago were long past — no one talked like this anymore.

"Why me?" he said.

Tirun leaned forward. "We've been very low key about our operation, but the fact is Trans-Illium has assembled one of the most capable and skilled teams of biologists and biochemists from across the Illium. Plus a security unit I picked personally. With an Illium League officer. What I *don't* have is a skilled negotiator. We have a signed and registered agreement with the Eëlians to conduct an expedition, ask questions, gather samples, analyze what we find. That's all. What we need to settle are rights and licenses to the products... the research spinoffs... the stuff of new technology, new products."

"And you want a minor official from a defeated planet, who's in prison on fraud charges?"

"But available," Tirun added quickly. "Available. And in his time, one of the most skillful negotiators Illium-wide, certainly on Toranga."

"Until I was, shall we say, overtaken by events," Leyden concluded.

"As you say."

Leyden thought for a moment. "Let me see if I understand. Trans-Illium has sent you here, to Rigel Prime, to try and recruit me. What are you going to do, organize a breakout, or just bribe the guards?"

Tirun smiled. "Not the guards. The government."

Leyden stared. "You're not serious."

"Absolutely," said Tirun, unable to hide his satisfaction at seeing Leyden's complete bewilderment. "You know why you're under arrest as well as I do. It has nothing to do with finances and fraud charges. Litigation is probably second only to banking and entertainment as a source of wealth and entertainment here. I'll bet every successful broker and investment officer on Rigel Prime has faced charges just like your own."

Leyden said, "You might say I share that view."

"Except for one thing," Tirun said, now leaning close to Leyden's face, beard actually brushing his nose. "Irina-Nakamoro. When DG Futures collapsed, the tabloid services all got photos and detailed accounts of your affair with... what's her name... the dancer from Patpong Row?"

"Tersis."

"Tersis," said Tirun. "Was that a stage name or a real name? Never mind. So there you are, two-for-two, the leading business news story, *and* the hottest tab story around, screwing a stripper at the same time you're engaged to one of the best-known women on the planet.... By the way, how *did* they get that vid?"

"No idea. You know, I don't need this," said Leyden, beginning to stand up.

With unexpected swiftness, Tirun reached out with a huge furred arm and forced Leyden back into the chair. "Oh yes you do. Because you haven't thought through what happened here, have you?" He stared at him.

"Maybe you're not the right one. Maybe all your political skills have deserted you after all."

"That could well be."

Tirun shook his massive head. "I mean, here you are, fighting with a bunch of squint-eyed, tight-assed Rigelian bankers over financial gimmicks like quantos and fourth-generation dynamic derivatives, whatever the hell that is. This from the man who once wrote the Toranguin Manifesto: 'The sacred territory of Toranga runs from its seas to its singularity. It is a fabric of time and space and land and water that are one and inseparable.'

"A little over the top, but *that's* the man I want to cut a highly profitable deal for us on Eëlios. Someone who can negotiate hard but also give the Eëlians a vision of what the future can hold for them if they become connected to the right Illium organizations. I *don't* want the man so caught up on making a killing on Illium futures that he can't see what's happening around him."

"Meaning what?" Leyden twisted with frustration in his seat, remembering the shock of the first wave of news reports. "As for Tersis, Patpong Row is off limits to everyone — tabs, virtual-reality news, the sims. Those are the rules here, everyone knows that."

"You're right. Absolutely right. Which means someone went to a lot of trouble, paid off a lot of people."

"I'm not following," said Leyden. "Are you saying Tersis was a set-up?"

"Of course she was!" Tirun roared again, the guard at the end of the interview room looking up finally from his monitor. "Where's your head? Look, you were a minor celebrity because of your engagement to Irina-Nakamoro. But otherwise, what the hell were you? Just another entrepreneur with a speculative Illium stock. This place crawls with thousands like you. Yet long before the DG Futures crash, someone went to the trouble of arranging for you to meet Tersis, someone who knew your weakness for women all too well. And offered enough money for the tabs to break their own rules and pursue a target into Patpong. Who goes to all that trouble? I'll give you a hint — it wasn't Irina."

Leyden breathed hard and stared at his prison footwear. "The Illium League government on Toranga."

"Target lock!" Tirun shouted, slapping his knee with satisfaction. The guard stared at Tirun with open curiosity. "What did you think? That they'd forgive and forget? Toranguin agents have been watching you ever since you arrived. Your new identity fooled no one. All they had to do was wait. And you were easy, so easy. They recruited Tersis, paid off the tabs, collected their vid coverage and waited. The collapse of DG Futures was just a bonus. Whether Irina wanted you in prison doesn't really matter.

You'd humiliated one of the most powerful families on Rigel Prime. Payback's a bitch."

"And now?"

"We've negotiated with the government and with Irina. For a price, everyone would like to see you go. You're an inconvenience now. The government would settle a messy civil case, Irina-Nakamoro and her family would get rid of an embarrassment. We've offered a settlement of your civil suits in return for the dropping all perjury and embezzlement charges."

"What kind of settlement?" Leyden asked.

"Drop your countersuits. Sign over all claims, licenses, investments and interests in DG Futures to the Rigel Prime Magistrate's Court. In addition, transfer all outside investments, cash accounts, and other financial instruments — on Rigel or off-planet — to Nakamoro Holdings. In return, you leave with me."

"What cost?"

"We estimate close to a quarter-million Illium talons to settle all the claims."

"Very generous of you. And what do you get out of this besides my services on Eëlios?"

"Trans-Illium will receive the rights to one of Delium Ghahan's better wine labels. If the sales projections hold, we'll recoup our investment in about ten standard years."

"*My* licenses, my marketing rights," Leyden muttered almost to himself.

"That's the deal."

"What's my deal with the Eëlios mission?"

"Standard mission fee," Tirun said briskly. "Fifty thousand talons upon successful completion, as certified by me."

"Come on. Prize money? Same cut as your mercs?"

Tirun laughed. "Not quite. But I am authorized to offer one percent of profit after costs and interest."

"One percent of *net*?" Now it was Leyden's turn to laugh. Calculating the costs of moving goods and people through the Illium required such fabulously complex calculations that companies almost never declared net profits on their enterprises. "One percent of gross."

"Not a chance," said Tirun, standing up. "And I'm afraid you're in no position to negotiate the matter." He loomed over Leyden, massive as a Toranguin wind oak.

Leyden stood as well, looking into his bearded, blazing face, eyes the intensity of dwarf blue suns. "Yes. All right."

"Excellent," say Tirun. "You'll be hearing from me very soon." They grasped right hands, placed their left hands on top and gave a ceremonial shake.

As Tirun turned to leave, Leyden said, "You know, I still think you're wrong about Tersis. I went to Patpong Row because it seemed the traditional pastime of successful Rigelian entrepreneurs. I found her, not the other way around."

Tirun paused, waiting for the guard, and looked back. "I know. You seem to have that illusion about all your women."

3 TUNDRA

Leyden could hear the sound of dripping, but whether water or blood, he couldn't tell.

In the pod's enclosed darkness, Leyden tried to move but couldn't; he felt immobilized and had no idea why. The side of his face seemed numb, his mouth frozen, and pressure on his chest made him wheeze. Twisting to the side only caused a shooting pain along his left side and the feeling of something tightening around his throat and choking him.

Alive, he thought. I am in pain, therefore I am. But whether living was preferable to the alternative seemed an open question at the moment.

Leyden tried his right arm. Yes, it felt relatively free. He touched the side of his face. Bad news: a strap cut into his throat and his nose seemed puffy and warm with blood, which he could now hear dripping onto the floor as steadily as a metronome. His eyes adjusted enough to see dimly.

The pod had hit and rolled upon landing, ending upside down. He hung from the harness, straps tight across his throat, chest and tangled in his legs. Twisting slightly to his right, Leyden began to sway slightly. As his eyes continued to adjust, he registered that he was looking down on the ceiling of the pod, the gravity couch behind him, anchoring his harness. Just above his head, he could see the control panel smeared with blood. Descent pods weren't equipped with air bags.

Get the hell out. He felt himself beginning to get faint from the pressure on his neck and the steady rivulet of blood from his nose. Leyden kicked his feet and managed to bang into one of them into the side of the pod, and starting swinging toward the control panel. On his third pass, he caught a panel edge and reached for the hatch release. He heard a muffled sound as the explosive bolts fired below him. The pod jolted, then nothing. He swung motionless for a moment, and realized that, of course, the top of the pod with the hatch was buried in the muck. The pod had a smaller escape hatch at the rear, which had to be opened manually. So instead of death by fire, he thought, I'll just swing here until I strangle. Instead of screaming as I burn to death, just die feeling stupid and looking ridiculous.

Another sound penetrated his consciousness. Leyden held his breath and listened: the dance of wind and rain against the pod, a chill, solitary sound made colder by the thought that they prepared exclusively for a mission to a place of constant heat and humidity.

Leyden tried vainly to wipe the blood from his swelling nose. His face throbbed. *Think.* He needed his backpack and kit, officially known as an ISSU — Individual Survival and Sustenance Unit — and usually pronounced as a mock sneeze. When he twisted hard to his right, pain hummed from his hip through the top of his head. He found the ISSU latched to the wall of the pod just in front of him. Feeling mildly foolish, he fumbled for a multi-blade, multi-function implement known as a Swiss for reasons that no one could explain.

Leyden sliced through the strap across his throat, then cut the tangle around his legs, feet dropping to the grounded ceiling of the pod. Eyes closed, he took several deep breaths without any sharp pain: no smashed ribs. Okay, this is better, he thought, die on my feet, even live a little longer.

Crouching in the dark confines of the pod, Leyden reached again for the ISSU, found the medpak, and pulled out antibacterial gel, packed wadding into his nose and crunched several painkillers. What else? he thought, checking the rack beside the ISSU: NavCom, translucent sleeping pouch, disposable filtration kits, extra food packets and a small pulse rifle wrapped just as it had been issued. Hawkwood had given the weapons orientation to most of the civilians, but Leyden hadn't had the slightest intention of enduring his instruction on any subject, especially weapons training.

The exit hatch jammed when he tested it. *Of course.* By now Leyden didn't expect even the simplest actions to be easy. Squinting in the dim light, he examined the Swiss again. Along with its blades, it had a set of complex tools, which latched into multiple positions to deploy ratchets, drill bits, odd-shaped edges, and a laser for cutting metal. He had no idea how to activate the thing. *Hell with it.* He stuffed it back into his pack and kicked at the emergency handle.

To his surprise, it moved. He kicked it again and the hatch popped ajar. Only at the last moment, just before he stepped out, did Leyden remember to seal his gloves, to pull the molded hood and transparent face mask over his head, and attach the micro-mesh respirator installed on the left shoulder of his carapace. He winced from the pain of the face mask pressing against his swollen nose and battered head. Humans could breath the oxygen-rich Eëlian atmosphere; the planet's microbes presented a far more uncertain threat. The rule remained: as close to zero direct contact with an alien environment as possible.

Leyden pushed his way out and stood. He felt an initial stab of disappointment: this is it? He had traveled a distance that had no conventional means of measurement, and dropped in fear and flames from the sky. And at the end of this experience, he found only a horizon bounded by fog, an uninteresting green plain spread across a wet treeless expanse, several small streams tangled in the distance, and a featureless sky filled with rain blurring his face mask.

His feet sank slightly into the saturated ground as he turned around; and then, without warning, the utter strangeness of the place engulfed him as thoroughly as if he had stepped into an ocean and sank to the bottom. Nothing had changed, no new sights except the sopping tundra, no sounds except the sigh and pull of mist-laden wind. Yet his vision suddenly snapped into focus and everything transformed.

The grasses stretched away at his feet in long, low runs of hexagonal leaves, pale green with white veins, punctuated every few meters by mounds covered with thorny plants that held bluish flowers, thick and curled against a heavy center stalk. The mounds themselves seemed to quake with the consistency of thick soup. When Leyden tested one of them with his feet, he sank up to his knee before pulling his leg back, his carapace black with mud. The only movement came from the streams, an intense silver color flickering against the muted tones of the tundra.

A peculiar blood-orange color suffused the clouded sky, the product, no doubt, of Eëlios's two suns. He noticed a smell: faint but so powerfully evocative that Leyden stopped and closed his eyes. He knew this odor: not from any outside field, but indoors, a house. His house. Leyden took a deep breath. Yes, the muffled smell of almonds from the kitchen of a distant childhood. He reached down and carefully plucked and crushed one of the pale grasses underfoot, but it was odorless, and there seemed no other obvious source of the almond smell.

Something disturbed the sky: a dark, flat shape that appeared below the cloud layer, circled for a few moments, then spiraled back up and disappeared. Only after it was gone did Leyden remember that he had high-rez, wide-spectrum glasses hanging from his belt along with a medpak, water container, and utility knife.

As he stared into the clouds, Leyden realized another reason for the strangeness of this place. Whether pale grasses, quaking bogs, or the spiraling shape in the sky, he had no names. With labels, perhaps, he could extract the alien quality that pervaded everything. But to do that, he needed others, those who lived here and could name the names that belonged to this new world.

Leyden climbed on top of the burned hulk of his pod. With his glasses in wide-vision mode, he turned slowly, twice, surveying the landscape. Nothing: no pods, no telltale white parachute patches, no movement of figures along the horizon. The NavCom emitted only random bursts of static. He was the sole inhabitant of a newborn world.

Closing his eyes, Leyden breathed deeply again: unmistakably almonds roasting, the dry, crumbling taste of almond biscotti. *How strange.*

He opened his eyes to contemplate his choices. He could head south, toward their original target, the Eëlian rainforest. Leyden turned one more three-hundred-sixty-degree circle with his glasses. The rainforest no longer offered a realistic goal: the distance too great, the mission a fiasco before it had begun. The only conceivable objective now could be to collect the survivors, set up an encampment, and wait out the time until the pick-up. And ensure that that total mission failure didn't scuttle his deal with Tirun and Trans-Illium and land him back in prison.

Leyden had been in the next-to-last set of pods. Assuming they all caught the same polar currents, they would have scattered roughly along a single wind-borne line. So keeping the wind to his back should give him the best chance of finding someone else from the expedition.

Leyden tried to recall his desultory review of the books and holos about Eëlios aboard the *Balliol.* For the most part, he remembered the discussion of the constant, intense radiation from Eëlios's suns, and their role in sustaining the densest known rainforest ecosystem in the Illium Archipelago. Of air currents and meteorology, he recalled nothing. But then, unlike the others, he hadn't been hired for any scientific, technical, or military-security skills.

Leyden shoved his glasses back onto his belt. Screw the wind currents, he thought. Better to move on than stay here and start hallucinating from hypothermia and isolation.

ISSU secured, Leyden took a final look at the remains of his pod and started walking, wind at his back, rainwater dripping off his carapace. Under the face mask, his packed nose throbbed in rhythm with the rasp of the respirator.

As he headed toward the nearest stream, feet sinking audibly into the gray, colorless earth, Leyden felt an odd, momentary bubble of comfort. He had, in fact, been here before. Not on this planet, but in this circumstance, following an inevitable path that led from hope to confusion and pain. It was the arc of his adult life. So he shouldn't be surprised now that the expedition to the Illium Frontier, which had promised escape and profit, had ended with him alone and lost in this uncelebrated place.

4 LIZARD PEOPLE

Thirty Illium-standard hours before the drop to Eëlios, the expedition assembled in the storage bay of the Flameship *Balliol's* Planetary Shuttle Vehicle. They were all encased in mottled green carapaces, which made them look as though they had just been removed from a defective plastic mold.

Each carapace, an extruded ceramic composite, had been fused into pebbled pliable fabric as durable as it was unattractive. From the neck down, the mission team resembled a congregation of large, two-legged lizards.

Such carapaces, or second skins, were standard protection against the biological hazards of an unknown planet. Off-worlders had no natural immunities against a new world's viruses or bacteria; no medicines, reagents or balms against poisonous plants or chemically toxic soils; or more rarely, no ability to discern the abilities and appetites of any large mobile life forms.

Tirun stood before them, huge, beard flame red in the harsh light, thick arms resting on a rack of Mutiphase Combat Weapons. In his own creaking carapace, he seemed more massive than usual, slumped under the low ceiling, scanning the mission team squeezed uncomfortably around a coil of polymer communications/computer units, air and water filtration systems, racks of food concentrates, mobile science and medical labs, and a disassembled surveillance drone. Standard package for a planetary drop. Hatches at their feet, along the corridor, marked the row of tubes converted from launching missiles and space mines to manned pods.

"In a few hours, we will launch the Eëlios Biological Mission," he said in a deep, building rumble. "It's been short notice for some of you, but we have trained hard and well, and I have no doubt of our success. We've traveled here to conduct what I believe to be one of the most important survey missions in the lifetime of many of us. And what we find here may well change life for millions living on the Illium Worlds."

Tirun leaned forward, hands gripping the exposed ceiling tubing over his head. "So much for the *official* reasons," he roared. "What's *really* happening is that, in a few hours, we man the oars and row to the shore of a new land. Whatever our personal reasons for being here — knowledge, fame, wealth, curiosity — we are truly explorers—Ulysses, Magellan, Cook, Kirov, and the Nova Prince."

He paused and stared at them: some sitting on pallets, most standing. Leyden scratched at the unfamiliar closure of the carapace around his neck. My god, he thought, everything they said about this guy is true.

In certain sophisticated circles, Tirun's generation of larger-than-life figures threatened to become caricatures of themselves. Certainly, some of the stories surrounding Tirun strained credulity: marrying the three daughters of the ruler of the Betelgeuse system to conclude a trade treaty; bringing a team out alive after crossing five hundred kilometers of arctic wilderness on Umlivik Four; ending a civil war on the Tsang Asteroidal Complex (which threatened a lucrative mining operation) in an individual stalking duel with pulse weapons.

But a decade had passed since the Viking's glory years, Leyden reminded himself. Now gray streaked the signature beard, the face eroded from the wind and suns of a dozen worlds, his movements hinting of retirement rust. Not for the first time, Leyden wondered just why Tirun had signed up for a routine biological survey, much less gone to the trouble of springing him from prison.

"You may be feeling tired or fearful," Tirun said, his voice falling as though sharing a confidence. "That's expected. But remember, we are a spacefaring species, and we were made for this. I can think of no better place and time to be than here, with you, in the moments before planetfall."

Tirun lifted his massive arms from the rack and turned palms toward them, as if in a benediction. "And when the history of this place is written, or sung, or celebrated, they will tell of these explorations, and, for better or worse, they will name our names and tell what we found here, and what we did." Another pause. "And what could be a better way to live than that?"

Leyden looked around at the assembled company, the colors and shapes of a handful of worlds, some staring at Tirun as though moved by what he had said, most expressionless. Tirun had probably given this speech twenty or more times in the hours before planetfall. But Leyden wondered how many of expedition members actually bought into it. Certainly not Tribune

Hawkwood, whose allegiance was to another organization and a different purpose. And probably not the veteran mercs — Chácon and Tranner — who had served on dozens of chaebol missions and commanded top payments for their services. But for the newer ones, Tirun remained a near-legend to whom they looked not just for leadership, but as a role model, however much they might laugh behind his back about overblown speeches.

Leyden knew the mercenaries least well, all of whom seemed to be tattooed in an inverse ratio to their age and experience. Chácon, square as a block of stone, seemed to have limited himself to an elaborate Arishima sea serpent coiled around a massive arm and shoulder. The other veteran, Tranner, a native of the Trapezium system who carried only minor ritual scarring around on his cheeks, stooped slightly from a great height, with the longest arms and saddest eyes Leyden had ever seen. The younger mercs like Ehrenburg and Zia from Ozumé, and Holmes from Rigel Prime, had the latest in holographic tattoos that appeared to writhe off their chests and arms.

But Tirun, Leyden realized, wasn't looking at the mercs, but at the civilian contingent. For many of them, this would be their first hard drop. And, in fact, they did look tired and anxious, hanging on Tirun's words. He might be an object of amusement among certain sophisticated circles in the Illium core, say around drinks on the Poseidon ocean resort. But now, in these wrenching preparatory moments before planetfall, his words felt quite different.

Leyden surveyed them. An San Kee, the coolly competent and striking exobotonist, and her planetary bioteam: Ka-Sung, Carpentier, and Modrescu. The meteorologist, Cabenza; Bois, planetary geologist; Bertelsmann and Chapandagura, biochemists; al-Saqua, physician; and Mkeki and Verlaine, representatives for Trans-Illium Enterprises. Only Ulam, a native of Eëlios, remained in his quarters, as he had throughout the trip. Another merc, Suslov, seemed to have disappeared.

Tirun straightened up as best he could, head grazing the overhead tubing. "Remember, you're a team. Stay together, help each other, stay focused on the mission, ask when you don't understand, but follow orders." He looked around. "Last questions?"

"Uh, just one. Why exactly are we here again?" came a voice from the back. A small wave of laughter. Verlaine, who, no doubt under orders from the home office, seemed to have taken on the role of morale officer.

Tirun nodded slightly in his direction. "*You're* here to see that we behave and that Trans-Illium makes a fair return on its investment. *We're* here to astound the Illium with our discoveries, make our names and our fortunes."

That caused a perceptible stir. The mercs, at least, appreciated a straightforward acknowledgment of what they were about. After all, Tirun, with fortune and reputation presumably secure, was simply one of the more celebrated and successful of their numbers.

"Nothing more? Good luck to you all. See you soon on the surface. Mr. Hawkwood?"

A figure who had been sitting back in the shadows on a storage crate stood. Leyden watched him carefully as he stepped forward, appearing almost slight next to Tirun's bulk. The featureless but distinctively gray carapace, a combat version of the units worn by everyone else, identified him as an Illium League officer, Tribune rank. Warrior and sworn defender of the Illium Archipelago. His dark skin and sharp, angular features gave him a gaunt, predatory look, the calm but intent expression of a raptor quietly determining the most efficient way to dispatch and consume its prey. Unless you noted that expression, however, or knew anything about his career, he probably would merit little more than a wary glance anywhere in the Illium.

"The PSV will disengage from the *FS Balliol* at eight prime, in approximately one standard hour," he said in a quiet voice that caused everyone to strain slightly to hear. "That's the time we have to complete all packing and stowage. You will then all enter the pods and be gassed for a sleep cycle of about three hours. During that time, we will launch both the mapsat and LZ probe. You will awaken for final systems checkout and launch."

He waited for questions, then continued. "The drops will be in sets of five," he continued. "Two or three individuals, and two or three equipment pods in each. I will be in the first set, Mission Leader Tirun in the last. At least one member of the security team will be in each set. Your places in the drop sequences will be on your screens when you enter the pods. You've all been through the simulations and practice runs, you're prepared and ready. Any questions?"

Yes, Leyden thought. Any chance I can destroy your life as thoroughly as you destroyed mine?

Zia, one of the junior mercenaries, raised his hand. Hawkwood nodded. "How old, exactly, is the information about Eëlios that we're working with?" Spoken by someone who had spent more time in martial arts simulations and weapons training than in reviewing the Eëlian briefing materials.

"Eëlios orbits in one of the more remote sectors of the Selucid Swarm," Hawkwood answered. "So even though the Selucids open to the Illium core every four years, expeditions to Eëlios have been relatively infrequent. The last mission was two cycles, or roughly eight standard years ago. With our interplanetary travel from the portal to Eëlios, the remaining aperture time for us to complete our mission and return to the portal is little more than three standard months. That's when the *Balliol* returns for the pickup after its other drop, on the Remora mining colony. In other words, the clock is running."

"No new information, no updates, since that time."

"None," Hawkwood answered. "Remember, there is no connection, no communication between burn cycles. During that period, it's as though this sector never existed. Just as it is in the core. But you tend to forget that, because the Core Worlds cycle so quickly. Anything else?"

"Is the reason for such a large security team?" asked Modrescu, a largely silent, almost sullen presence. "Because of what might have changed on Eëlios in eight years? I mean, do Illium officers like yourself usually accompany a strictly scientific mission like this?"

For the tiniest of instances, Leyden sensed Hawkwood pause, as though he might pass the question to Tirun. But he didn't.

"The answer to your second question is, not always, but sometimes," Hawkwood said. "And to your first question, yes. On some worlds, eight years can be a long time. On others, hardly time to breathe."

5 FOG

After an hour's trek across unbroken tundra, Leyden spotted another pod, marked by the shredded ribbons of its parachute, sodden and flapping in the wind.

He tried the NavCom, as he had every fifteen minutes. No response. Even its GPS didn't function, although identifying his exact location meant relatively little at the moment.

In spite of his vow to pace himself, conserve energy, Leyden found himself beginning to stride, then jog toward the pod, his breath rasping hard in his ears. As he drew closer, a worm of dread twisted in his gut. The pod had landed almost identically to Leyden's own, except with the hatch skyward, skin blackened and torn, a ragged, water-filled gouge showed where it had crashed and tumbled, one end buried in a small hillock of thorn-infested plants.

But something felt wrong as he approached — a body slumped against the side of the pod. Leyden stopped and caught his breath before he wiped his face mask and squatted, carapace joints squeaking. Dead surprised eyes stared up at the rain, respirator torn away, mask dangling against his shoulder.

It took Leyden a moment to recognize the face — Cabenza, the expedition meteorologist and climatologist. A quick, nervous man with the typically freckled face of a native of Tarn — a dry, cold planet whose lack of weather produced a remarkable number of professional meteorologists. For Leyden, Cabenza had been merely a face in the crowd aboard the *Balliol*, someone who gave briefings to the expedition on the Eëlian weather patterns that Leyden had dozed through or skipped entirely.

As a formality, Leyden placed a gloved hand on the man's face. Cabenza was very wet and quite dead.

Leyden climbed up on the pod and peered through the hatch: blood smears inside the opening and on the console, the floor of the pod already filling with rainwater. It appeared that Cabenza had been injured on landing, barely managed to open the hatch, and collapsed. Leyden jumped down. He should at least try to bury him.

Dropping his ISSU to the ground, he extracted the closest thing to a shovel from his Swiss and looked for place to dig. Then he noticed the footprints: faint, water-filled and leading away from the pod and back again. Cabenza had apparently hiked away from the pod, looking for help, then returned.

Leyden studied Cabenza's dead dripping face. In his pain, perhaps, he had torn off his mask and respirator, and unprotected from the Eëlian environment, quickly succumbed to a fast-acting virus or microbe. The thought chilled Leyden more deeply than the cold rain: the carapace and mask served as precautions against insidious, slow-acting diseases. Pumped full of a pharmacopeia of serums and antibodies aboard the *Balliol*, the expedition members operated on the assumption that they were resistant to 99 percent of disease-bearing organisms. The environmental carapaces defended against the remaining one percent.

Leyden continued to stare at Cabenza's slumped body. No one had ever suggested that, within minutes or hours, merely breathing the unfiltered air of Eëlios could be fatal.

He dug. The ground had the consistency of pudding, and the trench almost immediately filled with water. By the end, he bailed more than dug, finally giving up and leaving the grave partially filled with water. Leyden reached under Cabenza's rigid shoulders and dragged him away from the pod. For a moment Leyden debated whether to remove his carapace, but decided it would take too long to extricate him. Leyden replaced Cabenza's molded face mask and slid him, half floating, into the grave.

A marker, he thought, just before he started to cover the body — if they did manage to return for him. He surveyed the treeless expanse for Cabenza's ISSU, then climbed up again to look inside the pod. He could find neither his ISSU nor his pulse rifle. Leyden jumped down, puzzled. Cabenza must have dropped them on his hike away from the pod. He traced the footsteps, but they disappeared within twenty meters into yet another flat stream.

Stop, he said to himself, you don't have time for this. Cabenza got hurt, tried to get away, lost his equipment somewhere, returned and died. Cover him up and move on.

Then he remembered the blood. Cabenza's face had no obvious cuts, and Leyden hadn't noticed where his carapace has been pierced or damaged. Yet the interior of the pod had blood smeared everywhere. Leyden waded into the shallow grave, water up to his knees, and straddled Cabenza's floating body. He found the seal at the side of the neck and pulled it open down to the armpit.

Blood filled the body suit. Cabenza's throat had been cut.

◆

The storm rolled in from the planet's southwest, preceded by a blaze of silent silver light that flamed beyond the cloud bank like the reflections of a distant space battle. The wind increased, driving the rain horizontally across the unprotected landscape and reducing visibility to a few spattered meters. Twice, Leyden blundered into a soupy bog that swallowed him up to his thighs, and he struggled for several exhausting minutes to free himself from the black mud. Finally, on a rare patch of firm gravel next to a wide-bottom stream, he deployed his sleeping hutch. After sealing the outer flaps, he stripped off pieces of his carapace in the outer chamber, crawled through to the inner section and collapsed into sleep.

Leyden awoke to silence, and to a world so disorienting that at first he thought he must still be in his pod, still dropping through Eëlios's atmosphere. The landscape had disappeared as thoroughly as if it had been erased, and it only after he had rolled to his knees that he realized he was looking out at the thickest fog he had ever experienced.

Leyden pressed his face against the translucent fabric of his hutch; he could barely make out a few wet, beaten leaves less than twenty centimeters away. Otherwise, the fog appeared impenetrable. Sitting back against his pack, Leyden closed his eyes. Impossible to travel now, he thought. Stay here and rest. If he couldn't move, presumably no one else could either, and anyone ahead of him would remain in place as well.

Then he remembered Cabenza: how he had hurriedly covered him up and marked the spot with a piece of tubing pulled from the storage rack inside the pod.

Only after he had left the pod behind did he even allow himself to consider the implications about how Cabenza had died.

There were only two realistic possibilities. With no knife at hand, Cabenza certainly hadn't killed himself. That left only an attack by Eëlian natives, or by one of the expedition members. Eëlians from the rainforest traveled through these regions, he knew, but the distance and difficulty made it a rare event. The more likely and unpleasant prospect was that someone on the expedition had murdered Cabenza.

As to a possible motive, he couldn't even begin to speculate. Quite deliberately, Leyden had remained as distant from everyone on the expedition as possible, with one exception. Only Verlaine had made an effort to win his confidence. But as a Trans-Illium representative, his job mandated knowing as much as possible about everyone.

Leyden had confided nothing of importance to Verlaine; besides, the larger failures of his past, leading to his imprisonment on Rigel Prime, were quite public.

Leyden pondered the congealed fog. Now he wished he had paid more attention the other mission members, since one of them apparently was a murderer.

After trying the NavCom several times, Leyden rehydrated some HiCarb rations, ate, and dozed.

The light changed. With two suns, Eëlios never experienced true darkness, even at these sub-arctic latitudes. The story of the suns, he recalled, formed one of the Eëlian creation stories, typically full of violence, deceit, and patricide. The suns, called The Ginn, killed their father, the sky, at the instigation of their mother, the earth. He didn't remember the details, but it had sounded like standard fare for founding myths.

If the light had shifted, the fog had not. He could no longer afford to wait for the weather to change. Somehow, Leyden couldn't imagine Tirun or Hawkwood sitting out this fog for more than an Eëlian day. And presumably Cabenza's murderer, native or not, remained on the move as well. He stood, stooped in the confines of his hutch and stretched, muscle sore, face still tender, and changed the blood-soaked packing in his nose. Even traveling blind, he should be able to make some progress by following the many streams, whose sound of falling water would presumably would give him a warning before he walked blindly off a cliff.

For the next hours, Leyden walked in a world stripped to only a few elements. He felt like a flatland creature confined to the two dimensions of length and width. Splashing through the pools at the edge of the stream, Leyden lost any sense of distance and direction. The numbers on his NavCom appeared arbitrary, but at least their indicators showed him following the rough path of a small stream. Moisture beaded on his face mask, and the fog continued to hold him in a tight grip. Branches along the embankment slapped him hard on the helmet as he strode, head down, watching his feet. If he looked upward, he found himself peering into a bright nothingness that seemed more absolute than a black starless night.

Leyden didn't notice the fog relenting until he heard the first sound of rushing water. For the first time, he could see midway into the stream. Still, the fog lifted with painful slowness as Leyden dropped to one knee and waited; ten minutes passed before it had thinned enough for him to see the stream dropping away in a long series of shallow, rock-choked falls.

Halfway down, pushing through a patch of resistant thorn bushes, Leyden stopped again. The fog had dispersed enough so that he could see the stream sink into a marshy valley where it met another water course, darker, deeper, moving swiftly.

Leyden could also see the ruins.

Several utilitarian-looking buildings were strewn alongside the confluence of the two streams, roofs open to the sky, sides collapsed. A larger structure stood next to an overgrown field that might once have been a tarmac.

A bulky figure encased in mottled green paced slowly among the fallen walls.

6 MUSGRAVE'S DANCE

Amid the ruins, the survivors waited out their stunned reunion.

Their losses, human and material, accumulated slowly. When Leyden arrived, he found the mercenary Holmes, along with biochemist Bertelsmann and company representative Verlaine. Hawkwood and two other mercs, Tranner and Zia, had arrived first, then left to search for others.

A standard hour later, Tirun appeared at the head of a column, following the same stream as Leyden down to the ruins. His group found an equipment drone whose wings had apparently failed to deploy. The pod that carried the team's disassembled drone had buried itself full force into the earth.

Leyden reported Cabenza's death but said nothing of the circumstances.

After he had rested and eaten, Leyden offered to join a search party. Tirun, grim-face, at first refused, then relented and sent him out with Tranner and Verlaine to bring back the contents of a nearby supply pod that had landed intact. Among other items, it held the Rendezvous Dome, a collapsible, airtight structure with medical, decontamination, hygiene, and sleeping compartments; it also held a space large enough for the entire mission to shed their carapaces and gather in one place.

After they erected the dome, Leyden walked the perimeter of the ruins. Overhead, the fog-bound sky darkened and flushed red: one sun of Eëlios was rising, the other setting — the planet's closest intimation of night at this latitude.

The walls appeared beaten from eons of fog and wind. The ubiquitous thorn bushes pierced the remnants of a wide tarmac; at its center, a small control tower slumped with abandonment, one side already collapsed. Rows of broken stone traced the former walls of warehouses and other service buildings. Nearby, a blackened circle marked a campfire of more recent origin. Perhaps Eëlian nomads had stopped for the night here on hunting expeditions, their fires lighting structures whose builders and purpose they had long forgotten.

Leyden tried to estimate when the buildings had last been used: fifty Illium standard years ago, perhaps closer to a hundred? Without a measure of the rate at which the northern latitudes chewed away the face of its human monuments, it was impossible to say. Still, he could see that it had once been a helio or shuttle port of some kind, probably for local planetary travel, since it seemed to lack any blast pits or superstructures associated with orbital launches.

Leyden squatted down so that the rubble of an ancient masonry wall blocked his view of the Rendezvous Dome, and tried to reassemble the pieces of Eëlios's past from his desultory research aboard the *Balliol*.

Following settlement of the first core worlds, early Illium explorers burned through to the Selucid Swarm, discovering eighteen habitable planets in a system with hundreds of planetary-size bodies — one of the greatest concentrations of liveable planets outside of the Rigel system. Eëlios, however, orbited in a remote sector of the Selucid system, requiring almost another year of interplanetary travel from the Selucid's portal site. Only the remote mining and research colony of Remora required greater travel time.

As a result, the Selucid Swarm remained a relative backwater and Eëlios an isolated outpost, especially with the evolution of the core worlds, where burn cycles shrank to weeks and days, so that travel between planets such as Rigel, Toranga and Arishima began to resemble shuttle flights, albeit with a measure of psychological trauma always associated with portal travel. As a result, Eëlios and Remora were abandoned for more than half a century.

Leyden reached down and picked up a chunk of wall that crumbled easily in his gloved hands. He wished he knew the weathering properties of the building material. Could this outpost have deteriorated to this extent in only fifty years? He shivered in the beat of the constant wind and wet, despite his carapace. His nose itched, cheek throbbed, and he tried in vain to scratch them both through his rain-streaked face mask. Somehow, the shapes, the dimensions of the stone remnants seemed wrong, as did the size of the tarmac, the angles of the slumping control tower. No, he thought, not wrong so much as very old, far more ancient than the summary history he had learned aboard the *Balliol*. The walls resembled ruins that had fought the wind and fog for centuries, not decades, perhaps back to a time of the earliest outward migrations through the portals — to the fabled era of Anton Kirov and the first plunge into Illium space.

◆

Inside the Rendezvous Dome, Leyden shed his carapace and joined the others in the slow process of decontamination, showers, scheduled injections, debriefings, and fresh clothes. He sat against a power pole, watching the blood-tinted fog through one of the Dome's transparent panels, when Verlaine walked over and silently handed Leyden a Toranguin apple. Hard and nut-brown, it tasted pungent and redolent of home.

"Thanks," said Leyden. "Wasn't aware these were authorized mission food."

"They're not," Verlaine answered, chewing his own. "But, hey, live on the edge, eat an apple. Now a peach — that might be too much."

"Or drop onto the wrong side of a planet?"

"Certainly one possibility," Verlaine said.

Leyden looked him over. Verlaine — thin, quick moving — wore clothes in the authoritative dark tones of his employer. As he talked, his face remained deadpan, eyes revealing nothing, his words squirting out of the side of his mouth like an act of ventriloquism. Leyden could easily imagine him maneuvering through the cool networks of power at Trans-Illium, carefully selecting the words to advance a position, skewer a foe.

Leyden pointed to a building barely visible through the fog. "This place seems old to me, very old. Where the hell are we?"

"Musgrave's Dance."

"What?"

"Not kidding," said Verlaine, pulling out a small flat-screen handheld from an inside pocket. One of the few late-model pieces of equipment that Leyden had seen anywhere on the expedition. "Look."

Verlaine punched in a set of coordinates, and Leyden watched an orbiting image of Eëlios zoom in on a chunk of the northern hemisphere spidery with rivers and widely spaced place names. The screen dissolved and leapt inward, displaying their river junction and location, complete with a rough grid map of walls and control tower.

"Musgrave's Dance," he said, pointing to a scroll line at the bottom of the screen. "Served as a shuttle port on Eëlios before it was deserted."

Leyden leaned back and swallowed the remains of the apple. "Still, an odd name."

"The survey information lines up pretty well with the oral traditions here on Eëlios," Verlaine said, punching through several more data levels before closing up the unit.

"There's little question that this is where the first flight landed. Every clan on the planet, wherever they are, knows about this place. And they all refer to it as Musgrave's Dance or Musgrave's Landing or Musgrave something. Named for the mission leader, an officer named Derek Musgrave."

"And the dance?"

Verlaine said, "The Eëlios tales imply that the landing was particularly difficult. Maybe their lightship was damaged in the burn. Hard to say. But Musgrave and most of the company must have made it, because they celebrated here for several days. Dancing, feasting, screwing, whatever. Right here. Became the planet's main port for awhile before most of the population moved to the rainforest. Abandoned over the years as they let go of most of the high tech stuff. Like a lot of the early frontier worlds. Still, should be designated some kind of historic landmark, don't you think?"

"They danced, we count casualties. Progress." Leyden glanced at Verlaine. "I don't remember any of this in the briefings we had on the *Balliol*."

"You weren't exactly teacher's pet, as I recall," Verlaine answered. "But no, you wouldn't have found most of this stuff without specific data requests."

Verlaine remained expressionless. "Since we weren't supposed to land anywhere near this location, it was considered irrelevant to the mission. Rule one for a happy relationship — I know more than you do."

Leyden said nothing.

"Look, we're not exactly here for the same reasons, are we?" Verlaine said. "You got your ass out of prison to join our merry band. I work for a company that's already spent billions for this mission — and had me preparing for the last three years."

Leyden shrugged. "Point taken."

7 MISSION STATEMENT

In the next hour, the last of the search teams returned, carapaces black with rain.

They totaled the losses: One dead, Cabenza, and one missing, Suslov. They had lost one supply pod whose wings had failed to deploy. Another had disappeared completely, presumably blown into Eëlios's arctic regions.

Inside the Rendezvous Dome, they gathered before Tirun in a grim semi-circle, scientists and specialists to the right, mercenary security team to the left. Hawkwood stood to the side, apart from everyone. Typical League posture, Leyden thought, aloof from all the quarrelsome, grasping Illium worlders.

Tirun began. "We'll begin with a moment of silence for Mission Specialist Cabenza. We remain confident that Security Team Member Suslov will rejoin us soon."

Leyden could feel his head throbbing; it was almost impossible to imagine that Suslov could be gone. And then he had another thought: presumably Cabenza's killer stood among them, too, head bowed in mourning.

After several moments of silence, Tirun, arms akimbo, continued. "I spoke before the drop, aboard the *Balliol*, that future generations would name our names and tell our stories. With what we already have experienced, no statement could be truer. Short of combat, I can recall few drops as difficult as this one. That responsibility is mine, and it is mine as well to find answers to *why* this happened. For now it is time to regroup, recover, and move forward."

Tirun's voice rose, his graying beard seeming to bristle and revive with life in response to its owner's words.

"In a moment, I will ask Ulam, who is returning to his home on Eëlios after many long years, to explain something about the terrain from here to our original landing zone. But first, I want to stress that, just as we have overcome the drop, we can overcome the challenges still before us."

He paused. "Now, any questions before we go on?"

At that instant, like a blow to the stomach, Leyden realized that all his assumptions since his landing were wrong. Tirun had no intention of waiting out the time until the *Balliol* returned. Despite their landing fiasco, he intended to continue to their original destination.

Leyden looked around quickly and saw the same realization flooding through the mission. The faces of several of the civilian mission specialists looked especially blank with shock. Even the younger mercs, like Ehrenburg, appeared as though they had shared Leyden's assumption. The exceptions were the corporate reps, Verlaine, whispering to Mkeki; bioteam leader An San Kee, meditative, rocking slightly back and forth; and the senior mercenaries, Tranner and Chácon.

Hawkwood remained stoic and unreadable, but Leyden had no doubt that, if necessary, he would sacrifice the entire team to continue the mission. In the account books of the Illium League, only success mattered.

He waited for the inevitable chorus of protests. The civilians, at least, had signed up for a scientific survey, not for the hardships and dangers that now seemed more associated with a planetary invasion than a research mission. The Illium League, in fact, actively discouraged the former; they tolerated the latter only so long as it remained confined to licensed mercenaries.

No one spoke, and to his surprise, Leyden found himself on his feet, in a role from his former political life, like putting on an old coat.

"Why?" he said flatly. "Why are we going on as though we can continue the mission as planned? We're thousands of kilometers from where we should be. Two dead, one missing. Equipment gone, destroyed. Maybe we should face the fact that the mission has been too compromised to continue. Maybe we should just sit tight here and wait it out until the *Balliol* returns. Or limit the teams that we send from here."

Several of the mission members turned slightly toward him in relief and puzzlement: relief that he was articulating what some of them felt, puzzled because he had previously held himself so far apart from the group. Undoubtedly, they had also heard the rumors that Tirun had gone to a great deal of trouble, personally, to bring him on board. Was he now challenging Tirun's authority?

Tirun, impassive, gazed out over the heads of the mission toward Leyden. "For one, the *Balliol*, when it returns here from Remora, will be looking for us at the planned LZ, not here."

"But she'll send probes if we don't show up," Leyden interrupted.

Tirun began pacing as he measured each word for its full impact. "Maybe. Maybe not. The *Balliol* might conclude that we're missing somewhere in the rainforest, not in the northern regions. After all, we have no indication that they registered anything out of the ordinary with the drop. Retrieval time is limited. I needn't tell any of you that the cycle time for the burn back to the core is absolute. The Lightship must be in position three Illium-standard months from this date. Precisely. Anyone or anything on this side of the Illium after that time remains here for another cycle of four-plus standard years."

Tirun stopped pacing and stood in front of them, hands on hips.

"Four Illium standard years until the Selucid Swarm opens once again," he said slowly. "Plus travel through the Swarm to Eëlios. Those aren't problems, they're facts. The *problem* is that we have been sent here, at great cost, to conduct a survey of what appears to be one of the great biological storehouses of the Illium Archipelago, even if largely overlooked until now.

"Now think of how the Illium evolved, of the exploration stories that are the common heritage of us all. And not just those we know survived, like Kirov and the Nova Prince, but the hundreds of missions that faced the unknown, the *absolute* unknown of the first burns through the singularities of the portals — and disappeared. Whether from the universe or only from our portion of it we don't know. How do the risks we face here compare with those? Have we really come this far to simply cower here and wait to be rescued?"

Tirun paused and stared around the semicircle. "That's a question for each of you to answer. If any of you choose to stay, so be it. As for me, whether alone or with you, I intend to complete this mission."

In the silence that followed, Leyden waited for everyone to digest Tirun's words. He had no doubt that Tirun would carry the mission as he saw fit, whether by persuading them, or through direct orders if persuasion failed. Still, Leyden felt a tug of professional admiration as Tirun summoned the memory of the ancient heroes. As he undoubtedly calculated, the mystery and myth of the Illium phenomenon gripped everyone on the expedition to a greater or lesser degree, soldier and scientist alike.

The offer to let those who chose to remain here at Musgrave's Dance was sheer bluff — the mission had been launched with a bare minimum of used and second-hand equipment, from pods to NavComs. Tirun had neither resources to spare, nor the slightest intention of splitting the mission personnel and equipment. Besides, the mercenaries were under his full command, and the idea that they could make individual decisions was out of the question.

Leyden spoke less from any expectation of change than out of old instincts, from the dim days of maneuvering in the old Toranguin parliament.

"I'm sure I join everyone in admiration for the vision that you have just given us," he said with what he hoped held a slight but unmistakably patronizing tone. "But it is my understanding that we're still a very long way from where we should be. Across terrain we are neither trained nor equipped for. Assuming we make it, we'll probably use up the three months or close to it."

"More precisely," Tirun said, "we are more than twelve hundred kilometers from our planned location. But we are only about eight hundred kilometers from the rainforest itself, if we enter it from another direction." He nodded to the side. "I have asked Ulam to explain how we can make the trip, with time enough to conduct at least a partial biological survey."

Ulam had been a silent, often invisible presence through the preparation of the mission. Two cycles earlier, he had been one of a small contingent of Eëlians who returned to the Illium core aboard a lightship that had made a similar circuit voyage to Eëlios and Remora. He was a stocky, moon-faced figure, smiling, intensely shy, with a greenish cast to his skin that reminded Leyden uncomfortably of bad meat. Leyden had barely heard him speak, much less address a group like this.

Ulam turned to a map section displayed on the wall. "For a great. . . long time, I have waited for this day," he began in a voice filled with odd pauses as he sought the words he wanted in Illium Standard speech. Unconsciously, he scratched the translator chip implanted at the base of his skull. "I am sad. . . I regret that this day has come so far from the home of our people."

He pointed to the massive, ill-defined area that sprawled across much of Eëlios's equatorial region, then to their location at Musgrave's Dance.

"As Mr. Tirun said, we are a great distance from our planned landing. But there is a shorter way, if we follow the river — the river that with the joining of two streams here at Musgrave's Dance becomes known as the Whitebone. It would be possible, I believe, to float rafts for a long distance before the Whitebone becomes more too difficult to travel."

Ulam traced the route on his crude overlay. "We would then cross here ... to this body of water, and to the forest." He stepped back quickly to the side of the room and Tirun took his place.

After a silence, as the entire mission studied the map, Bois, planetary ecologist, spoke. "Float downriver on what? There isn't a tree worthy of the name anywhere near here."

"Pods," said Tirun with a fierce grin. "We're planning to pull in a number of pods, empty them out and cut them in half on their long axes. They've been burned down to their last layers of skin, so they're light. They're durable and they float. Attach some kind of outrigger piece to stabilize them and they should work."

Perfect timing for that piece of information, Leyden noted. He wondered if Bois's question had been a set-up. He might have done something similar in similar circumstances.

An San Kee spoke. "Do we know the condition of the river? Deep or shallow, rough or smooth? The name Whitebone would suggest the presence of rapids."

Tirun looked over at Ulam, then thought better of it.

"Ulam has told me that his people have explored this region only on rare occasions. He knows of at least two groups who have traveled parts of the Whitebone, at least to the point where we plan to leave the river. Yes, there do appear to be rapids, and we may have to portage around those sections. The point to remember is that the river is going to save us weeks of travel time, even with portages."

Tirun rubbed his hands in a concluding fashion. "If there are no more questions, I suggest that we all sleep well. We have much to prepare for our river trip."

So much for personal decisions about staying or going, Leyden thought.

◆

Later, under a dim red sky, Suslov returned. Leyden, sprawled on his back, asleep, felt sudden hands on his face and chest. He awoke with a start, started to struggle, then saw Suslov's face.

"Forgotten me already, my sweet?" she said, leaning over him, where he could see the tattooed Ohzumian pipe snake twitch under her left bicep.

Leyden fell back with a sigh, pulling her down beside him with a sigh. "You're alive, dammit. We thought you were dead."

"Not dead yet."

Leyden pulled his hands through her thick hair, dark now in the sleep shelter, auburn in the light, and still damp from decontamination and a shower. He nipped at her shoulder. "What the hell happened?"

"Must have been blown way north," she said, sitting up, pulling off his shirt in her no-nonsense manner, then pausing to strip off her own shirt and leaning over him. Suslov, he had learned quickly, made love as directly and efficiently as she conducted her duties as a senior licensed mercenary.

"The pod augured into a stream bed. Took me half a day just to dig out," she said as they both shed the remainder of their clothes.

"NavCom smashed," she continued, "so I kept walking a wider and wider circle until I found an empty pod and footsteps heading south... oh yes," she said with a sudden intake of breath. "Yes, that's better."

They lay side by side, rocking slowly as he lazily traced the sinuous path of her intricate dragon design — creature from a series of celebrated mythological tales that had spread from the Trapezium Cluster throughout the Illium.

"Turn over," she whispered finally. "My turn."

◆

It had been like this from the beginning: the quick, hushed meetings, the urgent rush to discard clothes, the whispered commands, instructions, suggestions. Aboard the *Balliol*, they had become, out of necessity, experts at lovemaking in small, difficult spaces: a steam-filled showers, gravity couch in a storage area, interior of an empty weapons locker, her feet braced against racks like stirrups, stretched across the all-purpose launch tubes.

They tried to be discreet, although neither had any illusion that their activity went unnoticed or unremarked upon. Liaisons aboard lightships were more the rule than the exception; affairs between civilians and mercs tended to be less common. Women had propositioned him in the past — especially in his brief prominence during the Toranguin independence movement — but this felt quite different. Suslov may have found Leyden attractive, but she also made it abundantly clear that his primary function was to serve her through some combination of no-frills sex and stress relief.

"Quiet," she would order him, or a preemptory, "Here," and begin stripping off her clothes in a half-filled storage container or next to a hidden bulkhead. Leyden had been startled at first; they had barely met each other on the shuttle flight from Rigel Prime to the *Balliol* before she made her intentions clear.

Not that Leyden objected, once he got over his surprise, since he had not anticipated any kind of involvement with expedition members. He quickly found that he liked the novelty, the role reversal of pursuer and pursued. After all, it had been his sexual appetites, or at least his inability to keep them under control, that had added such momentum to his final failures.

Leyden knew very little about Suslov except that she was from Ohzumé, one of the wealthiest but most violent worlds in the Illium; she had the planet's distinctive olive skin, pale eyes, and sharp features — features similar to those of another Ohzumian native, Tribune Hawkwood.

Even if Suslov hadn't approached him, he would have noticed her: the only female merc, her well-muscled arms and dragon-decorated shoulders. She had blocked him in a corridor outside the *Balliol* mess and said, "Looks as though we have twenty minutes before the next briefing."

She gazed at him, unblinking, small white scar on her temple, a splash of freckles at the base of her neck. She smelled of gun oil and coffee.

He checked his watch. "Yeah, about twenty minutes."

She smiled. "Think you can handle it?"

Leyden tried for a quizzical expression but had no idea if he succeeded. "Your place or mine?"

"Mine."

He had followed her downward through a maze of passageways to an unfamiliar cargo bay with container modules and a pallet piled with blankets and pillows where she fell upon him like an animal downing its prey; his job, he soon learned, was largely to follow orders and keep up.

Only once had she talked briefly about growing up in Ohzumé, a world of magnificent hill towns, celebrated for their wealth and art, along with murderous port cities that spawned some of the Illium's most violent criminal organizations – and many of the soldiers who joined the Illium League.

Like all such expeditions, the Trans-Illium had a nominal non-fraternization rule for security personnel and civilians, but in the months of travel within the Selucid Swarm to Eëlios, Tirun and Hawkwood were either unaware or uncaring about their activities, recognizing that such relationships were inevitable. If anything surprised Leyden, it was not the Suslov was willing to ignore the rules, but that she seemed indifferent to whether she appeared to be flouting Hawkwood's authority directly. An added benefit as far as Leyden was concerned.

Only one person spoke to him directly about Suslov, the head of the bioteam, An San Kee. Despite his vow of relative isolation, Leyden found himself occasionally drifting over to her section of the lightship and helping her inventory and pack supplies and science equipment. He wasn't the only person outside her team who sometimes stopped by to chat and help out, he noticed. Another was the Trans-Illium representative, Verlaine.

"Are you being careful?" Kee asked as the two of them took a break and she heated water for one of her exotic herbal teas.

"Careful? With what?"

"Suslov. You know, it's hardly a secret. . ."

Leyden flushed despite himself. "I assumed."

Kee turned away to pour the tea. "As long as you remember to take care of yourself."

He felt mildly astounded; she sounded as though she were an aunt or another older relative. "Care of me?" Not sure I understand."

She handed him a cup, and when he inhaled its aroma, it smelled of cloves and crushed flower pedals.

"I first met Suslov during my time on Tushangura. She was part of the security team there too."

"I have no idea."

Kee seemed to be suppressing a small laugh that ruffled her centered expression like a breeze rippling across a lake. "I don't imagine you do. What I recall is that she had a partner on Tushangura."

"Oh." That hardly sounded like unexpected news.

"Partners, actually. One was a woman."

Leyden sipped his tea. "Ah."

"I'm not telling you this to gossip, Leyden. We all have complicated pasts of one sort or another. We also have patterns. I wouldn't necessarily expect Suslov to act any differently now."

He was genuinely bewildered. "Are you telling me this to protect me from STDs, or to protect my heart?"

"Neither, Leyden," Kee said. "I'm merely telling you to be careful."

PART II: FLOATING

8 RUNNING THE WHITEBONE

They launched the eviscerated space pods in fog and confusion.

Sectioned and gutted, the thin-skinned blackened pods floated high in the swift waters of the Whitebone River. But they were also unstable: easy to tip in flat water, unpredictable when caught in currents and rapids.

The first pods to push off quickly thumped into a large boulder jutting in the middle of the stream, turned slowly and casually tipped everyone into the river. The occupants slogged to shore, pulling their swamped pod with them, amid jeers and nervous laughter.

The second pod managed to stay upright, but the crew paddled so ineffectually they simply turned in circles. Leyden and Verlaine — in the prow of an another pod with three others — tried to reach over and point them downstream; they succeeded only in tipping over their own pod and dumping everyone into the chilled water.

Nearby, An San Kee said quietly, "I think I'll walk after all." Knee deep in water, Hawkwood shouted orders to little effect.

Tirun stood on the shore, first glaring, then roaring with laughter. "Illium's finest, up the river without a paddle!"

The veteran mercenary Chácon, a native of Arishima who had sailed its island chains in his youth, finally succeeded in coordinating his paddlers and aligning the pod downriver. Amid shouts and curses, the others followed.

Despite their inauspicious beginning, they traveled the first section of the river without incident. Following Chácon's example, they learned to stroke with their makeshift paddles in pace with whoever occupied the prow position, while those in the stern used their paddles for steering. They settled into a rhythm and managed to remain pointed downstream, avoiding the obvious problems — frequent gravel bars and half-submerged rocks covered with spidery red lichen.

The waters of the Whitebone ran swift and cold, but also flat and relatively wide. The fog relented and then, a surprise: the clouds scuttled apart for an appearance by the Selucid Swarm's two suns. Wedged against bio equipment in the middle of a pod next to Verlaine, Leyden paused and trailed his hand in icy, dark water that immediately numbed his fingers.

He squinted upward. Thanks to Ulam, they were all familiar with at least a few Eëlian names now. The Selucid suns, collectively known as The Ginn, were son and daughter of mother Eëlios and father Kronos. The fat, red male sun, Naryl, hung just above the horizon; the yellow-blue daughter, Nevea, climbed the first quadrant of the sky. Leyden knew from his reading that, in astronomical terms, Nevea's compact, powerful gravitational forces were rapidly ripping out the heart of the older, more diffuse Naryl.

Beyond the gravel banks of the river, gray with shafts of white sediment that gave the Whitebone its name, the Eëlian landscape unfurled in fog-smoked tundra that appeared to have the consistency of thick soup. The Chaga Sea, Ulam called it, using an Eëlian transliteration for a term that literally meant water-land. Chaga salt grass, the ubiquitous plants with long runners of pale, hexagonal leaves, spread across the tundra. Bogthorn, the mounds of spiked plants Leyden had encountered outside his crashed pod, pocked the landscape, although Verlaine quickly named them "limp dick" after the shape of their bunched blue flowers.

The land undulated but held no elevation at all; occasionally it sank into outright swamps and networks of small lakes where the salt grass gave way to thickets of bamboo-like growths and water plants with floating leaves as big as serving platters. Ulam stood up in his pod, perilously unstable, pointed and shouted, and Leyden saw his first Eëlian animal — a small, blunt-nosed creature with warty skin and wide, paddle-shaped feet, snuffling around the edges of a marsh, oblivious to the passing flotilla. Bog bear, Ulam called it.

Leyden's second animal emerged from the daughter sun, flying straight out of Nevea's blue glare so suddenly that Leyden's first impression was of a dark, compact cloud racing overhead. He looked up in time for only a momentary glimpse: anvil-shaped head, beak studded with teeth, gray featherless skin and a wingspan the size of a commuter plane. By the time he ducked, along with the others in the pod, it was a dwindling shape climbing into the sky.

Everyone called on their NavComs, sucking hard on respirators and chattering to Ulam. Hawkwood, who had already uncased his Multiphase Combat Weapon, scanned the sky, overriding the comline and cutting them off. In the unilateral silence that followed, Ulam named the creature a kyte, rare to the rainforest but more common here, where they could hunt on the open expanse of the Chaga. From what he knew, Ulam continued, they usually didn't attack anything as large as a human. He paused. "I've never seen one that big before."

Leyden found nothing reassuring in Ulam's explanations. He punched the private comline on the chest panel of his NavCom and coded in Suslov's access number, even though they had agreed to keep such communications to a minimum. She acknowledged with an uncharacteristically soft, "Yes?" Leyden could see her ahead, in another pod, crossing a gravel bar so shallow that she, Zia and Tranner poled their pod, instead of paddling.

"I know I skipped briefings and didn't do my homework," Leyden muttered quietly, "but I think I would have remembered something about flying reptiles."

Suslov's responded with a quiet curse and small explosion of heavy breathing from the effort of pushing off the gravel bar. "Ulam's not exactly widely traveled. Eëlians stay pretty close to home, in the rainforest."

Leyden could still hear the steady pulse of her breathing, evoking the most vivid sound of their lovemaking.

"Kytes are the least of our problems," she added. "Better not call me at the office anymore, my sweet. Suslov out."

◆

In the dimming light of the Eëlian afternoon, they beached the pods on a wide gravel expanse in the middle of the Whitebone. Hawkwood sent Tranner and Ehrenberg on patrol downriver; the others installed the Rendezvous Dome and used river water, after boiling and chemical decontamination, to prepare High C/P, a carbohydrate/protein, vitamin-enhanced stew that combined the textures of pudding and bubble tea.

Leyden took his ISSU into one of the dome's sleep zones and found a spot along its translucent perimeter for his sleeping hutch. With no prospect that Suslov could join him in the confines of the Dome, he pushed a wafer-book in a polymer vid and started a new hypertext biography of the Nova Prince, which he had bought with a slew of other new multimedia pubs before the mission.

For virtually everyone, the Illium Flame Portals were both the barrier and the entrance to new worlds; the burn merely a necessary rite of passage. But the man who became known as the Nova Prince had little interest in finding inhabitable worlds. An explorer like his father, the legendary Anton

Kirov, the Nova Prince was fascinated by the experience of the burn itself. More so than anyone else, his life was shaped by the desire to become one with the singularities themselves. In the end, he succeeded, although in a manner neither he nor anyone else had anticipated.

After reading for an hour, Leyden flicked off the vid and stuffed it into his pack. Nevea, a weakening blue light, settled in the southeast while Naryl, blood orange, climbed overhead. A planet that never experiences darkness, he thought. Too bad: the nighttime display of the Selucid Swarm was supposed to be spectacular. Or was Eëlios so isolated that its sister planets appeared little larger than distant stars?

A soft gong sounded across the sleep zone; Leyden turned his hutch opaque and lay back. In a few moments, he could hear the soft rush of the gas that would ensure them all an uninterrupted sleep cycle.

♦

In the morning, with Naryl setting and Nevea rising, they gathered on the graveled edge of the river and listened to the report from Tranner and Ehrenberg. The rapids began about a klick from their location, they reported. Of the three sections before them, the middle part looked like the trickiest. The only good passage seemed a narrow twisting chute close to the right embankment. Below the rapids, the river flattened again, but they could hear what sounded like bigger rapids in the distance.

"One problem at a time," Tirun responded. "Let's get through these first."

Lulled by the shallow, swift river they had navigated since Musgrave's Dance, the Whitebone's sudden teeth caught them all unprepared. Only Chácon's pod made it through all three rapids unscathed. For the rest, the run brought disaster. One pod swamped in the first set of frothing waves, catching on the rocky bottom, slewing sideways and filling with water. None of the other three pods could follow Chácon's example and align themselves with the hard right twist of the chute through the second, steeper rapids. One overturned, and the other two, including Leyden's, survived upright but suffered the indignity of sliding down the chute backwards, paddles flailing as helplessly as a water bug on its back.

They beached themselves again, this time on a inlet of pale rock that contrasted with the near-black color of the river. Leyden felt as if he were standing on an overexposed black-and-white photograph.

Three of those in the overturned pod, Chapandagura, Mkeki and Modrescu, had their face masks ripped off and had swallowed river water. Within thirty minutes, all were suffering violent diarrhea and vomiting. The rest of them waited in unspoken dread while al-Saqua and An San Kee dosed them with a compound mixed from the drug extracts of three Illium worlds. Leyden felt a sense of secret relief. Now they would know if the Eëlian environment proved lethal to off-worlders, or just unpleasant for those lacking its natural immunities. Leyden noticed Hawkwood inspecting what looked like small tears on several of the team's carapaces.

Al-Saqua's potion worked, and within another half hour, all three began recovering. Moreover, al-Saqua pointed out, they would now probably be immune to any more ill effects from river water. If anyone else wanted the same protection, now would be the time to take a drink. There were no takers.

Verlaine walked over to Leyden who, squatting by the water's edge, watched for the reappearance of an odd-shaped crustacean with a single eye, which he had glimpsed scuttling under a submerged rock.

"Don't look," said Verlaine. "Listen."

Leyden stood up, adjusted his auditory control. It took a moment but then he heard it, the deep-throated mutter of water moving fast and steep over large rocks. It made the sound of the rapids they had just come through sound tinny by comparison. He grimaced silently.

"Yeah," said Verlaine. "I don't like it. If we quit the river, we'd have to march through this damn bog for days. Use up most of our time just getting to the rainforest. But we're like a damn slapstick comedy on this river, and if we're not careful, we're going to start losing people."

He pointed downriver. "Starting there."

9 CAUGHT IN THE KEEPER

Chácon shouted something over the riot noise of the river. Leyden could hear the note of desperation, but not whether he said, "High side!" or "Right side!" The problem was: they were different. The right side of their tipping, jury-rigged, pod-raft had buried itself in a froth of river, the left side wavered several meters above the maddened water. A bit higher and they would flip. Again.

"*High* side!" Chácon screamed.

Leyden stumbled over a tangle of carapace-coated legs, leaned over and thrashed at the water with his paddle. The left side of the raft hovered momentarily, flopped back into the water, slammed hard into a lichen-streaked boulder, and bounced down the chute.

The water poured over a series of washboard ridges and rocks in convex-shaped waves that slopped into the raft.

"Bail!" Chácon shouted this time. Leyden, Verlaine and An San Kee grabbed an assortment of cooking containers and helmet liners and began heaving water back into the river. Bois and Zia continued paddling at the prow, Chácon piloting from the stern. The rafts may have been a good idea, but no one had yet solved the problem of making them self-bailing.

Chácon stopped, paddle trailing in the water as a rudder, and peered down river. "Shit!" he said, followed by a series of other expletives. Verlaine looked up at Leyden through a water-spattered facemask. "Somehow I don't think that translates into 'Nice camping spot.'"

"Paddles!" Chácon shouted to him, Verlaine, and An San Kee. All three had been chosen for the lead raft with Chácon, who, as an Arishima native, had experienced white water in both oceans and rivers.

Leyden pulled himself to his position on the left side of the raft, paddle in hand. The landscape had lifted and dried somewhat, with the river beginning to cut deeply into the ground, carving raw, eroding embankments that dropped to the water's edge. A wasteland of boulders, gullies, and water-strewn rocks marked the height of the river at flood. He wondered if it would have been a better to navigate the Whitebone with higher water but fewer rapids.

Amid one jumble of boulders they passed a huge pile of bogthorn that clearly had been ripped from embankments farther upstream. It smelled of decay, and Leyden could see several bog bears rooting around its edges.

The sky become sullen again, and a mist rose from downriver. The river seemed to disappear into it.

This time Chácon spoke quietly. "Drop-off. Waterfall. All across the river. Keep it straight and hang on."

Leyden liked it better when Chácon shouted. They bobbed along in silence, with just the slap and sigh of the water around them, the sound of the invisible falls growing.

Chácon tried to see over the edge and gauge the size of the drop, then sat.

"Brace!" The front of the raft fell into a boil of whitewater, and Bois and Zia tumbled headfirst over the side. The raft plunged in, rose and spun sideways. Zia managed to hang onto the safety rope strung around the side of the raft, but Bois disappeared. They kept spinning, caught in a slow steady whirlpool. Ahead, Leyden could clearly see a constant wave that seemed to break back against the current. Chácon had even given this phenomenon a name: a keeper.

Chácon shouted again and threw Leyden a line. "Bois. He's in the rope in your corner of the raft."

Their eyes locked, but Chácon, standing, fighting the raft's spin, said nothing and gave Leyden the slightest of shrugs. *Choices, really only the illusion of a choice.* Leyden wrapped the line around his fist, tore off his respirator and facemask and went over the side.

The water, so cold his eyes throbbed, held him with a muffled furiousness, tumbling him. Leyden gripped the rope, feeling his hands begin to grow numb. His eyes adjusted, and looking up, he could see the violent, frothing surface. For a disoriented instant, he felt as though he were flying high above the clouds, watching a massive storm break breaking below. He pulled himself forward and saw Bois under one of the four pods, facemask gone, right arm caught in a tangle of rope.

Leyden moved toward Bois with slow hands that slipped again and again against the river's insistent pull. By the time he reached him, he could feel his lungs swelling against the lack of air. The rope had bitten so deeply into Bois's carapace that he couldn't even loosen it, much less pull his arm free.

Leyden surfaced. "Knife!" he gasped into the raft. Chácon kicked an ISSU toward Verlaine, who yanked out several blades from the Swiss and handed one to him.

"Come in!" Verlaine shouted over the sound of the rapids. "I'll go." Leyden shook his head and ducked back under.

By the time Leyden reached Bois this time, he looked completely unconscious and limp, his neck and shoulders slamming helplessly against the black bottom of the raft. Leyden slashed at the rope, slicing into Bois's carapace, freeing his arm.

Bois immediately swept down the length of the raft. Lunging, Leyden just barely managed to grab a foot. Fighting the current, his hands numbing, he pulled Bois and himself up the rope to the side of the raft.

♦

Leyden lay in the center of the raft, sickened, shaking uncontrollably from the cold, barely aware of An San Kee trying to resuscitate Bois and shouting over to Verlaine for al Saqua's river-water medicine. Crawling to the edge of the raft, Leyden retched violently before Verlaine could force the medicine past his clenched teeth.

"Bois?" he whispered.

"Sicker than you, and broke an arm," Verlaine said, "but he'll make it. If any of us can make it out of this goddamn current." Only then did Leyden once again feel the trapped motion of the raft, shuddering against the circular draft of the water.

As the medicine took effect and his nausea receded, Leyden revived enough to see Chácon and Zia struggle to keep the raft centered between the waterfall behind them and the ugly lip of the backwashing keeper in front. If the raft bumped too close to the waterfall, it immediately filled with water, triggering a frantic scramble to bail before it swamped. But the keeper proved worse, threatening to suck them under and churn them in place like a massive washing machine. A grim morass of beached driftwood, bones, and debris encircled them, looking like corpses that had been trapped in this same patch of grinding water for a very long time.

Through the mist, they could hear shouting from the shore. The rest of the expedition had landed above them, and Leyden could see them struggling to pull their rafts around the falls.

"Bail!" Chácon shouted. When Leyden looked up again, Tirun, Hawkwood, and Tranner had a raft in the water, straining to paddle upstream toward them against the current. As they approached the backwash of the keeper, with Tranner standing in the prow with a coil of rope, the raft began buck uncontrollably. They pulled back and made another run at the keeper, this time with Tranner on his knees. As Chácon maneuvered closer, Tranner heaved his rope again. Short. He threw again and the end slapped into the water several meters from the revolving raft.

"No! Back!" shouted Chácon as the edge of the backwash caught the raft and started to pull it under. Bois, along with a mass of equipment, packs and gear in the center of the raft tumbled toward the side of the raft that was burying itself in the powerful down current of the keeper. The raft started to fill again.

"Turn!" Chácon shouted this time, "Fast as you can!" They dug hard into the water with their paddles, slowly pulling the water-filled end out of the slough of the keeper, then spinning the raft so that the sides bounced off the wave instead of burying itself in it. After five minutes of exhausting struggle, they had the raft back in the center of the whirlpool. Below the keeper, Tirun and Hawkwood backed off and watched. Even those on the shore were silent; everyone seemed exhausted and out of ideas.

At least I've already been in the river, Leyden thought. He began stripping off his carapace, a loud ripping sound that cut through the throaty roar of the Whitebone. "What the hell are you doing?" Verlaine shouted above the pounding noise of the keeper. Chácon, whom Leyden suspected understood immediately, said nothing.

"If they can't get a rope to us," Leyden answered, "we'll get one to them. Tie it around my waist. I'll get on someone's shoulders and jump out as far as I can."

"That's crazy."

"Got a better idea?" Leyden shouted. "Besides, I've already been in the water. I may drown, but at least I won't get sick again."

Verlaine looked over Chácon. "Yes," Chácon shouted. He looked at Leyden. "One foot on your shoulder, one on mine. Count of three, toss him."

Verlaine shouted something in the jarring clamor, but Leyden couldn't hear him. Chácon knotted a rope around him and handed his makeshift helm to Kee.

Chácon and Verlaine bent down; Leyden wrapped his hands around their helmeted heads and kneeled on their shoulders. They waited for the raft to revolve toward the keeper.

"Now," Leyden said, as their slow orbit brought their side of the raft downstream. He struggled from knees to feet, still crouched, still clutching their helmets. Leyden could feel Verlaine beginning to lose his balance,

Chácon staggering. Leyden leaped in an awkward half-dive, his feet slipping off both shoulders. He flopped into the river, gasping from the cold.

Leyden could immediately feel the grip of the water, but in the spume and froth, he had no sense of direction. He tried to thrash to the surface but the current held him under.

The hell with it, he thought, and forced himself to stop struggling and allow the current take complete hold of him. *Let it carry me one place or another — either I will be downstream or back in the keeper.* For a moment he held an image of his pod landing, the dark, river-segmented landscape rushing to meet him, the sense that, well or badly, the issue at hand would now be resolved.

He popped to the surface ten meters below the keeper, the Whitebone whisking him downstream and into the shallows.

Leyden lay on a flat rock, shaking, not even looking as the others took his rope and finally worked the raft to the sanctuary of the shore.

10 PORTAGES

Leyden stretched, carapace crackling, and tested the soreness in his left leg where he had been slammed against a rock.

The expedition lay camped below yet another falls, this one dubbed Kyte's Head for a narrow, hammer-shaped rock formation resembling the flying reptiles, now constant witnesses to their journey. Nevea, more blue than green, hovered low in the northwest; in the southeast Naryl's bloody edge squinted over the horizon. An Eëlian twilight, or dawn, depending on one's sleep cycle.

Everyone was exhausted and muscle sore. After the near-disaster of the keeper, Tirun had decided that they would scout the Whitebone more carefully, run only the smaller rapids, and portage the rafts around dangerous sections of the river. No more rafts overturned, but as the Whitebone narrowed, its velocity increased. Heavy rapids appeared more frequently, scouring the shoreline into little more than slippery, lichen-covered ledges of broken rock too narrow to drag the rafts. Instead, they had to portage everything up steep embankments and back down to the river.

The alternative, to line the rafts through the rapids with ropes, avoided the heavy lifting but held its own dangers. Upstream, one or two members of the crew held the raft against the shore, while the other team, roped to the raft, climbed downstream. When the upstream team released the raft, it would shoot through the rapids, sometimes upright, sometimes not. The downstream team braced themselves with ropes wrapped around arms, backs and stones, and tried to rein in the raft as it shot past.

Simple enough in theory. In practice, the combination of slippery rocks, the increasing speed of the river, and the sheer weight of the raft made lining a difficult, injury-racked process. Several of them had already been badly bruised, even wearing carapaces, after taking hard falls off the rocks into the river as rafts spun away like frantic animals. Another, Chapandagura, pear-shaped and perennially hapless, had suffered a mild concussion after being dragged almost a hundred meters through the water before Suslov and Chácon retrieved the rope as the raft hit a pool of flat water. Other teams had opted for the safer but more tiring procedure of portaging their equipment around the rapids. As a result, the expedition had barely progressed three kilometers in two days.

Leyden pulled off his face mask and respirator, and lifted his head to feel unmediated Eëlian air on his face. The breeze still held the cold bite of the subarctic Chaga, but joined now with the signature scent of a humid southland, a fecund mix of humidity and decay, and unmistakably, the almond scent of his childhood kitchen.

Leyden stretched again, walking over to join a small group watching the blue chem flame boiling water for Ohzumian spice tea: Verlaine, Mkeki, and Chácon.

"Almonds," Leyden said. "I've been smelling almond cookies in the air since we landed."

"Not almonds," Verlaine said, snorting loudly through his respirator. "Wood smoke. We used to camp in the Aref Mountains on Delios Major during the sun season. Hated it then, couldn't wait to grow up so I would never have to camp in the wilderness. So where am I now? All grown up and camping in a wilderness. But I remember those night fires, roasting sausages and hard-skin chocolates. The smell of Delian pine burning. *That's* the smell now. Your dips in the Whitebone have soaked your brain, Leyden, to the detriment of your senses."

The others joined in the laughter.

"Verlaine," Mkeki said, "with your scented corporate suites, you couldn't tell the difference between smoke from a Delian wood fire or a fine Cold Moon cigar."

More laughter. With her shaved head and dark skin, Mkeki resembled the dark, succulent sugarberries that were a prized, and expensive, delicacy of her homeland, Cold Moon Rising, one of a crowded mix of satellites orbiting a much larger dead planet. She was slight and quick and unfazed by Verlaine's cutting barbs, her face and body adorned with a remarkable number of jeweled piercings.

Suslov appeared out of the dusky light, standing behind them; Leyden turned toward her just as she chose to sit between Mkeki and Chácon. He tried to catch her eye but she leaned forward to whisper something in Mkeki's ear.

"Is that what you smell?" Chácon asked, repairing small rents in his carapace. "Tobacco smoke? For me, it's the air on Arishima's Red Turtle Beach. Sea air. Not smoke or tobacco at all. And nothing like almonds."

Normally, the mercenaries kept largely to themselves, but Chácon, with sinews that ran like fault lines along his heavily muscled neck and arms, had joined his fellow survivors of the keeper.

"Pheromones," said a quiet voice behind them. An San Kee had walked up noiselessly behind them, a talent she must have learned in years of stalking biological samples on a dozen Illium planets.

Verlaine signaled for her to join them, as he poured aromatic tea for everyone. "No requests for sugar or honey, please. It is considered sacrilege with this particular blend."

Chácon, still following Hawkwood's alien-planet protocols, slurped his tea through the liquid intake tube with his respirator still in place. Everyone else followed Verlaine's example and detached their respirators to drink.

Mkeki laughed and nudged Suslov with an elbow as they swirled and slurped their tea. Leyden was struck by the similarity in their appearances. Mkeki leaned more toward body-and-tongue piercings than tattoos, but she was as well muscled as Suslov, with a wary, cat-like expression that, in the wavering firelight, mirrored Suslov's. For a moment, Leyden imagined encountering both of them in his sleeping hatch.

Leyden turned to An San Kee, who sat cross-legged in a position that Leyden suspected she assumed for study, meditation, even sleep if necessary. She continued to hold Verlaine's undivided attention.

"Almost every account we have of the Eëlian rainforest mentions smells that evoke powerful memories of childhood," she said. "Even sounds in a few cases. But always related to some intense memory of the past, usually when young."

"They're just unique chemical compounds in the atmosphere, right?" Verlaine asked.

"One theory is that, in the competition to survive and propagate, a number of species have learned to generate powerful pheromones that work not just on the senses, but actually activate parts of the brain associated with memory."

"Wait, wait," Verlaine said, holding up a hand impatiently. "Insects communicate with pheromones, right? Are you saying that the insects of Eëlios produce pheromones so complex they can affect humans, even people like us, who haven't been sensitized to the planet's environment?"

"Not insects," Kee said quietly. "The vegetation. The trees, the rainforest itself."

"But we're almost two hundred kilometers from the tropics," Chácon said.

"I know," Kee said, "which suggests that Eëlian pheromones are so powerful they can affect us even after being blown this far from their source."

"Is that why we're here?" Leyden said. "I mean, pheromones aren't exactly an unknown phenomenon."

"They're not," Kee said. "They're most closely associated with insects, as Verlaine suggested, and they play a role in many types of animal behavior, including humans. But we've never seen anything like this before."

"I assume that you're talking about more than chemical scents emitted by jungle plants," Leyden said.

An San Kee smiled and nodded over her neatly folded hands in a manner that Leyden found both restrained and enticing. "Yes. It has become clear in recent years that Eëlios is a remarkable place."

"Oh, don't lead us on like that," said Verlaine, with a quick elbow into her arm. "I bet you say that about everywhere you go in the Illium."

"Yes," Leyden said, seizing the opening. "You were on one of the first expeditions to explore those fungal life forms on. . . what? Luxor Six?"

"I'm a biologist," said Kee, choosing her words carefully. "I don't need to tell you that I feel greatly honored to have been selected by Trans-Illium, and Mission Leader Tirun, to join this expedition."

"Excellent answer," Leyden said. "Keep up that naïve-scientist front. Should serve you well."

Kee flipped him off and Leyden pretended to be insulted.

"You earned that one, Leyden," Verlaine said with a laugh, taking the opportunity to pull Kee in tighter.

Leyden breathed the alien air deeply. Almonds, still. Suslov was whispering to Mkeki again, refusing even to glance over at him. Another image flashed before his eyes — Suslov and Mkeki together, naked and panting, making athletic, evenly matched love, with no need for an extraneous third-party male like himself.

"What do you expect to find, other than strange pheromones?" Leyden asked. "There must be a dozen Illium worlds with rainforests. The Languishing Swamps of Imhotep. The river-jungles of Rigel Two, Blackwood forests of Bright Green Moon. Parts of Delium-Ghahan, where I spent a cycle. Luxor Six. The Ohzumian Preserve, what's left of it."

He paused. "There are others."

Suslov had a hand on Mkeki's thigh and continued talking to her in a steady undertone. By this time, everyone in the circle was both aware and trying to avoid looking directly at them.

"Indeed," Kee said. "Arishima's Polygon Island. The mist valleys of Farland Peninsula on Tushangura. I spent a year there gathering research for my dissertation. All of them storehouses of biological wonders. All unique. The destruction of much of the tropical habitat on Ohzumé is tragic. But Eëlios may turn out to be the most remarkable of them all."

"I love it when you talk mystery biology," said Verlaine cheerfully.

What the hell was going on? Leyden thought. Was Suslov trying to send him a message? Or didn't she care who knew that she might be acquiring a second lover, one for the *Balliol,* another for the Whitebone.

An San Kee continued. "Consider the combination of a relatively small, low-gravity planet, combined with the intense radiation effect of double suns. One result is a rainforest canopy almost two kilometers tall in places. A canopy that high and extensive means competition for sunlight that produces, among other effects, pheromones so strong that you can sit in the subarctic and smell the almond cookies that your mother baked for you as a child."

"You mean certain trees that tall," Leyden said, "not the entire area." These extraordinary heights were what immediately struck anyone studying the initial surveys of Eëlios.

Kee smiled. "It is unfortunate that you missed so much of the orientation. The areas bordering the rainforest are lower in elevation, but in the core, about a hundred and fifty thousand square kilometers along the equator, aerial surveys indicate that the canopy averages 1.7 to 2.1 kilometers in altitude."

Leyden glanced at Mkeki and Suslov again, unable to quite register what Kee had just said. Not individual trees, but an entire jungle canopy that, in old measure, rose more than two miles into the sky. He shook his head; unable to form any image at all.

Suslov abruptly stood up and disappeared as quietly as she had arrived. Mkeki looked distracted but didn't move to follow her.

Kee was still talking. "A complexity of interactions, predation, symbiosis that will probably take generations to understand. Not to mention the sheer number of new life forms to identify and catalogue. The computer projections suggest that, if Eëlios's rain forest is as extensive and dense as the surveys indicate, there could be several million new species here."

"Most of which probably sting, bite, fly up various orifices, or inject nasty venoms into your system," Verlaine said, leaning over to nuzzle Kee's neck. "But don't stop on my account."

Kee startled a bit, pushing Verlaine away and transferring his hand from her shoulder to her knee. Mkeki stood, waved vaguely, and left.

No one looked at Leyden.

"Plenty of insects, yes," she said. "But the most remarkable life form on Eëlios is undoubtedly the rainforest itself, especially the dynamics of plant life in the canopy."

Verlaine yawned, lifting and examining Kee's hand as if he had just discovered it. "Which is where our merry little band is indeed headed."

He began kissing her hand until she gently pulled it away from him.

Leyden said, "And where we'll all count plant species for An San Kee and her team."

"Count, hell!" Verlaine said, rising to his feet. "*You* count. Eëlios is a pharmacological storehouse. I'm here to harvest drugs and make myself and my company very wealthy indeed."

He stepped in front of the fire. "And when I'm old and doddering, I'll pull my twelve grandchildren onto my lap and say, `Yes, I went into the jungle an unknown man and came back rich! I say rich!'"

He looked straight at Kee. "I'm off for a good night's sleep, my children. Don't have too much fun without me and keep the noise down." He left.

"Charming man," Leyden said to Kee. "But perhaps someone else to be careful of, I should think."

"Indeed," said Kee, unmoving, staring into the pale darkness. "For both of us."

11 THE DRONES

The rapids ran from shore to shore: loud fast water smashing hard against gray-black rocks. Leaning back against the insistent pull of the rope, Leyden waited for the decision: to run the rapids or line the rafts. Both prospects dismayed him: Moments of speed, precariousness, and terror, accompanied by the distinct possibility of being flipped once again into the river. Or the laborious, muscle-wrenching process of pulling them through with ropes — taking an hour and gaining a mere five hundred meters.

Downstream, high on the cliff side, he could see Tirun and Chácon, making the same calculation. He had barely spoken to Tirun since escaping the keeper, but Leyden sensed his growing anxiety over the expedition's inability to gain any substantial distance in their daily assaults on the Whitebone. And from the frequency of his huddled consultations with Chácon and Hawkwood, he suspected that Tirun now faced the realization that Ulam, despite being born on Eëlios, had little practical knowledge of this part of his world.

A delta-wing shadow hurtled past the flotilla of rafts, followed by a harsh cry and the clacking of toothed bills. The kytes had become bolder in the last several days, sometimes gliding so low that, when they swiveled their claw-hammer heads to look downward, Leyden could see their eyes, the size and color of egg yolks. He glanced up: a smaller one this time, disappearing over the lip of the deepening canyon that was slowly swallowing the Whitebone River.

Leyden recognized the mission's serious, perhaps terminal trouble, but within his cocoon of fatigue, he hardly cared. He would lose a hefty fee — fifty thousand Illium talons could reestablish himself in moderate comfort. But the expedition never offered the prospects of real wealth that presumably drove Tirun, Verlaine, and the mercenaries. Whatever the outcome here and now, Trans-Illium or another corporate expedition would descend on Eëlios in the next four-year cycle. But with this failure, Tirun had little chance of being part of a later effort. Impressive as his past exploits might be, the corporate leaders of the Illium Archipelago dealt only in results, as they made calculations with consequences felt decades later and unfathomable distances away. At least a failure here would make Hawkwood's star burn a little more dimly inside the League, a pleasant thought that Leyden held along with the rope tied to a bucking restive raft.

Upstream, Leyden saw Tirun pass hand signals to Hawkwood at the river's edge. "Run it!" he heard Hawkwood cry both over the sound of the river and in the buzz of the NavCom.

Leyden breathed into the sky without his respirator or helmet. He had decided that the discomfort of wearing his respirator outweighed the abstract risk of inhaling a deadly Eëlian microbe. Plus, he had the satisfaction of defying a direct order from Hawkwood. The mercs felt too constrained to disobey Hawkwood, but many of the civilians, especially those who had fallen into the river, had abandoned their respirators and begun to discard damaged pieces of their carapaces as well.

Zia, Bois, and Kee piled into the raft. Leyden dug his heels in and waited until Chácon returned, then pushed off. "You figure we can handle this one?" Leyden shouted at Chácon. "Or is Tirun getting desperate?"

Chácon shook his head. "Paddle left!" he shouted, and to Leyden's amazement, they bounced through the rapids wet but upright. The other rafts followed, also without incident. Next, they found a stretch of smoother water that carried almost another half kilometer before they beached the rafts for what passed as night on Eëlios, although one or both of the suns lit the skies as brightly during their sleep cycles as it did when they were awake and fighting the Whitebone.

◆

The bad news spread through the expedition well before Tirun assembled them in a semicircle next to the river. Even Hawkwood, normally the most expressionless of men, looked grim.

Tirun stood, legs apart, arms folded, in the pose that Leyden now associated with his past pronouncements on board the *Balliol* and at Musgrave's Dance.

"As I'm sure you've all heard by now," Tirun said, "the Whitebone appears to descend into an extremely deep and narrow canyon around the next bend. From this end, anyway, it looks like almost continuous rapids, with no opportunities to portage. We don't have any useful surveys of this section of the river and Ulam is unfamiliar with the area."

Ulam, Leyden noticed, was practically shaking, his skin a more peculiar shade of green than usual.

Tirun continued. "We have only two options. One, we can pack up the rafts and portage around the entire canyon. The problem is that we really have no idea how far we would have to travel before we can get back on the river. Or we can abandon the rafts and head cross-country. The elevation is slightly higher and drier here than the tundra we've already passed through. But we will almost certainly have to cross a number of streams and marshlands, since this entire region is basically a mass of water flowing the toward the rainforest."

From the center of the assembled group, Verlaine asked, "If we leave the river, how long to reach the forest?"

"With light loads, limited rations and reduced sleep cycles, perhaps two-and-a-half, three weeks."

"And if we try to carry the rafts around the canyon?"

Tirun looked over at Hawkwood and Chácon. "We don't know. We do know that, somewhere below the canyon, the Whitebone widens and is relatively free of rapids where it empties into a bay. But we don't know how far upriver that wider section starts."

"How much cycle time do we have left?" An San Kee asked.

Hawkwood appeared to do a calculation on a flat, wide device attached to his wrist that almost certainly performed a number of classified military functions. "We have 3.1 standard Illium months before the Selucid Swarm closes off to the core."

No one spoke. Two choices, but Tirun had really given them only one. Dragging the rafts and equipment an unknown distance around the canyon was not an option at all. Tirun could have proposed sending a scouting team downriver, of course, while the rest of them remained here, but he hadn't mentioned that possibility. And Leyden was sure that, if someone were to propose such a plan, Tirun would reject it. Tirun's first priority was to keep the expedition moving at all cost. And he suspected Tirun had the support of the company reps, Verlaine and Mkeki.

We'll rest here for a day," Tirun announced. "Repack with the just the minimum to cross the Chaga."

◆

Leyden awoke to the invisible cry of a kyte, and a faint humming that, despite the noise of the Whitebone River, steadily grew louder and more insistent. Leyden straightened up from packing his sleeping hutch, listening. Nearby, Verlaine and several mercs, looking puzzled, also stared upward. Fog hung heavy over the river, and tendrils rose from the shore. The opaque sky continued to fill with a strange yet oddly familiar noise.

A section of the embankment behind Leyden gave way with a sudden crack and began sliding into the river. Downstream, a geyser erupted hugely into the sky. Leyden stood, disoriented, trying to comprehend.

An intense light flashed across the river, followed by an explosion that tore out another section of rock and gravel. The whining noise grew louder but the sky remained empty. The air smelled of river-bottom mud.

"Kytes!" someone shouted insanely, but Leyden didn't recognize the voice. Upstream, he saw several people running. Then he remembered his NavCom, and started to fumble for it in his pack. He heard a sucking sound, glimpsed another flash from the corner of his eye, then an explosion knocked him over, rolling him into the shallow water at the river's edge.

As Leyden lay stunned and gasping, a shape materialized out of the fog, followed by a second. They both hovered — rounded, blunt-ended objects with delta wings, mottled green-black shells pocked with air intakes, sensors, and weaponry.

Leyden cursed to himself as he lay in the freezing water, probing his numbed side to see if he were bleeding. Illium combat drones, he realized, identical to the ones that had attacked by the thousands for the League's final assault on Toranga. The sound then had seemed unbelievable.

But here, now? Under attack on Eëlios by armored, remote-controlled drones? From where? Leyden rolled out of the water and tried to stand. The drones, descending below the fog bank, fired directly into the camp. A raft exploded, shards arcing high into the air. Another pulse charge tore again into the cliff side, plunging a mass of rock and earth down on the Rendezvous Dome. Somewhere in the mist, Leyden heard screaming.

His leg still numb, Leyden grabbed his ISSU pack and half-ran, half-limped to the shelter of a patch of bogthorn growing next to the embankment. He found the NavCom and inserted the receiver in his ear. A succession of pulse charges exploded along the shoreline in soupy geysers of rock and water. He expected the comline to be filled with static and confusion, but it was in combat mode, with only Hawkwood's clear, cutting commands audible to him, not the responses. Even Tirun had apparently pulled himself offline so that Hawkwood could control the entire expedition.

Leyden listened for a moment.

"Can you reach it?" Hawkwood asked. A pause. "Yes, we'll cover." Leyden realized Hawkwood's problem: most of their weapons were packed away in the pile of supplies in exposed areas along the river's edge. Leyden had the impression that at least one merc had already been hit trying to retrieve them.

"Fire, all!" he heard Hawkwood call.

From along the shore, upriver from his location, Leyden saw a series of flashes burst in the sky around the drones; several seemed to be direct hits. A second burst of ground fire flickered around the drones. At least two mercs had managed to retrieve weapons, Leyden thought. Both drones wavered, climbed slightly and turned away from Leyden and toward the source of the ground fire.

Firing standard combat infantry weaponry would have only a negligible effect on a heavily armored combat drone, as Leyden knew all too well from Toranga. So did Hawkwood.

Fuel pellets and recyclable chem units detonated amid the ruins of one of the rafts, starting a fire that sent a pillar of eye-stinging, black smoke into the air. He saw a second round of ground fire, and one of the drones blasted back, sending yet another small avalanche into the river.

Leyden thumbed his NavCom and buzzed Hawkwood, who came on the line instantly. "Give me your location."

"About thirty meters downriver from the fire. In a goddamn thorn bush. What's happening? Where did these things come from?"

Hawkwood ignored his questions. "Hold position. Don't move."

Hawkwood cut the line. As Leyden watched, a carapaced figure emerged from the base of the cliff and ran toward the supply containers by the water's edge. The trailing drone rotated, tracking, then opened fire. A sudden trail of pocked water raced across the river and passed across the running figure. The merc fell without a sound. Leyden closed his eyes and turned away. Flechettes.

The ground fire intensified and the drone turned back upriver. Smoke continued to billow over the river. Hawkwood came back on the line. "We're pinned down here. Suslov and Zia have weapons and are trying to draw them upriver, away from the rafts and equipment. Chácon's trying to get to the cliff top. But I need our own Dragon. It's the only thing we have that can knock these things down. You're nearest. In one of those containers."

"Who just got hit?"

"Never mind," Hawkwood said. "If we can get the drones out of range, I'll send al-Saqua out to check him." He paused. "It should be safer for you. This smoke is starting to cover everything. With the temperature difference, it should screw up their infrared."

"Let's hope," said Leyden.

Hawkwood ignored his comment again. "Wait for my command, then go to those containers and find it. Along with a rack of kinetics and pulse charges. Get those too."

The smoke thickened, and Leyden could barely see the drones as they turned, then hovered above the river like bloated dragonflies. Flashes of ground fire blazed in the air around them, with little apparent effect.

"Go!" Hawkwood's command seemed to come from inside Leyden's head. He could see only one of the drones through the smoke.

Leyden ran down the river's edge. He stopped for a moment, crouching behind the fire burning alone the shoreline, then waded through the shallows around the flames and wreckage. The first container, almost empty, probably had held the Rendezvous Dome. Rapid, stuttering sounds; both drones must be firing flechettes upriver. He ran to the second container, and found the Dragon in two sections, wrapped in thick, transparent padding, along with the rack of shells, some smooth projectiles, others shaped like stubby arrows.

Dragon S-11. Sabot- and kinetic-equipped, laser-guided weapon that fired medium-caliber munitions that, on Old Earth, required forty-ton tanks. Leyden had seen them often enough but never held one before. The Multiphase Combat Weapon, the Illium infantry standard, could fire fifteen different types of projectiles, flechettes, explosives, and caseless ammunition. But it couldn't penetrate hard targets like armored vehicles, or combat drones. The Dragon, larger, heavier, slower to recharge, could.

"Got it," Leyden said, wheezing into his NavCom.

"Hold," said Hawkwood. The line went silent.

Leyden crouched beside the container, listening to the whine of the drones and the impact of pulse charges into the ground. And another sound, a gasping. He whirled around, then looked over the container. The merc who had been hit lay on the other side, half in the river, legs twitching slightly. Leyden dropped the Dragon and splashed through the water to his side.

It was Ehrenberg. He lay on his back, unseeing eyes staring straight up, mouth agape, his body shuddering with the effort of each unconscious breath. He appeared to have been hit in the groin and chest. The entry wounds in his carapace were small and irregular shaped; Leyden had no wish to turn him over see the horror of the exit wounds produced by high-impact flechettes. He pulled off Ehrenberg's helmet and tore open the carapace, just as he had done to Cabenza, in what now seemed like another life.

Stop the bleeding, he thought, even as another part of him knew that Erenberg was probably moments from death. He must at least find a way to perform that one meaningless act. Rummaging through the container, he found cushioned packing materials; that would do. He patched Ehrenberg's chest with ragged clumps of padding and tape, reached under his shoulders to turn him on his side when Erenberg's eyes fluttered, blinked into consciousness and focused on him. His hand tightened momentarily on Leyden's arm and he whispered something urgent and unintelligible, then repeated it.

"Yes," said Leyden to his unbearably young face. "It's going to be fine. You're going home."

Ehrenberg gave a barely perceptible nod and was gone.

Closing Ehrenberg's eyes, Leyden held him, rocking slightly to comfort himself as much as the lifeless body in his arms. He lay Ehrenberg back on the gravel beach and wiped the blood from his hands.

The NavCom came alive. "Leyden." Hawkwood's clipped voice. "We can't move at all. You're going to have to move closer to our position, activate the Dragon and take out the drones."

Leyden look down at Ehrenberg and said nothing.

"Leyden, you there? Acknowledge."

"I'm here. It was Ehrenberg. He's dead."

"Leyden, listen to me." He could hear Hawkwood's voice hardening. "We're *all* going to be dead very quickly if we can't get these drones off us. You understand? They're very low, scanning. None of us can even move without giving away our position. Our weapons are about depleted and we don't have recharger units."

"What do you expect me to do?" Leyden answered, almost shouting into the NavCom. "I have no idea how to operate this goddamn thing."

"We'll deal with that. Now move upriver, I'll talk you through the activation and firing sequence. But get up here. Stay under cover as much as you can, along the base of the cliff. Move. Now."

Leyden cursed to himself loudly enough for Hawkwood to hear. He slung the two sections of the Dragon across his shoulder and hoisted the shell rack. It was as heavy as he had feared: explosive pulse charges along with even heavier the kinetics, non-explosive but filled with depleted uranium for maximum penetration.

Scrambling up the narrow shore the base of the embankment, Leyden worked his way upriver through bogthorn and rock. After ten minutes he was exhausted, the leg numbed from the earlier explosion almost collapsing on him, the shell rack so heavy that he began simply dragging it.

"Location," snapped Hawkwood. "Can you see the drones?"

"Not yet." Leyden made out the outline of a drone through the rising smoke. "Yes. One of them. Just barely."

All right," said Hawkwood. Leyden heard a burst of static that, after a moment, he realized was an explosion. Hawkwood came back on the line, voice unchanged. "You will activate and arm the Dragon there. Then move out nearer the river so that you have the drones in clear sight. Acknowledge."

"Yes," Leyden said. Listening to Hawkwood, he tore open the fastenings on the padding and pulled the Dragon free. It looked like a large tube filigreed with triggers and valve-like devices that reminded him of a Toranaguin spirit flute. The only feature he recognized immediately was the fitting for his shoulder.

Hawkwood's instructions were precise and relentless: Attach the two sections. Find the keypad and input screen. After pressing the activation switches, Leyden could feel the powerful fingers of the shaped magnetic field that the Dragon generated come alive in his hands. But Hawkwood's directions for deploying the laser guidance system proved incomprehensible.

"Forget it," Hawkwood said after several futile minutes. "Just aim it at the goddamn things and shoot. You'll be firing an explosive, so all you need to do is get close. Now on the keypad, punch in XHE2. That's the munitions you're using, then a dash, then the distance to the target. What do you figure from your location, when you move closer to the river? Fifty meters?"

"I don't know. Maybe seventy."

"Close enough," said Hawkwood. Leyden could feel the pressure in his voice. "Find the pulse shells. Load two, close and lock the cover. Take the safety off, flip up the trigger guard, aim, and fire. Move out."

Dragging the shell rack behind him, Leyden ran in a half crouch to the shoreline, looking for a rock, a rise, anything that could serve as cover. There was nothing. The smoke was dissipating, and he could see the drones clearly now, not firing at all, but floating slowly over the river, scanning and waiting. They gave no indication that their sensors had picked him up yet.

"All right, all right," Leyden whispered to himself. "No problem now." He breathed deeply but was unable to stop the shaking in his hands. He closed the trigger guard closed, aimed. Sweat from his forehead stung his eyes as he squinted along the top of the Dragon.

He fired.

The Dragon seemed to give an enormous gulp, then torqued so hard in his hands that he fell to his side.

He looked toward the drones. No explosion, nothing. He had missed.

Only a slight vapor trail marking the shell's trajectory even indicated that he had fired. Something splashed into the river; for a moment, Leyden thought the drones had fired back at him, but it was the sabot, the covering, which had peeled away from the shell as it cleared the Dragon. An explosion reverberated invisibly in the distance.

Leyden scrambled to his feet and struggled to seat the Dragon once more on his shoulder. Trigger guard off, he said to himself. Deep breath, steady. He fired again. As he did, he heard Hawkwood over the NavCom: "No!"

Leyden kept his footing this time, but the results were the same. The gasp and torque of the Dragon, splash of the sabot into the river and, after a pause, a distant, heavy explosion.

Only now, one of the drones turned slowly toward him.

Hawkwood came back on the NavCom with a blistering string of obscenities. "Seventy *meters*!" he yelled. "You fired the fucking thing 70 *kilometers*!"

Fuck you, too!" Leyden screamed back.

The drone shuddered, and a geyser of rock and gravel erupted behind him. Leyden dropped the Dragon and turned to run up the shore to the shelter of the cliff. A shower of gravel and stones rained down on him from the explosion. He flattened himself on the ground.

"I'm spotted," he gasped into the NavCom. "Can't stay here."

"Leyden, this is all we have. This is it." Hawkwood's voice was low and controlled again. "I need you to get back and try again. We'll give you covering fire."

Leyden looked again at the small crater that the drone's shell had carved out of the ground. Crawling back to the shore, he grabbed the Dragon and shell rack and inched his way into the crater. As he did, the drone fired a burst of flechettes that stitched their way across the shore.

"Now what?"

"We go kinetic," Hawkwood said. "How may do you have?"

Leyden looked. "Seven."

There was a pause. "Load three. Just like the shells, then close the cover. No settings."

Leyden felt numb, the kinetics so heavy that he had to use both hands to unlatch them from the rack and fit them into the Dragon. He paused for a moment on his knees, head down, gasping, before hoisting the Dragon onto his right shoulder.

"Ready," he said in a hoarse whisper.

"All right," said Hawkwood. "You don't have laser targeting. Use the scope and walk the kinetics into the drone. I mean, we'll set the velocity low, so you can see them in flight. Aim the first and fire. You'll miss. Watch its path, adjust and fire the second, adjust, fire the third. . . see? Walk them right into the drones. Understood? You can do this."

"Sure."

"You can do this," Hawkwood repeated. "On my mark, stand, take your time, fire."

"What about distance and altitude?"

"Forget it. Aim and shoot."

"Yeah." A moment later, he heard a burst of ground fire from the canyon walls, followed by Hawkwood's command. "Now."

Leyden stood, stumbling under the weight of the Dragon. He couldn't crouch, couldn't run, only stand straight and walk toward the water's edge, watching the bursts of pulse charges around the drones. One drone began firing flechettes back into the cliffside, but the trailing drone rotated back toward him.

Three more steps, Leyden said to himself, feeling the sweat soak his chest and drip down his face. His eyes blurred and stung, the drone still turning. No, a few steps more, out into the shallows for a better angle. The drone hung motionless in the smoke-infested air, head on to him.

Leyden dropped to one knee in the water. *Okay*. Safety off, trigger guard up. The drone fired a rope of flechettes that foamed the water in the middle of the river and raced past him. Leyden could hear them travel up the shoreline.

He squeezed the trigger and fired, steadied himself with a hand at the bottom of the shallow water from the recoil, and watched the kinetic arc over the drone. A miss. He adjusted downward and fired twice more in rapid succession. The second shot slammed into the drone and tore off the front end in a cloud of white smoke, obscuring the trajectory of his third shot entirely.

The drone spun down wildly and crashed in a gout of flame on the far side of the river. The other drone executed a three-hundred-sixty-degree circle, then climbed swiftly into the fog bank and disappeared.

Leyden dropped the Dragon into the shallow water and sank to both knees in a moment of triumph, desolation, and complete exhaustion.

12 CHAEBOLS AND TRIADS

The expedition wrapped its dead, Ehrenberg and another mercenary, Carpentier, in coarse, Rigelian linen and laid them beside the river.

Tirun placed small expedition medallions on their chests, and for several minutes they stood in a semicircle, listening to the steady pulse of the Whitebone. No one spoke. Later, Zia and Chácon dug graves and buried them at the base of the cliff, amid flowering bogthorn.

Laser and pulse charges had ripped the shoreline apart and transformed the camp into a ruin, strewn with burned equipment and fragments of pod material. Small avalanches, torn from the cliff sides, had smothered whole sections of the shore, burying Carpentier and the Rendezvous Dome under rock and debris. A large piece of one raft floated upside down in the shallows, revolving slowly in the river's eddies. Chemical fires still smoldered, spitting black smoke into the sky. The air reeked of charred polymers.

Leyden, Verlaine, and Chacon joined An San Kee and Mkeki in helping the physician, Al-Saqua, set up a makeshift hospital under the skeleton of a container draped with salvaged sections of the Rendezvous Dome.

Chapandagura, who had been trapped in the Rendezvous Dome with Bertelsmann, had escaped with a fractured leg. Holmes and Modrescu had minor flechette wounds, Zia and Mkeki had bandaged heads from flying debris.

"Look at it this way," Verlaine said to them, "the company will have to bump your fee by fifty percent for combat pay. I think I can find the clause in your contract."

"My head hurts," Mkeki replied, eyes closed. "*You* tell me what fifty percent of zero is."

"Never mind," Verlaine said. "So we don't make it to the famous Eëlios rainforest. I'm trying to figure a marketing strategy for bogthorn as an ornamental shrub. Could be quite the rage. Like ice palms from Umlivik a few years back. Remember?"

"I have a hard time seeing you running a string of nurseries," Kee said.

"Ah, but you miss the point. The bogthorn franchise would only be a cover."

They all looked at him; Kee feigned indifference. Verlaine sat smug and silent.

Zia, youngest and most heavily tattooed of the mercenaries, couldn't stand it. "I give up. A cover for what?"

"Kytes," Verlaine whispered. "We smuggle back a batch of fertilized kyte eggs, and raise them in the bogthorn nurseries for nature parks. What I have in mind is this — while we regroup here, we get a couple of you mercs, and our local hero, Leyden, here, to start tracking these things back to their nests. No weapons, though, we don't want to hurt the little darlings."

Chácon stood. "We'll get right on it. But first, Illium Officer Hawkwood has requested that I undertake a little survey mission down river."

Leyden felt both restless and drained in the aftermath of his Dragon duel with the drones. "I'll go too."

As they started to leave, Verlaine said, "Oh Leyden, if I forgot to mention it, nice work on that drone."

Chácon stopped. "I was talking with the others." He paused. "Did you really set the first charges at seventy *klicks* instead of seventy meters?"

Leyden could feel himself go into a defensive mental crouch. "Apparently."

Chácon shook his head. "Hawkwood forgot that the default settings on the Dragon are in kilometers. So it's on him."

"Fine," Leyden said. "But those things didn't fly seventy kilometers, did they?"

Chácon shook his head. "They max out at something like fifteen, eighteen."

Verlaine said, "But an impressive display of Illium might, nonetheless, I'm sure."

"No doubt," Leyden said, turning away. "Probably scared the hell out of any kytes hanging around these parts."

♦

When Chácon and Leyden returned several hours later, they found the rest of the expedition clearing away wreckage and collecting equipment. Along with the Rendezvous Dome, the attack had destroyed much of their food and fuel, one full container of research equipment, communications gear and spare hardware. Two rafts were destroyed, the remaining two heavily damaged.

An San Kee sadly reviewed her surviving plant samples. Modrescu, normally An San Kee's gloomy shadow, sat in the hospital shelter talking with Mkeki. An odd couple, Leyden thought, but he could now recall seeing them together several times before, onboard the *Balliol* and at Musgrave's Dance. He couldn't find Suslov anywhere.

After everyone downed a grim, short-ration meal, Leyden joined Tirun, Hawkwood, Verlaine, and Chácon in a corner of the hospital shelter.

"Tribune Hawkwood will brief everyone later," Tirun said, "but I thought we should talk first." He was sitting forward, elbows on knees, looking like a larger-than-life portrayal of melancholia. Not the figure who had promised them wealth and adventure aboard the *Balliol*.

Leyden looked over at Hawkwood. His pale eyes seemed to gather and focus the light like small lasers in the dark frame of his face. Hawkwood had nodded to Leyden when he returned to camp and disassembled the Dragon. They had not spoken.

"I imagine there are some questions," Tirun said dryly.

"Yeah," Leyden said. "Like what the hell just happened?"

"Obviously, we're not alone," Tirun answered. "Someone is here who doesn't want us around."

"There's no possibility these are a group of high-tech Eëlians, then?" Leyden asked. "With equipment left from the last survey mission?"

"None," Hawkwood said. "Those were current-issue Illium-standard combat drones. Full array of pulse and antipersonnel weaponry. With ASVR upgrades, from the look of them. The League's latest models, not yet authorized for anyone, even licensed mercenaries with letters of marque."

"ASVR?" Leyden asked.

"Advanced sensor and virtual reality controls."

"Meaning what?"

Hawkwood's tone was dispassionate. "Meaning that, along with blasting the hell out of us, they made a complete sensor sweep of the entire area. The remote drone controllers are wired in extensively at conscious and unconscious levels. They basically fly the drones as extensions of themselves."

Leyden thought for a moment. "And the drone we shot down?"

"Generally, the operator spends a day or so under heavy sedation to recover. The experience is about as close to being blasted to death as you can be without the real thing."

"My, my" said Verlaine, "how did I ever miss *that* experience in Poseidon's sensory deprivation tanks?"

Leyden looked back at Tirun. "You're saying that another Illium expedition has made the Burn to Eëlios, and they mean to have the place all to themselves."

Tirun stirred heavily and gazed out at the Whitebone. "It would seem."

"How is that possible?" Leyden demanded. "Trans-Illium has the exclusive expeditionary rights to Eëlios on this cycle, doesn't it? If that's so, how could the Illium League have permitted anyone else through?"

"Well, there are several possibilities," Verlaine answered. "All delightfully entertaining. Remember, they weren't burning through to Eëlios, just to the Selucid Swarm. I don't need to tell you that the Swarm is one of the hottest frontier systems around now. So probably fifty expeditions passed through the Selucid portal with us to the Swarm, and a couple of dozen, maybe, going the other way."

Leyden could feel himself in the pull of a powerful current from his past, one that caught him up in all the intensity of his past life on Toranga, when he had joined the alliance that revolted against the League's monopoly control of the portal connecting Toranga to the Illium Archipelago. Toranga had counted on support from other Core Worlds. When it failed to materialize, the Illium League moved swiftly to crush the rebellion, occupy the planet, and execute the leaders in the traditional manner — by ejecting them through launch tubes from planetary orbit. The man who led the final assault on the Toranguin capital was Illium Tribune Hawkwood.

Leyden tried to suppress any emotion in his voice. "So another expedition had a cover story taking it to one location in the Selucid Swarm, then presumably diverted to Eëlios?"

In the silence that followed, Leyden noticed that, while Tirun seemed depressed, Hawkwood, his ice eyes closing momentarily, appeared uncomfortable, even angry.

Verlaine glanced over at Hawkwood as well. "We assume that's what the official Illium League records show." he said.

"The *official* records?" Leyden asked.

Tirun cleared his throat with a deep rumble and dug his fingers deep into his flaming beard. "Whatever the records show, an expedition of this size couldn't have made the transition to Eëlios without the compliance, formal or not, of the Illium League. With its set of distance-array sensors on this side of the portal, the League can easily track the trajectories of the lightships once they enter the Selucid Swarm. The League units handling this burn cycle knew where this particular expedition was going — or found out very quickly. How far up that knowledge goes up the League chain is another matter."

Leyden could feel the tension radiating from Hawkwood at that statement. They all remained silent for a moment.

"What about a Ronin expedition?" Leyden asked. "Isn't it possible a group of freelance mercenaries hijacked the expedition *after* the Burn and diverted to Eëlios?"

"We've considering that," Verlaine said. "But there are several arguments against it. This is a high-risk operation to a largely unknown, unexplored planet. Ronin takeovers, when they have occurred, generally have been disguised to avoid League retaliation — and been to places with confirmed wealth that can be easily marketed back in the Illium. Ronin are big on cash and liquidity. Also, there are a number of classified security measures that would be triggered in a takeover like that. Finally, the question remains, if such a takeover took place, why didn't the League launch a pursuit when it saw a lightship divert from its authorized trajectory? We have no idea, but for the moment we have to assume there was no Ronin takeover."

"So if it's not Ronin, who?"

Verlaine sighed. "Remember, we're talking mega-resources here. Flameship investment, portal transition, intra-system fusion travel. Not to mention Illium League licenses and any payoffs to let them travel undisturbed to Eëlios. Crew and expeditionary equipment. There are really only a couple of possibilities. . . chaebol or triad, or some combination. Nothing else could have pulled off something of this magnitude."

Leyden took a minute to digest Verlaine's observations. On one level, what he was saying surprised no one. Leyden, like everyone else, assumed that one or more of the vast, Illium-wide conglomerates known as chaebols financed at least part of their own expedition. If he had bothered, he could have conducted some discreet research and found out which chaebol was most closely associated with Trans-Illium. But the chaebols, like myths and clouds, tended to dissipate upon close examination. Chaebols avoided publicity if at all possible. No corporate, financial, or other entity listed their names. And although several were quite well known, no one could agree on exactly what they did or how many actually operated in the Illium Archipelago. More critically, no one admitted to knowing whether, as the stories implied, they controlled not just commerce, but entire worlds.

The triads were another matter altogether. Although heavily invested in any number of legitimate enterprises, their wealth rested on drugs. From the moment the first portals opened, smugglers realized that few items had a greater return per unit than illegal narcotics. Initially, drug traffickers moved the usual array of hallucinogens, amphetamines, opiates, fake aphrodisiacs, bear bile, folk remedies, and unlicensed meds — often in combination with other small items that could be easily concealed to avoid the League' tariffs. But as new worlds joined the Illium, so did entirely new generations of drugs, notably Black Dust, processed from the mushroom fields of Cold Moon Rising. The Cold Moon traffickers had plenty of rivals, especially the deadly urban-based triads of Ohzumé. But Cold Moon remained the largest and most successful of the Illium triads, with resources reputed to rival those of the chaebols themselves. The relationship of Cold Moon and other triads to the chaebols remained an explosive political issue on a dozen Illium worlds.

Leyden looked over at Verlaine. "Are you saying that Cold Moon could be the ones out there, equipped with the latest combat drones? That would suggest that the triad had managed to infiltrate the League itself. For what? New drug varieties?"

"Why not?" Verlaine said. "On the other hand, we've never heard of the triads trying anything this big before. The more likely possibility is one of the chaebols — the Sidereal Collective, Taranazuka, or SkyFlame."

"Why not JKH2?"

Verlaine shrugged. "Perhaps, but less likely."

Verlaine had named the largest chaebols, although others existed as well. Verlaine had dismissed JKH2, Jong Kirov Hathaway Holdings, perhaps the most secretive and least known, but also one of the oldest, with ties to the legendary Anton Kirov himself. The Sidereal Collective certainly had the size, and perhaps the greatest financial resources of the four; but it tended to be associated less with Illium expeditions and frontier planets than with vast real estate holdings throughout the Core Worlds. SkyFlame and the Taranazuka had appeared more recently — both growing, hungry, and willing to deploy mercenary forces when crossed.

Leyden looked at Hawkwood. "Remarkable. It would seem that someone has bought off a piece of the League."

He could see, with satisfaction, as Hawkwood's eyes momentarily squeezed shut, that he had hit home.

Tirun held up a massive hand. "I'm not interested in having you win any debating points right now, Leyden. The immediate problem is what to do next. Whoever is out there came well equipped and knew exactly where we were."

"Do we have any idea how many or what they're carrying?" Leyden said.

Hawkwood finally spoke. "If they have combat drones, it means that they dropped heavy — with drones, sensor and comm nets, perhaps ground-effect vehicles, weapons stocks. In other words, along with whatever scientific personnel they brought, they've probably brought a full combat team."

"How many?"

Hawkwood shrugged. "They probably dropped at least forty to maintain all that gear. Maybe sixty total."

"Where are they?" Leyden asked. "Close enough for a ground attack next?"

"We don't know," Hawkwood said. "I've got Suslov and Tranner out on patrol. They report nothing. They've also installed scanners, so we'll know of anything within thirty klicks coming from the direction of the Chaga Sea. Our guess is that they're not based here at all, but operating from the edge of the rainforest. Which is where we were supposed to be in the first place, if the Drop hadn't been sabotaged."

"That's confirmed?" Leyden asked.

"We've been analyzing what happened," Hawkwood said. "An accident or miscalculation by the *Balliol* is very unlikely. The drone attack simply confirms sabotage by the other expedition, chaebol or triad."

Leyden stared out at the smoldering wreckage, rockslides, and iron-gray skies. It was hard to imagine ever missing the prison on Rigel Prime, but he did.

"What's their next move?" Verlaine asked.

"Right now, they have a lot of raw data and video to review," Hawkwood said as flatly as if he were delivering a weather report. "That will tell them almost everything about us — approximate numbers, how we're equipped, and armed. They will also have surveyed downriver."

"You know," Verlaine said, "I once had the chance to go into accounting, believe it or not. Well, Mr. Hawkwood, what does your chaebol counterpart do now?"

Hawkwood pondered. "If they don't know now, their scans will confirm that we are a small, damaged, lightly armed expedition. They will know that the river becomes virtually impassable and that our supplies are low. They will assume that, sooner or later, we have to make a dash across the Chaga Sea to our original objective, the rainforest."

"No need to sugarcoat this for us," Verlaine said. "We can take it. Option one, we can hunker down here and run out of everything. Or hike out and they nail us when we're in the open, exposed, knee-deep in Chaga Sea muck."

Hawkwood voice remained neutral. "Depending on what they're carrying, they could launch a low-level drone attack to neutralize our Dragon, or use stand-offs, if they have them. Or even bring up a combat team in a ground-effects vehicle."

Verlaine heaved a theatric sigh. "I can't decide whether I prefer that, or surviving to explain to Trans-Illium management how we managed to squander close to half-billion talons on a bad raft trip."

Tirun rumbled deep in his throat. "Plan on survival, Verlaine, and writing your highly entertaining memoirs. Those are *their* options. What are ours?"

Hawkwood cleared an area on the table in front of him and activated a NavCom hologram that projected a map stretching from Musgrave's Dance, across the Chaga Sea to a body of water called Kronos Bay, which separated the Chaga from the rainforest. The holo provided detailed imagery of the river portion, recorded and analyzed as they rafted down the Whitebone, but much of the rest of the display showed only large-scale features from space-based surveys.

Hawkwood generated longitude and latitude gridlines along with a small light marking their current location. He adjusted the hologram's intensity and outlined a plan to split the expedition into four groups, scatter, and push hard and fast across the Chaga to Kronos Bay. Then find a way to sail across. They listened in growing dismay and gloom.

Hawkwood paused, looking at Leyden. "There might be an alternative. Do you and Chácon have anything to report?"

Leyden turned to Chácon. "Tell them about our adventures."

"We hiked a couple klicks down the Whitebone," Chácon said, looking to his leader and fellow mercenary, Tirun. "The river drops into a narrow gorge. Solid rapids. Narrow shorelines in some places, just but otherwise not much but rock walls."

Leyden interrupted. "Meaning we couldn't run it with the rafts we have now."

"I'm not following," Verlaine said. "We swim it?"

"No," Chácon said. "But we could take the pods that are still intact, and whatever we can salvage. Build two large rafts, as heavy and durable as possible — and run the river. Also, I think I can stretch fabric over a frame for two kayaks we could use to scout ahead of the rafts."

They all fell silent. Tirun spoke. "How do we guide rafts that heavy?"

"Basically, you don't," Chácon said. "We just build them strong enough to bull our way downriver. The pod skins are resilient stuff, so we just figure we're going to smash into a lot of rocks, bounce off and keep going.

If we hit truly impassable stretches with any kind of shore, we can line the rafts through them with ropes, like we've done before."

Verlaine seemed to be examining his fingernails with great intensity. "And what if we don't bounce, but flip?"

Leyden said, "We use the packing materials to make life rings that attach to the rafts. If the raft flips, the rings should help keep you high enough in the water to avoid getting pulled under. That plus the protection of our carapaces. Ropes keep you with the raft until you hit a section of water calm enough to make a recovery."

"Let me get this straight," Verlaine said, chewing a nail. "I'm on an alien planet, tied to an upside-down raft, swimming through some of the worst rapids we're ever experienced, watching overhead for another drone attack, wearing a homemade life preserver. Am I close?"

Leyden and Chácon looked at each other. "That's about it," Leyden said.

"Hawkwood?" Tirun didn't bother to look up from the hologram.

"I don't like it at all," Hawkwood said. "Except for one thing. It's the one move the opposition won't expect."

◆

In the lingering twilight, Nevea dropped from the sky and Naryl floated, purple red, on the edge of the river gorge. The river lay in deep shadow, its sides oozing water from the Chaga Sea like a saturated sponge.

The expedition hid itself in the dubious shelter of cliff edge and bogthorn.

When everyone seemed to have disappeared into their hutches, Leyden emerged from his in search of Suslov.

As he splashed quietly through the shallows, around rock slides and shell holes, Leyden heard voices near the hospital shelter. The wounded, he assumed, Chapandagura, Zia, and Holmes. But moving closer, he saw only motionless, sleeping forms.

He heard the sound of laughter: a woman's voice, and another, male. Leyden stepped behind a piece of fabric that covered one side of the shelter and looked around the edge.

"No, no, really," a voice was saying. "First assignment after being recruited. Fast-track corporate intern. Junior-league master of the Illium. Space services and maintenance firm on Rigel Prime. And I'm saying, 'No, sir. I'm *sure* you're fifty-*million*-talon lightship is not lost, sir. It's just not here in the inventory. And yes, sir, I will take *personal* responsibility and find it immediately. And yes, you have my *personal* assurance that it will be in *pristine* condition, ready for *multiple* burns to the Illium world of your choice.

"Of course, I had *no* fucking idea where the goddamn thing was. Back then, I couldn't have told you the difference between a White Dwarf freighter and a Magellanic lightship."

Verlaine, of course, but with her back to him, he couldn't immediately identify the woman. Only when she turned slightly did Leyden recognize An San Kee. She sat in her customary lotus position, but Leyden could see that Verlaine was already holding her hands and stroking her arms.

"What happened?" Kee asked in a voice full of laughter. "Was it just not listed properly?"

"Of course, that's what I assumed," Verlaine said. "A recordkeeping problem. I mean, you can't possibly *lose* a lightship. *Wrong*. It was lost. Meaning it had been in the spaceport maintenance yard, logged in, then disappeared. So this guy sues me, the company, the spaceport, the Rigelian government — compensation and punitive damages. Maybe five hundred million talons. And personally promises that I will be flayed, Tushangura-style, and dropped in an Arishima salt bath. So I figure this is it — goodbye glorious corporate career, hello mutilated beggar-monk on Salamis Minor. I mean, I'm suddenly feeling *very* spiritual."

Kee tried to muffle her laughter. "And?"

"Repos had taken it."

"Who?"

"Repossessed. Turned out the guy ran a string of shell companies and had defaulted on the payments. SpaceNet Financial Services hired a repo firm to take it. Apparently they brought in three Tatanka dirigibles one night, paid the spaceport crews to take a long coffee break, attached mag halters, and lifted it away. I mean, I have to file *a lot* of paperwork on that sucker. Decided that maybe accounting was not my best career move. But at least my future in monk-like contemplation got put on hold."

Verlaine reached for her hands again, leaning forward and quieting her laughter with a kiss, a hand touching her face and dropping to the top button on her tunic.

◆

Leyden found Suslov's sleeping hutch off by itself, wedged between a large boulder and a log blanched white by the river. He stood uncertainly for a moment while she unsealed the opening and looked out at him. Alone.

"Leyden," she said, squinting up at him. "Allow me to add congratulations for your work with the Dragon."

He could see the spray of freckles on the upper part of her right breast. "Someone said you'd been hit."

Suslov held up a bandaged forearm. "Flechette cut. Nothing, really."

"Glad to hear it."

Silence. Leyden shifted his feet. He felt awkward and exposed standing next to her as she kneeled in front of her hutch.

"Was there anything else?"

Leyden gazed up at the dripping, eroded shelf of the river. "No, guess not."

Suslov started to back into her hutch when she paused. "You're not really hurt, are you?"

"Hurt? No. Not even a scratch. Very strange."

"I didn't mean that."

He wondered how far downriver the splintered white log had traveled to end up on this shoreline. It must have been a long way, from the forests of the far north, since nothing that size grew in the Chaga Sea.

"Puzzled maybe, that's all."

He realized immediately that it was a mistake to have said anything.

Suslov looked amused. "Oh, my. And you'd like some kind of explanation, something comforting, along the lines of the things you'd say to the women you dropped, you know, back in the day."

Leyden stepped back. "Rest well, Officer Suslov."

"You, too, Leyden." It was impossible to register any inflection in her voice.

Suslov sealed up the entrance to her hutch. Leyden watched as she turned its translucent surface opaque to eliminate all outside light for sleeping.

13 FISHING FOR CYCLOPS

The rain changed. In the trip from Musgrave's Dance to the drone attack, the expedition had become resigned to suffocating fogs and abrupt, bone-chilling rainstorms. But now, as they attempted to recover from the drones, they began experiencing warmer, lingering showers. For the first time, they heard the distant cough of thunder. The rainforest of Eëlios beckoned, yet still out of sight, out of reach.

Despite being soaked through his torn carapace, Leyden felt slightly comforted; the thick clouds provided a virtual guarantee that the drones would not return soon. The Whitebone danced beneath the downpours, the blur of water erasing any discernable line between rainfall and river surface.

Leyden knelt by the water's edge and activated a small cutting tool with an intense blue laser edge, carving up the Dome's storage unit into slabs for the sides of the two large expedition rafts. He found it easy but tedious work. As he finished two vertical cuts from top edge to the ground, someone walked up behind him.

Without looking, he said, "Turn this thing over, will you, so I can keep going."

Someone flipped the container onto its side and he made a horizontal cut. The first panel thumped onto the ground, edges smoking from the laser burn. Leyden looked up. Hawkwood waited, carrying the two sections of the Dragon, which he placed at his feet.

For a moment, Leyden considered a sarcastic "by your leave," the traditional acknowledgment of an Illium subordinate to his superior, but thought better of it. "Yes?" he said. The last thing Leyden wanted now was a private conversation with Illium League Officer Hawkwood.

"Verlaine said that you had some information that you forgot to mention at our talk yesterday."

"I told Verlaine that I needed to tell Tirun something, yes."

"Tirun sent me."

Leyden straightened up and deactivated his laser cutting tool. Hawkwood's helmet and carapace were streaked with rain. Leyden remembered another rain day, when black smoke filled the skies of Toranga from a hundred burning buildings, bunkers, and mobile armored units. He had stood, rope-bound, before Hawkwood and other League officers, one of a collection of Toranguin prisoners to be inventoried, interrogated, and shipped out in a prison ship. That same day, the League forces detonated an enhanced neutron device inside The Citadel, Toranga's government complex, rendering it uninhabitable for generations.

Leyden shook his head slightly, bringing the river back into focus. "It's about Cabenza. The meteorologist."

"What about him?"

"He didn't die in a pod crash."

"No? What happened to him?"

Leyden paused, watching gouts of water pour into the river from the far bank. "Someone cut his throat."

Hawkwood remained expressionless. "And you decided not to mention this until now?"

"Yes. My little secret."

"Any reason I shouldn't treat this as a confession?" Hawkwood said. "Payback for Toranga."

"Treat it any damn way you want, Hawkwood," Leyden said. "When I found Cabenza, I naturally figured it was someone in the expedition. And there was no one I trusted. Now the situation's changed. If we assume that a chaebol or triad sabotaged the drop, they must also be responsible for killing Cabenza."

"There's no evidence the second expedition, whatever it is, was anywhere near our drop zone on the Chaga Sea."

"Why not?" said Leyden, beginning his second cut. "They have drones. Why not a small air shuttle too? With that kind of mobility, it would have been easy enough to travel north and monitor our movements, pick off an isolated member like Cabenza. Before the fog set in for real."

"Why bother?" Hawkwood answered. "They had us scattered all over the tundra. Probably assumed the we'd do little more than wait out the cycle for pick-up. Later, when we surprised them by running the Whitebone, they realized they had to finish the job."

"Meaning what?"

"Meaning you were right the first time. For whatever reason, someone on the expedition killed Cabenza."

Leyden straightened up and looked at him. "Well, the consolation is that if we all die, the murderer goes too."

"I don't know about you, Leyden, but I'm planning on finishing the job and going home."

"And save your precious League, no doubt."

"If necessary," Hawkwood said. "Which brings me to the other reason I came here." He pointed to the Dragon. "This."

"What's do you want? My autograph?"

"Close." Hawkwood dropped to one knee, snapped open the case and twisted the two sections of the weapon together. "From here on, I need to have patrols out at all times. That means keeping security armed and mobile. Along with Cabenza, we've already lost two mercs — Carpentier and Ehrenberg. Holmes is wounded. We're too few to tie down one of them with the Dragon, especially with ammunition stock so low."

"What are you suggesting? I couldn't even activate the goddamn guidance system last time. Not to mention the business of meters and kilometers."

"You'll be trained this time."

"Really. Who by?"

"Me."

Leyden deactivated the laser again. When he looked directly at Hawkwood, he noted that they were identical heights, which for some reason seemed exceedingly odd. "I don't think so. You were just about to arrest me for confessing to Cabenza's murder. Is this your fallback position?"

"Your feelings about the past, about Toranga, aren't of the slightest concern to me now," Hawkwood said in irritation. "I have a job to do, which is to help lead this expedition out of here as intact as possible. You may be a civilian, but you've actually fired the weapon in a combat situation, and unlike most of the rest of the expedition, you have no specific technical or security function to perform now. Therefore, I am assigning you to carry, maintain, and be trained on the Dragon. Is that clear?"

"Let me make something clear to you," Leyden said. "I work for Tirun, not you. That was the deal."

"Mission Leader Tirun has apprised me of that fact. He would be happy to confirm this assignment personally. Does that make matters clearer?"

Hawkwood held out the Dragon in his arms; Leyden debated for a moment before dropping the laser tool and taking it from him. It seemed heavier than he remembered. "This was the prime anti-armor weapon in the assault on Toranga, wasn't it?"

"One of them," Hawkwood said. "Now on your shoulder, lock in the brace and activate mag power, just as you did before. First, we'll work on the laser-guidance system."

◆

The river was a mass of torn brown water ripping through the earth and stone of the canyon before them. When they pushed off, the current caught them so swiftly that Leyden didn't even have time to glance back at their wrecked campsite.

Their world transformed. Sheer canyon walls closed in over them, leaving only a narrow corridor of fog-laden sky overhead. The sound of the river reverberated, a sustained roar as palpable as the regiments of waves that broke over the tops of the rafts and swamped the small kayaks tied to the sterns. Constant river spray saturated the air.

Kytes appeared overhead; smaller than the vast, solitary creatures that had cruised over them in the Chaga Sea, now in small flocks of three and four. They also seemed more active, dipping low over the river and emitting hoarse, hooting cries that echoed off the canyon walls.

The first kilometer of the Whitebone ran straight as a highway, coursing at enormous speed as the rafts heaved and spun in its grip. Chácon shouted commands from the helm of one raft, Tirun the other. More often than not, Leyden and the others flailed against the current helplessly. The water crested, and instead of encountering low-water, rock-edged rapids, they rocketed down stretches of intense white water that ran shore to shore, slamming them repeatedly into the canyon walls.

After the first stretch, their fortunes changed. The river narrowed yet again to little more than a gorge with a huge boulder wedged in the center. The river spewed twin gouts of white-yellow water on either side. After gazing at it in puzzlement for several minutes, Ulam announced that he recalled a description of this part of the river known as Stone Birth. Leyden immediately saw the image: the two arching currents of water were a woman's massive, sprawled legs, giving violent birth to an unformed stone child so massive that its top remained dry. It took two painful, cold-soaked hours to line the rafts through the gorge, scrambling for tiny foot- and handholds along the canyon face to brace against the weight and pull of the rafts.

Half a kilometer below Stone Birth, they found a shallow-water inlet and a shoreline wide enough to beach the rafts and recover. Verlaine promptly named the location Afterbirth.

They ate half-rations again, and for the first time Leyden felt a spike of real hunger. He was not alone. Ulam, Chácon and Suslov waded out and cast fishing lines into the deeper pools. With that act, the expedition acknowledged that they could no longer limit food consumption to Illium-supplied foods, just as most of them also shed their masks, respirators, and remaining pieces of carapaces.

Within half an hour, the three had hooked five of the ubiquitous, single-eyed crustaceans that the expedition had named cyclops, although Ulam insisted on referring to them by their correct, unpronounceable Eëlian name. These cyclops grew larger and more numerous than any they had seen before, transformed from the small, feathery creature that Leyden had poked from under a rock far up the Whitebone.

Modrescu, as expressionless as a shadow, waded out in the shallows, twisting a piece of soft, bright alloy onto a hook, and tossing his line into a hole under a rock downstream from the others. But when he caught a cyclops, he brought it to An San Kee, where they weighed, measured and extracted fluid from it, and then packed it into preservative salts with perhaps a dozen water-plant samples they had collected.

Several others, watching from shore, had already started boiling a large pot of water, when Ulam, who had weighted his line and thrown it far out into the river, gave a cry as he was swept off his feet. Chácon, who was nearest, lunged and caught him by the leg, quickly joined by the solitary planetary geologist, Bois, who helped pull Ulam to his feet. All three strained against the rigid, vibrating line.

Leyden joined others who splashed into the water, and soon they clung to the line, shouting, slipping on the rocks, slowly pulling in the largest cyclops any of them had seen. Once on shore, they stood back, well clear of its flailing, serrated claws. The beaked mouth, guarded by rows of fringed mandibles, opened and closed, and its single, pale eye revolved frantically on a fat, viscous stalk.

The cyclops, more than three meters from end to end, managed to heave itself toward the water; its outer shell, pliable and soft in the water, had become rigid enough to hold itself upright on land. Leyden realized that he had already seen at least four distinctive species of cyclops, each adapting to a different environmental niche along the river.

Ulam, more excited than Leyden had ever seen him before, pulled the cyclops over on its side. "We eat well now!" he cried, and expertly seized the two front claws, immobilizing them and slipped a long flat blade into the base of the eye stalk and twisted. The cyclops convulsed once as a clear liquid bubbled from the wound, and was still. Leyden turned away as Ulam began tearing off the limbs and tossing them into the boiling water. Like the others, however, Leyden stuffed himself on the bland, sweet meat. They piled the remnants on the fire.

He used the column of smoke from the burning cyclops carapace as a target for practicing with the Dragon's laser guidance system. Later, he timed himself on stripping down and reassembling it, Hawkwood's instruction manual by his side.

14 THE ABYSS

The Whitebone offered no other convenient fishing spots as it cut into the Eëlian rock, chiseling a deepening canyon; the sky receded to a slender path that could only be seen intermittently between the canyon walls. Leyden, estimating that they were almost a kilometer below ground level, tried to imagine a forest whose crown rose to such a height. He couldn't.

The river resembled a tunnel in an advanced state of disrepair, as sections of canyon wall broke loose far above them, triggering small avalanches of rock and soil that plunged into the river in massive geysers. They felt under attack, and during rest periods the expedition anchored under overhangs to protect them from the constant bombardment.

Chácon and Tirun tried to plot their course through each section of violent water, but once on the river, the current usually hurled them along as casually as a leaf. When they weren't fighting mountainous rapids, the Whitebone ran as dark and gray as liquid metal. The narrow shoreline disappeared entirely, and instead of landing, they pulled the rafts into flooded caverns during the rest cycle, secured them to outcroppings and tried to sleep on the Whitebone's shuddering flow.

Twice, Leyden's raft overturned in narrow chutes, and along with the others, he had to pull himself hand over hand along his safety line back to the raft.

As he grew ever more exhausted, Leyden found the ceaseless, uncontrollable strength of the river frightening. In his deepest moments of fatigue, he conceded that he would never survive this place; the Eëlian rainforest seemed like a place he would witness only in an afterlife.

The kytes grew more numerous and more agitated. For the first time, one slammed into the side of a raft on a low pass, floundering messily across the surface of the river, beak clacking at the water, before recovering and gaining altitude. During the next relatively quiet stretch, Modrescu and An San Kee, using high-rez scanners, pointed out that they seemed to have entered a nesting area — the nests themselves wedged invisibly into crevices in the canyon walls. Only the sight of kytes continually flying in and out gave away their locations.

Verlaine shouted to Chácon and Leyden against the pounding of the river. "Climb up and get me those damn eggs. Your Illium fortune, guaranteed."

But An San Kee, in the trailing raft, didn't joke about kytes. "I want the next one!" she shouted to Modrescu, who seemed neither surprised nor dismayed at her demand, only more grim than usual. Leyden wondered if he were always so withdrawn or was still brooding over not being chosen bioteam leader instead of Kee.

Modrescu dug through one of the packs lashed to the center of the raft and assembled a device that looked like a discarded piece of plumbing. The kytes circled overhead, with one or two breaking off from the spiraling formation to skim the river next to the rafts.

Kee stood. "This one," she shouted, pointing to the smallest of three kytes approaching low from downriver. Modrescu aimed, and as they passed by, fired from a distance of less than ten meters. The kyte continued to glide for a moment before pausing in midair with a shudder and nosing down into the water. Kee and Modrescu threw out a dilating net and caught the kyte as the current swept it next to the raft.

As the rest of the expedition watched from bobbing rafts, the two of them drew blood samples, carved off small patches of skin and flesh, measured and photographed the kyte. Even across the expanse of nervous water, Leyden could see the astonishing narrowness of the kyte's head and toothed bill; glaring, stunned eyes; skin as mottled and pitted as the rock walls where it nested. When Kee extended one of the delta-shaped wings, the hairless, featherless skin pulled taut.

She looked up at them, still holding the extended wing. "Not a great flyer, but wonderful gliders, especially with the air currents here."

Kee nodded to Modrescu, who filled a large syringe and injected the kyte with a clear liquid. It revived immediately, lashing frantically as both of them struggled to control its head and clawed feet. Finally, they heaved it out of the raft. The kyte flapped its way through the water to shore, its hooting cries quickly picked up and repeated by others circling in the narrow confines of the canyon.

♦

They overturned again on the next stretch of rapids.

It had begun to rain, a slowly thickening mist; and the lead raft, with Leyden, Verlaine, Mkeki, Al Saqua, Zia, and Chácon, shot through a narrow chute of seething water, slammed into a hidden rock, spun and tipped high up on its right side. Zia, still recovering from his head wound, and Mkeki, kneeling along the side, tumbled into the water but managed to cling to the safety rope strung around the outside. That slight reduction in weight kept the raft upright; it continued downriver on its side for another long moment, then slapped back into the water. But the trailing raft rose on end, hung for a moment and flopped over, upside down.

The river exploded into chaos. From downriver, Leyden could see everyone in the water, life rings around their waists, trailing behind their safety ropes. The sliver of sky reverberated with thunder and the rain's intensity increased.

"Go!" Chácon shouted. They began paddling across the river to intercept the raft when something slammed into Leyden and knocked him sprawling. He grabbed for the safety rope to keep himself from going over the side. Looking up, Leyden could see a phalanx of five or six kytes advancing upriver past them, wings in a slow beat, descending to attack those in the water.

"Weapons!" Chácon shouted to Zia, who dropped his paddle to scramble over the packs lashed in the center of the raft. It took him precious seconds to dig through the pile of equipment and extricate a multiphase rifle. By that time, the kytes, sensing the swimmers' helplessness, had clawed and lashed at them with their toothed beaks before spiraling back up high and disappearing into the rain. Zia fired once, helplessly, in an empty, water-filled sky.

Leyden couldn't see the swimmers clearly, but those wearing helmets against the rock falls seemed more stunned than hurt. Several others, bare headed, appeared to be bleeding.

Chácon bumped into the overturned raft, and Zia leaped across with a rope to secure it. Verlaine and Leyden followed, reeling in the lines attached to the wounded, Holmes and Chapandagura. It was only then that they realized that Modrescu and Suslov had swept past them: somehow, in the kyte attack or their fall into the river, they had become detached from their safety lines.

Thunder rippled overhead, joining the constant, pounding roar of the Whitebone. The rain fell in heavy sheets, and Leyden could barely see that Bois, hurtling downstream, had managed to catch the side of a rock, and pull himself out of the current. Modrescu, who was trailing him in the water, grabbed Bois's hand and pulled himself alongside. Leyden turned back to yank Chapandagura aboard, his face tight with pain.

As Leyden and the others hauled in the rest of the swimmers, Hawkwood pushed off in the kayak, heading toward Bois and Modrescu, motionless on the rock. Only then did Leyden see the shape materializing out of the rain from downriver: a kyte whose wingspan seemed to extend across the river from one canyon wall to another.

"My god," Leyden whispered. They had been in the company of kytes from almost their first moments on Eëlios, but nothing had prepared him for anything this size.

Modrescu must have sensed its presence first, because he rolled off the rock and back into the water. But Bois, head bleeding and dazed from the first attack, could only raise his arms as the enormous creature struck. The first attack slashed through his carapace with its sawtooth beak. The kyte banked sharply, circling so low that its wing tip dragged through the water. With its hammer-shaped head, it appeared more like a piece of deranged industrial machinery than a living creature. It dropped once more on the rock and seized Bois by his neck and rose again.

Standing in the raft next to him, Zia fired a burst of flechettes, but the unsteady raft made him miss. The blast seemed to have distracted the kyte however, because it suddenly dropped Bois, who fell limply into the river, and turned back toward Modrescu.

By then, Hawkwood had pulled alongside the rock his kayak, pulling his knifesword and extending the retractable blade. As the kyte slashed down toward him, Hawkwood thrust the sword inside the kyte's jagged beak where it wedged, vibrating. Hawkwood leaped for the kyte, wrapping his arms around its ropelike neck, and for a moment they both hovered in the air above Modrescu and the rock.

The kyte, wings pulsating, rose in the air, twisting violently, until Hawkwood fell back into the river. Zia, who had dropped to a sitting position in the upriver raft to steady his aim, fired another burst of flechettes that seemed to pass through the kyte's wing. The kyte gave a hoarse, honking cry and circled up into the rain-thick sky and disappeared.

By then, Hawkwood had climbed back onto the rock with Modrescu. Bois had disappeared. Another retort of thunder sounded through the canyon, sharp and somehow different. Leyden looked up to see rock explode from high up on the canyon walls and begin to arc down toward the river. It was followed by a second, then a third, and the river went wild as torrents of stone and earth fell into the river.

Verlaine and Chácon took up the cry. "Drones!"

Looking up, Leyden could barely see the mottled, cylindrical shape appear momentarily over the river.

As the rafts approached the rock, Leyden stood up and shouted as much to himself as to Hawkwood. "What now? What the *hell* do we do now?"

15 KYTE'S FLIGHT

In the panicked moments following the new drone attack, the expedition turned to Leyden with a cry for the Dragon. He peered up through the unrelenting rain, then turned to the wet faces around him and shrugged. The Dragon was inaccessible, secured deep in the bottom of the overturned raft.

"Everyone to shore!" Tirun roared over the din of the water. "Get the rafts to shore!"

They strained to cross the heavy current, paddles biting deep into the water, aiming toward a shallow spit of gravel and rock barely rising above the river's surface. On shore, they heaved the overturned raft right side up. Amid the confusion of securing equipment and retying safety lines, al-Saqua sprayed antibiotic bandages on those who had been hit in the first wave of the kytes's attack: Modrescu, Ka-Sung and Tranner. Only three Multiphase Combat Weapons remained with the expedition; Suslov, Chácon, and Zia attached them to their shoulder harnesses.

Leyden kept scanning the sky, but the drone did not reappear. Hawkwood splashed ashore beside him. "Assemble the Dragon," he said to Leyden. "Load a single sabot charge, but don't fire, except on my command."

"Why not?"

"My guess is they're going to try and test us, force us to expend ammunition. They don't know what we've got left, but with the damage they've done, they must figure we're running low on everything."

He watched Leyden unwrap the lashings around one pack and pull out the two thickly wrapped pieces of the Dragon.

"Don't even activate the thing," Hawkwood said. "Their probes will pick up the energy signature."

"You've got this all figured out," Leyden muttered to himself, attaching the two segments. "You handle the goddamn thing."

Hawkwood turned away to survey the beach, ordering Chácon on ahead in the kayak. Meanwhile, Tirun had everyone repacking and lashing everything down as tightly as possible. "Now, push off," he called out. "Everyone in and push off now. Now!"

As they did, the NavCom line crackled in Leyden's ear. It was Tirun again, broadcasting to everyone. "Make sure everything, I mean everything, supplies, paddles, weapons, yourselves are secure. Unless we hit an impassable section that we have to portage, we're not stopping, not for anyone or anything."

Tirun's continued, his voice heavy and urgent. "By Ulam's estimate, we've got to be close, no more than twenty kilometers to Kronos Bay, maybe less. If you overturn, stay on your ropes and pull yourself along back to the raft. If need be, ride the goddamn thing upside down until there's enough calm water to flip it over. If you get separated, ride your life ring and try and catch up. But don't expect a raft to hold back for you because it won't. The drones are out there to finish the job. All we've got now is the Whitebone to take us to the only safe place left. The rainforest."

The rafts pulled into the main current and began picking up speed downstream. After a crackle-filled pause, Tirun said, "Good luck to you all," and cut off the transmission.

◆

In a practiced unison borne of many Eëlian cycles on the Whitebone, the expedition's paddles bit into the racing water. Since the beginning of the expedition, they had seen the river change in color from crystalline to slate gray, and now, to an opaque brown, full of suspended soil. Leyden's raft, with Hawkwood now at the helm, smashed through walls of high water, sheets of spray pouring over the edge of the pod and soaking them all. Leyden reached out with his paddle, bending hard into his stroke, arms and shoulders already numb with fatigue, resisting the temptation to look behind him. The Dragon and its rack of charges were tied to the floor of the raft at his feet.

Zia, in the prow, scanned the cliff sides and the sky with high rez glasses as the rain finally eased. Suslov did the same in the other raft. Chácon, scouting to their front in the kayak, broke through fitfully on the NavCom, and Leyden guessed Tirun had a secure line to Chácon, which he opened to the full expedition when he saw fit.

"Heavy rapids," Chácon reported. "Steer right. Repeat, steer right."

The raft with Leyden and Hawkwood plowed into heavy water, spun and wedged momentarily on a rock shelf. The second raft, with Suslov in the prow and Tirun at the helm, shot by them, and traveled twenty meters downstream before they managed to push off.

"Oh no." Even over the din of the river, Leyden could hear the shock in Chácon's voice. "Kytes. . . ten, no. . . twenty, maybe more. Heading upriver.... Overhead now, I'm rolling over. . ."

"Suslov! Tranner! Zia!" Hawkwood's voice cracked over the NavCom line. "At the ready. Flechettes. Wide dispersal."

Zia unslung his weapon. In the lead raft, Leyden could see Suslov and Tranner doing the same.

Another voice cut in, clearly on emergency override, An San Kee's. "These are living creatures. Please. This is their world. Please, only shoot to ward them off. . . harm as few as possible."

"All right Kee," Hawkwood snapped "Off channel. This isn't alien empathy time. Fire at your discretion, but track only the ones attacking the rafts. No need to take out the entire flock."

The kytes rounded a downriver bend, flying toward the rafts in a ragged formation just above the water. Leyden tried to count them — at least twenty. All sizes, but none seemed as big as the one that had attacked Suslov and Modrescu. As they approached, Leyden could hear the chorus of hooting cries, the clacking of toothed bills.

Two of them dropped from the formation toward the lead raft. Suslov and Tranner opened fire. The kytes seem to halt in midair, their hoots transforming into cries, then tumble into the water. Several continued upriver toward Leyden's raft; the other kytes broke off toward the shoreline, circled and began to fly downriver, parallel to the rafts.

"Wait. Wait for the attack." Leyden could sense Hawkwood's voice steadying Zia like a hand on his back. The kytes banked and began to pour in from both shorelines toward the rafts.

"Now," Hawkwood called. Zia fired, and Leyden could hear the muffled impact as the flechettes tore into the lead kytes and knocked them into the water. Downriver, he could hear Suslov and Tranner firing again.

Leyden heard a new sound and looked around, up. The river attack was a diversion.

"No!" he yelled before remembering to hit the NavCom override button on his chest.

"Overhead!" he screamed. "Dammit! Overhead!"

With their wings tightly closed, the kytes seemed at first glance like boulders ripped from the cliff sides. But Leyden could see their enormous egg-yolk eyes and the involuntary snapping of their bills as they dove on the rafts. Five of them. All huge.

Sprawling on the bottom of the raft, Zia fired wildly upward and missed.

"Everyone down! Down and against the side!" Hawkwood shouted. "Zia, pulse charges!"

Leyden dropped to his side and rolled against the Dragon. They had only seconds now.

Zia fired again, heavier munitions that left a white-smoke trail. One kyte disintegrated in midflight from a direct hit; another, caught by a shell exploding nearby, burst into flames. A third kyte missed the raft entirely and smashed heavily into the river.

But the other two screamed down on the raft, spreading their wings only at the last moment to break their free fall. Leyden grabbed the Dragon and lifted it in front of him as a kyte, claws extended, slammed hard into him. Its bill slashed at his face and he swung the Dragon, heavy with the loaded kinetic, against the side of its leathery, hooting head.

The kyte turned away from him; Verlaine and Mkeki were swinging their paddles at it, an action both distracting and ineffectual. But it gave Leyden enough time to bring the Dragon up and smash it hard, once, twice, into the side of the kyte's head. The kyte screamed again, its head suddenly limp, wings flapping madly, knocking Leyden down. Verlaine and Mkeki, scrambling on hands and knees, grabbed the kyte's branch-like legs and pushed it toward the edge. Leyden gained his feet and charged into the kyte's side below the wing, and together the three of them heaved it over the side and into the water.

In the middle of the raft, Hawkwood, his knifesword out once again, dueled the second kyte, parrying the slashes of its heavy bill. Hawkwood forced the kyte's bill upward and, dropping to his knees, slipped underneath to slash at the animal's leather-like neck. Yellowish blood spurted into the raft.

Hawkwood swung again, severing the kyte's head.

16 THE MOUTH OF KRONOS

Leyden pushed away from the convulsing body of Hawkwood's headless kyte and glanced out in time to see a huge geyser bloom in the center of the river between the two rafts. A splintering sound echoed off the cliffs.

He turned around and looked upriver. The drone trailed the rafts, hanging low over the water, apparently matching the speed of the rafts.

Leyden cursed and reached for the Dragon, now smeared with kyte's blood. Hawkwood looked over at him. "Hold, Leyden. Don't fire. And get this goddamn bird out of here."

Zia and Verlaine lifted the heavy body over the side, al-Saqua and Mkeki the severed head. The surviving kytes, hooting softly to each other, spiraled up the cliff sides, some disappearing into the persistent mist, others continuing to fly parallel to the river.

Hawkwood, watching the drone, spoke on a secure NavCom line to Tirun. The raft shot into another set of boiling rapids. Verlaine, Mkeki and al-Saqua scrambled for their paddles. Zia started to level his weapon at the drone, but Hawkwood shook him off. "Don't even bother. Get a paddle. We need speed right now."

The drone fired again, and Leyden could feel the heat and impact of the shell as it exploded in the water next to the raft.

Hawkwood shook his head. "All right, Leyden. We've got to push that thing off our tail. You have a sabot charge. Go ahead and fire."

The raft caught a chute of water, sloughed sideways into a rock and recoiled back into the current. Waves crested and slopped into the raft, mixing with the kyte's blood into a viscous mess.

"How the hell am I going to hit anything now?" Leyden shouted.

"You aren't." Hawkwood said. "But you'll confirm that we still have a functioning Dragon and force it to back off. Go."

Leyden cursed, hoisted the Dragon on his shoulder and activated it. The drone jittered around in his laser sight, the target-acquisition signal flicking on and off as the raft surged through the white water.

He gave up trying for a lock and fired. The charge, set on the slowest, close-combat mode, flew flat and straight across the river, the sabot casing peeling away and immediately exploding in front of the drone.

"Close enough," Hawkwood said, as the drone immediately dropped back and gained altitude.

Tirun opened the NavCom line so the entire expedition could hear. "Chácon, report. We've got a drone on our back. What's ahead?"

"Flat water," Chácon answered. "Then the river divides three ways. Looking for the main channel now."

Hawkwood cut in. "Find it fast. They'll be back real soon."

"Paddle! Get your backs into it!" Tirun shouted over the NavCom.

Hawkwood turned to Leyden. "Kinetics this time. Load three and stand by."

"Three."

Hawkwood frowned at the river "Set range at a hundred meters. Up on the acceleration scale to four. If they've got only this one drone left, they'll probably play it safe, increase their distance."

Payback, Leyden thought. Maybe that's the thought which would keep him alive: even the remote prospect that he would find the opportunity to settle accounts with Hawkwood — for the river, the Dragon, Toranga.

"And if they've got more than one?" he said through his teeth.

Hawkwood pulled hard right with his paddle, dragging it deep in the water to turn the raft away from a section of broken rocks. "They may copy our kytes and try to stuff it down our throats. Drop down from overhead, very tight, and open up with everything."

"And then?" Leyden said.

"It will be very fast, no time for sighting, range, anything. Just aim, track and shoot. Like the camp."

They hit a stretch of fast but relatively quiet water. Chácon came back on air. "Left channel. Take the far left channel."

The drone remained out of sight, presumably above and behind them. With the rain ending, the persistent mist began to thin and burn off under the glare of the double suns. For the first time, the abyss seemed to open slightly as well, the canyon walls sloping away from the river. Along with the crisp feel of the Whitebone itself, Leyden again smelled his childhood almond biscotti, but now mixed with a deeper, more fertile scent of plant and growth. The sanctuary of the rainforest must be near.

The Whitebone widened into what might have been an extinct volcano, with a shoreline of pitted black rock. Reptilian creatures, sprawled on the rocks, splashed quickly into the water ahead of them. The river changed color again and ran clear. Peering down, Leyden could see the dancing shapes of cyclops and schools of eel-like fish. Kytes continued to patrol along the now-receding cliffs with soft hoots and clacking bills.

They paddled into Chácon's channel. "Stay ready," Hawkwood said to Leyden. "If they want to use the mist for cover, they're going to have to make a move soon."

Chácon came back on the NavCom. "I'm picking up the sound of heavy rapids, maybe a large waterfall. Any ideas?"

Leyden doubted anyone had a clue at this point. Ulam possessed only rudimentary knowledge of the Chaga Sea and probably knew very little about these lower stretches of the river at all.

Tirun came online. "We're looking for a place where the river empties into Kronos Bay. Ulam wants to know if you see any kind of large cave along the river."

"Cave? No," Chácon answered. "But I'm hearing one large goddamn big set of rapids. Stand by."

For the first time since they had entered the gorges, the Whitebone River ran flat and undisturbed. The mist dissipated completely, the sky rapidly filling with the colorless glare of Nevea and Naryl shining through high clouds in the Eëlian sky. Leyden got a good look at one of the animals inhabiting a lichen-coated rock: a lizard-like creature with a dorsal crest that opened like a sail to the suns. It reared back on squat hind legs and tail to peer at the procession of rafts sailing by, its head wreathed in a cloud of brilliantly colored insects.

The crested lizard turned and disappeared in a blink into the river. The kytes, still flying along the riverbanks, maintained their chorus of gentle, almost mournful hoots and clacks.

Chácon came on the NavCom, his voice barely audible above the din of the river. "The Whitebone's gone, just gone. Whole goddamn river seems to flow right into an opening in the rock."

"We need shelter from the drones," Tirun said. "Can we get under the rock?"

"Negative," Chácon answered, and even over the NavCom and the noise of the river, Leyden could hear the frustration and exhaustion in his voice. Chácon, after all, had been fighting the Whitebone continually, alone, in his kayak.

A new unfamiliar voice cut into the NavCom. Soft, hesitant. "A cave, yes, this must be it," Ulam said. "The Mouth of Kronos."

"What does that mean?" Tirun asked, keeping the NavCom wide open to everyone. "You mean the bay?"

Both rafts began to accelerate again in the building current. In the distance, Leyden could hear and feel the rumbling of massive volumes of falling water.

"Yes. . . this. . . the end of the Whitebone." Ulam's voice filled with excitement. "The stories talk of this. Whitebone River passes through a great rock wall. . . a cave known as the Mouth of Kronos. Other side is Kronos Bay, the rainforest. Home."

Chácon cut him off. "I'm telling you there's no way through! Barely enough clearance for a kayak. Not even close for the rafts. Unless we're all going to swim for it."

"Can you see what the river looks like at all beneath the cave?" Tirun said.

"Barely," Chácon answered. "Maybe twenty meters, no more. Totally dark. But there's no clearance for the rafts at the entrance. None."

The rafts rounded a bend, and for the first time they saw Chácon, close to the left bank of the river, back-paddling to hold his position. A sheer rock face rose in front of them, barren except for Eëlios's ubiquitous lichen. As they approached, Leyden could see the wide Whitebone River sliding into a ragged opening that ran the length of the rock formation. It resembled the smile of something that had just played a clever practical joke upon them all.

"No," came Ulam's quiet insistent voice. "This is it. We must find a way through. The rainforest waits for us on the other side. This I know."

Leyden looked around the raft, its interior smeared in sloshing water and kyte's blood. Hawkwood searched the rock face with a hi-res scanner; Zia, al-Saqua, Verlaine and Mkeki sat motionless, paddles in hand, waiting.

"Goddamn dead end, Hawkwood!" Leyden shouted through some combination of fatigue and fear. "We just rafted down the damn river to nowhere. Ulam's never been here before, we all know that. How the hell would he know about getting through an underground river?"

"He may or may not know the way," Hawkwood said, turning and scanning the sky behind them. 'But they certainly think he does."

Upriver, Leyden saw two mottled silver-gray cylinders sliding slowly over the wide, volcanic-rock section of the river, glinting in the weak sunlight.

"Shit!" said Leyden and reached for the Dragon. "They know what?"

"They must know that the river can take us to the rainforest," Hawkwood said. "If they didn't, they wouldn't risk their drones like this, in clear skies."

As they watched, the drones slowed and hovered. Leyden tried to imagine the operators in their distant consoles — probably inside a tent somewhere on the tundra.

Hawkwood spoke for a moment privately into the NavCom, then scrambled over to the munitions rack for the Dragon.

"Reload with these," he said, handing Leyden two sabot charges. "Now. Quick."

"The drones?"

"No," said Hawkwood. "The cave. We've going to give Kronos here one hell of a facial."

As Leyden loaded the charges into the Dragon, Tirun came on the NavCom to everyone.

"Listen carefully. In a moment, we're going to fire Dragon charges into the cave and try to create enough clearance for the rafts. As soon as you see the explosions, paddle like hell for the opening. We'll have only seconds, a minute at best, before the drone operators figure out what's happening and attack. I have every confidence that Ulam is right and that we're going to come out on the other side, safe, in the rainforest. God's grace to believers, good luck to you all. Stand by."

Leyden tried not to flinch as he felt Hawkwood's hand on his back. Hawkwood had done the same thing to Zia, steadying him just before the kyte attack.

"Setting should be SH-2," Hawkwood said. "Forty meters. Midrange dispersal. Sight it right into the cave, upper edge, clear of the water. Move ten degrees right for the second shot." Hawkwood took his hand away. "Fire when ready."

The cave glowed in the circle of the laser sight. Leyden took a deep breath, let it half out. At least the river held only a steady rocking motion. He fired.

A section of the cave exploded into white smoke and shards of stone. An instant later, the concussion swept over them like a warm wave. Another breath, adjust. He fired again. Pale smoke enveloped the entire rock face.

"Pull for it!" Tirun roared. "Pull hard!"

The rafts lumbered into the main channel as Leyden reconfigured the Dragon and loaded kinetics.

They had stroked halfway to the cave entrance before the drones reacted, dropping low and accelerating down the center of the river. Zia,

Suslov, and Tranner opened fire, but the drones were not kytes and the results were no different from the camp attack.

Leyden knelt with the Dragon, leaning against the edge of the raft. The drones, growing larger with each moment, flew so low that they carved a fantail in the river behind them. Explosions pocked the air and water around them.

"Wait...wait," came Hawkwood's voice as Leyden squinted into the hard glare of the river.

The drones opened fire. The water foamed white with the tracks of flechettes stitching downriver and past the rafts. Spray hissed into the air and showered the rafts.

"All right," said Hawkwood, his voice as flat as if discussing a meal. "Track and fire."

Leyden took a breath, let half of it out, and tried to hold the Dragon steady on the lead drone. He fired twice.

One kinetic flew low and clearly missed, but Leyden had the impression that the other had passed directly through the lead drone. It continued on an unwavering trajectory before discharging a gout of flame and black smoke, veering sharply down into the river. A geyser of fire, smoke and water erupted from the water.

Leyden heard someone give a whoop of delight just as a huge explosion smashed into the raft, enveloping him in a cocoon of hot light and white noise.

In his next conscious instant, he found himself in the river, tumbling at the end of his safety line, choking on river water. Gasping, head still echoing from the concussion, he fought to pull himself along the line to the raft.

As he came closer, Leyden realized that the drone strike had torn a ragged chunk out of the raft, which was now listing heavily under a heavy wash of river water. He lifted his head from the river for a moment; he could see Verlaine and Mkeki looking stunned but otherwise unhurt. Zia was firing overhead while Hawkwood fought to hold the raft steady in the center of the current. Al-Saqua had disappeared.

Leyden, struggling against the rush of water, sensed a sudden shadow as the second drone screamed overhead, followed by the sound of more explosions and the chewing sound of flechettes on water.

Clinging to the ragged end of the raft, Leyden looked up to see them passing into the cave entrance. With the gaping, still-smoking holes created by the Dragon, the cave's smile seemed transformed into an insane laugh.

The Mouth of Kronos swallowed them all.

PART III: CLIMBING

17 BLACKBONE SWAMP

The Eëlios Biological Mission floated upon a sea as still as glass beneath a silent sky. After living for so long with the constant din of the river, they now drifted in a vast, soundless bowl broken only by the quiet sweep of their paddles, which sent silent ranks of ripples marching away to an indeterminate horizon.

The featureless water appeared as devoid of fish as the sky of birds, or kytes. Between river and forest, for this space of time, they floated alone.

The cliff side from which they had emerged had now disappeared behind them in the glare of Eëlios's double suns. Looking ahead, they stroked across Kronos Bay toward a pale mountain of haze and cloud that seemed without perspective, as close as the end of an outstretched hand, as distant as a suspended world. Even the NavComs succumbed to their battering on the Whitebone and produced consistently unreliable coordinates.

Only the air, growing hot and humid, hinted at their destination, its flower fragrances mixing with the deeper scent of furious growth. The water grew thick with scum and algae.

Finally, even the paddlers stopped and slumped down beside the others in the pod-rafts to sleep. A creature invisibly broke the surface with a gasping exhalation; an unknown bird cried out once in the distance. Only Ulam, awake and alive to his approaching home, heard them. But even his eyes closed at last.

The water quieted once more, without ripple or wave; the air, heavy with moisture and scent, remained utterly still. The two rafts floated, nearly as motionless as a painting.

♦

They awoke slowly to the pain of multiple cuts and other wounds inflicted by the Whitebone rapids and successive drone attacks. Tirun had them lash the two rafts together as they attempted to inventory their supplies and equipment. Leyden slowly stripped off the remaining pieces of his shredded carapace. Except for Hawkwood, the others — Zia, Modrescu, Verlaine and Mkeki — followed his example.

Their raft presented the most immediate problem. The last drone had killed al-Saqua, their physician, and torn away most of the back section, leaving it uncomfortably slanted and awash. More seriously, they discovered that the explosion had destroyed most of al-Saqua's medical supplies, including his pharmacy of anti-bacterial, fungal, and viral agents. They had only their individual medkits to treat cuts and other wounds, now dangerously exposed to the Eëlios's alien microbes.

Their food supplies had fallen low, a concern that Ulam found incomprehensible. Once across the bay, he pointed out, the rainforest offered a inexhaustible banquet for them all. But he had no answer to the question of how off-worlders, with their unpredictable immunities and vulnerabilities, could distinguish Eëlios's delicacies from its poisons. They had three functioning Multiphase Combat Weapons, all half-depleted, and only five kinetics and three sabot pulse charges for the Dragon. One micromesh water purifier still functioned.

Together, they scanned the skies for the drone. Hawkwood ticked off the alternatives. The attackers, possibly as disoriented as they were, couldn't find where the Whitebone emerged from the mountain. But more likely, they had brought their surviving drone back for refueling, calculating that its preservation took precedence over the risks of another open-sky attack. Plus, they themselves had at least one casualty: another drone operator in deep shock and in need of heavy tranks and recovery time.

The expedition alternatively drifted and paddled for two more revolutions of Eëlios's suns. When Leyden awoke on the third Eëlian day, they were entering the mountain of mist that had hung before them like a vision. The air filled with the weight of heat, and the water darkened with the rich detritus of the rainforest. For the first time, their destination felt both close and real.

Ulam stripped off his clothes and plunged into the water. After determining that he was not being consumed by large or small predators, Leyden and the others joined him in the tepid, brackish water. Closing his eyes, Leyden let himself sink below the surface, one hand on his safety rope. Despite the uncertainty and discomfort of the current situation, he suspected they all welcomed this respite of emptiness, silence, and heat. Not only did they need to recuperate from the battles on the Whitebone River, but also from their experiences in the Mouth of Kronos.

As Leyden bobbed on the surface, others splashed into the water around him: Mkeki, Chácon, and Verlaine. They all floated behind the raft. Mkeki, he noticed, had rings through her right nipple and her navel.

"Kronos," Verlaine said. He spat a mouthful of water into the air. "One of the truly disgusting experiences of my life."

"And you can't wait to do it again," Mkeki said.

"Absolutely," Verlaine answered. "And I know I can count on all of you to rejoin me there as soon as possible. Why, we can collect. . . god knows how many fascinating specimens for our dear Kee and company?"

Leyden closed his eyes and sank back beneath the water, tasting its rich suspension of earth and vegetation.

◆

As soon as they had entered the Mouth of Kronos, the river enveloped them in complete darkness, and they struggled to rig several small searchlights that illuminated the river cave for perhaps twenty meters around them.

The lights revealed good and bad news: first, that the river widened slightly, leveled, and slowed to near-drifting speed. The bad news appeared when someone shone a light around the cave to reveal that the walls were alive with the Whitebone's cyclops creatures, some the size of dinner plates, but others much larger than those they had fished and eaten from the river. Night caimans lay in unmoving piles along ledges by the river's edge, similar to the daylight versions they had seen in the lake of the extinct volcano, but with adaptive red eyes that glowed like stoplights.

Unfortunately, as the river slowed, both species seemed to share an equal curiosity about the rafts. They could hear the caimans splash into the water, and feel their movement as they circled the rafts.

The cyclops made no sound whatsoever, and only slowly did they realize that swarms of them were crawling up the sides and into the rafts. They began tossing cyclops back into the river, trying to avoid their painful claws, but more poured over the rails, their single viscous eyes revolving like out-of-control searchlights. As they threw, swatted, squashed and kicked cyclops back into the water, the caimans grew agitated, beating the water into a froth and finally attacking the rafts directly. Wheezing with excitement, eyes aflame, the caimans twice bit hard into Leyden's paddle, almost jerking him over the side.

It seemed to Leyden that they were trapped for hours in the cave, fending off cyclops and caimans, able to see little more than the dim shapes and fiery eyes of the creatures as they circled, slammed, and crawled toward him. The cyclops grew so numerous that Leyden and the others began simply stomping them into the bottom of the raft. For the first time, he felt grateful when they heard the sound of a waterfall, which finally drove off the caimans.

Unlike any other fall that they had encountered on the Whitebone, the water at the end of the Mouth of Kronos ran smoothly, but dropped so steeply that they all tumbled into each other in the front of the raft, along with a nauseating slop of dead and living cyclops. Their last moments on the Whitebone were hardly dignified ones: they did not so much sail out of the Whitebone as fall off it.

◆

Leyden took a deep breath and floated face down, peering into the dark water of the bay, listening to the conversation of water in his ears, unaware of the moment when the mists first parted, like an opening-night curtain Verlaine said later, and revealed the expedition's goal.

Leyden had rolled over for a breath and opened his eyes before he noticed that everyone had become very still.

He, too, gazed upward, and into the double image of the Eëlian rainforest. The ranks of black trunks and knotted greenery seemed to hover in the sky, while the same image floated on the still waters, a second underwater jungle growing downward into the depths of the bay. Thunder sounded in the distance. The atmosphere mixed a stew of a hundred scents, some acrid, others sweet, all alien. The chorus of a myriad of unseen birds and countless other hooting, singing creatures filled the air.

Along the edges of the water, the trees grew squat, with smooth black trunks that rose to conical-shaped crowns. Behind them, the rainforest didn't so much grow taller as vault into the sky, climbing at a near-vertical rate until it disappeared into a band of pale gray clouds.

The band of mist and clouds, he estimated, floated at least half a kilometer in altitude, and the density of the growth disappearing into it suggested that the final canopy, spread beneath the suns of Nevea and Naryl, stood unimaginably higher.

Having given them this preview, the Eëlios rainforest withdrew behind a squall line that advanced out from the jungle and encased them in a vigorous thunderstorm. Ulam, who seemed a brighter green with each passing day, stood bare-chested, arms wide, and gloried in it. The rest of the expedition huddled down to escape the raindrops that blew into them with the force of pellets.

They only escaped the rain when they passed beneath the outer rank of trees into an understory of branches and tangled vines that rendered the light muted, shapes blurred and indistinct. They had entered Blackbone Swamp, Ulam said, and indeed the water seemed to smother all the remaining light. In spite of themselves, they began whispering.

Leyden sat paddling in his accustomed left-rear position, uncomfortably aware that he was only a meter or so away from where the water washed over the ragged end of the raft destroyed by the drone strike. No one felt like swimming here. If he stared up hard, he could see what appeared to be a glow associated with a distinctive warbling sound. Otherwise, the low light level drained all colors into shades of gray and brown; they were too far below the jungle's verdant growth to experience even a shaft of sunlight. The water occasionally rippled with silent movement, but the source remained unseen. Twice Leyden saw growths on trees that, as they approached, scuttled upward, revealing themselves to be centipede-like creatures.

For the most part, however, they saw surprisingly little of the rainforest's fabled life. The massive tree trunks rose smooth and straight, without even a hint of a branch until high up in the shadowy understory. Plant life requiring even a modicum of sunlight would have a difficult time surviving at water level, at least until one of these giants fell before age, storms, or parasites.

Leyden dipped his paddle soundlessly into the black water, and for the first time, he felt it nudge the swamp bottom. Hillocks began to appear out of the water along with the movement of creatures slithering out of their way. Instead of paddling, they soon were poling their way, with Ulam standing, smelling the air, and pointing the way.

"We are close," Ulam announced, trembling with anticipation.

Leyden looked around at the silent swamp stretching around him, ranks of tree trunks like monoliths to forgotten gods, the black water spread motionless before them.

Close to what?

18 LARGE CHARISMATIC FAUNA

Leyden's legs made a repulsive sucking sound as he pulled them from the muck of Blackbone Swamp and leaned into the rope.

The misplaced planetary drop, the Whitebone, the drone attacks, and now this: towing rafts through a malodorous swamp. At least he had company. On one side trudged Chácon, whose square-built body seemed expressly designed to hump heavy equipment and weaponry across alien worlds. On the other, Verlaine ran through the curses of twenty Illium worlds plus a few imaginative variations of his own.

Soon, Ulam assured them, we are very close. But the water thinned to a few centimeters, and their paddles simply sank into the black mud when they tried to keep poling. Lighten the load and pull, Tirun ordered, and rotated them in teams of three: suited in spare, lower-body carapaces and dragging the rafts for two-hour stretches. The swamp receded before them: dark, smelly, unchanging.

"Tell me again," Leyden said, straining against his rope at a near forty-five degree angle. "Tell me again how Eëlios is going to make you seriously rich. Not planetary rich, Verlaine, but real money. Illium money."

As they pulled their boots from the muck, they could see segmented worms, white as bone, twist wildly and burrow down into their tracks, which immediately filled with water. The air smelled with the putrefaction of centuries.

"They say every great fortune starts with a crime," Verlaine said. "Might start with knocking you off. Drop your body in the swamp where no one finds you for millennia. Take along an ear for verification. Or a tooth. Collect a *big* award from the folks on Toranga."

"One possibility," Leyden said. "I got another. You could export this swamp shit. Stuff could probably could make Umlivik glaciers sprout vegetables. Sell it in the nurseries with your damn kytes."

Verlaine cursed as he caught a foot on a buried root and almost fell. "Which you and Chácon neglected to collect from the nests when you had the chance. Just don't come whining to me when I stand with the Illium at my feet."

"Fine," Leyden said. "Once you clean the shit off them."

Even Chácon laughed.

They reached a water-filled channel and climbed aboard the rafts once more. The trees dispersed and the overhead foliage thinned enough to allow a modicum of light. The Eëlian version of an open field.

Ahead, Leyden could hear a chorus of enormous slaps on the water and what sounded exactly like sustained farting. As they approached, Leyden spotted a group of large gray animals diving and blowing in the muck and water. Either mammals or hot-blooded reptiles. He could see only small parts of their anatomy at any one time: a distinctively flat tail, a blow hole on the top of their head ejecting a column of water vapor, a blunt snout that looked designed more for grinding through swamp vegetation than animal flesh. Leyden tried to compare them to known Illium species. Water hogs of Luxor Six, he decided, or the hut-building beaver tribes of Bright Green Moon.

Ulam was looking distinctly uneasy as the rafts floated near them.

"Is there a problem here?" Tirun said to him, loudly enough for everyone to hear.

Ever since entering Blackbone Swamp, the NavComs had surrendered completely to fitful bursts of static and abrupt breaks in communication. With no time for maintenance, the expedition had simply abandoned them and resorted to calling out when necessary. Hawkwood, Leyden noticed, occasionally resorted to a series of hand signals for the mercs. Leyden assumed that the land-space com link remained functional; if not, the *Balliol* would return, conduct its sweeps, and with no response, depart.

Ulam shook his head, and unconsciously played with the ridge at the base of his skull where the translator chip was implanted. "No. These are called. . . hyloons. . . river hogs, perhaps, is the closest term. They are quite harmless, as long as they don't start playing with the rafts. But where there are hyloons, there are predators. We should leave this place quickly."

"Hey, Modrescu! Kee!" Verlaine called out, as they all dug in with their paddles, skirting the hyloons along the opposite bank of the channel. "Want to throw out that net and grab one for a blood-and-tissue sample?"

Modrescu, face frozen with his unchanging frown, stood to make holo recordings. An San Kee, scooping swamp soils through a fine-mesh device, nodded her head and smiled. Leyden suspected she had already been calculating the difficulty and disruption of immobilizing one of them.

Despite their efforts, they soon found themselves among the hyloons, which floated alongside with frank curiosity, watching the rafts with large colorless eyes that had migrated to the tops of their heads, blowing snot and spray over everyone. The bow shape of their mouths gave them an expression of vacuous hilarity.

Hyloons seemed to be as fun-loving and unselfconscious as they looked. They employed a remarkable repertoire of whistles, grunts, belches, snorts and sustained farts to communicate among themselves during the ten minutes that they accompanied the rafts to the end of the channel. Of course, if he enjoyed life and the water as much as the hyloons appeared to, Leyden thought, he'd probably be farting with happiness as well.

The water thinned and the forest closed in upon them once more. Again Leyden, Verlaine, and Chácon climbed into the muck and adjusted their halters; Ka-Sung, Bertelsmann, and Suslov on the other raft. They had been pulling for at least two hours, thirty minutes to go. Leyden could feel the fatigue and ache in his legs migrating upward to his back and shoulders.

"Just there!" Ulam called, pointing. "They are waiting for us there!"

Leyden looked up and squinted, wishing he had his Hi-Rez optics . For the first time, the foliage closed down to ground level; the swamp appeared to end in a ridge of dry land and dense growth. A few more meters and he would have this halter off his shoulders and his legs free of swamp mud.

A new sound. One that began as a hushed tone, a long, extended sigh, like the passionate breathing of lovers. Leyden and the others stopped and listened. The sound filled the air, held for long seconds before dying away with a cry of intense sadness, followed by a series of percussive clicks and concluding in a noise that resembled suppressed laughter.

Ulam looked ashen as he turned in a nervous circle. Leyden could barely hear his words.

"They shouldn't be here," Ulam said in a choked voice. "Not here."

The sound pattern repeated, the volume intensifying, filling the air so that it was impossible to establish its direction.

"Ulam!" Tirun called.

"Weapons." Ulam was almost whispering. "Need your weapons."

The heavy breathing began again, cut off by a series of building roars and heavy movement in the underbrush.

Leyden heard Ulam crying, "Away! Run!" but he had no idea in which direction. Ulam had his arms outstretched, palms upward as though beseeching, his cry guttural and unintelligible.

Leyden dropped his halter and started to run for the raft, but, like a bad dream, the swamp resisted and held him to a slow-motion stumble.

And then something the size of a small horse emerged from the foliage and the dream became worse. Much worse.

In his recollection, what happened next remained as vivid and unreal as a hallucination, a set of images with little connection or continuity, severed from each other by blank moments when, mercifully, his memory failed entirely.

He first registered the creature's odd, loping gait, caused by forelegs considerably longer than the rear ones, and its massive, avian-shaped head. As it closed upon him, Leyden remembered his astonishment at its textured, glistening skin, green with splashes of red and yellow around the eyes. Similar creatures were dropping from the foliage all around him with roars and clicks that ended in hysterical laughter.

Leyden found the laughter almost as unbearable as the sight of the creature as it leapt for him. It was a carnivore's mouth, filled with hooked teeth that seemed to retract and extend in rapid succession, creating the distinctive clicking sound that hammered the air. Behind him, he could hear shouts from the rafts, and the first screams.

He remembered the fetid, sickening smell as he dropped into the mud, trying to kick at the creature with his mud-covered, lower-body carapace. Then another smell, the stink of carrion, as the creature held him immobile in the muck, those curved, almost beak-like teeth raking across his arms and chest, those taloned arms pressing him so deep that mud poured over his face and filled his mouth.

The creature's skin felt dry and pebbled as he hit and clawed back, spitting mud, pulling a utility knife from his belt. He tried to stab an eye, missed, and slashed a nostril.

The creature reared back with a roar, and Leyden tumbled through the air, landing in a tangle of vegetation. Before he could move, the creature sprang on him again, pinning his arms, its claws lacerating his chest and raking his face. He felt an incredible pressure on his head, pushing his chin up and back, exposing his neck, leaving him with one flashing moment to contemplate his end. *Now. Let it be quick.*

But the fatal moment, the descent of those reeking teeth, never came. He sensed another presence, and the creature twisted away, releasing him. Leyden had only an instant to glimpse a humanoid figure, green skin, face obscured with a ragged crown of hair, astride the creature, plunging a long dagger repeatedly into its throat. A gout of hot blood burst from the creature as it shook itself violently, throwing the humanoid off, trembling violently, then collapsing. The blood became a stream, a lake, which rose around him.

The numbness began to ebb and an advance guard of pain flowed through him. Somewhere, Leyden could hear a voice screaming, pleading, a voice so loud and ceaseless that he grew impatient with it even as he realized it was his own.

19 BLUE BOY

The water bubbled down between fissures in the rock, and speckled yellow froglets swam in green pools.

"It won't be long now," his father said to the boy. "Not too tired, are you?"

The boy, Leyden, shook his head no, even though he was cold and had scraped his leg and it still hurt. The wind oaks of Toranga, tormented by seasonal storms, clenched their branches into hovering fists over his head, and he could see only fragments of a pale sky.

Later, Leyden sat in the kitchen, eating almond biscotti, and telling his mother how steep the trail was, how brave he had been. If he could, he would have spoken to her of the monumental stillness of rock and oak, and the look of the mountain with the fog flowing down its sides like spindrift off the ocean.

Sitting there, eating biscotti and drinking Toranguin apple juice, he noticed that the stream, still filled with tiny froglets, wound through the kitchen.

That was odd.

◆

Leyden paced slowly in the transit lounge, savoring the feeling of his entrance onto a new, larger stage. Occasionally, he was even recognized, and people bowed to congratulate him, graduate of Toranga's Ifé Autonomous University, winner of a coveted Kirov scholarship for study at an elite school on Antares Minor. Bowing back, he would hold out his aromatic wind-oak branch, Toranga's traditional acknowledgment of achievement.

He returned to his seat, too preoccupied for reading or holos, waiting for the shuttle to the lightship and his first burn through Toranga's portal.

But why had the crowds gathered again, faces contorted in hatred? And why were they holding burning evergreen boughs this time, their smoke and stink filling the air, shrieking that he was a betrayer, a traitor?

◆

Her hands, as they wandered over his face, smelled of cloves and exotic garlics and of the hot Rigelian oils that bubbled on the stove. Her neck and her breasts were cinnamon and sandalwood from Luxor, and he dipped his finger in the red wine of Delium Ghahan and trailed it down to her navel.

"A good year," he said. She laughed, and he delighted in the thought that the evening would bring the twin feasts of her kitchen and her body.

But no, she was pushing him away from her now, almost vibrating in anger as she catalogued his multitude of sins and failures. In another moment, she slumped against the burnished counter, exhausted by her own fury, filled with regret, saying only that he was a memory now.

This meal, the wine, this night of lovemaking, he realized, were for another.

◆

As the reports flooded in, the Com Center grew still. They watched the displays and the readouts, trying to comprehend the enormity of what was occurring half-a-million kilometers away, staring at explosions like tiny novas around the singularity, the numbers spinning out the advance of the Illium League fleet through the great wheel of the portal complex.

But why were the screens now filling with static, a twitching blue mass that advanced off the screens and spread across the floors, up the walls and staining the ceiling? The hiss of a thousand galaxies filled the room, growing in intensity.

And why was he in such constant tormenting pain?

◆

Leyden heard a spectral voice, someone with a bad connection speaking to him with an odd accent. He tried to see, but his eyes were covered and bound. He had no sensation when he attempted to move his arms and legs.

The voice returned, and in the distance Leyden could hear a soft roll of thunder. He started to struggle. Where the hell was he? The voice was soothing but he couldn't understand the words over the constant static ... static?

He tried to relax. Start over. He knew that his eyes were covered, and for some reason his arms and legs immobilized, But someone was trying to speak: concentrate on that. Ignore the noise, the static, whatever the hell it was. He listened.

"You must remain still," the voice said. "Do not try to move."

Leyden attempted to open his eyes again, and through the covering or bandage or blindfold, he could see only a blue cloud full of twitching movement.

"We are with you," the voice behind the blue cloud continued. "You are not alone. But you must remain still, and as soon as you can, go back to sleep and dream your dreams. They will be strange dreams, but they do not carry..."

Here the voice halted. An *Eëlian* voice, of course. "These dreams do not carry truths or prophecies, so they should not trouble you. They will pass."

Leyden tried to speak and realized that his mouth, like his eyes, was covered. The static remained loud, persistent, and he had the sensation of movement all around him. He began to shake.

"I will bring another," the voice said. "One of your own."

He waited, suspended in his buzzing blue cloud.

He felt more movement, and realized that someone was carefully pulling away part of the binding over his mouth and inserting a mouthpiece and tube so that he could breath more easily. And talk.

A new voice, one that he knew. An San Kee. "Can you hear me, Leyden?"

"Yes. Where am I?"

"Recovering. Along with several others. You were injured. Do you remember?"

Leyden thought for a moment. "Some of it. Are they gone?"

"Yes."

"I hurt all over, and I can't seem to move my arms and legs."

"I know. But you're going to be better. But you must remain still. Whatever sensations you have, don't resist."

"What is all this noise around me? I hear constant static."

"I know. I'll explain later."

Leyden felt more fully awake now, sensing the prickling movement, sucked down by the enveloping pain. "I don't understand. Could you just take my hand for a moment?"

"I'm sorry," Kee said. "I can't."

"Why not?" He paused. "Are my hands gone?"

"No. Your hands have some bad cuts, like other parts of you, but basically they're fine. And no," Kee said, anticipating his next question, "as far as we know, you're not paralyzed. Or blind."

"As far as you know," Leyden repeated. "Why can't you take my hand and why are my eyes covered?"

Kee said, "Because, at the moment, you are covered with several thousand bees."

Somewhere inside the territory of his pain, a trickle of laughter leaked out. "It must be an interesting sight."

"Oh, it is. You are one large, twitching mound of blue bees. Quite fascinating, actually"

"Good for you. Can I ask why?"

"The Eëlians brought you up here. You and Bertelsmann and Ka-Sung. All three of you were mauled pretty badly by these things. I laser-sutured your wounds, but there wasn't much I could do about the infections. They brought you here and mixed up this foul-smelling paste, smeared it all over you and... within a few minutes or so, the bees arrived."

Somewhere behind Kee's voice, Leyden could again hear a beat of thunder, like someone flapping an enormous carpet. "What, exactly, are these bees doing to me?"

"As they collect and masticate this paste, apparently each of them is injecting you with a tiny amount of venom, which seems to contain an incredibly powerful antibiotic."

Even through the fog of buzzing bees, Leyden could hear the scientist's detached excitement. "I've already collected some samples. In fact, I was running some tests when you became conscious."

"Happy to help your research, Kee. But am I going to get any better? I don't feel better."

"Oh, yes. You were dying when we brought you here. Now she thinks you'll make a near-full recovery."

Leyden tried to squint through his eye covering and focus on the dim shapes crawling on his face. "Who?"

"Eëlian. A combination doctor and herbalist, I guess you could say, an expert on the properties of Eëlian plants. She found the berries and leaves we ground into the paste. She's making more now."

"A native botanist," Leyden said. "Just the person you've been looking for."

"Oh yes," Kee said. "She's one of ones we were supposed to meet on the Drop."

Leyden could feel himself begin to shake again. "If she's so good with medicines, what about something for pain?"

"Soon. As soon as most of the bees have left. Meanwhile, try to go back to sleep."

"I've had such dreams. . ."

"I know," Kee said. "The venom. It's an hallucinogen."

◆

When Leyden awoke the next time, his eyes remained covered, but the cloud of blue bees had flown from his head, although he could hear them still swarming around his chest and legs. His arms, he discovered, could move, and he reached for his face.

He felt a hand on his wrist. "It may not yet be time for the binding to come off." The accented Eëlian voice again.

"Why not?"

"It has been suggested that the sight of the bees might be disturbing to you. They are large. . . and quite dramatic looking."

The pain from his wounds had lessened, but he had a pounding headache. "I'll have to think about that."

He heard nothing more. "Are you still there?"

"Yes. Let me give you water now." The accent was unique, but the hesitancy had the familiar cadence of an implant, an Illium Standard translator chip at the base of her neck.

He swallowed several mouthfuls of tepid water. "What is your name?"

"You wouldn't be able to pronounce it." He could hear a note of amusement in her voice.

"Say it anyway. I don't seem to be going anywhere."

Her response was full of sibilants, ending in a guttural click that almost seemed to mimic the call of the creature that had attacked him.

He tried the first combination of syllables and gave up. "You're right. Unpronounceable. . . I mean for an off-worlder like me."

"I have talked with your companion. The one called Kee. I can give you something for pain now, and to sleep."

"Please, yes."

He felt a set of fingers on his lips, and when he opened his mouth, it was stuffed with a ball of what felt like damp leaves. Vile tasting.

He tried to spit it out, but her hand remained firmly over his mouth. "If the taste is. . . unfamiliar. . . just chew and swallow quickly."

"What is this?" he mumbled.

"Wadi leaves. A very good painkiller with. . . no bad effects. The leaves are tough, but I chewed them first to soften them for you."

Leyden began choking. "*You* chewed them already?"

"Of course." Her voice carried a note of impatience. "Now swallow and I will give you more water."

He fought his gag reflex and did as he was told. After several drinks, he could feel the wadi leaf's effect. The sound of the blue bees faded and he felt himself floating, the edge of his pain dulling.

After another silence, Leyden asked if she was still there, but there was no answer. He drifted and again slept through alternate dream-world versions of his past life.

20 WOMAN IN GREEN

When the day came that the last of the blue bees departed, Leyden opened his eyes to a new world. The pain had eased, if not the itching, and he could see.

His eyes teared as he blinked and brought into focus a dappled place of piercing light and cool shadow. Leyden stared into a mass of green foliage so dense it took several minutes before he could begin to decipher the patterns and identify any single element. A cacophony of sound that slowly resolved into discernable melodies and chords: a slow fugue of branches heavy with leaves and berries, accompaniments of hanging vines and mosses, themes of fancifully shaped ferns, short interludes by pot-shaped plants with spiky leaves and tiny red flowers as small and random as the notes of a Toranguin harp. He felt suspended as the plant music circled in constant variation around him.

Insects with the brilliant wings of butterflies and the darting speed of dragonflies appeared and disappeared, along with what looked like his blue-colored bees. Invisible birds sang their little hearts out to challenge all comers. Leyden could hear the rustling sound of constant movement all around him.

This is no tropical idyll, the noises said: life here is earnest and hidden and very, very serious.

A new image appeared in his field of vision, and it took Leyden a moment to recognize it as a woman's face, with curious dark eyes, mouth biting unconsciously on the tip of a tongue, hair as tangled as the growth around him, skin a forest green.

Then the face spoke the most astonishing thing anyone had ever said to him in his life.

"We have never met before, but I know your eyes."

Later, he would he learn that it was a traditional Eëlian greeting. But at that moment, suspended in his new world, the words fell indelibly upon his brain, and he often wondered what effect they had upon later events.

The green woman wore a loose-fitting tunic of deep emerald, with an intricate, embroidered design in scarlet and blue that spilled from her collar over the left shoulder and short sleeve. A simpler version of the design adorned the left side of her face, around and below the eye. She wore thongs on her feet with crisscrossed ties that extended to her knee, and her skin glistened as though covered with a thin layer of wax. Her arms looked powerful. At that moment, he decided that she was the most exotic-looking woman he had ever seen since the blended-gender women of the Patpong night world.

Leyden said, "You. Are you the one who brought the bees? The one with the unpronounceable name?"

"I am."

"I don't know your name, or your eyes, but I thank you."

The green woman gave the barest of acknowledgements. "*Uh*. It is my job."

Leyden looked carefully. She seemed both young and ageless. "Tell me, though, how old are you? Are you a child or a woman?"

For a moment he thought the eyes looked hurt. "I am. . . older than you think. I am a gatherer of plants, maker of medicines. Sometimes. . . a healer."

Leyden closed his eyes. "For me, certainly."

"It is time for you to get up," she said abruptly placing her hands underneath his shoulders, lifting him to a sitting position. Either he had become quite a bit lighter or she was stronger than she looked. Her grip felt like a vise.

Two remaining bees, glistening in the thin shafts of light, were probing his knee for remnants of the paste that had coated him. He bent his leg and they flew off.

His body looked unrecognizable: ribs and pelvis jutting from a body covered in swellings and welts from his thighs to chest, hundreds of tiny red pinpricks from the bee-venom injections. His soft stomach had disappeared, replaced by ridges of scar tissue scrawled across his torso, pale and still tender to the touch. Overall, his skin seemed an odd color, as though he had been rinsed in a thin green lacquer.

He remembered his face and probed his eyes, cheek and nose: a scar ridge seemed to extend from below his left eye to the corner of his mouth. If the rest of him were in such bad shape, what about his face? Early in his career, Leyden had been called, in a sneer by his political opponents, the

Adonis of Toranguin politics. An effective slap, but true; his story-book looks had, for a time at least, served him well in public and private affairs. No longer, apparently.

"I need a mirror," he said.

"That wouldn't be wise."

Another voice. "Not yet."

An San Kee sat in her customary lotus position on the platform next to him. The green Eëlian woman squatted beside her, knotted hair spilling over her face.

"That bad?"

"One thing at a time," Kee said. "You look fine. Just different, like the rest of you. Right now, you need to recover your strength so we can travel."

Leyden probed his face once more. "What about the others?"

"Bertelsmann had only minor injuries compared to yours. Ulam is guiding him and Verlaine to the rest of the expedition. The three of us will follow as soon as you are ready."

"Any messages?"

"Messages? For you?" Kee thought for a moment. "Verlaine sends his regards."

"I trust he sent more than regards to you."

"He did," Kee said, unperturbed.

"What the hell were those things? Another unpronounceable name?"

"Actually, yes," Kee said. "We've decided the best approximation of the Eëlian's name for them is *Saar*."

She looked at the green woman, who nodded.

"Think of them as arboreal raptors," Kee continued. "They probably hold the same ecological niche as the kytes in the Chaga Sea."

"Stop trying to make me feel better," Leyden said, who now realized that, even relatively pain-free, he was wasn't feeling well at all. "Are we going to run into those things again?"

Kee looked over at the Eëlian woman, who remained expressionless. "It is our understanding that attacks like this, in packs, are uncommon," Kee said. "The Saar are usually solitary hunters. They were probably tracking the hyloons and were attracted by the disturbance we caused traveling through the Blackbone Swamp. Ulam said they followed us from overhead, then attacked when we hit dry land."

"Did we get any of them?"

"Two, I think," Kee said, "including the one that attacked you."

"Saar." Leyden tested the word on his tongue."I thought Ka-Sung was hurt too."

"He was."

"And?"

"He didn't make it," Kee said.

Leyden took a deep breath, the air thick with a thousand unnamable scents. Odd, but now he could barely discern the almond smell. How many had they lost now? Leyden tried to run through the list. Cabenza murdered by parties unknown. Ehrenberg and Carpentier in the drone attack. Bois by the kytes and al-Saqua at the Mouth of Kronos. Now Ka-Sung: unflappable, silent. Even in the upper reaches of the Whitebone, he had carefully gathered specimens and compiled field notes. In any but an arbitrary world, he would be a survivor.

"What happened? I thought these were miracle bees or something."

Kee held up a vial, and Leyden could see three blue bees suspended in a thick, clear liquid. "They do have a remarkable antibiotic capability, but they're not miracle workers. Actually, Ka-Sung was not as badly injured as you, but he was attacked by a particularly virulent infection. No one, not even the Eëlians, had an antidote."

"Why didn't it infect me?"

Kee stuffed the vial back into her pack. "No reason. You are a lucky man. This time."

The green woman rose to her feet. "You were chosen to live. I am pleased to bring you the healing life of this place." She left quite suddenly, without a sound.

Leyden looked after her. "Was it something I said?"

"Think for a minute. Asking whether she was a girl or a grownup probably was not the best way to introduce yourself. After all, she's been taking care of you and your bees for more than a week, with very little sleep as best I can tell."

Leyden wrapped himself stiffly in a length of rough Eëlian cloth that lay beside him; he felt exhausted. "I will prostrate myself before her at the first opportunity."

Kee said, "Since she saved your life twice, the first time from the Saar, it might not be inappropriate."

"Her? Really?"

As soon as he asked the question, the image of the figure astride the Saar snapped into focus before his eyes, and Leyden realized why she had seemed familiar.

Leyden closed his eyes. "God, I feel lousy. Bring back the damn bees."

Kee rose to her feet. "I'll bring you some food. Something called a williwaw fruit. Remarkable. Like a kind of citrus banana."

"Sounds like something with a big sales potential back in the Illium."

Kee said, "I believe Verlaine was already drawing up the marketing plan."

"And something for headache if you have it," Leyden said. "I'll even take those pre-chewed leaves."

When Kee returned, Leyden was almost asleep again. He choked down another wet wad of wadi leaves

The williwaw turned out to be an ugly misshapen ball with a brownish yellow skin and lumps like tumors. Tasted far better than it looked or smelled.

"What now?" he asked Kee. "Have we got a plan?"

"You recover so that we can travel and catch up with the rest of the expedition."

Leyden opened his eyes and looked around. "And where is that?"

"Little more than a kilometer. The local village."

"Okay. Not far."

Kee smiled. "Not a kilometer *away*. A kilometer *up*."

21 SPEAKING IN TONGUES

Leyden awoke to distant thunder, an invisible fluttering, and the sound of water falling through layers of leaves. The light had dimmed.

Turning his head, he could see the green woman squatting on her heels next to a half-open sack, quietly grinding with mortar and pestle. She looked up at him with an opaque expression that seemed somehow uncomfortably familiar. Was he really here, scarred and bitten, trying once again to placate a woman? That's what he had liked about Suslov. She had required no placating, no weighing of emotions and needs. Or so he thought until the very end, when he had been left feeling he wanted. . .what? The minutest flicker of regret? He had no idea now.

"It seems I owe you much more of my gratitude than I realized," Leyden said. "Saving me from the Saar, then saving my life again with the bees."

"It is well known that the Saar are vulnerable in the neck. Since its attention. . . was upon you, I had the opportunity to cut the vessel. . . the word is unfamiliar. . ."

"Artery."

"Artery, yes."

Leyden watched her working for a moment. "More Eëlian medicine?"

She continued grinding without looking at him. "In part. It is a lotion, from the Amaranth. . . How do you feel?"

Leyden could see nothing but the top of her head. "The truth? I'm nauseated, hungry, constipated. I itch all over, I haven't had a bath in longer than I can remember. I've got huge scars and my head hurts again. Other than that, I'm fine."

"Then perhaps it is time." She paused and put down her pestle.

"Time for what?"

She didn't answer but gave a trilling sound that ended in a series of clucks, again a mild version of the Saar's percussive sounds. She waited. Leyden heard a rustling sound somewhere around him.

A lizard-like creature, the size of a Rigelian cat, dropped out of the foliage on to her shoulder, rotated one eye toward Leyden, the other eye downward, then stuck its tongue into the woman's ear.

She smiled. "This is Twen."

"All right," Leyden said slowly. "What is it? Your pet?"

"Not mine. Yours. And not a pet but a. . . partner, a guide."

"I'm not following. It's a lizard, isn't it?"

"Careful what you say. Twen has a limited vocabulary, but he understands more than you might think. He may or may not appreciate being called an off-world animal."

The woman wiggled her fingers in front of its head; the animal removed its tongue from her ear, wrapped it around her thumb and climbed up on top of her head. There, Twen draped a remarkably long tail over the woman's shoulder like a piece of ornamental jewelry. One eye rotated in random movements around the forest, the other remained unblinking and focused on Leyden.

"Are you saying this thing is intelligent?" Leyden asked.

"The Iksillia are very advanced, yes. They have been our companions and helpers from the first time we came to live in what you call the rainforest."

She sounded as if she were giving a lesson to a child, which in many ways she was.

"The Iksillia." Leyden's pronunciation seemed approximate this time.

"Yes. I have been told that in your terminology, they are not lizards but theropods. Warm-blooded, with. . . upright legs. More like birds than lizards."

Leyden took a closer look. Twen was a variegated green color, like the forest around him, but with a blood-red sagittal crest, yellow slashes around the eyes, and the longest legs he ever recalled seeing on a reptile of any size. The legs seemed to end in retractable claws.

"You mean this thing is related to the Saar? A raptor?"

The woman laughed. "Oh, yes. Except that they have been always been attracted to humans. We don't know quite why. Perhaps an evolutionary development, or just a function of their intelligence and perception."

"Don't fight them, join instead."

The woman pondered Leyden's words as though he were making a significant statement; casual humor rarely translated well.

"Perhaps. They eat plants and insects, mostly..."

"Mostly?"

"They seem very careful to assure us that they are vegetable eaters, but we suspect that, away from us, they do hunt down small animals and birds."

"That can't be very reassuring."

Once again, the green woman looked confused, even frustrated. Leyden had difficulty accepting the fact that, as powerful as the universal translator chips were, they could never escape what their developers called "the deep well of cultural context." The problem wasn't necessarily that of unfamiliar references — one of the program's strengths was coping, or at least alerting the user to terms with potentially misleading equivalents. The problems were more those of inflection, irony, humor, sarcasm, multiple meanings — and lies.

"The Iksilla have been our guides for many years," she said after some hesitation. "And they can be yours. But first, you must learn to communicate with them. With Twen."

"You know," Leyden said slowly, "I'm not following this conversation at all. Why would I want to communicate with your lizard or theropod or whatever?"

She looked disappointed now. Had he done it again? Loaning this animal to him probably represented the highest honor an Eëlian could confer on a stranger. Or possibly she had forged a web of obligation and commitment with him, like it or not, by the act of saving his life. It occurred to him that, despite the research he had done for his negotiator's role, he hadn't the slightest insight into the culture that produced this woman. Beyond the interesting fact that Eëlios natives lived in the rainforest canopy, he knew virtually nothing about who these people were or how they regarded off-worlders like him.

Leyden stood, stretching, testing his stiff arms and legs. He tried again. "Does your... does Twen communicate with sound or in some other way?"

"Not sound," the woman said. "The Iksilla are silent. They communicate with their tongue. Later, after bonding, they communicate directly. For our part, we use both words and sign language. I will show you."

She ran through a series of movements with her hand in front of a phlegmatic Twen, who watched with one eye while the other continued to roam the trees. When she finished, Twen unrolled his tongue and held it upright. It was a fat, three-pronged affair, and Twen manipulated each prong separately, then corkscrewed his entire tongue into a dozen different shapes in rapid succession. Twen concluded the demonstration by twirling his tongue back into the woman's ear before swallowing it again.

Leyden said, "I assume that last bit is a sign of affection?"

"Yes." She seemed mildly pleased at his discomfort. Payback.

"As for the rest," she continued, "Twen communicated that he is prepared to follow my wishes and take you to a place for cleaning and healing."

"He said that?"

"Yes. If you will follow Twen, he will take you there now. The next step in your recovery."

"What kind of place?"

The green woman looked impatient again; answering his questions must be like talking to a very slow child.

"A traditional place for bathing, for becoming well. Not far. But first, you should learn some basic signs to communicate with Twen, and Twen with you."

The woman held up her hand, and after a pause, Leyden did the same.

"*Stop*," she said, and waited until he copied the shape of her hand. "*Wait. . . Slower. . . Help. . . I don't understand. . .*" After they had run through the sequence several times, the woman signed to Twen, still perched on her head. Twen extended his tongue and made a shape that looked like a warning of bad road ahead. "*Follow me. . .*" the woman said, ". . . *Danger. . . Wait here. . . Faster. . . Let us return. . .*" As with Leyden, she had Twen run through the signs several times.

The green woman paused and looked at him. "Are you ready?"

Leyden stretched again, watching Twen watch him. "I suppose so."

She signaled and Twen climbed down and landed on the platform with a plop. One eye never left Leyden's face.

"I don't quite understand," he said. "Does Twen belong to you?"

"Not really," she said, assembling what looked like a collection of berries, branches, powders and a bars of brightly colored soaps into a small bamboo basket. "Twen is unattached. That's why I chose him for you. I have another partner."

The green woman gave another clucking trill and a slightly larger version of Twen appeared, without bothering to climb onto her head. It took Leyden a moment to realized that the woman's tunic and face decorations mimicked the scarlet-and-blue markings of her Iksilla.

"This is Twon," she said. "Twen's mother, or sister. We're not sure which."

Leyden shook his head. Twon and Twen. They sounded like a circus act. In fact, if they were really so intelligent, they could probably join one of the Illium's traveling exotica shows.

The green woman placed the basket before him. "When you arrive, here is what you do." She began picking up items one at a time. "Wadi leaves for headache and stiffness. Since my chewing them disturbs you, you can begin with them dry, like this. It will simply take you longer. The berries are for constipation. The Aramanthian powder should be mixed with water into a paste and spread over your skin. Keep it on for a few minutes before washing it off. Repeat twice, use all that I have given you. These are your soaps. But first, take these branches here and scrub your skin well, scrub as hard as you can. Use this caälyx wax bar last and keep it with you. Use it daily. It will protect you against many skin irritations and biting insects."

She handed the basket to him. "Any questions?"

Leyden poked through the basket. *No, Mom. And I promise that I'll wash behind my ears.*

"Does Kee know about all your wonder lotions and soaps here?" he asked.

"Oh yes. I have also told her of others, too, and she is away collecting plants right now. With another from our colony of Iksilla."

Leyden stood and stretched, still nauseous, feeling the scar tissue across his chest tighten and burn. His whole body congealed into one large itch. "I'm ready."

"Oh, one other thing," the green woman said, looking somewhat embarrassed. "If Twen becomes upset. . ."

"Yes? Is there a sign for that?"

"No. He just spits."

Leyden gazed at Twen's unblinking, appraising eye. "I guess I'll have to be careful and not upset him."

The woman seemed relieved. "Yes, yes. It is the wisest course, especially at first, until you have. . . bonded."

Leyden felt slightly taken aback: had she entrusted him to a creature that could become full of spitting anger if he didn't follow its instructions precisely? All Leyden could think is that he wanted to be alone so he could scratch and curse and spit himself. He wedged the basket over his shoulder.

"Bonding with a hot-blooded lizard is not high on my list right now," he muttered.

Twen led him out of the bower of foliage that had been his home for weeks and along a branch as wide as a footpath. Twisted vines served as a rudimentary handrail, clearly marking an established travel route. For the first time he could see downward through a patchwork of thin light for at least fifty meters, although ground level remained invisible.

The branch ended in a trunk as wide as the side of a house; Twen scrambled straight up, twisted his head around and stuck out his triple-forked tongue. *Follow me.*

"Yeah? How?" Leyden muttered to himself before discovering a rope ladder hanging almost invisibly against the trunk. After climbing for several minutes, his hands and feet scraping away small sections of bitter-smelling bark, he paused, out of breath.

Slow, he signed, then said aloud, "How much farther?"

Without looking up, he could hear Twen skitter down onto the top of his head. His tongue fluttered into his ear: a swirl and two taps.

"Hey!" Leyden jerked his head back, but Twen remained unmoving and repeated the pattern: a swirl and two taps.

He tried to look up. "Does that mean, *Not far,* or what?"

Twen leaped off and continued up the trunk far enough so that he appeared in Leyden's line of vision and stuck out his tongue once again. *Yes.*

They shortly left the trunk for another wide branch that sloped upward at an easy angle. As they moved away from the trunk, a dappled world enfolded Leyden in a tangle of vines, branches, flowers, mosses, and molds. He quickly became disoriented, without any sense of their direction and distance, the growth pressing in around him, brushing his face, twisting around his wrists and ankles. Insects the size of small birds buzzed his head, suspended splashes of color, and the air filled with a spectrum of sounds: hoots, purrs, trills and bursts of song as sudden and liquid as water spilling.

Twen moved in short bursts, loping forward, hanging from a branch with a retractable claw or tail, listening, darting forward again. Leyden slowed; in this enclosed world lacking any clear sight lines, touch and sound became as important as vision.

A new but familiar sound joined the chorus; but one that he never expected to hear climbing trees: running water. They entered a region with flattened, rubbery leaves the size of small rugs: Leyden could have rolled up completely in one without even his toes showing. A thin layer of water flowed along the surface, deepening as the leaves intertwined and took on a more bowl-shaped appearance.

Soon he stood in an ankle-deep sheet of flowing water. Twen disappeared just as Leyden slipped down and slid around a corner, landing with a large splash in the waist-deep water of an arboreal pool.

CLIMBING THE RAIN

Leyden stood up, cursing and looking around for Twen. The pool was a misshapen bowl of matted vegetation, with water sliding in from several directions on the same rug-sized leaves, and dripping down from above in a constant rain. Birds and winged insects bisected the air in sudden slashes of color, and pairs of red eyes seemed to float on the surface until he realized they were attached to small frogs hanging motionless in the water. Phalanxes of slumping, trumpet-shaped plants enclosed the pool and appeared to be actively drinking from the surface.

Twen appeared and wagged his tongue in front of him: *Follow. Now.* He disappeared down a branch that angled under the pool.

"Okay. No spitting," Leyden said, as he balanced on one branch and held another to follow him.

Beneath the pool, Leyden found a rough platform that he was beginning to recognize as typically Eëlian in look and structure. Above him, water poured through entwined vegetation in a second steady rain, and more trumpet stems reached out from the green walls of the surrounding forest to collect the flow.

He felt a wet tickle in his ear. Twen, perched on his shoulder, twisted his tongue in front of his face. *Here, Now.*

Leyden looked around: a jungle rainfall perhaps, but also an Eëlian shower room. He stuck a handful of wadi leaves in his mouth, and immediately realized why the green woman had earlier taken the trouble to chew them for him.

Stiffly, he stripped off his clothes, collected the various paste and soaps and waxes from the basket, and stepped into the falling water. He shivered slightly, although the water felt tepid, the air warm and humid.

Leyden closed his eyes and felt the water pour upon his damaged face and arms and chest. For a moment, he smelled the scent of almonds.

Let it be healing water.

22 ANCHORWOOD

Leyden scratched his scarred chest, stared at the Dragon, and cursed. "What the hell did Hawkwood tell you when he left it?" he said to An San Kee.

"That he would take the pulse charges and kinetics," Kee answered. "But since the expedition already had enough weight, you should continue being the designated Dragon carrier."

"Nice try, Kee. And the truth?"

"His exact words were, 'The Dragon stays with Leyden no matter how much he complains. The truth — your relationship with Tribune Hawkwood — is another matter.'"

Leyden stared at her. Sometimes Kee seemed as unreadable as much of the plant life she studied. He had no idea if she thought she were being ironic, sarcastic, or serious.

"My *relationship*?" he said. "My relationship with Hawkwood is quite simple. I'm betting only one of us is going to leave this planet alive. The other can become good fertilizer for your favorite Eëlian tree."

Kee turned away. "Few things are that simple. And certainly not between you, from the rebel world of Toranga, and an officer of the Illium League."

"*Former* rebel world, now occupied colonial territory. In large part due to the efforts of the League and great warriors like *Tribune* Hawkwood."

"And yet here you are. Together again."

Now *that* was sarcasm, wasn't it? Leyden looked down at the Dragon and cursed again. Rumor had it that the newest models, the eighty-eights, were lightweight enough to be carried in one hand. The model eleven

Dragon-class railgun wasn't just heavy, but antediluvian. Yet cheap, Leyden knew, like everything else on this cut-rate expedition.

The Dragon lay at his feet, dismantled in two sections, encased in a transparent wrap with attached carrying straps. Within the confines of this vegetable world, it would be useless in any close-quarter encounter with the Saar or whatever other large surprises awaited them in the Eëlian rainforest, with or without any munitions. Well, he could throw the goddamn thing at them, or just tell Hawkwood that he lost it on the climb. That sounded like a much better idea; Hawkwood couldn't keep putting him in the line of fire if he no longer had a weapon.

"Designated Dragon carrier. Designated to be killed carrying this damn thing," Leyden said, wanting Kee to realize how sorry he was feeling for himself at the moment. Besides, he was scarred and ugly and turning an unpleasant shade of green. "That's what Hawkwood really meant."

"You're everyone's hero after shooting down the drones at the campsite," Kee said calmly. "And again, at the Mouth of Kronos."

Leyden said nothing; he had no wish to be comforted

"Other than being martyred," Kee said, "how are you feeling physically?"

"Well enough."

Kee nodded and looked pointedly over the green woman, crouched at the other end of the platform, preparing her pack. It was a complicated-looking affair of tightly woven bamboo strips with numerous small compartments and closures. Her belt, stitched from a material that looked like reptile skin, held more small pouches, as well as several waxy looking gourds that he assumed contained water or other liquids. She had piled climbing gear in front of her: a coil of sticky looking rope, wooden clips, spikes with foot straps and several small, very sharp picks. The scarlet-and-blue markings around her left eye looked freshly reapplied.

Twen and Twon slept in a patch of weak sunlight.

Leyden scratched his chest and felt the mark of the Saar's claws across the face. The scars ratified the truth of his exile life: never again the wonder boy of Toranguin politics, nor again the easy charmer of men and women. The object now? Survive the Eëlian ordeal. Cut a deal with the planetary locals to Tirun's satisfaction. Get far, far away from Hawkwood and anything related to the League. Take his pitiful fifty-thousand-talon fee and construct a new life on a new world. Shed the past like an outgrown skin and invent a new future.

After all, wasn't that the central meaning of the Illium Archipelago itself? Starting over. Conquering more. Didn't that constitute the great lesson of the Illium's heroes: Anton Kirov, pioneer of the portals; his son, the Nova Prince; Ma Win of Arashima; even Zeon Tutilo of Rigel Prime, builder of Poseidon, the celebrated orbiting ocean resort?

The green woman stood and said something with a click in her voice, causing Twen and Twon each to each pop open a single eye. Her fingers engaged in a flurry of signals.

"Time we should go. Find the others."

"Are they waiting for us?" Leyden asked.

"No. They have been climbing." The green woman paused, looked at An San Kee. "We are going to take a different way. One that is shorter."

"Shortcut?" Kee said.

"How does that work?" Leyden said. "We got an air shuttle stashed away?"

The green woman shook her head, the tangle of hair obscuring her eyes. "No. Something different."

◆

They began by retracing the path Leyden and Twen had taken to his bath: along the pathway branch, up the rope ladder hanging off the crumbling bark of a massive trunk, and out another wide branch. Twen and Twon skittered ahead, disappearing and reappearing like forest apparitions. They could have been on an outing with two odd-looking dogs. For a moment, he thought they would pass by his arboreal pool, but the green woman took another turn, and soon they entered unfamiliar territory. The light dimmed and the branch pathway they climbed grew even wider and more massive, more like a highway.

They passed into a darkened section of the canopy's vast understory, a twilight world cut off from even dappled sunlight. The familiar rainforest vegetation retreated. Instead, networks of branches fought silent battles with entwined woody vines as tough and tight as nooses. Pale clumps of sponge-like mosses sprouted on tree limbs.

The green woman led them on an easy level walk along the flattened branch, actually the fusion of dozens, perhaps hundreds of smaller branches, and he had a clear line of sight downward for what seemed several hundred meters until the light failed completely. They arrived in a dim, vault-like arena, and for the first time, he found himself overwhelmed by the sensation of enormous height. But he still had no clear idea of their altitude, although any measurement seemed beside the point. Whatever their elevation, they were no longer connected to the surface of Eëlios at all. The Chaga Sea, Musgrave's Dance, Whitebone River, Mouth of Kronos, Blackbone Swamp — all belonged to another world, as though, in their climb, they had burned through to another Illium planet. Here, with its sense of twilight enclosure, Leyden felt as if he were moving through a larger space than any he had ever before experienced.

Looking upward for yet another hundred meters or so, Leyden could see a backlit wall of vegetation that seemed to be holding back the sun. Just below this pale ceiling, clusters of slowly pulsing colors — scarlets, blues and yellows — seemed to turn and rotate.

The green woman looked up with him. "Glowbirds," she said. "Feeding on insects. They communicate with the brightness and pattern of their colors."

"Some kind of bioluminescent chemical, we believe," Kee added. "Each bird secretes an enzyme that activates its own unique color or shade. We haven't caught any specimens yet."

They watched for a moment in silence as the flock of lights coalesced and scattered and reformed far over their heads, as if they were watching a Rigelian Ferris wheel from a distant shore.

"Good eating," the green woman said. "We will net them. . . as many as you want."

Leyden thought that An San Kee looked momentarily pained.

"Can't wait," he said cheerfully.

The Iksillas returned, with Twon skittering up the green woman's leg and perching on her shoulder, so that Leyden had a good look at the matching scarlet-and-blue markings on their faces. Twon paused at his feet and the two of them looked at each other.

"Should I be doing something now?" he asked.

The green woman glanced at them. "Just give him the hand greeting you learned. You will know when you have bonded."

"I was afraid of that." Leyden slowly shaped the traditional hello.

Ahead of them, the branch ran into a sudden cliff, black and vertical, a wall massive enough to divide worlds.

"Wait here, please," the green woman said. She advanced to the cliff and pulled a nondescript piece of cloth from her belt and draped it over her shoulders. As she did, Twon jumped off her shoulder. The green woman knelt, her hands covering her face, and began nodding silently.

"What's happening?" Leyden whispered to Kee. "Are we praying to the forest gods or something?"

"Something like that."

"I hope her prayers include a short course in rock climbing."

An San Kee looked at him. With her dark clothes, her face seemed to swim in the half-light like a moon. "That's not rock."

"What the hell is it?"

"A tree. Two of them actually."

Leyden looked again. Impossible. It had to be a wall that the green woman was praying to. Staring down its length, he tried detect the hint of a curvature, but the wall disappeared in the weak darkness. The green woman pulled the cloth down over her shoulders and gazed upward, palms open.

Leyden could hear her words, a slow repetition of an Eëlian phrase, punctuated with the clicks and whistles he found so unpronounceable. As he listened, Leyden realized how closely her odd sounds resembled the calls and cries of the rainforest itself. It seemed remarkable that the Eëlians had developed such an alien language, yet one so attuned to their environment, in little more than a hundred Illium standard years or so.

She finished and motioned to Leyden and Kee. Twen and Twon skittered up the wall, stopped and peered down at the three of them, hanging by only front claws and the serrated edges of their tails. Leyden walked up to the wall, a mass of pits and crevices, with a crumbling surface and an acrid smell. Bark.

The green woman sensed his questions. "This is one of the six. . . pillars of our world. One of the six places where tree. . ." She looked at Kee.

". . . where tree entwines tree," Kee said.

"Where tree entwines tree," the green woman repeated, "and in constant struggle and prayer together, seek to rejoin mother Eëlios with the Ginn, our sacred suns, Nevea and Naryl."

"There are six trees this size on Eëlios?" Leyden asked. The scarlet markings around the green woman's left eye appeared luminescent in the semi-darkness, her expression ageless and opaque. She could be feeling exalted, bored, curious, tired; he hadn't the slightest idea.

"There are only two," the green woman said. "But their gift is the six anchors that lift and create our world, give us life."

Leyden turned to An San Kee. "What are the size of these things. And what does she mean, there are only two?"

"No one has examined any of them at the base," Kee said, "so we really have no idea of their maximum size. Besides, a good portion of both trees are buried underwater in Blackbone Swamp. Higher up, the earlier expedition estimated the diameter at a quarter of a kilometer. But as best we can tell, we're not measuring a single tree, but sets of two, and only two. Genetic tests of the core samples from at least three of these anchors are identical."

"Meaning?"

"Meaning that we're dealing with only two individual trees as the foundation of the entire Eëlian rainforest canopy. In other words, two of the largest known life forms in the Illium Archipelago."

Leyden tore off a chunk of bark and crumbled it as he craned his neck upward again. He felt another hand in his, toughened and smooth. The green woman had taken his hands in hers; Leyden looked into the darkness of her young-old eyes.

She opened his hands and took away his bark, and with a blunt nail, split the bark twice again, revealing a dark, charcoal-colored vein. Peeling away more of the surface so that she exposed a point, the green woman placed a hand carefully on Leyden's face and lifted his chin. Very slowly, she drew a line across his forehead and two slightly curving lines around his eyes and down each cheek to the corners of his mouth. Still holding his head, she moistened two fingers and retraced the lines, smudging them and making them thicker, a crude approximation of the decorative markings on her own face.

When she finished, the green woman broke off another piece of bark and repeated the process with An San Kee. As a final step, she streaked her chest and the tops of her breasts with the charcoal bark, repeating a short phrase, first in Eëlian then in Illium standard: "So it is done."

"The first meeting of strangers with the anchorwood is a sacred moment," she said to him, "one that must be marked with ceremony."

"And always with the bark of the anchorwood tree?" Leyden asked.

The green woman gave the smallest of shrugs. Some gestures seem universal. "Not really. It could have been done with water. And there is a prayer, of course, which you do not know. Also, if you had been Eëlians, coming of age, I would have drawn the lines in blood, with a knife."

Leyden glanced at Kee. "I appreciate your restraint."

With a series of soft clicks, the green woman summoned Twen and Twon, hand-signaled, and sent them scurrying up the vertical side of the anchorwood trunk and out of sight.

"We will wait here a few minutes while they check the light — the place of Nevea and Naryl in the sky."

Leyden took a breath and sneezed at the bitter smell of the bark. "Six anchor trees but only two species," he said to Kee. "I don't follow."

Kee said, "The Eëlians use the term anchorwood for the six locations where these trees attain their full size. Whether they are all connected to the same root system, or have grown from separate seeds, we have no idea. The DNA tests are quite clear, though — we're not dealing with two species, but with two *individuals*. If only we had more time. The structures are too massive for us to investigate without a lot more time and resources."

Leyden stood close to the trunk, his chest pressing against the bark, and looked up. "Two trees in six places. I only see one here."

"They're fused and hard to tell apart in places, but you'll see soon enough. The anchor tree and the strangler."

"Strangler?"

"Choke trees, strangler figs, death firs. Strangler trees are common on almost any world with a sizable forest," Kee was speaking in her unmistakable classroom voice.

"If you think about it, there are only so many ways to beat the competition and reach the sun in a jungle. You can grow fast, you can grow big, or you can hitch a ride on another plant, which is what all the vines and lianas around us are doing.

"You can even give up on rooting in the ground altogether and become a parasite, like many kinds of mosses. Or an epiphyte, like the bromeliads, which attach to another plant and get their nutrients largely from the air and rain. Or you can start out as an epiphyte, then send roots *down* to the earth. A hemi epiphyte. With its altitude, you can pretty well assume that the high canopy of Eëlios consists mostly of epiphytes."

"And the anchor tree and the strangler?"

Kee nodded. "Well, they're the most dramatic example I've ever come across. Right now, our best guess is that the Eëlian rainforest is a product of their struggle."

Leyden said, "So the tactic of the strangler is to entwine itself around the anchor tree. Like a vine."

"Yes, but with one important difference," Kee answered. "Choke trees or stranglers can literally crush the tree inside them and kill it. If you were to see a grove of death firs on Tushangura, or strangler figs on Old Earth, you could see a corkscrew shaped trunk that is hollow in the center, where the other tree has died and crumbled away completely."

"But that hasn't happened here?"

"Oh yes, it probably did. Many times. But in six instances, at least, it didn't. Our best guess is that the anchorwood trees here, or at least one species of anchorwood, countered the Eëlian stranglers by becoming larger and more massive. The strangler tried to match its size, and as a result, they literally exploded into the sky, creating the tallest trees and the highest jungle canopy in the Illium. Today, presumably, the anchor trees are too huge to crush. Or maybe not. We have no idea. They're either living in relative symbiotic peace, or the struggle goes on. Slow. Silent. Whoever is around in the next millennium may see the winner."

Twon reappeared and scrambled onto the green woman's shoulder. Twen did the same with Leyden, and before he quite realized it, Twen had wedged himself between Leyden's neck and shoulder, forked tongue waving in his face.

"Time," the green woman said, pulling on her backpack.

Leyden tried to brush Twen away diplomatically but succeeded only in getting his hand licked with Twen's sticky tongue. He gave up and reached down for his ISSU and strapped on the Dragon.

Twen climbed on his head, claws digging uncomfortably into his scalp. Like it or not, it felt like the beginning of bonding.

"What now?" he asked the green woman.

She handed him a set of webbed spikes for his feet and short-handled pick. "The usual. We climb."

23 LIGHT GAPS

As the Iksillas raced in aimless circles, Leyden, An San Kee, and the green woman scaled the massive side of the anchorwood tree.

Almost unbelieving, Leyden found himself in a vertical climb — without ropes, net, or a clear understanding of the distance they had to travel. The pitted ridged surface of the anchorwood bark offered numerous foot and handholds. It also proved relatively easy to kick the spikes on his feet into the soft bark. At the same time, he could swing the pick into the wood above him to establish at least one secure handhold. Leyden, gaunt and much lighter since his recovery from the Saar attack, also found he had the routine strength, if not the endurance, to climb against the planet's relatively mild gravity.

On the other hand, if he drove his foot spikes or pick in too hard, the bark tended to crumble and break away unexpectedly, leaving him scrabbling for the next step. And though he felt lightweight, Leyden was still in an absolute vertical climb, and he quickly became soaked and gasping, the straps of the ISSU and the Dragon cutting hard into his shoulders, neck rigid and sore as he craned it back constantly to spot his next move. An San Kee didn't seem to be doing much better.

Leyden suspected that the green woman, born to this world, was dismayed at their difficulties. From his eye-stinging, blurred perspective, she appeared more like a forest sprite than a full-size human, climbing with astonishing ease, using only a pick. Waiting for them to struggle upward, she would occasionally hang from the trunk with only one hand as casually as if she were leaning against a wall.

They finally reached small ledge, apparently where a branch had long ago splintered and broken off. Kee and Leyden wiped their faces and drank from yellow water gourds. The woman pointed up. Instead of continuing to rise vertically, the trunk bulged outward.

Leyden suppressed a curse of dismay. "Is that. . .?"

"Yes," Kee said, "one of the coils of the Eëlian strangler around the anchorwood trunk."

Leyden looked at the green woman and shook his head. "I don't think we can make that. A piece of bark breaks off and we fall."

She stared at him impassively, the Iksillas on either side of her as motionless as small gargoyles.

"Wait here," she said and gave a series whistles, clicks, and hand gestures to the creatures. Twen and Twon raced up the trunk and disappeared.

As Leyden and Kee watched, the green woman scrambled up the trunk and out under the swelling of the strangler so that she was hanging at an oblique angle. She reached into her belt and pulled out a kind of rung, pushing it into the bark, moving farther out and pushing in another. By the time she made a series of regularly spaced holds around the bulge of the strangler coil, the Iksillas reappeared carrying lengths of vine in their mouths. The woman, again hanging by only a hand and foot, looped and tied the vine through the rungs before climbing back down to the ledge.

"This will be enough, yes?" she said, hardly breathing hard at all.

Kee and Leyden looked at each other.

"We'll certainly try," Kee said carefully. "How much farther do we climb the trunk this way?"

The green woman considered. "For me, one more hour. For us, with rest. . . perhaps two."

She noted their dismay, and added quickly, "There are many places to rest. And then, a very easy way into the high canopy, to my home, and the others."

Leyden looked up at the vine loops hanging from the strangler. "Did the rest of the expedition go this way too?"

"No. With all their equipment, they went an easier way, along connections of branches and rope bridges. But longer than us. Too long."

Stretching and standing, Leyden felt two pairs of eyes on him, measuring, considering: the green woman's and his Iksilla, Twen. He awkwardly signed what he remembered as the hand gestures for *go, now*. If Iksillas could look surprised, perhaps it would have registered on Twen's face; instead, the Iksilla stuck out his tongue and signed an acknowledgment.

Kee stood and gathered the science packs that attached to her modified ISSU. "Why not leave it here?" she said.

"What?"

"The Dragon."

Leyden picked up the two sections and considered. If the Saar attacked, it would take him twenty seconds minimum to charge and fire the thing. By then, they would be picking their teeth with his bones. Leave it, make the climb easier, and confirm all of Hawkwood's prejudices about him, Toranga and Illium worlders generally.

Cursing silently to himself, he slung it over his back and tightened the straps. "Let's go," he muttered more to himself than to Kee. "Let's just go."

With the security of the green woman's vine loops, the climb out and over the strangler swelling proved easier than he expected. Next, they encountered another long vertical stretch, scrabbling and clutching for each new crevice and outcropping. Kee and Leyden alternated in second position behind the green woman, since the one bringing up the rear caught all the fragments breaking off in front. Anchorwood bark coated his face and hair.

After twenty more minutes, sweat once again almost blinding him, Leyden heard the swift clucking sound of the Iksillas. The green woman froze. She turned slowly and looked down at them. "Back down. Now."

Leyden tried to rub his eyes with his arm. "Why? What's wrong?"

"Back down," she repeated. "Now. slowly." Her voice was flat and urgent.

That proved harder than climbing up, and they had only dropped back ten meters or so, when Leyden felt something warm licking his face. He looked up into a pebbled, green lizard face. Twen twisted his tongue into the unmistakable signs for *danger*, and *follow me*.

"Follow us," Leyden repeated downward to An San Kee, now in last place. "Don't ask."

They climbed down at an angle before beginning another vertical ascent. Somewhere above him, out of sight, he thought he heard the sound of fire, followed by the unmistakable smell of burning wood. After climbing hard for several more minutes, they found a branch and heaved themselves onto it in exhaustion. Moments later, the green woman appeared, hands and face smudged, like a child who had been playing in dirt.

"What happened?" Leyden asked.

"We passed a nest of. . . dangerous ants. It was important that we stay far away from them."

"We smelled fire," Kee said. "Did you burn out the nest?"

"Yes. Here I brought you some specimens."

The green woman held out two huge black ants with enlarged heads and front legs modified into enormous scythes. Somehow, she had managed to stick or glue their legs together so that they were immobilized. Their antennae flailed madly, very much alive.

Kee popped them into a tube and sealed it. "Tell me about them," she said with undisguised excitement.

"The closest Illium translation would be. . . head-chopping ants," the green woman said. "They attack other insects in swarms and bite off heads whenever possible."

"Outstanding!" Leyden said. "I can think of a dozen uses already."

Both women ignored him and continued to examine the ants, which were now rendered completely immobilized by a compound coating the inside of Kee's specimen jar.

"Ah. Let's call them guillotine ants." Kee mimed the basic operation of a guillotine.

"Yes! Yes! Guillotine ants." It was the first time he had seen the green woman laugh.

Leyden said, "But not quite large enough to behead us, I should think."

The green woman glanced at him, still smiling but with the same changeless expression in her eyes. What would it take to change?

"Guillotine ants are very aggressive," she said. "They swarm over any living animal within reach, no matter how large. For something as large as us, their manner of attack is to enter any body openings and burrow into the flesh. Extremely painful. If they sensed us, we would not have been quick enough to out-climb them. Also, this is an important pathway for my people. So it was necessary to burn the nest away."

"What about the danger of fire? Couldn't you set off the whole rainforest around here."

The green woman shook her head. "No. Anchorwood is very..." she looked over at Kee.

"Fire resistant," Kee said.

The green woman nodded. "If I took you back, you would see only a small burn mark, soon gone."

On the next stretch, Leyden had the sense of the anchorwood tree and the strangler diminishing in size. The light strengthened with their altitude, and he could begin to see a curvature along the trunk. The glowbirds flew closer, and Leyden could pick out individual birds, their wings and throats blinking on and off like warning lights.

The green woman stopped and pointed silently. For a moment, Leyden was unable to pick out anything in the foliage until he realized that she was pointing to a small blue cloud of insects.

"Blue bees!" he shouted in sudden recognition. "My saviors."

She smiled down at him before turning away and continuing to climb. A laugh and a smile. She seemed to be less guarded the higher they ascended.

For the next forty minutes they climbed through a zone of constant mist: the Eëlian cloud forest. Water soaked his clothing and beaded on his face. Their world shrank to damp shades of gray, fog streamers hanging from black, dripping branches or drifting like suspended islands. Ferns proliferated and fuzzy blankets of moss and fungi coated the surfaces of both branches and trunks.

When the cloud forest thinned at last, they found themselves in the lower reaches of the high canopy, surrounded once again by vegetation and dappled light, the vault-like sense of elevation and space gone. Their climb had also brought them to a relatively temperate zone, with the heat and humidity noticeably less than in the lower elevations. Apparently, their vertical anchorwood climb was over.

They continued along a branch with vine-twisted railings. At intervals they encountered ragged squares of vertical netting made of woven vines and climbed them to the next level. As the light levels increased, so did the activity around them. Vegetation pressed in around them in more shades and intensities of green than Leyden thought could exist. He brushed by leaves rounded and soft, or slender and sharp as knives. The fragrance of flowers intensified, accompanied by the darting brilliance of Eëlian dragonflies, bird calls, the cries of indeterminate creatures, and the first suggestions of wind.

When they paused, Leyden examined one of a clump of bell-shaped leaves that had begun to appear on stalks along the branch, almost at eye level. Each leaf cluster held a viscous-looking amber liquid along with a flotilla of struggling insects.

The green woman knelt beside one, flicked away the larger insects and, tipping back the edge of the leaf without plucking it, drank down the contents.

"Sweet, good for a trip like ours. Try one."

Leyden took a look. A large multicolored ant and several smaller insects hung on the surface, legs churning. "I think not."

"Oh, come on," An San Kee said, already tipping back a plant and drinking.

Leyden unclipped the Dragon webbing and pulled it off his shoulder. The two women waited for him. He plucked out the colorful ant, gave up on the smaller ones and drank. The sensation felt akin to an ice cube down his back: the most intense experience of sweetness he had ever experienced, followed by an aftertaste of rich berries.

"Remarkable," he said. "Maybe I'll have another."

The green woman shook her head. "Later. Here, fill this up." She handed Leyden one of the small gourds on her belt, clearly a kind of seed pod or thick-skinned fruit with its center carved away and closed with a kind of waxy cork. He filled it with the liquid of two plants.

"What is it called?" Leyden asked. "This plant."

The green woman used an Eëlian word, then paused. "Nevea's Nectar."

"Nectar of the gods," Leyden said. "Very appropriate. Kee, you've got all this, including samples?"

"I do. But you better move fast before Verlaine beats you to marketing it."

"No doubt."

Twen appeared, sat back on his rear legs and tail, and wrote long sentences in the air with his triple-forked tongue. With a quick wave, the green woman sent him off again.

"We will wait here a moment," the green woman said. "The suns will soon be right."

Kee looked at him. "This Nevea's Nectar?"

"Yes."

"A good example of a bromeliad, one of the most important types of epiphytes."

"And a personal favorite of yours, no doubt?"

"Absolutely," Kee said. "The Illium variations of epiphytes are fascinating. They have to deal with some very special problems. One is holding onto water. It may rain a lot, but the water dissipates rapidly. Nevea's Nectar, like many bromeliads, is shaped like a cup to hold liquid, and in this case to produce a sweet fluid to attract a nice supplementary diet of insects. A very common adaptation in environments like this."

Twen and Twon reappeared, each carrying one end of a long piece of vine. "Time," the green woman said. "We must hurry."

The green woman moved so fast that Leyden fell into a half jog, hands out to protect against passing vines and thorns.

"Have we got an appointment with someone, or what?" he muttered to Kee.

"More like something, I should think," she answered.

They stopped in a bowl-shaped mass of entwined vegetation where the upper reaches of the canopy, still far above them, seemed to have thinned, increasing the light level markedly. He looked more closely. This wasn't a natural bowl in the rainforest, he realized, but an artificial space cut by human hands.

Stump-like bromeliads stood in waist-high clumps throughout the bowl. They had a central pod topped with mottled green tendrils that reminded

Leyden of the sea anemones on Poseidon. A rim around the pod held several centimeters of water and the usual contingent of floating insects.

The green woman took the vine from Twon and Twen and cut it into three lengths. When she handed one of them to Leyden, he found it so gluey that he could barely unpeel his hand.

"I will answer questions later," the green woman said. "For now, stay close and do exactly as I do. Immediately. This is our way upward to the others. But we have only one chance. Am I. . . understood?"

Kee and Leyden nodded silently, and followed her into the middle of the bromeliad field.

The green woman unclipped what appeared to be a small flute from one of the belts across her chest. But the note she blew was unmusical, shrill, and loud. She repeated it several times. Following a quick wave of her hand, Twon wrapped himself around her neck and remained motionless. A moment later, Twen did the same with Leyden.

They waited in the buzzing glade, with only the slightest suggestion of a breeze. Leyden could feel the sweat tracking down his back, the bite of the straps from the ISSU and Dragon cutting into his shoulder, the odd rapid beating of Twen's heart against his neck. *Waiting, for what?*

The sound came from far overhead: the cracking and splintering of wood, as if lumberjacks were felling an arboreal forest above them. The canopy parted and shafts of full sunlight, unbroken by leaf or branch, fell upon them. And upon the heavy epiphyte stalks.

"Do you have any idea what is happening?" Leyden muttered to Kee.

"I think we're going to see another way of climbing through the canopy. Something we've never seen before."

A second crack rolled down and the hole in the canopy widened until sunlight flooded the entire glade. Minutes passed. The green woman remained as motionless as the vegetation surrounding her. Leyden wiped his face as the temperature increased noticeably.

He felt a vibration, a field of movement around him along with a hissing sound. The bromeliad stalks began to tremble and wave in unison.

With a percussive snap, the cap popped off the end of the bromeliad next to An San Kee, followed by a second, and then a volley of explosions that sent a litter of caps arcing through the air from the rest of the plants. The hissing sound was more pronounced now. From the plant next to Leyden, an inner stalk as thick as a fist and pale as a succubus emerged from inside the plant, inflating as it rose above the stalk. He looked around: wet, swelling stalks appeared everywhere. As they lengthened, the stalks continued to grow, from pods to balls to pear-shaped hissing balloons twice Leyden's height.

Leyden looked at Kee. "Hydrogen gas," she said. "They're generating hydrogen gas and climbing through the canopy to the sun." She nodded to the green woman. "And we're going to hitch a ride."

Still motionless, the green woman waited until the field of inflating bromeliads filled the sky, waving in the still air. The indiscernible moment arrived, and she seized two of the stalks at the base of the inflated top, threw her sticky length of vine around them, then looped it around and under herself in a rapid series of turns so that she was both tied to the stalks and seated against them. Twon twitched his tail and licked her face.

"Do the same," she said to Kee and Leyden. "Be quick."

Leyden got his vine around several stalks nearest him, but found he had to untangle and unstick himself several times before he had even a half-satisfactory knot. The single strand that he managed to loop under him cut uncomfortably into his butt.

They ascended slowly, rising past green walls toward the sun-flecked sky.

He looked over at Kee, almost level with him, and to the green woman, riding perhaps ten meters overhead. Twen stirred around his neck, licking his face and unwinding from his neck to perch on his shoulder. Leaves and branches brushed by his face. Glowbirds and insect clouds floated past.

The green woman looked down at them, frowning at their arrangement of loops and knots. "Are you all right?"

"Yes," Kee called back. "What is this called?"

The green woman hesitated, looked up, then down again at them. "The Eëlian word means, Floater-to-the-Sun."

"You use this all the time?" Leyden asked, calling up to her.

"No. This is only for special times like this. Emergencies. We must keep this section always cleared of growth. But the hardest part is there," the green woman said, pointing upward. "We must collect heavy logs to drop and pull aside the trees and open the canopy to the sunlight."

Within an hour, the floater vines pushed into the high canopy. A platform woven of rope and twisted vines swam into view; the green woman cut herself free, hung for several moments with one hand, then stepped off. As she did, she casually slashed open the hydrogen-filled sack of her balloon vine. When Kee and Leyden approached, she leaned off the platform and cut their balloons as well. The vines shuddered and deflated, hanging in the air, twining around themselves and hooking onto branches as they started to collapse and fall.

Leyden pulled himself onto the rope platform as Twen leaped off his shoulders and into overhanging branches, where he joined a collection of other Iksillas. Kee busily cut and tagged samples.

As he pulled the ISSU and Dragon from his shoulders, Leyden saw a group of Eëlians standing a short distance away in a tangled litter of wood fragments and overhead ropes where they had launched the deadfall.

"Have we arrived?" he said.

"Yes," said the green woman, the tone of relief unmistakable. "They are from our village."

The scars on Leyden chest itched and throbbed; he would need to ask for her medicated oils and wadi leaves soon.

She looked at them. "Let us go, then."

"Wait," Leyden said, his hand on her arm. She paused and looked up at him, and he realized for the first time that the top of her head just reached his chin. He wanted to reach out and touch the scarlet-and-blue paint around her eye. He dropped his hand away.

Leyden felt suddenly awkward. "After this trip, it seems time that we should settle on a name," he said. "Something we can halfway pronounce."

He looked over to Kee for support.

The green woman repeated her name slowly: sibilants, whistles, and clicks. "It will be a long time before you could say my name, or many other Eëlian words."

True enough," he said. "But let's compromise on something easier. For now."

She shrugged and repeated it again slowly.

Leyden tested several parts of it. "Sh-yal. . . Shil-la. . . Sylla." He looked at both of them. "Sylla."

An San Kee made a face. "Not even close."

"Yes, but short, simple. Easy."

The green woman stepped away, her face in shadow, only the slashes of color visible. "Yes, Leyden and Kee. I will be Sylla."

PART IV: BALANCING

24 NAUSICCA'S FEAST

The Eëlians lit torches, and somewhere behind the veil of foliage came the sound of flutes and small plucked instruments. A solemn line of children appeared with the first course: small, anonymous creatures, crusted and brown, arranged on a bed of yellow-green leaves that smelled of unfamiliar spices and hot oils.

Leyden examined his plate carefully. "Any guesses?" he asked the group.

He sat in a semicircle with Suslov, An San Kee, Verlaine, Mkeki, and Chácon. A second group, also arranged around a low table of tightly woven bamboo, consisted of Modrescu, Bertelsmann, Chapandagura, Tranner, Zia, and Holmes. As guests of honor, Tirun and Hawkwood sat in the center on a slightly raised platform with Cleanth, the village headman, Ulam, and several women whom Leyden assumed belonged to Cleanth in some capacity.

High-ranking villagers ate at several other tables; but most of the Eëlians seemed content to hang back in the foliage, standing and eating with their fingers, not particularly quiet and respectful — chatting and pointing as small children played around their ankles. A collection of village Iksillas, including Twen and Twon, clucked and raced through the overhanging branches, raining down small showers of twigs and generally causing a nuisance.

Torches burned around the perimeter of the amphitheater, clearly designed for ceremonial occasions. The overhead vegetation, woven into a ceiling, kept everyone in shadows, even though Nevea and Naryl hung high in the invisible sky.

A procession of women emerged from the cooking shelter with large gourds, Sylla among them. She separated herself and approached Leyden directly, knelt before him, and poured a dark liquid into a carved anchorwood cup. As she turned to fill An San Kee's cup, Leyden sensed a quiet stir among the Eëlians — quick glances all around, as though something unexpected had occurred, a subtle but unmistakable breach of decorum. Leyden wondered if her act somehow announced the connection of their journey together. Sylla herself revealed nothing as she moved around the table.

"Is it permitted for you to join us?" An San Kee asked.

"Not tonight," she said. She gestured in the direction of the group seated with Headman Cleanth. "I am helping my sister. She is the chief cook."

Leyden had met Nausicca when he first arrived: a voluble, round-faced woman who seemed the complete opposite of Sylla in temperament. Yet the connection between them also struck him when he looked into Nausicca's black, distant eyes, set off with bright green and scarlet slashes of color in a pattern similar to Sylla's. Oddly, he had seen no other women in the village with the same type of markings.

"Well, then," Verlaine said to Sylla. "Tell us what we are about to eat and drink. Promise or threat — for off-worlders like us?"

Continuing to kneel, Sylla placed her gourd on the table. "You are drinking Aramanthian wine, made from the fruits of three or four different Aramanth plants. The first course is a delicacy especially prepared in honor of your visit — Musgrave beetles, trimmed, lightly dusted in flour and marinated in kanjin, which is. . . a mix of ingredients." She paused and looked around at them. "It might be considered an insult to the village, and an embarrassment to our honorable Headman, if you were to refuse such a dish."

The wine, while drinkable, tasted heavy and sweet, not at all to Leyden's liking, trained on the ravishing bouquets of his ill-starred Delium Ghahan venture. The Musgrave-beetle sauté was another matter: al dente, succulent, the marinade light but distinctive. Leyden looked around for seconds.

A clear soup with an arrangement of pale floating blossoms replaced the beetles. It looked delicate but held a delayed bite that brought water to their eyes. Eëlian soup with liriope chilies and wadi blossoms, Sylla explained.

The servers returned with another round of wine and the next course: spitted glowbirds on a bed of coarse-looking grain, sautéed in red Naryl garlic and yellow-gourd oil and seasoned with mixed-vine peppers.

"Quite an entrance on those blimp-style vines," Verlaine said, carefully testing a mix of glowbird and peppers. "An improvement over our four days. Up one goddamn branch after another."

"Special treatment for those injured in the line of duty," Leyden said.

Verlaine looked him over carefully. "Yeah. I heard about your bee treatment. Glad it worked. Gives you a rugged appearance in a nice shade of green. Improvement over your pretty-boy looks if you ask me."

Leyden reached involuntarily for the scars on his face. "You're so kind." He cut a slice of glowbird breast meat, the skin blackened and seared, the inside suffused with juices. An alien but seductive taste.

"An uneventful trip?" Leyden asked Verlaine. "Didn't bump into the items that will make your fortune yet, or Trans-Illium's?"

Leyden waved a piece of glowbird between a pair of fluted Eëlian chopsticks. "Franchise this. Musgrave beetles and glowbirds. Become owner of the trendiest restaurants on twenty worlds."

"No doubt," Verlaine said. "But why just a restaurant chain? Think bigger, think like an Illium entrepreneur, a chaebol."

He waved his hand to encompass their setting, the canopy, the rainforest. "Think about a hotel more than a kilometer in the sky serving food like this. Think about a rainforest resort on the scale of Poseidon. *Now*, you're thinking like a chaebol."

"Is that the plan? Is that why Trans-Illium is here?"

Verlaine shrugged. "No. We don't have those kind of resources, not with our limited permit from the Illium League. Until we got hit by the competition, whoever they are, the plan was simply to lock up as many licenses for medicinal plants and genomes as possible. Find out exactly what this place has to offer. That's plenty. If the big boys, the chaebols, want to develop something else, build another Poseidon, that's quite another matter."

"And you, personally?"

Verlaine pulled his second glowbird off the spit and started nibbling it with his fingers.

"I'll tell you my feeling about this place, Leyden. It's too much. Too big, too high, too complicated. Look at our dear Kee. Three lifetimes, or ten, plus a hundred more researchers like her and she still couldn't begin to catalog half the life forms here. Same for Trans-Illium. How many plants, chemicals, enzymes, organic compounds, medicines—your blue bees—are here? We frantically stuff a couple thousand into specimen containers and sail away on the *Balliol* — if we're lucky and steer clear of whatever the hell is out there. Anyway, I have something specific in mind to find. One item, market-tested and reliable."

"Is this little side venture cleared with your employer?"

"Absolutely. I'm on straight salary here, not even per diem, can you believe it? Deal is, I look out for Trans-Illium's interest, let Tirun run the show. If I find what I'm looking for, it's mine, with a percentage cut for

Trans-Illium and their promise to help fund any Core World franchise operation."

"And our competition, out on the Whitebone, how do they factor in?"

Verlaine bared his teeth as he consumed his glowbird. Juices ran from the corner of his mouth.

"Everyone realized that Eëlios would begin to attract a lot of interest after the main Selucid Swarm planets were settled. But we have only a limited-time permit here. No one figured that any chaebol like the Taranazuka or the Sidereal Collective would risk their investments across the Illium. . . for what? Plus bribe someone inside the League in the process. If, in fact, that's what happened."

A chorus of furious whispering and stirrings from the Eëlians signaled the next course. Snake on a spit, Sylla explained: Eëlian emerald boa, blackened and seared with spiced oils, covered in strips of Eëlian bamboo flesh melted over the top. Leyden prided himself on having successfully consumed the specialties of a dozen Illium worlds, but blackened boa tested the limits of his ability. His eyes watering, he gulped down another glass of Aramanthian wine, hoping he wouldn't regret it. The others experienced the same difficulty, except for Mkeki, who smiled and consumed the whole thing, her tongue ring shining momentarily in the torchlight as she sucked the meat off the skewer.

Leyden turned back to Verlaine; perhaps his best shot at squeezing out more information about the expedition. "What is this magic item you plan to franchise? Something Ulam and the others brought back last time?"

Verlaine wiped his mouth and licked his fingers. "Ah, this is all very proprietary stuff, Leyden, you know that. But yes, it's not hard to guess that the stuff Ulam and the others had with them has been of great interest to everyone."

"Yet a small player like Trans-Illium wins the exclusive license for a return expedition. Remarkable." Leyden looked around for his water gourd. "I figure Trans-Illium is fronting for one of the chaebols, after all. And I'll bet another one is out there, maybe claiming foul in the whole licensing arrangement with the League. The way I see it, this started out as a chaebol race. Now we're in the middle of a chaebol war. I wonder if the Eëlians have a clue about the bright future in store for them."

"Logical and persuasive, if wrong," Verlaine said. "But then, no one ever questioned your intelligence or your oratory." He smiled and Leyden realized that Verlaine understood exactly what was going on and would now change the subject entirely.

"It was always your judgment that sometimes left something to be desired, wasn't it?" Verlaine continued. 'It was one thing to speak out for the interests of Toranga and the other Core Worlds. Quite another to raise the issue of controlling the portals themselves. Because then you weren't just taking on the Illium League, but the interests of the chaebols themselves, who are quite happy with the current arrangement. You crossed a bright red line there, my friend."

Leyden said nothing. Verlaine was right, of course: in the end Toranga had overreached. By isolating Toranga and refusing to join either its political or military challenge to the Illium League, the chaebols guaranteed the rebellion's failure. They much preferred the certainty of monopoly control of the portals to the potential chaos of having them run by up to a hundred separate worlds.

Hawkwood and the League invasion forces merely administered the *coup de grace*.

Somewhere behind the screen of foliage, the sad, thin notes of a solitary harp replaced the dulcimer and flutes. The servers reentered with a platter of arboreal fish, also sautéed in red garlic and yellow-gourd oil, but plated with marinated fungi and a dried fig-like fruit from the tracasandra vine. Next came dishes of sweating rivertree fruit, red, sweet, cool.

Leyden was definitely feeling bloated when Kee pulled him away from Verlaine.

"I've been asked to tell you that you may have a little business after dinner with our Mr. Tirun and their leader, Cleanth," she said.

Leyden grunted.

"Don't look now, but I think we're being watched," she added.

Leyden looked up to see a group of Eëlians from the kitchen shelter gathered in the entrance, observing the proceedings. Nausicca stood in the center, wiping her hands, arms coated in brown flour, whispering to Sylla.

Leyden leaned back, wine cup in hand, and raised it in a silent toast to Sylla and Nausicca. Sylla remained expressionless; Nausicca smiled, and some of her assistants covered laughs of embarrassment with their hands. They all disappeared back into the shelter.

"Did Tirun say anything about whether our heavy-weapons attackers are around here?" he asked Kee.

"It's odd. I get the impression that the village is as surprised at the news of another expedition as we were. Much less that we were attacked."

Leyden signed. "I'd like to think that maybe, if we're lucky, we'll both flounder around in the canopy and not even run into each other again."

"Think so? Really?"

"No. They tried hard to wipe us out on the Whitebone. Why stop now? If they have a functioning NavCom satellite, they'll find us if they want to."

He looked down as Kee picked at her food. "What's wrong? You could probably write a book on tonight's dinner alone. Not to mention what you've collected in the rainforest already."

"If we survive long enough to get back."

Leyden could only put an arm around her for a brief hug. "Point taken. Now who do you think is out there?"

"I have no idea." She smiled at him. "But I suspect you have a theory, especially if it involves the League."

"Everyone says only the chaebols have the resources for something like this," Leyden said. "But why not Cold Moon Triad? Or some chaebol breakaway fronting for one of the triads? You're the exobotonist — you know better than anyone that Eëlios probably has narcotic, hallucinogenic, psychotropic, and pleasure-activation substances. A whole new product line to market to the zoned-out masses on Ohzumé, the high trippers of Rigel Prime and New Kirov. The Earwigs, the Rockheads — they're always ready for something different — why not exotic Eëlios?"

"You're forgetting something," Kee said. "The League. You really think they would knowingly let one of the triads launch an unauthorized expedition to the Selucid Swarm?"

Leyden hesitated. "Not the League. Maybe just a corrupt officer. The League colludes with the chaebols. How big a step would it be, really, to make a deal with Cold Moon? Two rival expeditions cross the Selucid Swarm to Eëlios, neither of which could have gotten here without the Illium League. Triad or chaebol, the League takes its cut. Only this time it looks as though they took it from both ends. Divide and conquer. Not the newest tactic around, but always effective."

"I'm a scientist, Leyden. We've been attacked by someone. That's a fact. But we really haven't clue as to who they are and why they're here."

"No, but they've certainly gone to a lot of trouble for something, whether it's wonder drugs or narcotics or medicines or gourmet food products. Sabotaged us, and failing that, attacked."

"Sabotage?" Kee asked. "Really?"

"Tirun confirmed it on the Whitebone. After the drone attack."

"Not to us. Not to the rest of the expedition."

"All we know is that it has to be someone with full access to expedition ops."

"And who does Tirun nominate? Civilian or merc?"

Leyden shrugged. "If he has a candidate, he's not telling me."

"And you?" Kee asked.

"What about someone a little higher up in the expedition?"

"Higher?"

Leyden sipped a spice tea that was the latest serving. He felt remarkably refreshed; no doubt the tea had its own pharmaceutical assets.

"What about our own Tribune Hawkwood?"

Kee patted his hand. "Oh, Leyden. That would be your heart's desire, wouldn't it? Your sworn enemy corrupted by one of the triads."

"Why not? Who would have had better access to every aspect of the expedition?"

"And let himself get blown away with the rest of us in the Whitebone attack?"

Leyden hesitated. She had pointed exactly to the problem with his scenario. A figure like Hawkwood would be an invaluable agent within the Illium League for any group. The League built its cohesive, even fanatic organization to fend off precisely such intrigues, offers of sex and money, blackmail, and other inducements that a hundred worlds could offer. Leyden had no compunction about trying to undercut Hawkwood, but he didn't really believe that Hawkwood would sell out. No, he was a true believer in what he undoubtedly called order, what Leyden and Toranga had once called oppression.

More pots of spiced tea arrived with servings of the banana-like williwaw, glazed in a kind of crystallized honey that jolted him into a powerful but obscure memory. He took another bite: not a distant memory, but a recent one, dreamlike but painful, one of smell and touch, not sight. He scraped off a ridge of the glaze and tasted it again. Honey of blue sky bees, his bees, the same smell that had enveloped him as the bees swarmed over his wounded body, severing his past life from the present.

Tirun was standing now, cup in hand, clearing his throat. The invisible harp stopped playing. Leyden could hear the Iksillas still racing and clucking overhead. He groaned to himself. How was it possible that, no matter where you traveled, the institution of the formal, often interminable, after-dinner toast remained universal?

25 GUELPH AND GHIBELLINE

Leyden shifted in his seat at the small after-banquet gathering and tried to assess the village headman.

Cleanth appeared as alien and unfamiliar as the Eëlian rainforest, but when Leyden looked into his eyes he knew him instantly: even paradise has politicians.

He was a man of big shoulders and a small, rock-hard pot belly. Instead of face paint, he wore decorative scars that extended below his right eye and down his cheek like the trail of an acid tear. A massive, elaborately carved chest plate hung from his neck. As best Leyden could determine in the unsteady torchlight, it depicted either a triumphant battle or a set of complicated sexual encounters.

At his side sat an equally familiar type: the hard, flat face of a man who on Rigel Prime would be called chief of staff; on Ohzumé and Cold Moon Rising, enforcer or consigliore; and on Umlivik Four, iceman. Like Cleanth, he had ritual scarification across the side of his face and unplanned scars on his neck, no doubt the result of close combat.

Tirun, full of fellowship, Aramanthian wine, and the triumph of having finally arrived at their intended destination, played the expansive guest of honor. Hawkwood stood in shadows behind him.

"Honorable Headman Cleanth," Tirun said. "Let me present my associate, Leyden of Toranga, a man whose name is known widely throughout the Illium Archipelago."

Leyden bowed. "It is an honor to meet you, Headman, as it is a privilege to have been permitted to ascend into your world."

Cleanth nodded. "You are most welcome. This is Nouvé, my Saarman," he said, gesturing to his enforcer. They all sat.

"Ah, then, let us begin," Cleanth said. "And since I know you are all practical men, men of action, let me begin with what I think you in the Illium call the 'bottom line.'" He gave a characteristic scratch at the location of his translator chip.

Leyden looked over at Tirun. It might have helped if Tirun had found the time for a short briefing before they launched into actual negotiations. He clearly expected this to be a purely ceremonial occasion, with the hard talks put off to a later, more sober time.

Leyden said, "Mission Leader Tirun, Tribune Hawkwood and myself join with Trans-Illium in this opportunity to build an alliance that will bring great benefits to all our worlds. We have spent our time traveling through a remarkable land that soon will be celebrated across unimaginable distances, throughout the Illium Archipelago. We have passed through a world, your world, of unimaginable splendor, and may I say wealth? A world that, through our alliance, can raise itself to the highest ranks of the Illium."

Cleanth looked skeptical. "Whatever the future holds, right now we have only what the Illium representatives have called a licensing agreement. Nothing more. Am I not correct?"

Nouvé nodded emphatically; the Headman was entirely correct.

"Indeed, you are" Leyden said quickly. "But with vision and mutual interest, that agreement can be a seed that will sprout in rich soil and grow from a mere sapling to become a great pillar for a new Eëlios... In fact, I suggest that we consider calling our enterprise just that — *Seventh Anchorwood!*"

In the awkward silence that followed, they all watched Cleanth. Tirun looked a little dazed.

Leyden knew he was taking a sizable risk here. An San Kee had given him the short course in Eëlian anchorwood-and-strangler biology, including the apparent fact that six massive trunks of two genetically identical trees undergirded this high-canopy world. And Sylla's ritual prayer and face painting when they first reached the trunk had confirmed the sacred view in which the Eëlians held the anchorwood. Hardly surprising. Leyden suspected the Eëlians had many more collective rituals and prayers associated with the most monumental fact of their existence. Quite possibly, therefore, his anchorwood reference could be regarded as odd, inappropriate, or more dangerously, blasphemous.

But the potential gain was equally great. Any agreement between Trans-Illium and the Eëlians would be the result of long arduous negotiations, and any one of a hundred small differences could harden positions and generate bad feeling. In such an undertaking, as he knew from experience, both sides must establish their common interest at the beginning and agree on their goals. If Leyden could associate Trans-Illium with anchorwood, it could potentially carry them across a dozen sticking points in the negotiations. Hammer home a vision of what regular access to the Illium Core could mean. Inculcate the idea that together they were growing a new, a seventh anchorwood for Eëlios. If he weren't executed as a heretic.

"A new anchorwood tree!" Cleanth gave a short, explosive laugh and smacked Nouvé hard on the shoulder. "A seventh anchorwood! I like the sound of that."

Nouvé nodded and rubbed his shoulder. Smiles and exhalations all around. Servers appeared with more Eëlian tea.

"I have explained to Headman Cleanth the struggles and losses we have suffered in our journey," Tirun said. "And expressed my deep concern about the deadly assault by an outlaw expedition."

"This is troubling news," Cleanth said. "We know nothing of these off-world attacks. Tomorrow, Saar-man Nouvé will lead a delegation to the territory of the Ghibelline. If these off-worlders have come with the same intentions as you, that can be their only other destination."

The Ghibelline, Leyden knew from his desultory research aboard the *Balliol*, comprised a loose confederation of villages and settlements. Cleanth led a similar alliance known as the Guelph. Several other smaller settlements appeared to be independent, but most Eëlians identified themselves as one or the other. The origins of the words remained obscure, although Verlaine insisted that Derek Musgrave, as leader of the original expedition to Eëlios, had named them after factions in a remote era of Earth's history known as the Renaissance.

"We look forward to your findings." Leyden tried to suppress any note of irritation in his voice.

In any properly prepared negotiation, he would have had extensive briefings on every aspect of the background, interests, culture, goals, and vulnerabilities of the other party. But the files he had seen aboard the lightship had proved thin and relatively uninformative. Tirun had promised more detailed information in preparation for their talks, but that hadn't happened, another casualty of the Whitebone. Leyden sighed. Perhaps he could make his own ignorance work to his advantage, play to Cleanth's vanity as a politician, the pupil to his instructor.

"May I be permitted to ask about the relationship of the Guelph and Ghibelline at this time?" Leyden could see Cleanth and Nouvé stiffen slightly.

"The Guelph and Ghibelline share this high world in a peaceful, open, and friendly manner," Cleanth said with a smile. "A relationship based upon a treaty of amity and cooperation that has served us for many years."

Leyden decided to play the intimate: another, smaller gamble. "That bad, Headman Cleanth?"

Again, a small silence. Unblinking, Cleanth and Leyden looked straight at one other. Then Cleanth roared and smacked Nouvé on the shoulder again. "Open and friendly. . . yes, that bad!"

Uneasy smiles and quiet laughter all around.

Tirun spoke. "In the last cycle, when the survey mission returned home, Headman Cleanth saw the wisdom of sending an Eëlian delegation back to the Illium. The Ghibelline were given the same opportunity but declined."

"Indeed, so," Cleanth said. "We sat in this very place, with Headman Shinsato of the Ghibelline. He refused any agreement, saying it could open the way to large numbers of off-worlders and the eventual destruction of Eëlios. My view was, and is, that the right alliance would give us the power to protect our world as we saw fit and open up new opportunities."

"A course of obvious wisdom and foresight, Headman," Leyden said.

Cleanth waved off the compliments with a motion somewhere between weary and pleased.

"There was no agreement in the end," Cleanth said. "Ulam and the three others who went to the core worlds were all Guelph. Only Ulam has returned. We mourn the deaths of those who did not."

Cleanth looked around the entire gathering. "Any further agreements we reach must honor their sacrifice."

"On behalf of Mission Leader Tirun and the Illium worlds that we represent, we make the same pledge," Leyden said. "It is our hope that these talks will both protect this world and open new doors of great promise to those who live here."

Cleanth nodded and stood; the others followed. "It is late. You have come far. We will meet again, soon, and we will await news of the Ghibelline from Nouvé."

Nouvé and Cleanth disappeared along a matted pathway out of the amphitheater. Leyden, Tirun, and Hawkwood followed several Guelph villagers along a swaying rope trail to the collection of wood-and-thatch huts given over to the expedition. They sat in Tirun's room, really more of an alcove, joined by Verlaine and An San Kee.

"Much as we feared," Verlaine said following Tirun's brief summary of their meeting with Cleanth.

"Meaning?" Leyden asked.

"This Guelph-Ghibelline rivalry," Verlaine answered. "We've always been concerned that it could seriously complicate reaching any commercial agreements. Now we seem to have confirmation."

Tirun dug thick fingers into his beard. "Only now the Ghibelline may well have Illium soldiers and heavy weapons to enforce any concerns they have about our arrangements with the Guelph."

Hawkwood spoke from his typical position in the back of the room. "It is vital that Nouvé and his people bring back as much detailed information as they can about the expedition. Numbers, equipment, weapons, health, everything. Basically, all we have now are three functioning combat weapons and a Dragon without any ammunition. I will speak to Nouvé before he leaves tomorrow."

"Wait," said Leyden. "What do you mean, no ammunition? We were carrying at least three kinetics and two pulse charges last time I checked."

Hawkwood said nothing and Leyden could see that Verlaine looked very uncomfortable.

"Afraid we had a slight accident on the climb," Verlaine said. "The pack apparently had a frayed spot or something. We were on a rope ladder when the goddamn thing tore open. Everything fell out. Lost the Dragon ammo and some lab equipment."

Leyden shook his head. "Wish I'd known this before we climbed up here. I would have dumped the damn Dragon."

"There's nothing to be done about that now," said Tirun. "And frankly, a couple of Dragon charges aren't going to change the equation much. Right now, our job is to get Cleanth's agreement to providing assistance and guides for us to collect as many plants and as much genetic material as possible. We have that now. We can't afford to waste any time, even waiting for news from the Ghibelline. With the understanding, of course, that nothing will leave Eëlios until we have a full agreement. In other words, a signed commercial treaty." He looked over at Leyden. "That's where you come in."

Leyden nodded. "Fine, but you and I need to have a long talk. So I know what the hell I'm talking about."

"Oh, I don't know, Leyden," Verlaine said. "You may do better improvising. Looked to me as though that anchorwood ploy went over just fine. Plant a seed, grow a tree. A really really big one."

Tirun's rumbling laughter filled the room, and An San Kee duck her head to hide her smile.

Tirun held up a massive hand. "But you're right, it's time to give you more background on what Trans-Illium wants to accomplish here."

He dug around in an open supply case and handed Leyden a tightly rolled polymer hypercomputer. "Databases, vids, hyperfiles, model agreements, economic estimates, biological analyses from the previous mission. Get through this and we'll talk."

Leyden ran his fingers over its knobby surface. "Including analysis of the Guelph-Ghibelline relationship?"

"You'll find summaries of the information collected from interviews with Ulam and the other Guelph who went back with us. But I doubt you'll find that it explains much about the current situation."

Tirun stood. "Let's call this off for now." As they rose to leave, Tirun signaled for Leyden to remain, as did the inevitable Hawkwood.

"When we begin our surveys," Tirun said, "we're going to have just about everyone in the expedition scattered everywhere. With Eëlian guides wherever possible."

"Yes?"

"If we've got someone working for the Cold Moon Triad here, this is when they'll make their move."

"For what?"

"The Triad wants the same things we do. Plants, seeds, chemical compounds, genomes. Some of it very specific material," Tirun said.

"What are you talking about? What specific material?"

Tirun looked uncomfortable. "Eëlios presumably has many potential narcotic substances. That's no secret. But you'll find references in the data to one in particular. A substance derived from a plant known as Mostera that the Eëlians call Looking Glass. Very powerful hallucinogenic, according to the research. And very addictive."

"Is that's what this is all about?" Leyden said. "The other expedition out there is run by Cold Moon? And they're here to collect Mostera so they can add a new product line?"

"Possibly," Tirun said. "Or maybe the Triad simply bought off someone on our expedition who's freelancing for them. That would be more their style. Either way, we need to know."

"I didn't exactly hire on as a narcotics investigator."

"No you didn't, but you *did* hire on to me, remember?" Tirun's icy eyes pierced the dimness of the hut. "The deal with Rigel Prime and the Nakamoro family can still fall through. Does that clarify the matter?"

Leyden stared back at him. "Somewhat. And if I bump into someone processing Mostera into Looking Glass?"

Hawkwood stirred. "That's on us to deal with. Right now, we simply need to know if Cold Moon has someone right here, on the expedition."

"Meaning this person was responsible for sabotaging us on the Drop and the Whitebone?"

Tirun sighed. "Perhaps, perhaps not. Unfortunately, these may well be two separate problems."

26 FREELANCING

Restless from the multicourse meal and heavy wine, Leyden woke well before the end of the sleep cycle, still groggy and exhausted. Outside his translucent sleeping hutch, Leyden saw a fuzzy shape and heard the sound of branches pushed away.

"Leyden!" an urgent voice hissed. He pretended to be still asleep.

"Leyden! Tirun needs to see you. Right now."

Leyden groaned to himself, rolled over and unsealed the entrance. Chapandagura, the biochemist, stood outside, a round soft man with a blinking, perpetually bewildered expression.

Leyden stared at him. "Go away."

His head felt melon-like. That's it for Eëlian wines, he thought. He didn't want to have to move anywhere or speak to anyone for another couple standard hours.

Chapandagura blinked furiously. "Mission Leader Tirun says he needs to see you immediately."

"I don't care. Go."

"What should I tell the Mission Leader?"

"Screw him. Go."

Chapandagura squinted down at Leyden's head as though it were out of focus. "I don't think I can do that. I will wait. Yes, I will stand here and wait until you are ready."

Leyden cursed and rolled onto his stomach, holding his melon head in his hands. Chapandagura was still standing there when he emerged, shifting from one foot to another, as if waiting for the next available public toilet.

Leyden brushed by him. "Let's go. What are we waiting for?"

Tirun and Hawkwood stood together. Low overhead branches bounced unexpectedly and several leaves floated down on their shoulders. Leyden looked up to see Twen uncork his tongue and present him with the traditional Iksilla greeting. He signed back.

"Cute friend," Tirun said.

At least Tirun had some version of Eëlian hot coffee or tea on a counter. He poured a cup and drank — that it was hot was about the only thing anyone could say in its favor.

"What are those, anyway?" Hawkwood asked. "They're all over the place."

"Iksillas," Leyden said. "Quite intelligent. Most belong to one particular person."

"Pets?"

"You could say."

"And that one?"

"Mine. Courtesy of my personal healer — the one who brought me here."

Tirun shook his head. "Never mind that. We have a problem. Exactly what we thought might happen."

"Meaning?"

"Someone has apparently gone off on his own with one of the Eëlians."

"To do what?" Leyden asked, still thinking with irritation of Chapandagura. "Whip up a batch of Looking Glass? A little alone time?"

"Who knows?" said Tirun. "In any case, no one is authorized to go *anywhere* for *anything* unless I approve it. I've made that clear enough."

"You have been most eloquent on the subject," Leyden said. "Of course, I remember that speech at Musgrave's Dance, where you seemed to give everyone the option of staying or going downriver."

Hawkwood shifted his feet; Tirun glared at him. "We don't have time for this."

"Who's gone, then?" Leyden asked.

"Verlaine."

Leyden wondered if another name would have surprised him more. Verlaine hadn't even bothered to hide his ambitions to seek out a source of personal wealth on Eëlios. He'd hinted at it to Leyden as far back as Musgrave's Dance, and joked openly about collecting everything from kytes' eggs to building a tropical complex to rival Poseidon. At the banquet, he talked of Eëlios as too big, too diverse — that, by contrast, he planned to target one market-tested item, with financial backing from Trans-Illium. Could he have been hinting about dealing drugs for the Cold Moon Triad as well? Perhaps he felt that his Trans-Illium connection provided enough cover. But Verlaine had always struck him as more indirect in his moves, not someone who would impulsively launch himself into the jungle and deliberately cross Tirun.

"Verlaine is Trans-Illium's official representative," Leyden said to both of them. "Your employer. Why are you assuming he might be something else?"

"We're not assuming anything," Tirun said. He held up a massive hand and began ticking off his points.

"Verlaine's Trans-Illium colleague is Mkeki, who *is* from Cold Moon Rising, and anyone from there always goes to the top of our list. Second, he's been in on the planning of this expedition for years — he knows the logistics as well as anyone. No one would be in a better position to sabotage the Drop or communicate to outsiders undetected. Third, his convenient accident in losing the last pulse charges and kinetics for the Dragon. Finally, if anyone is going to make a move for something like Mostera or another drug, they're going to have to do it soon, since there's no guarantee about how long we can remain here."

"So go after him, and good luck to you," Leyden said.

Hawkwood shook his head. "Nouvé and I are leaving within the hour for the Ghibelline."

"Send a couple of mercs."

Tirun shook his head. "They already have assignments. Besides, I'm not trying to arrest anyone. I just want to know what the hell he's up to. You're the closest thing he has to a friend. Take a guide and go find them."

"Them? I thought he was alone."

"No. He apparently made an Eëlian an offer she couldn't refuse. The one who served the table last night. Your pet provider. . . your beekeeper."

"*Sylla?*"

"If that's her name, yes."

What kind of offer could Verlaine have made? You don't know if they'll say yes until you ask: a maxim that Leyden suspected Verlaine had used frequently in his corporate climb.

He thought for a moment. "I still need a merc. I mean, if Verlaine is a Cold Moon trafficker instead of a corporate raider, he's presumably armed and dangerous."

"All the weapons are accounted for," Hawkwood said. "He's not armed. And I have no mercs to spare." His mouth compressed with amusement. "And even if someone like Suslov were available, would you really want her with you now?"

"Fuck you."

Tirun slammed a massive hand down on the table, spilling Leyden's drink. "We have no time for this nonsense!"

Leyden's head actually felt better. Tirun's anger was directed primarily at him for being a smart-ass, he knew. But all three understood that Hawkwood had allowed himself the slightest break in his iron self-control with his dig about Suslov. It was enough for now.

"Where the hell do I find him?"

"We've talked to Cleanth," Tirun said, "and he is providing Nausicca, the cook from last night. She's some sort of relation to your healer."

Tirun continued. "You're just out for your own little survey. Gathering fruits, herbs, Eëlian foods with Nausicca. Samples for analysis and cataloging by An San Kee and the bioteam. Or for tonight's dinner. I don't care. You just happen to run into them."

"Nausicca is going along with this?"

"She has her instructions."

◆

Although it remained hidden beneath the jungle canopy, Leyden could hear the sky: the slow tear of thunder, the push of distant wind, the sound of invisible rain that sifted through the canopy in a vast whispering conversation. Ahead, in the mottled light, he could see Nausicca waiting impatiently for him to negotiate his way up a series of ladder-like branches along with Twen and her own Iksillia, called something like Tarn — a yellow-green creature that appeared extremely wary of Leyden. Tarn kept climbing up Nausicca's back, peering over her shoulder, and sticking its tongue at Leyden in the unmistakable signal meaning, depending on context, "no, not, never, you've got to be kidding."

They had left the last rope bridge fifteen minutes earlier, picking their way through vine-wrapped, moss-encrusted branches, amid clouds of tiny insects that buzzed in Leyden's ears like nanotech tools. His waxy coating of calyx lotion warded off most of the biting insects, but the tiniest ones seemed especially attracted to his head. He had been told to exercise restraint and not rub them out indiscrimately since — like the blue bees — they injected various disease-resistant compounds into his bloodstream in return for the opportunity to sip fluids from the corners of his mouth and eyes.

As he blundered through the foliage, his hair became flecked with pollen, the glowbirds snatched at the insects he dislodged, and yellow butterflies fluttered in front of his face, apparently getting high from his exhalations of carbon dioxide. Scaly white leeches seeking a blood home slid off his waxy skin. It was as though the Eëlian rainforest was chewing and changing him into a kind of lumbering symbiotic creature carrying its own burdensome, if fertile, ecology wherever it went.

When he reached Nausicca, Leyden felt wrung out, a condition increasingly familiar with each effort at climbing or traveling for an extended period through the Eëlian canopy. He had asked about the distance several times, but Nausicca only laughed awkwardly, cutting herbs and other greenery for wide-mouth bamboo baskets attached to both their backs.

Twen skipped onto his shoulder with his uncomfortable claws as Leyden stopped for a drink from his water gourd.

"How can you be sure they came this way?" he asked.

Nausicca tried to remain expressionless but without success. Something about him seemed to amuse her vastly and she laughed again, covering her mouth with her hand. "This is as good a direction as any."

"Yes, but is it where Verlaine and Sylla went?"

"Don't know. Ask your Iksilla. He's the one who has brought us here."

Leyden corked his water container and reached up an arm for Twen. He poured water on Twen's head, which he promptly mopped up with his versatile tongue. *How far?* Leyden signed, trying to remember his hand positions. Twen stuck out a prong on his tongue in his ear and seemed to sign a message that combined *close* with an indecipherable measure of distance.

He wiped the side of his face and turned to Nausicca. "Let me ask you this. If you were going in search of the Mostera plant, would you climb in this direction?"

Nausicca looked puzzled. "Mostera?"

"Yes, the plant that is the source of the drug called Looking Glass."

She giggled. "Looking Glass, yes. A fine tea. You and the others drank it at dinner last night."

"Mostera tea?"

"Oh, yes."

"And Looking Glass. . . by itself?"

Nausicca looked away. "Only the chosen ones can enter the Looking Glass. No others."

"But what if others wanted to enter the Looking Glass? Off-worlders who promised great wealth. Are there Guelph and Ghibelline who would be willing to show them how to make Mostera into Looking Glass?"

Nausicca contemplated him, no longer laughing. "Perhaps. It. . . you are all so new."

"And your relative, Sylla. Is she one of those chosen to enter the Looking Glass?"

"She is a healer. Yes, she knows about Looking Glass."

"And many others of the Guelph?"

"We are not Guelph."

Leyden watched her carefully. Unlike Sylla, Nausicca's face markings were symmetrical: deep indigo stripes that curved under her eyes and around her mouth.

"I don't understand."

"Sylla and I are not Guelph. We are Ghibelline."

He waited, watching, saying nothing. The discomfort of silence, he had found, often eroded one's commitment to secrecy, even fear. Leyden had little confidence in his ability to read the Eëlian culture; but Nausicca's behavior, alternating between laughter and vague answers, suggested that she felt conflicted about what to hide, what to reveal.

Nausicca stood, nervously looking about. "We should go now."

Leyden didn't move. "I still don't understand. Explain it to me."

She wrung her hands, then sat again as though conceding to some irrefutable ultimatum.

"The treaty between our people says that when Nevea and Naryl have circled Eëlios five hundred times, the Guelph and Ghibelline will meet, and each will present the other with five of their most favored children. Those children will be raised in the homes of the other."

"As guarantors of the peace?"

"Yes. We are two of the five."

"But you are grown now," Leyden said. "Can you go back to the Ghibelline? Or can you choose to be Guelph?"

Nausicca shook her head. "No. I am promised as consort to a leader of the Guelph. So I can never go back. But always, I am Ghibelline."

"And Sylla. A consort too, but Ghibelline?"

"Of course."

Several branches bounced overhead; Twen appeared, hanging by his tail and uncoiling his tongue. Nausicca glanced over. "They are here. Come."

Nausicca literally swung through the trees, balancing for an instant or dangling in the gaps before gathering in the next branch and disappearing into a dappled wall of greenery and flaming color.

Leyden lumbered after her, trying to remember the few hints that Sylla had passed along back at the beginning of their journey. Pick younger, flexible branches to swing out on, stay away from dead ones that might snap. Also, avoid vines: they grow upward, and if you try to swing out on the end of one, you likely will plunge downward rather than end up on the adjoining branch.

Twen jumped on his head, then off again to scurry out of sight along a curving branch, then back, leaping on and off Leyden's head.

"Cut it out!" he shouted. "I'm going as fast as I can."

Just ahead of him, Twen turned, sat up on his tail and spat on Leyden's chest.

Leyden didn't need an interpreter for that expression. He felt clumsy, stupid and furious. "Do that again, you miserable excuse for a lizard, and I'll twist your tail off!"

Leyden looked up to see that he had blundered onto a small, makeshift platform of matted vegetation, with Nausicca, Verlaine, and Sylla all staring at him. He stopped, trying to recover his breath and some fragment of dignity. The Iksillas, now including Sylla's Twon, raced through overhead branches like hyperactive children, showering leaves down on them.

"We need to teach that lizard some manners," he said to Sylla.

She said nothing, and Leyden looked over at a mass of plants with slender glossy leaves spread fanlike in front of Verlaine.

"And hello to you too," Verlaine said. "Just happen to be out for a morning stroll, you and the misbehaving Iksilla?"

Leyden shrugged the bamboo basket off his shoulders. "Collecting a few goodies. And you?"

Verlaine held up a similar wide-mouth container of bamboo. "You are looking at the next great sensation to sweep the Illium Archipelago."

"Travel via Looking Glass, perhaps?"

"Looking Glass? Drugs? Oh my, no." Verlaine reached into the pail and cupped two handfuls of dark reddish brown berries. "When these suckers are dried and roasted, look out. All I need to do now is to cut a licensing deal."

Leyden looked at the berries more closely. "Dried and roasted. Are we talking about what I think we're talking about?"

"Yes, indeed. Coffee. Eëlian Premium Tropical Roast. Eight, maybe ten different varieties. The featured offering in an Illium-wide chain of coffeehouses. I even have the name."

"Which is?"

Verlaine smiled. "*Eëlios High: Coffee Blends from the Illium's Greatest Rainforest.* You like?"

"Depends on my cut."

"You negotiate a deal and get us out of this jungle in one piece and we'll talk."

Leyden watched Sylla and Nausicca, who apparently knew how to turn off their translator chips, talking rapidly and incomprehensibly to each other as their fingers darted up and down each other's forearms to punctuate their words.

He suddenly wished he were drinking one of Verlaine's brews in a remote coffee shop, looking into Sylla's face with the same intensity as Nausicca's.

27 JKH2

Verlaine's unripe coffee beans tasted raw and bitter. Leyden spat out the remains and uncorked his water gourd. Sylla and Nausicca appeared more stoic, he noticed, but neither looked as though she were enjoying the experience. They might be regular drinkers of Mostera tea, but appeared to be unfamiliar with the concept of coffee.

Verlaine didn't care. In his enthusiasm about his discovery, he insisted they all try a handful of green berries.

"Treetops," he was saying. "I might stick all the coffeehouses up in trees, real or artificial depending on location. Tables in a jungle environment, sounds, holos, vids. . . the usual. Serve authentic Eëlian food. Maybe not Musgrave beetles or glowbirds, but blackened Eëlian treesnake, and williwaw fruit with blue-bee honey glaze. Sponsor symposia on Illium ecology. Listen, Nausicca. . . may I call you Nausicca? Perhaps you could pass along some of your recipes?"

Leyden recognized that much of this ironic free association was for his benefit, the words seeming to tumble sideways out of Verlaine's mouth. But Sylla answered him directly and seriously.

"Perhaps someone could go with you, from here back to the Illium. . . to assist in your venture," she said. "Perhaps one of us."

Verlaine stopped, genuinely surprised; clearly not a response he had anticipated.

"Why sure," he answered after a pause. "Yes, why not? I mean, you could supervise the menu, organize the kitchens. Hell, Nausicca could be executive chef." He stopped and looked at both of them. "Why, either one of you could be the centerpiece of a high-impact advertising campaign."

He looked at Leyden. "I can see them now, emerging from the trees, wearing someone appropriately suggestive and preparing a big cup of Eëlian

Premium Roast with a shot of Rigelian apple liquor and foamed Umlivik milk-curd."

"Enough," Leyden said. Even joking, the thought of this place, and his experiences here, sinking into the maw of Illium chaebol culture unsettled him.

Verlaine took a breath. "Of course, we'll have to clear this with Headman Cleanth. I'm sure..."

Nausicca suppressed a gasp, and Sylla seemed to pale despite the rich color of her skin.

"You must say nothing to our Headman," Nausicca said in a rush. "Nothing of such things at all. Not a word. You must promise us this."

Verlaine looked startled. "Of course, of course. Just an idea. Strictly *entre nous*. I will say nothing to anyone. Eëlian or off-worlder."

Nausicca turned to Leyden. "And you too?"

Leyden shrugged. "Of course. Not a word. But why? Headman Cleanth agreed to send Ulam and others during the last cycle. Why not now? Because you are both Ghibelline?"

Sylla stiffened and turned to glare at Nausicca.

"Yes," Nausicca said. "We are Ghibelline promised to the Guelph, to Cleanth, by treaty. A suggestion that one of us might leave could be considered... treason."

"Still," Leyden said, "you've considered the possibility."

Sylla tried to be dismissive. "These are a child's dreams. Perhaps one day, when we have made agreements and joined these Illium worlds of yours. Perhaps then. Perhaps many of us will travel to other worlds. Or our children."

She nodded to Nausicca and the two of them abruptly rose and disappeared into the foliage. Overhead, Leyden could see the swift shapes of the Iksillas trail after them. Twen returned and draped himself on a branch over Leyden's head, devouring what appeared to be a large moth.

Leyden found a resting place against a vine as thick as his thigh, with paper-thin, flaking bark and an oily, oddly soothing smell. He closed his eyes and listened as the silence filled with the sounds of the rainforest: the constant aural background of insects; the hoots, trills, coughs, and musical scales of glowbirds, parrots, and nectar-sippers with bills like small trumpets — and something else.

He listened again: something deeper than the flurries and calls of animal life, deeper and slower than just the push of the wind through a thousand plant species. His breathing became the breath of the rainforest itself, the inhalation and exhalation of a vast entity that had risen to these heights and lived in a constant embrace of sun, rain, and wind.

"Tirun sent me, you know," he said, eyes still closed. "He is not at all pleased at your little freelancing expedition."

"And worried that I might have another employer, eh? Like Cold Moon?"

"It crossed his mind."

"This too shall pass. Hell, I'll give him the option of investing."

"Generous of you."

"Not at all. Prudent."

Leyden opened his eyes. Verlaine was tagging his samples and softly muttering notes into a NavCom clipped to his collar. The jungle seemed to have swallowed Sylla and Nausicca and their Iksillas completely.

"Get rich quick," Leyden said. "Is that what this is all about? I thought your object was climbing the corporate rungs at Trans-Illium."

"The object is independence," Verlaine said. "If the coffee thing takes hold, then I've got a power base independent of Trans-Illium. Freedom of maneuver, freedom to take risks I otherwise couldn't."

"If things aren't to your liking, you walk."

"Or threaten to."

"Why would Trans-Illium be interested in helping create an independent executive who might one day turn on them?"

Verlaine spoke into his neck. "Off," he said to the NavCom. Verlaine began gathering up bundles of Eëlian coffee branches and securing them in the bamboo basket. "They're not," he said. "But others play the long game and are willing to take the risk."

"Like the people you actually work for?" Leyden said, watching Verlaine's face. "Let me guess. Chaebol. . . Jong Kirov Hathaway Holdings."

"Very perceptive. Go to the head of the class. How did you know?"

"After the first drone attack, we said that if it weren't the Cold Moon Triad, it must be one of the chaebols. You seemed certain that, whoever it was, it wouldn't be JKH2. The question is, why bother to hide the chaebol connection from the mission at all?

Leyden waved off a cloud of tiny annoying insects hovering around his mouth. He needed to apply more calyx lotion as soon as possible.

"Any number of reasons," Verlaine said, stacking his collection of coffee cuttings. "Some economic, others political, even psychological. Think of the chaebols as night creatures. They don't like light or exposure of any kind. Without their names and prestige attached, they retain more flexibility, more room to maneuver. Full deniability. The ability to cut their loses quickly in high-risk Illium ventures like this if things go wrong."

"Like now."

Verlaine shrugged. "All the more reason for me to line up Eëlian High Coffee."

"That still doesn't explain why a chaebol would encourage you to open a coffee chain throughout the Illium."

"See, you keep thinking of the chaebols as large companies. They aren't. They're alliances. There's no *there* there. No center. Chaebols don't want to run companies, just maintain a degree of connection and control. If the coffee thing takes off, they will have a satisfactory return on their investment. More important, they'll have another presence on multiple Core Worlds."

"Plus they'll have you."

Verlaine twisted his mouth into something between a grimace and a smile. "They have me already. We're just establishing the price right now."

"I've been over some of the background Tirun gave me for the negotiations," Leyden said. "Parts of it seem pretty thin. Especially anything about what happened to the Eëlians who left with the last survey mission. Just that Ulam was the only survivor. What's not in the official records?"

Verlaine pulled an expensive, animal-skin flask from one of the pouches on his belt: Arishima walrus hide from the look of it. He took a long pull and handed it to Leyden. Toranguin apple liquor: dark, sweet, burning. Home.

"In many ways, it was a typical Illium probe," Verlaine said as Leyden handed back the flask to him. "And a very expensive one, too. Financed in the usual manner, by a consortium. Several Illium Core interests from Rigel Prime, Delios Major, Tushangura. Of the chaebols, Sidereal SkyFlame, took a piece of the action. So did JKH2, which took the largest, in fact, twenty percent, but still a minority holding." Verlaine took a drink. "The survey itself went smoothly, but from the point of view of the investors, it was still a disappointment."

"Why?" Leyden asked. "They got a bio research license, didn't they? With options to negotiate marketing rights."

"Do you have any idea what it costs to burn through to the Frontier Worlds? The investment in computer power to calculate Illium paths? Outfitting lightships? Probably not, because it is not in the interest of the chaebols, or the Illium League, to reveal those numbers. To get an adequate return on that investment, they didn't want the rights to some hot new pharmaceuticals. They wanted the rights to the whole goddamn *planet*."

"What happened?"

"The mission returned with four Eëlians and several thousand biosamples. The test results were intriguing, even quite promising in many cases. Pharmaceuticals for the most part, fruits and nuts with possible commercial value, even my coffee plant."

"And Looking Glass."

"Yes," Verlaine said. "And a demonstration of how to process Mostera plants into Looking Glass as both narcotic and hallucinogen."

"But?"

"All intriguing findings, but hardly surprising, really, for an extensive tropical environment."

Verlaine took another pull of Toranguin brandy and passed the flask back to Leyden. "But the big payoff didn't seem to be there. Most of the survey mission partners decided to drop out — the Core Worlds and SkyFlame. JKH2 was left holding a marginal investment without much prospect of a significant return anytime soon."

"Some of this is in the records," Leyden said, "except that the reference to Looking Glass is cryptic, to say the least."

He drank again; this time the brandy went down warm and soothing. There was a saying about Toranguin liquors: first cold, second warm, last unconscious.

"No one wanted to publicize Looking Glass," Verlaine was saying, "not with Cold Moon and the other triads sniffing around. But JKH2 had a different problem — the commitment to outfit another expedition and, at a minimum, return the Eëlians home."

Leyden set down the flask. "But when the cycle opened the next time, you didn't go back."

"No. There was a huge debate on this point. I know, because I was in the middle of it. One side said we should cut our losses and wait for however long it took to find new partners. My side pushed for paying the price, going back as soon as possible, and trying to recoup some of the costs with exclusive licenses to whatever products and drugs we could."

Leyden thought for a moment. Something hooted in the foliage below them and was echoed in the distance. The air hummed with shadow, sunlight, and the bewildering flight patterns of Eëlios's birds.

"The compromise was to wait two cycles, continue the research — and try to do the return expedition on the cheap?" Leyden said.

"More or less. But by then, another complication had arisen. The Eëlians began getting very sick. Despite all the precautions. Meds were useless. Two died. The two survivors were placed in sterile isolation wards on Rigel Prime, which finally stabilized their condition. But they had no prospect of living any kind of normal life outside Eëlios. Not until we learned a helluva lot more about Eëlian biology."

"Obviously Ulam survived. What happened to the other one?"

Verlaine picked up the flask, started to drink, thought better of it, and returned it to his belt pack.

"Ulam was reasonably accepting of his situation. But the other one couldn't deal with the isolation and managed to escape. We regarded it, in effect, as an act of suicide and assumed that he died shortly thereafter."

"Assumed?"

"He disappeared into the city. We never found him or his body."

"But now we're working with a different set of assumptions," Leyden said.

Verlaine puffed his cheeks. "Afraid so. Now we have to assume that he was either kidnapped or helped to escape. In any case, someone took him away, very possibly off Rigel Prime altogether."

"But why would he be worth the risk? JKH2 itself regarded the Eëlians as a marginal investment. I'll bet you would have jumped at the chance to sell the research, along with returning the Eëlians."

Verlaine said nothing.

"Wait," Leyden said. "I'll bet JKH did just that, didn't they? Shopped the Eëlians around to see if anyone was interested. That's how word got out about them in the first place."

"Sure. But no takers."

"But your guy got taken."

"We figure now that word leaked out about Looking Glass," Verlaine said. "To someone connected to the Cold Moon Triad."

"You never considered that possibility at the time?"

"Not really. They were both still sick when he disappeared. And our biosample of Mostera was intact. If he had survived, all anyone would get from him was a personal account of Looking Glass. The uncorroborated testimony of a sick off-worlder. Hardly enough basis to launch an expensive, possibly illegal Illium Burn, even for Cold Moon."

"But someone has," Leyden said. "Presumably they got corroboration somehow. From the inside — from someone at JKH2 familiar with the Eëlios mission."

"Presumably." Verlaine sighed and swatted at the omnipresent insect cloud.

The platform began vibrating beneath them, and Leyden looked up to see Sylla and Nausicca emerging from the cool moss-drenched canopy. Tarn and Twon matched their pace overhead, creating a shower of twigs and moss.

"Nouvé has returned from the Ghibelline," Sylla said. "There is urgent news. We must return now."

Leyden felt disoriented. "Where did you hear this? You haven't been back to the compound already."

Sylla signaled with her hand, and Twon skittered up her leg and perched on her shoulder with a quick lick to the ear. "No. The Iksillas from the village passed the message to Twon."

"We were looking for bamboo to cut for baskets," Nausicca added. Sylla glanced over at her. Nausicca wasn't particularly well versed in dissembling, Leyden decided. Clearly, they had been engaged in something other than bamboo hunting.

Verlaine heaved his load of coffee bushes onto his back. "Well, let's face the music."

Sylla and Nausicca stood unmoving, looking uncomfortable. "There is more," Sylla said.

Verlaine and Leyden looked at each other. "Yes?" Leyden said.

"One who went to the Ghibelline with Nouvé," Sylla said hesitantly.

"Hawkwood? The Illium soldier?"

"No," said Sylla. "The other."

"Suslov? The woman?"

"Yes."

"What about her?"

"She did not return."

28 THROUGH THE LOOKING GLASS

With bundles of coffee and other plants tied to their backs, the four of them and their Iksilla companions returned as swiftly as they could to the Guelph settlement.

Sylla and Nausicca appeared as insubstantial as shadows as they danced along quaking branches and slipped down rudimentary vine ladders into the fragmented light of the understory. Verlaine and Leyden, by contrast, followed at a ponderous pace. Overhead, the Iksillas slid through the branches, joined gradually by an increasing collection of other Iksillas from the village, all hissing in excitement.

The villagers, already gathered for Nouvé's return from the Ghibelline, clustered in whispering knots along the collection of rope-lined branches and bamboo platforms that bore the closest resemblance to a central gathering place. The expedition members stood apart, and when Leyden first saw them, their numbers seemed pathetically small compared to the twenty two who had assembled aboard the *Balliol* for the Drop. And now Suslov?

Before Leyden could speak to anyone, Tirun took him into an enclosed space off the central area where they had attended the banquet. He found Hawkwood there, standing alone in a starkly furnished room with only two stools and a table that obviously followed the contour of the trunk from which it had been cut. Tirun left the two of them alone.

"What happened?"

"She fell."

Leyden watched Hawkwood's face as he spoke, but it revealed nothing. "Fell," Leyden repeated as though he were attempting to translate a non-Illium word. "How?"

"We don't know," Hawkwood said carefully. "No one saw it. We were maybe halfway back, in a relatively open area, big gaps in elevation between the layers of tree branches. Suslov went on ahead. When we couldn't find her, we turned back and retraced our steps. Nothing. One Eëlian found a spot where a branch had snapped off — a section slick with moss, some of which appeared to be torn away. We assume that she was hurrying, slipped, reached for a branch, which broke off, and fell. At that point unfortunately, there appears to be a fifty, sixty-meter drop before you reach the next layer of growth."

"And her body?"

"The Eëlians climbed down and searched, but couldn't find anything. They said that wasn't surprising."

"Why not?"

Hawkwood shifted uncomfortably. "Scavengers. Anyone, anything that falls, they gather it almost immediately."

"Scavengers. You mean the Saar?"

Hawkwood nodded. "Yes. Believe it or not, the Eëlians fall too. Not often, but it happens. Usually a child."

Leyden said nothing, trying to blur any possible image of the Saar carrying off Suslov's broken body, or if she had been conscious at the time.

"This is a real blow," Hawkwood said finally.

Leyden looked into his pale eyes. "You must be quite practiced at this, I would think. Telling people that someone under your command has died a violent death in some odd corner of the Illium, trying to snuff out the odd rebellion here or there."

Hawkwood rubbed his hand against the polished wood of the wall and said nothing. At least he didn't say he was sorry for Leyden's loss.

Leyden began pacing across the room and back again, trying to resist the flood of memories, the rage, the humiliation of his past with Hawkwood, the League, and Suslov. He, too, as a leader of the rebellion, had received the families of the bereaved. The initial casualties had been light, although that had not lessened the grief of the families he met. Later, of course, the deaths grew to such proportions that individual sorrow was swept away in the collective horror of total devastation. And the anguish of loss had turned into a cry for vengeance against everyone responsible, including him.

Leyden blinked himself back to the present. Hawkwood continued to stand beside the gleaming table as though waiting to continue the conversation. Why? He had spoken the words required of an expedition leader.

Leyden sat back down. "Was there something else to talk about? Memories of the good times?"

'Yes. Suslov's death."

"I thought we just did that. You expressed your condolences. And the information that some treetop reptile might be cracking her bones as we speak. Maybe I'll join her soon. Maybe we all will."

"Perhaps," Hawkwood said. For the first time Leyden heard a note of deep weariness in his voice.

Leyden shoved his stool against the wall and tipped back. "All right. What else is there to say about Suslov's death?"

'The possibility that it wasn't an accident."

Leyden froze. In trying to block out any mental image of what had happened to Suslov, he hadn't considered any alternative explanations. "You mean Cabenza's killer?"

"And the person who sabotaged the Drop. And called in the drones. Assuming, of course, that he or she survived the Whitebone River and Blackbone Swamp attack. By no means a certainty."

"Who? Someone working for a triad, Cold Moon Rising?"

"Maybe," Hawkwood said. "Maybe one of the chaebols. I'm also betting that Verlaine knows a lot more about this than he's told us."

Hawkwood confiding to *him* about Verlaine? Verlaine, along with Hawkwood and Tirun, were the big three of the expedition. Leyden felt disoriented again. Why confide in him? He ran his hand against the dark, knot-riddled wall.

"You've bet wrong about him once already," Leyden said. "His Looking Glass expedition turned out to be coffee beans. Eëlian Tropical Blend. The next big thing. Besides, why would Verlaine be conspiring against his own expedition? I mean, he's a chaebol rep himself, as I'm sure you already know."

Hawkwood nodded. "That's beside the point. This expedition has been compromised from the beginning. Unless we find out who is responsible, and soon, our chances for survival will be barely above zero. Tirun agrees."

"What's your evidence that Suslov was killed? You just said there was no sign of a struggle, just a broken branch and some torn moss."

"There would be no struggle if she met someone she knew. One push at the right time and you're gone."

Leyden found himself unable to sit any longer. He got up and paced. Three steps to the wall, turn, three back.

"Wait a minute," he said. "Is this an interrogation? Am I a candidate for Suslov's murder?"

Hawkwood wiped his hand from his face. "Actually, no — spurned lover or not."

"Drop it, Hawkwood. I mean it."

Hawkwood gave the barest of shrugs. "You were a suspect when we learned how Cabenza died. But since Tirun found you locked up on Rigel Prime, we've always considered it unlikely that anyone would have managed to locate you, much less find the opportunity to turn you. But that's not the case with the others. They've been out collecting bio samples for Kee in the last several days, and it's not impossible that someone slipped away to meet Suslov. Perhaps with help from an Eëlian guide. Maybe a Ghibelline."

Leyden rubbed his face. His hands smelled of anchorwood and he had a sudden vision of Sylla marking his face with a piece of crumbling bark. If only he, too, could fall now, fall as gently as those gas-filled floaters that carried them to the high canopy. Let him deflate and die as mildly as falling asleep on a soft, soft bed.

"Here, take this," Hawkwood was saying, and Leyden looked up to see him holding a small hypercard.

"What's on it?"

"Profiles, timelines, a small matrix program. You have a DataHed unit that still works, don't you?"

"Yes." It was relatively primitive, but enough for the multimedia readings he had brought with him, notably the large biography of the Nova Prince. Most matrix programs contained huge relational databases and ran some of the Archipelago's most advanced software.

"Tirun and I have to go and meet with Cleanth about the Ghibelline now," Hawkwood said.

"What did you find? Triad or chaebol?"

"Does it matter? We didn't see any off-worlders. But yes, they're there, they're heavily armed, and they've formed some kind of alliance with the Ghibelline."

"You're sure?"

"Yes. The message from the Ghibelline is that a delegation will be here in six settings of the Ginn. They will come with proposals for the future of Eëlios and the Illium."

"Ultimatums, I imagine," Leyden said.

Hawkwood nodded.

"What was Tirun's reaction?"

"Care to guess? Come on, we need to meet with him now."

"Instructions?" Leyden asked.

"Use every asset the Guelph possess to get accurate intelligence about who's out there and what they have. Play for time. But first things first."

Leyden held up the waffle-shaped hypercard. "Meaning this?"

"Yes. If we have an agent on the expedition, we need to find out who. Now, fast, or we'll have no options at all. We've gone over it again and again, but there's nothing conclusive. Tirun thinks we need another view. Right now, our thought is to set a trap, see if we can force a wrong move."

"And the bait?"

Tirun's shadowy bulk loomed before them. "With what presumably brought them here in the first place," he said in hoarse rumble. "Looking Glass."

"Is that the reason we're here too?" Leyden asked.

Neither of them answered.

◆

Later, when Leyden returned to his sleeping hutch, he pulled out a dark piece of polished rock on a twisted leather thong that he had brought from Toranga many years ago.

Leyden rubbed the stone, talisman like, as he loaded the hypercard into his DataHed and scrolled through the information sets. The Hed had a conventional flat screen for text and visuals, but most of the information it contained coalesced into solid, if slightly quaking holograms that seemed to hover above the entry keys.

It held brief, multimedia bios of everyone on the expedition except Hawkwood: League security would never have permitted that. An San Kee's proved the most visually interesting, with image sequences and analyses of her findings in the mist valleys on Tushanguara's Farland Peninsula and Imhotep's Languishing Swamps. The bios of the mercenaries, by contrast, were brief, almost cryptic, with formulaic military summaries of their assignments, accomplishments, wounds, and awards.

As he examined the matrix setup, Leyden could see that Hawkwood and Tirun had run standard data-mining programs against everything to try and determine who had the skills and opportunity to sabotage the Drop and call in the drone attack. But they were already on Eëlios, of course, and had no access to the Quanta, the vast reservoir of information and AI applications of the Illium, so it was impossible to rule out anyone conclusively. The matrix could suggest patterns and probabilities of time, access, and opportunity, but anyone, for example, could have found hidden moments during the long slowtime flight to sabotage the ship's software controlling the Drop.

Suslov's bio, which he viewed last, held the only real surprise. She had indeed been raised in a wealthy, mountainside city, as she had told him. But Suslov had been adopted at age five from one of the planet's vast orphanages, a celebrated breeding ground for criminal enterprises as well as Illium League recruiting. However much she remembered, Suslov, like

Hawkwood, had indeed experienced the trauma of the most extreme deprivation and poverty anywhere in the Illium Archipelago.

Leyden continued rubbing his Toranga stone to a high gloss. In the end, the DataHed had shown him a piece of the truth about Suslov after all.

Leyden darkened his hutch and tried to sleep. Maybe he should consider the man who wasn't in the matrix at all. Still, Hawkwood made no sense as a suspect. He could have destroyed the expedition in a hundred different ways, or simply left them all stranded at Musgrave's Dance. With his access to the *Balliol* and the shuttle, for that matter, he could have ensured that virtually everyone ended up in out-of-control pods slamming into the Eëlian tundra.

He stared into the enclosed darkness. There simply wasn't enough information for the matrix to produce any definitive answers. But as he thought about the information concerning each of the expedition members, Leyden felt sure of one thing.

Hawkwood was right. Suslov had not died in an accident.

29 SYLLA'S CHANT

    The air felt like being submerged — full of refracted light, blurred sounds, and the constant weight of water that impeded every reach and step. Overhead, thunder again rolled across an invisible sky like the surf pounding a remote shoreline; twenty minutes would pass before the rainwater percolated through the canopy in beaded rivulets.

    The saturated air soaked Leyden so thoroughly that he found he coped best by thinking of himself as swimming underwater. He floated through an green ocean reef, he imagined, where fish were birds and corals branches. And like the sea floor, life crowded in upon life in the rainforest canopy, with layers of mosses, epiphytes, flowers, ferns, vines, bromeliads, insect nests, and trees knotted in coils of competition and cooperation that defied human unraveling.

    But it was an inverted world. Instead of descending downward into a sea of increasing darkness and pressure, the new territory of Eëlios lay upward, beyond overlapping lattices of the canopy, toward an expanse of sky still hidden by partitions of leaf and branch.

    He climbed toward that light, along with Sylla and the Iksillas. But Leyden felt so completely lost that he could no longer be certain of anything except that hours had passed since they left the Guelph settlement. He hadn't seen the sky since their pods slid into Blackbone Swamp weeks ago.

    For the first part of the journey, they followed aerial paths already familiar to Leyden: highways of wide anchorwood branches, worn smooth from constant traffic, and quaking bridges of woven bamboo and railings of living vines. Moving from one platform cluster to another, Leyden could almost forget that he was more than a kilometer above the surface of the planet — until he came upon a near-vertical ladder knotted from woody lianas. Sudden reminders that the Eëlians lived suspended in the sky, without roads or streets.

As they traveled beyond the wide settlement branches and easy ladder climbs, Leyden found the mental aspect of their travel as difficult as the physical, especially with the light but bulky collection basket on his back. To move even a few meters required a fresh decision about the intricate nature of the plant growth ahead of him. In some places, the branches grew large and relatively unobstructed. But more typically, the jungle growth appeared impenetrable, forcing him to climb up or around, laboring for tiring minutes through a stretch that Sylla, wraith-like in the fractured light, seemed to float through as effortlessly as a diver above the sea floor.

Leyden's choices of branches and handholds often proved precariously wrong, forcing him to back down and try another route. The Iksillas raced up to Sylla and back around Leyden in circles, obviously bewildered at his difficulty in moving through a world as open to them as to fish in the sea.

He lost all sense of the distance they had traveled, primarily because he had no feeling of moving laterally at all. Beyond the anchorwood highways, movement consisted of vertical climbs, three meters or thirty, up or down. Horizontal progress felt incidental. Were they moving a hundred meters above the Guelph settlement, at a distance of a kilometer — or three meters below, but only a quarter kilometer away? Leyden had no idea.

In tortuous degrees, however, he slowly understood one fact about their direction: they were climbing *out*, away from the massive base of the anchorwood tree toward smaller support branches and unbroken foliage. At last, as Leyden feared, they passed beyond the last of the vine ladders. Somehow, it felt as though they had crossed the border from what passed for Eëlian civilization into a genuine wilderness.

Since they carried coils of vine-rope like bandoliers, Leyden knew this moment would come. What he had not understood was the role of the Iksillas. When they came to their first major climb, a vertical stretch of anchorwood, one Iksilla took the rope in his mouth, the other a wooden, pulley-like device, which Sylla had removed from her belt. Together, the Iksillas and raced upward, disappearing into the vegetative maze above them. Moments later, the end of the rope thudded down from overhead.

"With short climbs," Sylla said, "this is faster than climbing tools."

Fashioning a slip knot, Sylla signaled Leyden to stand next to her, feet inserted into the loop. Together, with alternating strokes, they pulled themselves upward. Her skin felt waxy from caälyx lotion where their shoulders rubbed, and he wondered again if the skin beneath her tunic, as brilliantly patterned as a bird's plumage, had the same green shade as her arms and legs.

Even this close, Leyden found it difficult to read the face beneath the tousle of dark hair and the bold slashes of scarlet and blue that descended off one side of her face and disappeared into her tunic. Was a single breast painted as well? It was a piercing, unexpectedly erotic thought. He had assumed that only someone whose body was thin and wire-tough could move as fluidly through the Eëlian canopy as Sylla did. But this close, he realized that she was much fuller and muscled under the drape of her clothing than he had assumed. Sylla's knowledge of the rainforest suggested long experience, but physically, he had thought of her as very young, little more than a teenager. No longer. Most disturbing, she reminded him of someone from his past. Someone he had no particular wish to remember.

They pulled themselves to the branch with the pulley, and repeated the process twice more before Sylla, pointing to a clump of Nevea's Nectar plants, signaled a rest. She wordlessly cut off a section of another unrecognizable plant, stripped the bark, and gave him a fleshy white section to eat.

Leyden, eyes closed, leaned back uncomfortably against a mat of mossy lianas and savored the nectar's intense sweetness, a perfect complement the slightly acrid taste of the plant stalk. He felt a rasping tongue on his face and opened his eyes to see Twen's marbled green-and-yellow snout inches from his nose.

What's wrong? he signed, but Twen didn't respond, but only draped himself around Leyden's neck and demanded pieces of plant stalk to eat. Iksillas, like most reptilian life, Leyden had discovered, were indifferent to touch, even though they were hot-blooded like birds. But the connection to human beings remained important nonetheless. Even back at the Guelph settlement, Leyden found that whenever he rested, or napped, Twen would climb up and doze on his back or chest. Twen slept soundlessly, but had an annoying habit of twitching his tail. Leyden could push him off, but Twen would eventually reappear and flop back on top of him. At least Iksillas tended to be out and active at night, so Leyden rarely had to put up with him then.

With their infallible sense of direction, Iksillas were indispensable for extended journeys through the canopy, although they possessed a sense of time and distance quite different from that of humans. Whenever Leyden signed queries for *how far* and *how long*, the Iksillas always gave vague and unsatisfying answers.

Sylla and Leyden were only one of several Illium-Eëlian teams spread throughout the canopy. Tirun had directed An San Kee to undertake as extensive a biological survey as possible before the Ghibelline arrived, and units of Guelph guides, Iksillas and expedition members were all searching different quadrants of the canopy, collecting plants and other samples reputed to have psychotropic, medicinal, or other biochemical qualities.

Leyden licked his lips for the last traces of Nevea's Nectar. "Sylla, how much longer?" he asked. "Are there no samples we can collect around here?"

Sylla's scarlet-and-blue markings made her seem as inscrutable as a totem. "There are many here. Beyond counting. But not for us. Not this time."

"Beyond counting," he repeated. "More, perhaps, than you and the Guelph will ever reveal to us."

She gazed out at the surrounding blizzard of vines and flowering growths, all with their halo of insects, as though doing sums in her head.

"Not that that's necessarily a bad thing," he added quickly. "I wouldn't give my secrets to this crowd either." Sylla didn't laugh but at least smiled.

Dropping the rope coil at her feet and turning away from him, she closed her eyes and began to chant in a voice hesitant with the effort of translating the traditional words into a lilting Illium Standard. Her voice floated overhead like a bird call joining the busy choruses already filling the jungle. He had to strain to hear in the dense, shifting air.

Can we name the names?
Oh, mother Eëlios, giver of our life,
Can we name the names of your bounty?

Let us drink,
Juice of the rivertrees,
Nectar of the Nevea.
And let us eat,
Flesh of the tracasandra,
Berry of the midnight acacia,
Leaves of the strangler vine.

Oh, can we name them all, oh mother Eëlios,
Name them all —
Except the nameless one,
which only you can call?

Heal us, care for us:
The hidden justicia to cool a fever,
Lycos seeds to knit a broken bone.
Thunberia moss to dissolve tumors,
And the koa-koa to summon another's love.

From the shelter of the anchorwood
Tearing at the sky,
Hear the calling of our hearts.

Oh, we can name them all,
Oh mother Eëlios,
Name them all —
Except the nameless one,
which only you can call.

She stopped, flushed, and opened her eyes, for a moment looking embarrassed and vulnerable. Leyden felt as though he were looking upon her for the first time, seeing the woman beneath exotic paint and glistening caälyx lotion. He wished he were close enough to read her eyes, as she had claimed to read his when she first saw him, unveiled by the blue bees.

"I'm sure An San Kee and the rest of the expedition will want it all," he said. "All the magic and medicine that will make Eëlios a wealthy and powerful member of the Illium. Why, the koa-koa, to win someone's love — that alone should be worth the fortune."

Leyden wasn't sure, but it seemed that Sylla blushed as she turned her face away from him.

In that motion, he remembered the dim figure from his past. Not someone he ever recalled blushing or looking vulnerable, not even someone he cared for deeply, but a woman whose exoticism and grace he had found unbearably seductive. Tersis, the dancer of Patpong Row on Rigel Prime. She ranked among the most spectacular misjudgments he had ever made: to have engaged in an affair, however discreet, whe he was engaged both to Irina-Nakamora and in the difficult negotiations for the wine futures of Delium Ghahan.

But here, watching Sylla amid this blazing green world, he remembered Tersis's combination of cool detachment and compliant, eager carnality. *What will be your pleasure be tonight?* she would whisper, biting his ear, and he knew that he could do with her whatever he could imagine.

Yet an hour later, she would scarcely acknowledge his presence as, her fingertips on his arm, they walked streets and alleys of the Patpong. His lover and, at least according to Tirun, agent for the new regime on Toranga.

He imagined himself, perched high in his Eëlian treetop lair, looking down at that man working his way through the glitter and seduction of the Patpong. A man unable to see that, as Tersis bent and arched to his happy desires, he was being well and truly manipulated.

He remembered a man who still refused to accept any permanent responsibility for his role in Toranga's disastrous rebellion; still grasping, still reaching for all the Illium's cornucopia of incompatible pleasures and rewards. He wanted the wealth of his Delium Ghahan wine investments and financial speculations; but he also wanted the social position of Irina-Nakamora, the erotic pleasures of Tersis and the Patpong — and the vindication of both his vision and innocence during the Toranguin rebellion.

In those days, he had been indistinguishable from hundreds of thousands for whom the Illium Archipelago represented an endless array of worlds to conquer and commercialize — a figure like the corporate leaders who had organized the Eëlios mission, and those who lurked with the Ghibelline.

Neither the Guelph nor the Ghibelline, however, realized the implications of the Illium's vast appetites and technologies. The lucky ones would succeed to great wealth, of course, but even those few could not comprehend that they were dispensable, tiny fragments in a power game already played out countless times on other Illium Worlds. Whatever Eëlios's future, it no longer rested in the hands of its people. Verlaine's coffee enterprise would be the least of it.

As he gazed out over the canopy, glowbirds blinking around the anchorwood trunks, Leyden realized, with a small shock, that he no longer shared in this insatiable hunger. When had the connection been severed? Perhaps it had begun to dissolve inside the stone walls of Rigel Prime's prison. But the clearest moment came later, when Sylla called down the swarms of sky bees, and their healing venom had taken him back through his life in a series of dreamlike scenes, dissolving one into another, vivid yet distorted. When he had emerged from that chrysalis of bees, his body and face were scarred and transformed. Until now, however, he had not understood that he had changed in more obscure ways as well.

Leyden felt neither anger nor disgust at what he imagined the fate of this planet would be, only a disconnect from the whole enterprise. What did he want? Survival, yes. To somehow make it off this tall, difficult world alive? Of course. But beyond that, he contemplated only the prospect of retreat to a remote part of the Illium, a place where these battles for possession and power had already been fought and won, and lost.

He blinked and looked again at Sylla's back, realizing he knew even less about her than he had of Tersis. Sylla and Nausicca referred to themselves as sisters, but apparently that meant only that they were somehow related, most likely as cousins. Born Ghibelline, they both came to the Guelph as part of a diplomatic peace treaty, but he had no idea what that really meant in Sylla's life. Nausicca seemed to indicate that they never lost their identity as Ghibelline. Did she have lovers, or even a husband and children? He had seen evidence of neither, but did he really know? Sylla seemed somehow ageless as she moved through this intense foliage. Yet she had looked so young in her chant to the floral bounty of mother Eëlios.

"What now?" Leyden said, standing. "Which of those wonder plants are we collecting here? Or just the nameless one? Is that a plant?"

"Yes, the nameless one is a plant. But no, we are not here for any of those," she answered, clicking her tongue and calling the Iksillas. "We are here for only one thing."

Leyden tried to peer into those distant, masked eyes. "Looking Glass?"

"Yes."

30 WILD BAMBOO

Harvesting the prime drug crop of Eëlios proved to be more exhausting than anything Leyden had done since pulling the pod through the muck of Blackbone Swamp.

The bamboo presented the toughest obstacle. They had to cut their way into the center of a bamboo thicket, invariably interlocked with anchorwood, to find the Mostera plants whose leaves the Eëlians ground and processed into tea, seasonings, and Looking Glass narcotics. Like everything growing in the high canopy, Sylla explained, the bamboo had evolved its own competitive and cooperative arrangements for survival. Unlike true epiphytes, Eëlian bamboo, small and slender, did not use other trunks and branches solely as bases. Instead, it sank its roots into the branches of larger trees, drawing nutrients directly from its host. But it was not entirely a parasite either, since the host tree could draw water and sugars from its porous rootlets.

Eëlian vegetation repeated such exchanges in a thousand variations throughout the high rainforest. Cut into almost any large branch, Sylla pointed out, and you will find that it is not a branch, but a network of tightly packed branch-and-root systems of a dozen intertwined species.

Leyden paused, stretching his back and taking another drink from his water gourd. He wiped the edge of the blade from his Swiss and looked back along the narrow, tunnel-like path that they had cut. Eëlian bamboo, scattered but indispensable for constructing everything from storage containers to bridges, often meant long harvesting expeditions from the settlements. For that reason, they had to cut carefully and selectively, leaving the stalks intact so they could later be carried back to the village.

Sylla stepped ahead of him, swinging a machete-shaped device with a sharp wooden edge that seemed to cut through vegetation as effectively as Leyden's ceramic blade. She passed the severed stalk to Leyden, who added it to the small pile behind him.

"Here," she said. "Mostera."

Mostera grew low and dense, with pale yellow spotty leaves. Leyden bent down to examine it more closely. It appeared indistinguishable from dozens of other Eëlian bushes except for its remarkably contorted branches, with odd, oblique angles so twisted that the plant seemed to be moaning in pain.

"This is what all the fuss is about?" he said, more to himself than to her.

Sylla knelt beside him and plucked a leaf. "We only discovered Looking Glass eight4 standard years ago. It was always present when we cut bamboo, but for many cycles we ignored it. Then we discovered that chewing the leaves relieved the exhaustion of the journey, the harvest. Later, we found that, for those who prepared themselves, special compounds of Mostera would permit us. . ."

Sylla stopped and frowned. "I cannot find the word combinations in Illium Standard."

"Getting off?" Leyden asked. "Getting high?"

She gave him a tired look. "I could show you a dozen plants whose compounds will drug you and make you high far longer and more deeply than Looking Glass."

"Really?"

"If you wish, Leyden, I will mix you a potion that will suspend you into an alternate state of consciousness for about an Illium standard month."

"Cool." He smiled at her but she remained expressionless, even solemn.

"Another will help sustain an orgasm for days."

He froze, not sure how to handle that one, although her deadpan expression suggested she might be putting him on. Leyden again tried to peer more closely at her eyes beneath a fringe of damp hair adhering to her forehead. Did Eëlians have a dry sense of humor? Or was that just Sylla?

"You might want to keep quiet about those other drugs," he said. "Still, I assume Looking Glass has special properties."

"It does. These compounds permit journeys of the mind. . . journeys where one can see Eëlios in different ways and times. One can learn to enter into the consciousness of its living things. You from the Illium call it Looking Glass, but that does not seem close to our Eëlian term. *Vision travel. Vision quest.* That might be closer."

She slipped her wide-mouthed collection basket off her shoulders and began filling it with yellow Mostera leaves. "But still, we don't really understand."

"Understand what?"

"Why, of all that grows on our world, the Looking Glass compound should be so important. Only the few, only after long preparation, can travel with Looking Glass. For escape, for pleasure, I can't believe there aren't hundreds of such drugs and liquors available throughout the Illium — without the bother of climbing here, to our world."

Leyden thought for a minute as he too began filling his basket with leaves.

"There are, of course. Usually illegal, and always very profitable. The last expedition discovered that Looking Glass was one of the most powerful hallucinogens they have ever encountered. But more important, they found that Looking Glass can be highly addictive. For the triads, that meant not only a potential market of millions of users, but a market that would come back again and again for their product. In many ways, that's the key, as long as they have ready access to supply, or can keep manufacturing costs under control."

As Sylla knelt next to him, plucking leaves and listening, Leyden could see the sweat and humidity beaded on the caälyx lotion covering her face, the slight smearing of her scarlet-and-blue markings. She smelled of a dozen rainforest fragrances, like one of the more complex varietal wines from Delium-Ghahan. You would need time and discernment to identify its flavors.

"In the Illium, as you might imagine," Leyden continued, "there is little interest in the role that Looking Glass plays in the life of Eëlios. Only the prospect of making immense fortunes for those who can control its manufacture and sale."

"We're aware of all this, even without traveling to the Illium. And it's not as though we are immune from drugs and addiction."

"Of course. I didn't mean — "

Sylla looked almost bored. "Is that why you think you are here, then? For Looking Glass?"

"No. At least I hope not. But it seems possible that those who have joined the Ghibelline might be here for that purpose. And one of their agents may be part of our expedition as well."

Sylla shook her head. "This strikes me as what your teachers in the Illium call reductionist thinking. You are all here for many reasons, some you may not even know."

"Reductionist. . . where did you. . .?"

Again, Sylla looked impatient. "Quit patronizing me, Leyden. I know how I must look — this exotic, green-skinned creature imparting the wisdom of the forest to you."

He took a breath. "I. . . okay. . . yes, I will admit that you are pretty damn exotic looking. . . beautiful too. . ."

"Spare me." Now she looked unmistakably irritated with him.

"But there is also the small fact that you and your jungle wisdom saved my life."

Sylla waved a hand as though swatting insects. "That is past. The answer to your question is to remember that you off-worlders were here before, and left behind large … amounts of Illium data. We have translator chips, you will recall, and believe it or not, we know how to read and write."

"And lots of time."

Sylla's laugh was sharp and abrupt. "Yes, Leyden, whatever else we have, we have plenty of time."

"I stand corrected, with apologies." He wasn't sure for what.

"There is no need. We should continue, yes?" Sylla looked around. "Any preferences?"

"Not really. My instructions are simple enough. Go with you. Collect whatever you tell me is worth collecting."

"Really?" Sylla continued to pluck off leaves in a rapid, practiced manner. "I thought you were here for the same reason I am"

"Which is?"

"Headman Cleanth directed that I bring back Mostera," Sylla said. "Nothing else. It was his feeling that those who came here for Looking Glass would show themselves." She paused. "He said you had the same instructions."

"You're right," Leyden answered, suddenly embarrassed at his small deception. "I do." He reached out and touched her hand as it rested on the basket.

"No matter." Her dismissive expression needed no further translation.

Leyden decided his best course was to shut up. The idea of baiting a trap with Looking Glass might or might not be a good idea, but he hadn't come up with any reasonable alternative. And that was the problem. In less than a standard week, if he understood their orbital pattern around Nevea and Naryl correctly, the Ghibelline and their off-world allies would appear with their demands. If the expedition couldn't identify and rid themselves of the agent in their midst before that time, what little maneuvering room they had would disappear.

◆

CLIMBING THE RAIN

They finished filling both baskets with Mostera leaves after another hour of sweltering work. Sylla handed him several crumbled leaves, saying the effect would be mild but reviving. Leyden dozed, chewing on the acidic leaves, feeling like a cow on its cud. Inevitably, as soon as his eyes closed, Twen scuttled down from the tops of the bamboo and arranged himself over his neck and shoulder.

Leyden awoke with no sense of how long he had been asleep. The Eëlians were acutely sensitive to the shifts in light levels and colors as Nevea and Naryl plowed invisibly through the sky overhead. But unless one sun had set and the other hung low in the unseen sky, however, creating a twilight effect, neither Leyden nor the other off-worlders could mark the passage of time without checking their DataHeds or other Illium devices, many of which no longer functioned in Eëlios's heat and humidity.

A glowbird called in the distance, but the rainforest otherwise seemed oddly quiet, with only the steady nimbus of butterflies and other insects whining overhead. His vision seemed sharper, and his hearing more acute, as though he could follow the movement of a thousand simultaneous leaves, accompanied by the distant fall of water. He still felt a dozen muscle strains from the long climb, but as Sylla had promised, he also felt refreshed. Apart from the Looking Glass question, perhaps Mostera could be processed into a line of brewed drinks that might rival Verlaine's coffee.

Leyden stretched and shook Twen off his neck. *Where is Sylla?* he signed to him.

Twen rotated one eye upward and stuck out his tongue. *Gone.*

Leyden nudged him with his foot.

"Wake up, lizard breath," he said, 'you can do better than that."

Where? he signed again. For a moment, he thought Twen was going to spit. But what emerged was his triple-forked tongue and one of the first terms he had learned from the Iksillas. *To the water.* Odd, he seemed to hear the words inside his head at the same time that Twen signed them with his tongue.

Although not particularly convenient in their high world, the Eëlians regarded frequent bathing as essential, if only to replenish the layers of caälyx lotion needed to ward off the ubiquitous biting insects. Rivertree locations, with their carpet-like leaves that collected rainwater, were always valued and carefully protected locations.

Take me, Leyden signed, collecting his kit of soaps, bushy scrubbing brushes and caälyx lotion required for any sort of travel through the canopy.

Twen's tongue flickered out and back almost as quickly as Leyden had seen him filch a Musgrave beetle off a branch. *No. Sleep now.* Leyden both heard and saw the words.

Leyden scratched his face. This presented a slightly new situation. He had previously expressed impatience in ways that Twen had understood. But he had been careful, as Sylla had instructed, not to cross or anger him. And in most cases, Twen had simply been his indispensable rainforest guide. The question now was: who's in charge here?

He nudged Twen again with his foot. Twen opened one eye and again rotated it upward. Leyden signed slowly and deliberately: *No. Take me now. I bathe. Now.*

A single reptilian eye remained locked into a staring contest with Leyden's eyes. Twen sat up on his haunches, cheeks swelling and spat; the glob whisked by Leyden's head and splattered against the bark. He continued to stare at Twen, unblinking. After a pause, Twen's tongue flickered again. *Follow,* he signed and disappeared along a branch pocked with stumps of freshly cut bamboo.

Leyden felt oddly elated, as though he had mastered some tiny piece of Eëlian practice. And there was no question about it: with the twistings of Twen's tongue, he had simultaneously heard the words inside his head. Did this mark the beginning of telepathic bonding that Sylla had mentioned when he first was introduced to Twen? He would ask her as soon as he could.

The sound of water grew as Twen led him through flowering thickets of orchids and trumpet-shaped bromeliads, and into the heavy shade of a grove of rivertrees. The noise of falling water increased and he felt a mist against his face. Twen darted away and Leyden parted a last heavy, green curtain of foliage.

The catch-basin was a small, irregularly shaped oval lined with a thick knot of vegetation and layered with rivertree leaves. A blaze of flowers hung overhead, and water lilies, populated with pale frogs, floated on the surface of the basin. Water fell as constant rain from a disheveled roof of leaves and lianas. At one end, a waterfall poured out of an ancient anchorwood trunk, its center long ago consumed by fungi.

Sylla knelt in the pool beneath the waterfall, naked, her back to him. She held her head back, exposing her neck to the swift-flowing stream, either in meditation or simply luxuriating in the sensation of the falling water. Her dark hair, normally tangled and threatening to cover her eyes, lay flat and straight against the nape of her neck. He knew he should move away or somehow signal his presence. He didn't, watching instead as the water beaded and ran down her green, muscled back and along the curve of her waist and hips. She twisted slightly, still unaware of him, and arched back to let the water beat on her chest. Her breasts appeared only a slightly lighter shade of green than the rest of her, with the slender tendrils of her scarlet-and-blue markings curving over the outside of one of them. Well, that answered *that* question.

She sensed him, then, startled, then turned slowly toward him, still kneeling in the waist-deep water. Even from across the pond, in the weak light slipping through the dense growth, he could sense the heat of her eyes.

She rose slowly, turning turning away from him, and disappeared into the waterfall.

Leyden waited for her to reappear. She didn't. Finally, he pulled off his Eëlian tunic and leggings and waded into the water with his packet of caälyx and soaps floating beside him. He examined his chest and shoulders. No question, he had turned an unmistakable shade of green. Submerging, Leyden could see the water lilies floating above him, and the rapid succession of concentric circles from the steady fall of water.

He surfaced and dove again, skimming against the soft masses of algae along the bottom of the pond, as clouds of translucent frogs burst away from him like shattering glass. Twisting upward, Leyden saw a figure quaking above the surface. Sylla.

He was wrong.

31 HOSTAGES

When Leyden surfaced from the pond, three figures stood along the edge, all unfamiliar: Eëlian men with stony faces the color of unripe fruit, decorated with circular brushes of color instead of the straight, brilliant slashes associated with the Guelph. Two carried feathered Eëlian pikes with serrated ax edges on one side, smooth sword blades on the other. The third held a sword of burnished anchorwood.

Ghibelline, he knew immediately, and they didn't seem interested in a round of recreational bathing. The one with the sword motioned silently for him to remain still.

Three more figures emerged from the foliage. Sylla, in a damp tunic, hands tied in front of her, expressionless, hair still wet and straight. Behind her, each holding a Multiphase Combat Weapon, stood Modrescu, wild-eyed and transformed from the sullen figure who trailed in An San Kee's wake. The other was Mkeki.

Leyden stood before them in waist-deep water, naked and numbed. For the first time since he had entered Blackbone Swamp, he felt chilled. With his hands crossed in front of himself, he felt stupid and afraid, and something else. He had a sliver of understanding at last. Finally, some questions had answers.

Modrescu looked furious and triumphant, but Mkeki seemed oddly diffident, almost embarrassed, and avoided looking directly at Leyden. Yet she was clearly the one in charge.

"Either you take off your clothes, too, or give me mine," Leyden said.

Modrescu answered. "First, we get things absolutely clear."

Leyden shrugged, and looked over at Sylla, her eyes wide but unrevealing.

"Sure," he said. "But I'd say things are pretty clear right now."

"Leyden," Mkeki said, "I regret things had to come out this way. Really. But we can all cooperate and end this matter quickly, no harm to anyone."

She paused and glanced at Sylla. "You have something for us. You need to take us to it now. Quickly."

As she spoke, Leyden caught a glimpse of the stud that pierced her tongue. Had that been one of her attractions for Suslov?

"No idea what you're talking about," he said. "Sylla and I are out collecting bio samples..."

"Shut up, Leyden," Modrescu interrupted, flushed and impatient. "No bullshit. You're out here collecting Looking Glass. We want it. And the location where it's growing."

Leyden waved his hand helplessly. "I don't know where you're getting your information, but it's flat wrong. You might check your sources and see if someone's setting you up. So embarrassing."

"Shut up, Leyden, I mean it," Modrescu repeated.

This almost felt like old times. "Charming. No doubt one of the reasons An San Kee was chosen bio leader over a mediocrity like you."

"Listen, you shit." Modrescu started toward him but Mkeki waved him off, bracelets of silver and polished stone sliding up and down her brown arm.

"Stop the nonsense, Leyden," she said. "No bargaining. We're not here to discuss this. No time. We need to move and move now." She touched the filigreed ring in her nose.

Leyden remained silent.

Modrescu exploded with a curse and signaled to one of the Ghibelline, who turned around and casually slapped Sylla's face with a sound that could be heard above the noise of the falling water.

Sylla staggered back slightly before regaining her balance and ducking her head. Her nose seemed to be bleeding.

"We can continue this if necessary, asshole," Modrescu said with a wide smirk. "I'm told that the Guelph and Ghibelline have quite an imaginative range of tortures they can inflict on their captives. Beginning with the insertion of guillotine ants into various body openings. That would be after she's been raped, of course."

Leyden ignored Modrescu and stared at Mkeki, who seemed shamed and near tears. "Verlaine was right. You can take the girl out of Cold Moon Rising, but you can't take the Cold Moon Triad out of the girl. Or is this more a favor for your girlfriend Suslov?"

Mkeki tossed her head to regain her composure. "Leyden. You know nothing... nothing at all. I left Cold Moon behind when I joined JKH2. All of it. But they have my family. I had no choice."

"There are always choices. . ."

"If I had made even an attempt to have had them protected. . ." Her voice dwindled.

Leyden watched in silence. The stories of the triads were lurid and familiar to everyone. With their wealth and access, they controlled much of the commerce of Cold Moon Rising, legitimate and not, but they reputedly infested other worlds in the Illium Archipelago as well. The Cold Moon Triad didn't hesitate to practice remarkable forms of physical and psychological torture, surpassing even the ritual sacrifices of the Ohzumian underworld. JKH2 presumably had checked Mkeki's family status very carefully; most likely, someone had bought off JKH2's own investigators to ensure that Mkeki was cleared.

"Who are you working for, really?" Leyden asked. "Is that a Cold Moon expedition out there with your new Ghibelline friends, or have you cut a deal with one of the chaebols?"

Mkeki shook her head. "No more talk, Leyden. We must go. The Looking Glass source. Now, or Modrescu is right. We turn the woman over to the Ghibelline."

Leyden had no more cards to play. Not now. "All right. Can I get out of this wet skin now?"

Mkeki signaled and one of the Ghibelline men threw Leyden's clothes to him.

"What I don't understand," he said as he dressed, "is why you went to all the trouble of sabotaging the expedition. And killing Cabenza."

"We had nothing to do with that," Mkeki said.

Leyden glanced up at her. "Nothing," she repeated.

He finished dressing and turned to Modrescu. "Then the killing was all you? Maybe your calling isn't botany after all."

Modrescu activated his MCW and shoved it into Leyden's face. "Last time. Shut your fucking mouth. You and the Guelph woman will take us to the Looking Glass, or we'll replace her face markings with scars."

One of the Ghibelline men, carrying a feathered pike, looked Sylla up and down and grinned.

Leyden brushed him aside and stepped in front of Sylla, lifting her chin to see the blood crusted under her nose and swelling on the side of her face.

"Call the Iksillas and let's go," he said softly. She nodded.

He turned back to Mkeki. "And if you want to make time, cut these damn ropes off her."

♦

Mkeki was installing a transponder to mark the location, the Ghibelline men hoisting the baskets of Mostera leaves, when the first shot sizzled through the damp air. A blood-orange laser pulse that blazed out of the foliage and caught the one of the Ghibelline in the thigh. He cried out and fell, yellow Mostera leaves spilling from his basket. The Iksillas hissed and disappeared into the overhead growth. A second shot smoked the air, just missing the head of another Ghibelline.

As Mkeki and Modrescu activated their pulse weapons and fired back wildly; everyone crouched in the tangle of bamboo stumps, then crawled backward into a wall of uncut foliage. The air filled with a burning smell of ionized air and charred foliage. The smell of death. In the sudden silence, lying next to Sylla, Leyden could hear the hoot of a distant glowbird.

Modrescu rolled to his side and turned his weapon on Leyden. "It's a fucking trap," he snarled, his face flushed. "You're a dead man."

"Stop it!" Mkeki hissed. "We need him. We need them both."

The wounded Ghibelline man groaned as his companions scrambled to his side. The laser shot had bored through his leg at such a high temperature that it sealed the opening with little bleeding. Classic laser-weapon injury. A pulse charge would have taken off the leg and seared the stump. Sylla crawled over to them, pulling a salve from her belt which she smeared over the wound before saturating a dressing with a liquid and wrapping his leg.

Another shot stung the air overhead and Modrescu fired back. "We can't stay here," he said to Mkeki. "We've got to take what we have and get the hell out of here."

"That's probably Hawkwood out there," Leyden said, "along with a couple of mercs and Guelph guides. You're in no shape to go up against a combat Illium League officer. Better give it up right now."

"Shut the fuck up, Leyden!" Modrescu hissed. He looked even redder than before, and close to panic. "We got you, remember? They make another move on us, you die."

Mkeki crawled over and shook Modrescu's shoulder. "It doesn't matter whether it's Hawkwood or not. We took two of the last weapons they've got. They have maybe a couple left, and no recharges. He can't afford to get into a firefight."

She signaled to the Ghibelline men. "We take Leyden and the woman and move out."

'What about your wounded man?" Leyden asked.

"Leave him!" Modrescu answered. "Let Hawkwood or whoever is out there take care of him. It'll slow them down."

Mkeki signaled again, and the two remaining Ghibelline reluctantly left the side of the wounded man. Mkeki looked at Leyden and Sylla. "You two carry the baskets."

◆

They dropped from the mottled light of the upper canopy into the perpetual mist of Eëlios's cloud forest. During their exhausting, increasingly panicked journey, Leyden accumulated rope burns, small cuts from sharp-edged leaves, and occasional blows as his captors hurried him along. Still, he doubted they had eluded their pursuers.

The baskets, light but bulky, banged his neck and caught in the dense undergrowth as they descended into the cool mist. Mosses and ferns grew huge in the saturated air, bark and branches blackened with constant moisture. Flowering plants retreated, replaced by pale, spongy growths that smelled like rotting meat and drew large iridescent flies. They could see clusters of carnivorous plants slowly digesting other insects behind their interlocking leaves.

Water permeated every surface, and small rivulets and streams coursed along branches and down tree trunks. The fog smothered sound and reduced objects to vague shifting outlines.

A new sound emerged from the indeterminate distance: a sigh, a cry full of mourning and menace, ending in a series of clicks and muffled laughter. It was echoed by a second voice, then a third, each rising to a sustained high note of almost unbearable sadness and frustration.

Leyden glanced at Sylla, drawn and grim beneath her slashes of flaking paint. She made hand signals for *Iksilla* and *large*.

The Saar. Leyden looked around at the congealing fog. His vision of Sylla under the waterfall seemed a lifetime ago.

This was not going to end well.

32 OSSUARY

The skulls swam out of the perennial mist, wedged between tree forks or hung in tangled roots, dripping with lichen. Some were the small, scattered remains of frogs, lizards, and birds, but many were larger Saar skeletons with hooked snouts and yellowing, curved teeth.

The sobbing laugh of the Saar again poured through the fog like an aural wind. Mkeki and Modrescu looked shaken, as did the two Ghibelline men, which Leyden found even more disturbing. Both Iksillas appeared out of the fog, standing upright on their haunches, tails twitching.

"Where are we?" he whispered to Sylla, as they crouched for a moment on a crumbling bamboo walkway. Humans clearly visited this place, even though it was at a far lower altitude than any of the Guelph or Ghibelline settlements.

"The name has no Illium equivalent," she answered in a muffled voice, as though her mouth were full. "Not a graveyard but. . . the place of bones. Where we bring our dead after the ceremony of joining their spirit with mother Eëlios."

"And the Saar?"

"They are here. Yes." Her voice sounded as though she were chewing something. "They come here to scavenge. The remains of all creatures of the high places descend over time to the cloud forest."

"The Saar eat your dead?"

Sylla looked at him, and he sensed how much he must try her patience: here they were, captured and on the run, and he was yet again asking another stupid question.

"What would you have us do?" she asked. "Carry their bodies all the way down to become food for the water-worms and eels of the swamp? The cycle of regeneration is here for us, in the elevations of the anchorwood, not there. The Saar and other creatures are merely the instruments."

Her mouth still looked as if she were eating.

The fog folded in upon them, cutting vision to only a few meters. Leyden felt as chilled as if he had been standing in a cold shower. "Why are *we* here?"

"The ceremonies are performed above. We bring our dead here, and leave. It is dangerous to remain. The Ghibelline must have convinced Mkeki that the fog and the Saar would cause your Illium soldiers to give up. Or become lost."

"Have they? I haven't heard anything since we hit this fog."

"They are still with us."

"How do you know?"

"They can be heard."

Sylla *was* chewing. "Are you eating something?" Leyden whispered to her.

"Yes. Mostera."

"*What?*"

"Quiet." Sylla glanced at him with exasperation. "The leaves provide me with better sight. As I told you. And hearing. We need both."

Leyden remembered how he refreshed he had felt after chewing several leaves himself. "Can the others hear that Hawkwood is still following?"

Sylla hesitated. "I don't think so."

Modrescu, guarding them from the rear, muttered something and they fell silent. The Ghibelline man with the anchorwood sword signaled to Mkeki and they all continued forward along the swaying bamboo walkway, down a stretch of vine netting that led to a wider platform of rough planking that twisted off to the left and disappeared into the mist. Fragments of white bone covered the splintered wood, and fog hung over the walkway like a discarded shroud. Puddles of wax from old candles appeared on the railings, accompanied by dead flowers. The smell of damp and decay intensified.

Another mournful cry and a series of clicks rang through the air; the Ghibelline guide signaled for everyone to hurry. Twen climbed up Leyden's leg and perched atop his basket of Mostera leaves.

Leyden heard a muffled, rattling noise. He looked up, and for a moment couldn't comprehend what he was seeing. He blinked and looked again: the human dead of Eëlios, a community of skulls hanging head down in the heavy growth overhead. Pieces of clothing and skin still clung to many of the corpses, but most were skeletal, encrusted with moss and fungi, plants growing out of eye sockets and mouths. They hung almost side by side in some places, scattered in others, where the Saar had apparently dismembered them, often leaving only a skull or part of a limb. Leyden felt suffocated.

Mkeki and Modrescu looked frozen in shock. Within the confines of the fog, Leyden couldn't tell how far this Eëlian internment extended, but it overhung the visible length of the platform. The bones rattled in the soft movement of the air. Skeleton hands beckoned to them, and skulls seemed to nod in greeting. Vines wept from their eye sockets and spilled onto the walkway.

Leyden sensed rather then saw another kind of movement — quicker, smaller. He stepped closer to see more clearly and wished he hadn't. The head and torso of a man dangled from a Tracasandra vine, and a colony of maggots and scavenger lizards still fed on his ravaged face.

One of the Ghibelline men hissed at them.

"Move!" Mkeki said. They hurried along the platform, the procession of hanging bodies unreeling above them. A Saar cried out, much closer now. Water beaded onto Leyden's face and his hand shook as he wiped it away. For an instant, he imagined himself head down in the fog, coated in blue bees, which suddenly flew away, leaving only a grinning skull.

The walkway widened into a platform bounded by a curtain of vine netting. The Ghibelline men scrambled up, followed by Mkeki. Leyden and Sylla lagged behind and Modrescu, who had been in the rear, brushed by them and started up the net.

"Now!" Sylla whispered to Leyden. They both shrugged off their Mostera baskets, causing the Iksillas to leap off and scrabble onto their shoulders. They turned and began running back along the walkway and into the obscuring fog.

"Idiot!" Mkeki shouted from halfway up the net. "Get them!" Modrescu cursed and tried to unsling and activate his rifle with one arm while holding to the netting with the other. Leyden and Sylla crouched and Modrescu's pulse shot sizzled overhead. He jumped back heavily to the platform and fired a dispersal of flechettes that spattered and splintered into the wood.

Leyden felt a hot stinging sensation on his lower leg. He kicked aside the Mostera basket in front of him and scrambled after Sylla into a mist as thick as gelatin. Modrescu fired again, missing so badly that Leyden couldn't even hear the impact. Looking down, he saw a piece of jagged metal sticking out of his calf muscle. He reached down and pulled it out, burning his hand on the still-hot ceramic fragment, and without thinking, dropped it into a pouch on his belt. His hand instantly began hurting more than his leg.

The fog, heavier than ever, absorbed sound as well as sight and direction. Leyden had no sense of where to run. He stopped, fearful he might find himself rushing back toward Modrescu and Mkeki — or over the edge of the walkway. Twice he called Sylla's name in a shouted whisper without response. Water continued to bead up and drip off his face. He had experienced fog like this only once before, on the tundra leading to Musgrave's Dance. Sylla had disappeared.

A blurred, darker shape loomed out of the white air.

"Sylla!" he called, at the same time realizing that the shape of the head was horribly wrong, the arms oddly jointed and clawed.

The Saar's head snapped into focus like a floating apparition, teeth bared and hissing, marbled green skin slashed with yellow and red. Leyden stumbled back, tripped and fell. Something dropped beside him. Picking it up, he realized he held the still-warm flechette from his leg. As the Saar lunged forward, he slashed at its head and gouged out a section under its eye. The Saar jerked back, but Leyden could already feel a powerful claw digging into his foot, dragging him along the platform. He wanted to scream but couldn't.

Something dropped out of the fog onto the Saar's head. Twen. In a screaming, hissing noise that Leyden had never heard from an Iksilla before, Twen dug his claws into the Saar's nostrils. The Saar roared in surprise, rearing up on its haunches, releasing Leyden's leg. It shook its massive head violently, but Twen remained attached, tearing at a nose and eye. The Saar, twisting up to its full height, clawed at the Iksilla and flung Twen into the fog in a squealing arc.

Meanwhile, Leyden pulled himself to his feet, only to feel his ankle collapse beneath him. He turned to drag himself away when he saw Sylla behind him, motionless.

Leyden kneeled, ready to slash again with the piece of flechette in his hands when the Saar lunged again in a hissing roar — but moved past him and into the fog. After a stunned moment, he looked over at Sylla, eyes still closed.

He called her name in a hoarse whisper. She blinked at him. "This way."

He struggled again to his feet, the pain firing from his ankle to the top of his head, and tried to follow. An instant later she disappeared again. Once more he found himself alone in the suffocating fog. Ahead, he heard the stinging explosion of a weapon and the choking cry of a Saar.

Leyden cursed his wound and himself as he gripped the railing. He had no idea what had just happened, but perhaps there were worse ways to go than dying clueless. Overhead, the assemblage of Eëlian skulls grinned down at him. *Care to join us?* They appeared delighted at the prospect of his company. The contortions of branches and vines filling the cavities of their eyes and mouth looked familiar. Sylla was leading him *away* from Mkeki and Modrescu. . . wasn't she?

In the next moment, Leyden had his answer.

A double cry rose from above him, Saar and human, as the curtain of netting materialized again out of the fog.

Leyden found himself with Sylla back where he had started.

The Saar that had attacked him, eye draining a mix of blood and ooze, was bolting up the net, as another was descended out of the mist. Modrescu, Mkeki and one of the Ghibelline clung in the middle. It took Leyden a moment to realize that the screams came from another Ghibelline, hanging between the masticating jaws of a third Saar crouched on the platform. As soon as it sighted Leyden, the Saar leaped off the platform and into the fog, the Ghibelline's choking screams trailing behind it.

Both Modrescu and Mkeki flailed about on the net, trying to fire their weapons with one hand. But neither was a trained soldier, and the two Saar closed in on them in an instant. Mkeki finally managed to get off a pulse shot that caught the descending Saar in the shoulder; it paused, roaring in pain — enough time for Mkeki to jump down to the platform. Sylla leapt upon her immediately, tearing the pulse rifle out of her arms and kicking it over the Leyden. She pinned Mkeki to the blood-spattered bamboo with her knee and reached around to grasp her nose ring, immobilizing her.

Modrescu fired one burst of flechettes, but it only grazed the climbing Saar, already half blinded and enraged from its encounter with Leyden and Twen. It lunged upward, caught Modrescu's arm in its front claws, and with an incredible twisting motion, tore it from the socket, and flung it into the fog, the hand still gripping the weapon. Modrescu looked down in stunned silence before a gout of hot blood burst from his side. In the next instant, the Saar buried his jaws in Modrescu's neck, cutting short his cries. Blood showered onto Leyden, Sylla, and Mkeki.

Leyden switched Mkeki's weapon to flechettes and fired a burst into the Saar's back. The Saar reared back, releasing Modrescu, whose torn body slid lifelessly down the netting to the platform. Before Leyden could fire again, the Saar hissed at them all and jumped free into the fog.

Shadows materialized into three more Saar in the netting above them. Before Leyden could fire again, a pulse shot chewed through the air from behind them, and he turned to see Hawkwood kneeling on the platform, with Nouvé and several other Guelph behind him. Hawkwood fired again and a Saar responded with a shrieking roar.

Sylla stood in front of them, Mkeki still prone before her, and held out an arm to both Leyden and Hawkwood.

"Stop!" she called out. "No more."

Hawkwood froze, as did Leyden.

"Don't shoot!" she yelled. "Don't move!"

Sylla turned toward the three Saar, which had dropped from the netting to the platform little more than ten meters from her, teeth bared, claws extended.

Sylla stood very still, arms at her side, eyes closed, Mkeki unmoving at her feet. Two of the Saar approached her slowly, as though examining which part of her body to tear away first. The third paced behind them as though contained in an invisible cage. Leyden, on one knee behind her, raised his weapon.

"No," she said very quietly, not turning her head. "Do nothing. Nothing at all."

Sylla shook her head at the Saar, which seemed to mimic her movements. She raised her hand in a motion that he found oddly familiar. Then he recognized it: the same hand signals she used to communicate with the Iksillas. *Go... Now... Go.*

The Saar twisted their heads to the side, as though confused and unable to focus. Other Saar howled in the distance. The three Saar turned, as if on command, swiftly climbed the net and were gone.

Leyden heard a small scrabbling sound next to him, and turned to see Twen crawling up beside him, cut, skin hanging in ragged tears and generally looking like hell. He found no way that he could hug a lizard, but he did cup Twen's head in his hands and look into his yellow eyes. Twen blinked and licked Leyden's nose with his fat three-pronged tongue.

As Hawkwood approached, with Nouvé and the Guelph behind him, he motioned for Mkeki to stand. She struggled to her knees, but as she did, Hawkwood raised his weapon.

Barely registering what was about to happen, she turned to Leyden with a mute appeal in her eyes. Hawkwood fired a full pulse blast that tore through her chest. Mkeki was dead before she fell back to the blood-soaked platform.

Hawkwood looked over at Leyden. "My experience has been that it's best not to prolong these matters."

PART V: BURNING

33 GHIBELLINE GAMBIT

From the deep mass of the canopy, the Ghibelline announced their arrival with the stutter of drums and throaty call of wooden flutes.

Cleanth sat on an elaborately decorated stool, flanked by Tirun, Hawkwood and Leyden on one side, Nouvé and an assemblage of Guelph retainers on the other. Behind them stood ranks of Guelph, all freshly painted and wearing ceremonial tunics brilliantly decorated with reptile skins and the plumage of a dozen Eëlian bird species.

The trees shook, and the first Ghibelline warriors appeared, ignoring the tangle of platforms, netting, and hanging bamboo walkways at the center of the Guelph settlement. Instead, the Ghibelline chose to advance through the trees with the fluid ease Leyden associated with Sylla on their Looking Glass expedition. The Ghibelline appeared in the webbed ceiling of vines and branches, faces painted in swirls and circles, in sharp contrast to the colorful slashes of the Guelph. Some of the Ghibelline remained in the branches; others dropped down to the end of the platform opposite Cleanth and the Guelph.

As everyone waited, the overhead canopy trembled, accompanied by the sounds of scrabbling feet, sibilant hoots, and small showers of vegetation. The Ghibelline had brought their own contingent of Iksillas.

The main body of Ghibelline emerged from the curtain of foliage: painted retainers accompanying a figure enveloped in a cloud of bird feathers even more elaborate than Cleanth's cape of pebbled skins. Shinsato appeared, the Ghibelline leader and Cleanth's cousin, according to the information Leyden had reviewed in preparation for this meeting. The face was gaunt and scarred, the shaven head an oiled golden green shell.

The Guelph stirred suddenly behind him with a fierce outbreak of whispering, and out of the corner of his eye, he saw Tirun jerk his head sharply, either from surprise or recognition. For a moment, amid the mottled brilliance of the Ghibelline assemblage, Leyden couldn't pick out the source of everyone's attention. Then he spotted him. The odd man out: as squat and square as a block of Umlivik ice, wearing an unadorned military-style tunic and a bandolier that held what appeared to be the latest issue Multiphase Combat Weapon. The face, too, resembled an Umlivik glacier: broad, pitted, and uninviting. An off-worlder's face, the face of a chaebol mercenary.

But also a face that Leyden vaguely recognized. He probably had seen him in a Quanta stream — those enormous, and enormously compressed bursts of news, information, vidbooks, holographic images, and other data that exploded through the opening phase of any Illium cycle prior to the appearance of transport vessels.

In the Illium Archipelago, the the cycle between worlds was open or closed, one or zero. Wars could be fought, technological breakthroughs achieved, cultural movements rise and fall on one world – and be utterly unknown, and unknowable in another until the Illium portal opened — whether every six months, six years, or six centuries. When the portals did open, it was vital that both worlds instantly share vital strategic data, with vast fields of information and news to follow. That was one function of the Quanta; if these data streams were not the first phenomena through an opening portal, a planet might well conclude that it could be in danger of attack.

"Braga," came Verlaine's quiet voice from behind him, as though reading Leyden's mind. "His name is Braga. One of the few, the disgraced, the extremely wealthy."

Leyden nodded without turning around. He remembered now: Braga, formerly of the Illium League. Over the decades, the number of Illium officers who severed all ties with the League remained small but important. If their League service didn't leave them either physical wrecks or mental burnouts, their skills and knowledge were so highly prized by the chaebols that the bidding for their services reputedly reached legendary figures. Some even owned private Illium lightships, otherwise unheard of except for a miniscule number whose fortunes were basically beyond measure. Needless to say, the League actively worked to prevent such defections through its own elaborate systems of indoctrination, rewards, and punishments.

"Do we know who he works for?" Leyden whispered out of the corner of his mouth.

"Braga works for one chaebol only. The Taranazuka."

"What about Cold Moon or another triad?"

Behind him, he could sense Verlaine hesitating. The flutter of wooden pipes and flutes fell through the air like passing rain. "Maybe. The Taranazuka are still young and hungry. If I had to pick one chaebol to risk such an alliance, they would be it. If the stakes were high enough."

They stopped talking as Shinsato advanced. Cleanth rose, and the two of them engaged in a greeting that was equally elaborate and incomprehensible. Leyden wished Sylla were nearby to explain what was happening, but he had seen neither her nor Nausicca among the assembled Guelph. Perhaps their Ghibelline origins prevented them from attending.

Leyden itched and sweated for what seemed a full standard hour, which included the Eëlian version of reviewing the guard. In this case, that meant slow elaborate greetings among the high officials in each retinue. Leyden, too, received an introduction, nodding his head as Shinsato repeated a formalized welcome to the world of Eëlios that he conferred on Verlaine, Tirun, and Hawkwood as well. Braga, he noticed, remained in the back of the Ghibelline contingent and took no part in the formal ceremonies. Leyden's ankle throbbed, an unwelcome reminder of his week-old encounter with the Saar.

With the formalities over, Cleanth led the Guelph and Ghibelline into the enclosed meeting space where Leyden and the others had had their welcoming banquet. This time, the Guelph served a green pepper-tea drink that Leyden had successfully avoided on previous occasions. The fragment of a white blossom floated in each carved anchorwood cup. Leyden touched the pepper-tea to his lips very tentatively and ate several nut clusters sweetened with syrup from Nevea's Nectar plants.

When the tea and food had been cleared away, Cleanth nodded for the smaller negotiating group to join him at an anchorwood table in the center of the room: Nouvé and several other Guelph leaders along with Leyden, Verlaine, Tirun, and Hawkwood. Shinsato brought an equal number of Ghibelline to the other side of the table. Both Guelph and Ghibelline onlookers stood back in the shadows of the thick foliage, and, as always, the Iksillas constantly raced overhead like undisciplined children.

Without preamble, Shinsato rose, unconsciously scratched the scar of his translator chip, and began speaking in typically accented Illium Standard Speech:

> The Ghibelline join the Guelph in welcoming those of you who have traveled such great distances to our world. However, we say this: the Ghibelline have never agreed to give Illium worlders the right to cut a single plant, collect a single seed, take a single leaf from our mother world, Eëlios.

And so we say this: The Guelph have no more right to enter into such agreements today than they did when the Illium worlders first fell into our skies. Nevertheless, they have done so, and thereby violated those parts of our treaty which require that all decisions concerning the riches of Eëlios be agreed upon mutually by Guelph and Ghibelline alike.

And so we say this: With such violations nullifying the Eëlios-Illium treaty, the Ghibelline are now free to enter into their own agreements, independently, with the Illium worlders. And we have done so. Moreover, we declare that the Ghibelline and their Illium allies have agreed, for their mutual benefit, to explore, and transport to the Illium, any and all of the natural wealth of our world in what is known as the Fourth Eëlian Zone.

And so we say this: the Ghibelline and their Illium allies will take all necessary and appropriate steps to enforce their agreement, and to ensure that no one enters this domain without the approval of our joint Ghibelline-Illium council.

And finally, we say this: In the spirit of peace and amity between Ghibelline and Guelph, we invite all inhabitants of Eëlios join us in this great new enterprise.

Shinsato sat down to rumbles of approval from his assembled Ghibelline retinue and stunned silence by the assembled Guelph.

Cleanth rose and responded in a similar vein of polite ultimatums. The Guelph, not the Ghibelline, had the only valid agreement for the exploration and collection of the biological wealth of Eëlios, he said. The Ghibelline had rejected the opportunity to join the first agreement made with the Illium worlders; they had no standing to unilaterally declare such an agreement now.

As for the Fourth Zone, the Ghibelline knew full well that this was sacred territory for all peoples of Eëlios, site of the first discovery of the flower from which their world took its name. For his part, Cleanth invited the Ghibelline to join the Guelph and its Illium allies in cooperative explorations, and ensure that Eëlios entered into the Illium Archipelago in a position of wealth and power.

Shinsato seemed to savor the moment before answering, his satisfaction perhaps too obvious, Leyden thought. That might offer a small opening.

The words of the Guelph were as empty as a yellow-tree gourd, Shinsato said. Their so-called allies were merely the remnants of a misbegotten expedition so inept that they had landed far away on the Chaga Sea and virtually destroyed themselves traveling down the Whitebone River. They were small in number and possessed few if any weapons. The Illium allies of the Ghibelline, on the other hand, were many and powerful, possessing weapons that could, with little trouble, annihilate both Guelph and their pathetic Illium friends.

But there was no reason for any such violence to occur, Shinsato said, arms wide and expansive. The Guelph must simply face the truth that he, Shinsato, leader of the Ghibelline, represented the new order on Eëlios.

As he finished, Leyden leaned forward and whispered in Tirun's ear, who in turn spoke quietly to Cleanth. Cleanth nodded, almost imperceptibly, stood, and suggested they stop so that the Guelph could consider what the leader of the Ghibelline had said and meet again after the setting of the sun Naryl. Shinsato, intoxicated over his ultimatum, quickly agreed.

◆

When they reconvened, Naryl had set and Nevea was rising in the first quadrant. Shadow and the pale plumes of smoky torches filled their enclosure.

Cleanth spoke first. He had asked a high official of the Illium, Leyden, to speak for the Guelph alliance at this time. Perhaps Shinsato would want the off-worlder present with the Ghibelline to speak for them?

Leyden could see a small ripple through the assembled Ghibelline before, in the rear, Braga frowned and shook his head in the negative. Shinsato said that wouldn't be necessary. And despite the obvious differences in their ranks, he would allow the off-worlder to speak for the Guelph.

Shinsato clearly relished this moment too much to give it up to anyone else, even if Braga had been willing. That was good. As Leyden had told Tirun and Hawkwood during the break, they had only two goals in this negotiation: information and time. At all costs, they must avoid agreeing to anything of substance.

Leyden arose and looked out over the gathering before turning to Shinsato.

Leader of the Ghibelline, it is indeed an honor for me, representative of many distant worlds, to address you in this difficult moment. I will, therefore, attempt to speak with complete candor.

Honorable Shinsato, you have been deceived. Those with whom you have reached agreement represent not the vast worlds of the Illium, but only themselves. They are, I must regretfully report, outlaws and criminals whose actions are neither recognized nor authorized by any authority, corporation, planet, or other Illium organization. Certainly not the Illium League, which rules the great space portals that brought your ancestors and now serve to link you with the planets and space colonies known as the Illium Archipelago.

Honorable Shinsato, it is true that you have joined with representatives of one of the Illium's large corporate entities known as the Taranazuka. But the Taranazuka have no legal right whatsoever to enter into agreements with the people of Eëlios for the exploration, study, and development of the biological riches that are your legacy, and indeed, your home. As for us, the Illium representatives, such a license was purchased, legally, at great expense I might add, by the organization known as Trans-Illium.

Moreover, Honorable Leader, I must regretfully point out that the Taranazuka have apparently entered into an alliance with a vast and dangerous criminal organization named after the Illium world Cold Moon Rising.

Honorable Shinsato, Cold Moon Rising has no concern for Eëlios, but only for transforming some of your most powerful and sacred plants, such as the Mostera plant, into illegal drugs that will enslave and destroy the lives of millions, including many here on Eëlios. They may indeed offer you the prospect of great riches. But in all honesty, I must tell you that, in the end, Cold Moon will destroy you and seek complete control of the narcotic plants that grow here. We have, unfortunately, seen this pattern on many other worlds of the Illium.

Let me conclude, Honorable Leader of the Ghibelline, by suggesting that we can, in fact, reach an agreement for the mutual benefit to all. The Guelph will agree to set aside the original accord with the Illium and negotiate a new one in which Ghibelline and Guelph share equally. In turn, we would ask that the Ghibelline to repudiate its illegal agreements with the Taranazuka and the Cold Moon Triad.

Shinsato responded to the last suggestion with a derisive laugh; indeed, he rejected any suggestion that his agreements be reconsidered. That was predictable. Leyden could only hope that he had planted some doubt in his mind.

When Leyden suggested another adjournment, he noted with satisfaction that it triggered a fierce round of whispered argument among the Ghibelline, including Braga, who clearly became increasingly agitated the longer Leyden spoke. In the end, Shinsato agreed only to a delay of one revolution of the Ginn, until Nevea's dawn.

♦

When they gathered again, Leyden opened the session. "Honorable Shinsato, we believe that we can prove the falsity of the Taranazuka's claims if we are permitted to review the license authorizing them to reach commercial agreements with Eëlios."

"The agreements are satisfactory to me," Shinsato said, his oiled head glistening in the filtered yellow-blue light. "That is enough."

"I understand. But if you wish the Guelph to accede to your demands, we should be at least be allowed to review the terms of the agreements — both yours with the Taranazuka, and the Taranazuka's with the Illium. It is the least that a gracious and powerful leader like you, one with the fate of a world at his command, should be willing to grant."

That triggered a prolonged and semi-private meeting among the Ghibelline, presumably with fierce opposition from Braga and the rest of the Taranazuka. But in the end, the appeal to Shinsato's vanity worked and the Ghibelline produced both items. For the few moments that Leyden and others viewed it, the Illium-Taranazuka commercial agreement appeared to be heavily encoded. But that mattered little, since they were able to scan and record it for later analysis.

The Taranazuka-Ghibelline document, however, held a real shocker. In addition to the usual research and pharmaceutical rights, one of the final clauses permitted the Taranazuka "to isolate and transport a sector of Eëlian biota, in its entirety, from the Planet Eëlios to a designated location in the Illium." The document then gave a series of coordinates that Leyden assumed fell within this disputed Fourth Zone.

Leyden spoke. "You are aware that the Taranazuka will have to bring in huge terra-forming equipment to remove, to literally tear away a part of your world?"

"We are aware of what we have agreed to," Shinsato said dismissively. "I am no fool. In this way, we will bring our biological wealth and wonder to the Illium and renown to the people of Eëlios."

He sat back with an expression of satisfaction at the shouts of anger and outrage from Cleanth and the assembled Guelph.

Leyden looked over to see Tirun and Hawkwood talking together. Extractive industries such as mining and lumbering operated among Illium core worlds with short cycle times. But the enormous expense of transporting massive objects from planetary bodies to the portals made such activity relatively rare. On those few worlds where processing plants proved impractical and raw-material demand high, chaebols had developed rail-gun technologies to blast massive quantities of gem rocks, titanium sands, and other ores into orbit, and then transport them using slow detachable ion engines to the portals.

Only in the case of the Alnitak Cloud Cluster could Leyden recall an instance when a chaebol alliance had invested in massive lifting vehicles to log and transport an entire hemisphere of prized, tropical hardwoods, known as Tyco Marblewood, through an Illium portal. It had been a typical Illium enterprise underwritten by speculative stocks and highly leveraged loans. With the successful delivery of close to a million Tyco logs to Rigel Prime, Casmir Four, Arishima, and the Cepheus Complex, the investment paid off in spectacular multiples that created a new stratum of wealth in the Illium. Hybridized Tyco Marblewood now grew in tree farms and small forests on a dozen Illium worlds.

But the scale on which the chaebols ravaged Alnitak's spectacular ecology produced an intense backlash that resulted in prohibitions against any similar projects. Now the Taranazuka proposed a similar undertaking on Eëlios. But why? The pharmacological potential of Eëlios remained potentially enormous, but still unproven. And harvesting Mostera hardly required such an operation.

Shinsato spoke again, nodding toward Braga and reminding them all that the Ghibelline possessed the power to enforce their agreements. The Guelph, he repeated, had no choice but to accept this new order.

"Once again, you have been deceived," Leyden said quickly, before Cleanth could respond. "We do not believe that your Illium allies possess the strength that they claim. Twice, we confronted them on our journey down the Whitebone River. And twice, we successfully defeated their attacks and inflicted heavy losses upon them."

Leyden could feel the stirring among the Guelph. Tirun coughed and leaned toward him. "What the hell are you going with this?" he whispered.

"Say nothing," Leyden said without turning his head, steadily watching Shinsato. "And tell Cleanth not to speak for the moment. . .with all due respect."

He could see Braga push his way forward and, gesturing emphatically, speak directly to Shinsato. "I have been informed that you are speaking untruths," Shinsato said after a pause. "Your story is little more than fiction. You are few in number, and after your losses on the Whitebone, virtually unarmed."

"Ask your allies how many drones they lost to us," Leyden answered. "On the contrary, we believe that it is the Taranazuka who are few in number, and without any weapons to speak of. I say it is the Taranazuka, and the Ghibelline, who are the *jeets* here."

Leyden was using a term he had learned from Sylla for a tiny frog with an incongruously deep voice that normally hid inside certain large orchid plants. Calling someone a *jeet* on Eëlios, especially a man, was a deep insult.

Shinsato flushed and curled his mouth in disgust. For the first time, Leyden sensed hands tightening on weapons around them. Shinsato opened his mouth, no doubt to explain the slow and painful ways in which he planned to remove Leyden's organs and appendages before he thought better of it.

"Games and nonsense, Representative Leyden, and too trivial for me to respond to your weak chatter. Your claims are nonsense."

Leyden leaned forward. "Prove it, Honorable Leader."

Beneath his rich emerald skin, Leyden could see Shinsato flush with anger. He stood, and signaled to his retinue. "And so we will. Now!"

Leyden noted with satisfaction that Braga openly tried to argue with Shinsato, but without success. Within a few minutes, the bulk of the Taranazuka expedition, which had been held out of sight, appeared.

Leyden counted. Hawkwood's earlier estimate on the Whitebone had been about right: the Taranazuka numbered close to forty, about half of them mercenaries. All of the mercs wore body armor and carried new Multiphase Combat Weapons; they also displayed three late-model Dragons. Shinsato also proudly stated that, despite earlier losses, they still possessed another operational drone and other "great explosives," which presumably meant an assortment of smart mines and missiles.

After the Taranazuka had withdrawn, taking an enraged Braga with them, Shinsato turned to Leyden, almost snorting through his nose, and prodded Leyden hard in the chest. "Who is the *jeet* now?"

Leyden stood and bowed to Shinsato. "You are correct. The forces you have shown us are formidable indeed. I can only ask, on behalf of my Illium companions, and the Guelph, for your patience in giving us time to consider this new situation."

Shinsato, swollen with a sense of victory, turned to Cleanth, and after several exchanges, agreed to give the Guelph three risings of The Ginn before meeting again.

After the Ghibelline had left, Tirun approached Leyden. "Not bad for playing a weak hand," he rumbled.

"Well, well," said Verlaine with a whack on Leyden's back. "No wonder the Illium League worried about you so much."

"We bought a little time," Leyden said. "That's all."

34 THE GINN'S SECRET

The canopy grew unmistakably thinner, the light richer, almost syrupy compared to the thin gruel that reached into the deeper recesses of the understory. But still, Leyden missed the sky.

As he waited, chewing on the sweet stalk of Nevea's Nectar, the branch began to vibrate.

Sylla appeared. "I saw no one. Neither Guelph nor Ghibelline."

"But are we there?"

"Yes. This is the Fourth Zone."

Leyden looked around. Although they had climbed higher into the canopy than usual, their surroundings appeared indistinguishable from any other part of the high-altitude rainforest. A trunk of one of Eëlian's six anchorwood trees, invisible under the profuse layers of growth, undergirded everything. From that base rose thickets of epiphytes, knots of lianas and vines, masses of fungi, and carpets of mosses and flowering plants that left the air heavy with scent. Glowbirds sifted through the undergrowth, flickering like dim searchlights, along with swarms of iridescent insects sleek as tiny spaceships. Translucent frogs and lizards, their organs suspended and pulsing, raced ahead of them, several blundering into the webs of large spiders with fringed legs that immediately injected them with a paralyzing venom. The muffled hoots, cries, and buzzing of a dozen different species populated the air.

Leyden found himself increasingly acclimated to these crowded sensations. He could not match the fluid movements of Sylla and the other Eëlians, but he had managed this climb with much greater ease than any previous trip through the canopy. His weight had dropped long ago, and as the green color of his arms darkened, he had become stronger and more sinewy. His body had finally acclimated to the steady humidity, and the layer of caälyx that covered him seemed as natural as the Eëlian tunics and leggings he now wore instead of his patched Illium uniform. Sometimes he felt as though he was in a race of unknown length, with his gasping mind trying to keep up with the transformation of his body.

A rapid scratching noise followed by a small downfall of leaves and twigs announced the arrival of the Iksillas, Twen and Twon. *Stay?* The words appeared and evaporated in his head like carbonated bubbles. Leyden could receive only Twen's most basic communications; typically, anything more involved hand signs and tongue twists to supplement Twen's telepathic messages.

Sylla sat carefully against a stumpy, moss-laden bromeliad pocked with yellow-green flowers; she seemed uncertain how close to sit next to him. Until this climb, Leyden had not had a moment alone with Sylla since their boneyard encounter with the Saar. He wanted to catch her eye but she persisted in looking away, and he sensed a weight, a sadness, that he had never before noticed.

As he had in the past, Leyden tried to imagine something of her interior life. Before, he had been unable to penetrate her surface exoticism and elusiveness; she invariably appeared as one with the rainforest, wrapped in its unreadable and unreachable depths. She knew exactly how she appeared to him, he suspected, and had taken the trouble to point it out, even mock it. To see her more clearly had once seemed neither possible nor even particularly vital; now it did. The image of her rising beneath the waterfall still burned in his mind.

"Why is the Fourth Zone so special?"

Sylla hesitated. "Some of the plants that we value most grow here in greater numbers than elsewhere."

"You mean Mostera?"

"Not Mostera. Others."

"Is that why the Taranazuka picked this place?"

"Perhaps. But the Fourth Zone is special, sacred. For Ghibelline and the Guelph."

"I'm sure it's the Taranazuka who are insisting on targeting the Fourth Zone," Leyden said.

Sylla gazed at him directly. Her scarlet-and-blue markings blazed in a shaft of light as thin as an arrow.

"The Ghibelline and their off-worlders are many, with powerful weapons. Do we have any choice in these matters?"

"You are Ghibelline Sylla," Leyden said. "What do you think?" His tone sounded too blunt; he could never seem to find the right balance between formality and familiarity in talking to her.

"It is no secret that Shinsato has been Cleanth's rival for years," she said carefully. "All agree Shinsato made a terrible mistake by refusing to join the Illium expedition in the last cycle. Now he has a chance to lead the Ghibelline to a final triumph over the Guelph. Although I understand that you had some success with him."

"A delaying tactic, no more," Leyden said, secretly gratified that she had heard some of the gossip. Leyden sucked the last bit of sugar from a piece of Nevea Nectar and threw it into the foliage. "We know about Shinsato. But what about the Ghibelline? Do they want revenge as well?"

Sylla regarded him gravely. "I truly know little of such matters. Like Nausicca, I was promised to the Guelph as a child. Once in a while I can visit my family, but I can never stay. There is little I could tell you of the Ghibelline now."

"Promised to the Guelph," Leyden asked. "What does that mean?"

Sylla drew up her knees and looked down, so that all Leyden could see was the tousled crown of her head. The swaying leaves created patterns of dappled sunlight on her hair and neck. "I was promised as a consort to the leader of the Guelph."

"To Cleanth?"

"Yes."

Water from an overhead branch dripped on Leyden's head and he shifted slightly. "I don't understand. Are you his companion now?"

"I was summoned to serve the Trans-Illium because of my knowledge of biology and medicine. That is all you need to know of me and my life now, Leyden."

I used to be considered charming, Leyden thought. Now I can't even manage 'so what do you do for a living' conversation. "It was not my intention to upset you," he said.

Sylla looked away.

"Quite the opposite. I wish to be your... friend."

She blinked at him as though he had grown a supplemental monster's head. "Friend? You wish to be my *friend*?"

"You have saved my life. Yes, of course. Your friend. Is your translator chip not functioning?"

"There's nothing wrong with the translation," she snapped. "Only your patronizing tone."

"What? I am not — "

Sylla stood and glared at him. "Do you think the word *friend* doesn't hold as many meanings on Eëlios as it does on Rigel Prime, or wherever you claim you're from?"

"I'm from Toranga. A planet destroyed and occupied by proxy rulers for the Illium League — meaning Hawkwood. I was imprisoned on Rigel Prime for financial fraud — which I was innocent of, for the most part — and for betraying a woman I claimed to love, for which I was most guilty. I am deeply sorry for troubling you, especially now, in the middle of all this."

Sylla made a hand gesture to the Iksillas. "We must go."

Leyden stood. "Tell me, what am I misunderstanding about the word friend?"

"Friend has many meanings."

"But you are referring to one in particular."

"Yes."

"Could you tell me — if only that I can avoid its improper usage in the future?"

Sylla looked upward into the canopy. "Most often. . . when you say *my friend* in a certain way, you mean someone you have sex with, without caring. A sex partner, not a lover."

"I see. Thank you."

Sylla looked at him with an expression that froze his face.

"You see very little actually."

◆

The Iksillas reappeared. *They come.*

Sylla turned in a single liquid motion; she had received the same message.

Following the Iksillas, Sylla and Leyden scaled a section of pitted, aromatic anchorwood trunk until they reached a cluster of broad-leaf epiphytes. They needed to find a location with reasonable lines of sight while still remaining hidden — a difficult feat in a canopy world where plants competed for virtually every square centimeter of space. The only option, even for Eëlians such as Sylla, was to rely on the Iksillas and their extraordinary sensitivity to every element of the rainforest. The two of them waited in silence.

As he had learned, vibrations first signaled that something substantial in size was moving through the canopy. Next they heard the scrape and wheeze of the climbers, followed by their first glimpse, perhaps thirty meters distant, of a group moving up the same massive anchorwood branch that Leyden and Sylla had traveled earlier.

Leyden scanned the party with his high-rez Optic. Preceded by an advance guard of Iksillas, two Ghibelline men appeared first, equipped with adhesive rope and slender picks, standard for canopy ascents. They were followed by two unfamiliar off-worlders, clearly Taranazuka mercenaries equipped with forest crampons made of a glossy alloy that shone in the light.

Another figure, still obscured in shadow, appeared in the rear, someone familiar. Not possible. Leyden adjusted the Optic for a tighter focus, but the figure climbed steadily and he could manage only glimpses. Yet no doubt. Suslov.

Leyden shook in spite of himself, so much so that Sylla noticed and took the Optic from him to scan the climbers herself.

"The two Ghibelline have equipment for climbing through the canopy to the high places," she said.

"Yes." Leyden could manage only a whisper.

Sylla looked over at him. "Is it the Illium worlder we thought had fallen?"

Leyden nodded.

"So she was a betrayer from the beginning."

"Apparently."

"Like Mkeki and the others?"

Leyden took back the Optic and tried focusing it again on Suslov, but the entire party had disappeared into the shadowy foliage above them.

"No. Not like the others, I think. They were simply paid by the Triad to get as much Mostera as possible for Looking Glass. She. . . Suslov must have been working with the Taranazuka from the beginning."

"A *friend?*" Sylla looked at him with frank curiosity.

"Look. . ." he started to say when he saw that she was quietly laughing.

"Yes, a friend. Exactly." Leyden tried to sound rueful. "I had no idea. It would have served me right if she had planted a knife in my back before she left." He flicked away an insect from the corner of his eye.

"One wonders why she didn't," Sylla said.

◆

As Tirun had instructed, Leyden and Sylla spent a full Naryl revolution moving slowly from one location to another throughout the Fourth Zone, monitoring any activity by the Ghibelline and Taranazuka. But no other groups appeared. During the sleep period, Sylla showed him where to find the interlaced fronds of the amber-musk for a hammock with scented air and comfortable sleeping. She asked no more questions about Suslov.

As he lay back, surrounded by the rainforest night sounds — different yet often even busier than the daytime chorus — he found he was no longer angry at what Suslov had done, only saddened to think of his own self-deceptions and indulgences. What an insubstantial man he had been, and likely still was.

Naryl rose, suffusing the canopy with broken orange light. For a rare moment, only one sun hung in the Eëlian sky. Several times, he caught Sylla watching him carefully, as though she had to make a decision.

After a sticky, uneventful morning, Sylla took his hand, her fingers roughened from a lifetime of climbing. "Come," she said, "I will show you a special place."

As they traveled along slender, trembling branches, Sylla, for the first time, began to take a critical interest in his technique. "You and the others are thinking constantly about how high up you are, about falling. Don't. In most places, the canopy will catch you even if you did."

"Easy for you to say," he muttered.

Sylla took that as a challenge. "Watch," she said, pausing to check her location, then simply collapsing and falling off the branch.

"No!" Leyden's shout was involuntary as she disappeared into a mass of flowering vegetation several meters below. A moment later, she reappeared laughing, and scrambled back up to him. "Now you."

"I don't think so."

Sylla again took his hands. "The branches of the anchorwood are many and broad. Physical balance is easy. The balance in your head is the hard part."

Leyden shifted the belts, attachments and travel pack on his back. "*Still* easy for you to say."

She smiled at him and he remembered the first time he had seen that expression: during their first anchorwood climb, when he had spotted a cloud of sky bees and declared them his saviors.

"We should go back now," Sylla said.

Leyden touched the scar under his left eye, legacy of the Saar, and looked around. "If we are close to the top of the canopy, why not take me all the way up? To the sky."

Sylla's eyes opened in surprise and closed both hands over her mouth to stifle her laughter.

Leyden frowned. "What is it? What did I say? I did not utter the word *friend*. Not once."

She shook her head, still trying to stifle her laughter. "Nothing."

"No, what?"

Sylla shook her head again. "No matter."

Now it was Leyden's turn to take her hands. "Please."

"It's only that the phrase 'take me to the sky' has a different meaning among us."

"What?"

"I can't really say."

Leyden moved closer to her, the scents and heat of her body. "Yes, you can. What?" He had a pretty good idea already, but he wanted to hear the words from her.

She pulled her hands away and gazed down, exposing the vulnerable nape of her neck, and whispered, "It is usually an offer from one to another to make love, for two people to reach the... heights of passion together."

"Let me guess. Not as friends."

"No. Not as friends."

"Well, then." Leyden reached for her hands again, but she was already retreating along the branch, glancing back only once, a dark figure in the blood-light of the sun.

Sylla seemed to dance before him, more vision than flesh, a wraith-like emerald figure moving among infinite shades of Eëlian green, the slashes of scarlet and blue as brilliant and momentary as the darting passage of glowbirds. The reflexive leap of frogs, bright as tiny prisms of light, preceded her like the bow wave of a ship. For brief periods she disappeared entirely into masses of arboreal bamboo and flowering bromeliads. Where the anchorwood branches divided, he would pause, and invariably a phrase, an image would surface in his mind. *This way.* The message from Twen, who remained overhead.

A new but familiar sound emerged: running water and the appearance of the rug-like rivertree leaves. Sylla stood, waiting for him, Twon and Twen each perched on her shoulders. He could hear the water rushing invisibly, in deep shadow, somewhere below them. Leyden paused in front of her, leaning forward, hands on knees, catching his breath. "Let's slow down a little."

Sylla shrugged the two Iksillas off her arms. She unhooked her belt and chest straps, and pulled a chunk of caälyx wax from one of her bamboo pouches.

In the distance, overhead, Leyden could hear the familiar rip of the sky as a storm broke and brought down a speckled rainfall.

"Here you do not need to fall," she said softly, watching him. "Only jump. Or dive."

She half turned from him, stripped off her leggings, reached behind her back and pulled off her tunic in a single, swift motion. A glowbird called and was answered farther away; the light dimmed as the rainstorm pressed down upon them.

Sylla turned sideways to Leyden, arms at her side, declaring herself in nakedness and silence. She smiled again and disappeared. For a moment,

Leyden had no idea what she had done until he caught a glimpse of her arched back and pointed arms as she dropped through the shadows, followed by an invisible splash.

He peered down but it was impossible to see into the deep recesses of the foliage. Twen sat on a branch just in front of him, head cocked.

"What!" Leyden said to him. "You have something to add?"

Will you swim? Will there be a joining?

"Joining?" Leyden squatted down so that he was almost on Twen's level and stared into his pebbled face. He signed: *Show me a way down.*

No way. Jump. Twen reinforced his telepathic message with tongue signals.

"Big help," he muttered. "Any other advice? What about Cleanth? What's the story there?"

Don't understand. You do not wish to join with her? Leyden found Twen's unblinking, reptilian stare completely disconcerting.

He peeled off his clothing and leggings and glanced over at Twen so that he wouldn't have to look down. "All right. Satisfied?"

Twen rolled one eye at him, then closed both of them and seemed to go to sleep.

He jumped.

Leyden surfaced in dark, tepid water, enclosed in shadow, unable at first to find Sylla. Trumpet-shaped drinking plants bowed overhead, and as he treaded water, the rain arrived in a soft patter after its travel through the upper canopy, falling from leaves and petals and dissolving into the surface of the pond.

And there, in a gentle shell of moisture and noise, he found Sylla, floating quietly under a flowering bush with distinctive quadrilateral leaves and small white blossoms.

He swam to her and seized her wrists, determined that this time she would not slip away so easily. He brought her to him and tasted her skin for the first time. Even as he did, memory and moment fused, and he knew that this combination of her caälyx-coated skin, pond water, and flower-scented air would remain one of the most powerful remembrances he would ever possess.

He submerged in the water and rose, exploring her face and shoulders above water with his mouth; her breasts, stomach, and back below the surface, rising again to breathe and return once more to those eyes that burned like blue-green fire in the darkness. She swam away and dove underwater, and he followed, seeking a dim, wavering shape as elusive as when she had danced ahead of him in the rainforest. When he caught her underwater, he kissed her until they both ran out of air and gasped to the surface.

Finally, they pulled themselves out of the water, and he stroked the length of her, neck to thigh, from bodies wet and dripping to merely damp. Pressing into each other, they rolled into the flowering plant that hung overhead, and white blossoms shook free and fell upon their backs and upon her neck and upturned face. She licked the flowers from his shoulders and swallowed them and whispered that he should do the same. He did and they rolled again into the plants and the blossoms fell over them like warm snow.

◆

When they awoke, the Iksillas guided them out of the pond to where their clothes hung like the skins of past lives. Now I will take you to the real sky, she said. After they had been climbing, she paused and said, this is the time of the setting of both suns and we will find only full night there.

Planets with double suns were more the rule than the exception in the Illium; and as a result, many worlds experienced little or no true night periods. Certainly, those living on many of the worlds of the Selucid Swarm rarely witnessed genuine nighttime skies. He thought he remembered quite clearly that Eëlios was one of them.

"No, Sylla insisted. "I have never seen it, but full night comes to Eëlios several times a year. The time of the little death, when both Naryl and Nevea are below the horizon for almost an hour."

Leyden took her hand. For those planets lucky enough to have a genuine nighttime, the blazing display of the Selucid Swarm's planetary and satellite bodies must constitute one of the wonders of the Illium.

"Take me to the sky, Sylla," he said. "Show me your local universe."

They made the final stages of the climb in the failing light, where they anchorwood trunks finally, reluctantly, shrank to slender, swaying branches. Leyden felt the first gusts of wind undeterred by barriers of rainforest growth. They began using Twen and Twon to carry sticky strands of Tracasandra vine ahead of them so that they could pull themselves up with Sylla's wooden pulleys.

When they finally broke free of the roof of the canopy, Nevea had set and Naryl hung as a bloody wound on the horizon. They gazed out over a darkening green ocean. Within minutes Naryl's light faded and the darkness gathered like a swiftly approaching storm.

But as the wind ceased and the night deepened, the sky remained blank and unblemished by a single planetary body. Even through his Optic,

Leyden could just barely make out the blush of a distant galaxy that might have been the Selucid Swarm. Or not.

And then he knew. Or more precisely, he knew now what he didn't know.

35 THE NEGOTIATOR

As Leyden contemplated the grim face before him, he imagined he could hear the sound of grinding teeth in the wet, torpid silence. Good. Despite his phlegmatic exterior, the frustrations of the chief Taranazuka merc, Braga, appeared to be mounting.

Leyden had managed to drag out this, their third meeting with the Ghibelline, for almost three hours without a break. In a moment, he would suggest that, without any substantial progress, they recess and agree to meet in three day's time, when Nevea was again at its apogee. Braga and the Ghibelline would refuse, and he would try and settle for the equivalent of one-and-half Eëlian cycles.

Leyden's tactics had changed little since the first sessions with Shinsato: delay, obfuscation, division, information-gathering. In each meeting, he had reinforced the Ghibelline conviction that they held all the advantages, and therefore could afford to emulate their leader's initial generosity in granting the Guelph time to consider and negotiate the terms of their surrender.

At the same time, he had raised a range of objections to minor matters in the Ghibelline-Taranazuka agreement, including the formality of recognizing Cleanth as leader of the Guelph settlement, and providing for written guarantees of safe passage for the Trans-Illium expedition. Clearly, too, if Braga was any guide, Leyden had managed to heighten tensions between the Ghibelline and the Taranazuka, who apparently wanted Trans-Illium and the Guelph disarmed and confined to the immediate settlement area as soon as possible. But whatever their differences, the negotiations had not, as he had hoped, created any open splits between them. Braga, moreover, seemed to have convinced Shinsato to stay out of the negotiations personally, and Leyden had been unable to gain any more useful information about the Taranazuka and their intentions.

Braga stood and leaned on the table with heavy, sloping shoulders and massive hands. "The talk of trivialities will stop. Now. We call for a break of ten minutes only. No longer. When we return, we will have someone new join the talks. One who will assist us in resolving these matters once and for all."

Leyden remained seated. "Very good. We will be waiting, willing as always to bargain in good faith."

Braga snorted and left the table, followed by a contingent of Ghibelline.

Leyden stretched and looked around. Nouvé and two other Guelph who had been observing rose and left as well, presumably to report back to Cleanth. He knew that he should discuss these latest developments with Tirun and Hawkwood, but since returning from the Fourth Zone with Sylla, he had spoken with both of them as little as possible. He needed to know more before he confronted either of them.

Verlaine was the obvious information source, but also a risky one: as the JKH2 representative on the expedition, he probably knew the most, yet had the most to hide. Whatever the level of their friendship, Leyden had no doubt that it was superseded by Verlaine's corporate mission. Leyden had recognized the hot flame of Verlaine's ambition from the moment they first talked at Musgrave's Dance. His freelance exploration to collect Eëlian coffee plants merely confirmed Verlaine's disguised but consuming drive — presumably for the usual — power and wealth. Verlaine, in short, undoubtedly held a cache of Trans-Illium secrets. Whether he shared them with Tirun and Hawkwood, fully or in part, was another matter.

He knew of one other, however, who might have answers, perhaps even a few gathered in pillow talk with Verlaine.

Leyden found An San Kee seated before a long table, cataloging plants under high magnification. Using gloves that regressed into tweezer-like appendages, she flash-froze seeds, pods, fruits, tubers, roots, leaves, and stalks, murmuring information into a DataHed clipped to her arm. She looked absolutely content.

Kee looked up at him. "What's the latest? How much time do we have left?"

"Hard to say. Except we're running out fast."

Kee looked around at the stacks of living and cryogenic samples. "Will we be able to keep what we have already collected?"

"I've insisted on that as a minimum basis for our recognition of the Ghibelline-Taranazuka agreement. They want the right to inspect all samples, and remove any that they feel infringe on their own agreement. In other words, anything valuable would probably have to go."

"Can we refuse to cooperate with them?"

"Braga has made it clear that his mercs are prepared to move against us at any time."

Kee shook her head. "That can't be. There is so much. . . richness here. For everyone. A lifetime of botanical study alone. I talked with one of their researchers—she is as excited and as eager to cooperate as I am. She also seems to have formed a friendship with one of the Ghibelline in particular."

"Good. Tell her and her new friend to talk to Braga, and to Shinsato for that matter."

"I will."

Leyden knelt on one knee so that he was at eye level with Kee, who had the husk of a brilliantly colored beetle with enormous mandibles pinned to her tunic.

"There is a small matter I wanted to discuss with you."

"Yes?"

"Nice brooch, by the way."

"Thank you. I like it. My understanding is this species allows itself to be consumed whole by a certain type of snake and then lays its eggs in the snake's stomach. When the larvae hatch, they grow these large mandibles and eat their way out. Isn't that fascinating?"

"Charming. . . and chilling, Kee. What are the odds that there's something out there that wants to chew its way out of *our* stomachs?"

"That's a good question," she said. "Is this beetle's life cycle unique, or is it the pattern for a number of insect species here?" She smiled at him. "You see how wonderful this place is, how many questions there are to be answered?"

"I do."

"All right. I'm digressing here, aren't I? You had a question."

"Why exactly *are* we here?" he asked.

"What do you mean?"

"Is Eëlios simply one big pharmacy? Is that all there is to Trans-Illium and this expedition? And is that why the Taranazuka are here?"

Kee slowly extracted her hands from her manipulator gloves. "Yes, this dreary business. What are you suggesting? That Trans-Illium itself is just a front for the triads? That we're really only here to export Mostera or some other illegal narcotic back to the Illium."

"Conceivable. Imagine the growth potential, the profit, if Looking Glass were to rival Black Dust as the Illium drug of choice."

An San Kee looked disgusted. If she had clearly considered the possibility, she had chosen to look away and focus instead on her unparalleled garden of delights.

"Do you believe this?" she asked.

"A few days ago, maybe. Today, I'm not so sure that Looking Glass can be the explanation. Not for the risk of a full-scale chaebol war. A simple scientific expedition to collect and research bio samples, that might explain JKH2 backing Trans-Illium on the cheap, But it doesn't explain the Taranazuka. Why would they bribe or otherwise buy their way to Eëlios after the League had granted the exclusive license to us? Something is missing."

He patted her hand "I thought you might know what it was. Or been told something during a late-night talk."

Kee made a face at him and pushed her hands back into her gloves. "No, Verlaine doesn't share his secrets in our bed, which is fine with me, because I'm so tired at night that I can barely — never mind. I think you should consider something else.

"What?"

"Not what. Who. Hawkwood."

"What about him?"

Kee bent over her next specimen. "When Trans-Illium decided to recruit a negotiator, it was Tribune Hawkwood who suggested your name. Not Tirun."

◆

Braga was already sitting impatiently at the conference table, digging his fingernails into the wood, when Leyden returned.

"The Honorable Shinsato has instructed me to conclude these talks now, on the terms already set forth." Braga said.

Leyden had heard variations of this opening before. "Yes, of course. I share your eagerness. There are, however. . ."

"Never mind," Braga said, allowing a grim smile to crack his unyielding face. "We have someone to assist us in bringing matters to a close."

Leyden looked up. Suslov.

She had on a uniform virtually identical to those she had worn for Trans-Illium, except that now it carried the insignia of the inward spiraling nebula, corporate logo of the Taranazuka. She looked tired; the work of a double agent must be quite exhausting.

"No further negotiations," she said flatly. "All terms must be agreed to unconditionally. Acknowledge the terms of the Ghibelline-Taranazuka agreement. Surrender all weapons immediately. Report to a location that we will designate where Trans-Illium members will be held for the duration of the cycle. And finally, recognize the authority of the Ghibelline in all matters pertaining to Eëlian-Illium relations. There will be no further discussion. Failure to agree will result in an immediate assault to enforce these terms."

Leyden ignored her and turned to Braga. "We do not recognize the authority of this individual. She has betrayed us all, and directly or indirectly, caused the death of members of our mission."

Braga smirked, freed of any pretense or formality. "Recognize her or not, Leyden. Doesn't matter to me. I'd as soon blow all of you out of the treetops as waste another breath on you. These are the terms."

He left with the Ghibelline contingent. Nouvé and he Guelph remained away from the table and Leyden found himself alone with Suslov.

"No more time," Suslov said, stone-faced, not even a twitch. "In three more standard weeks, the cycle ends and we burn back to the Illium."

Leyden stared at her. It was almost unbelievable to recall that they made love or had sex, depending on your definition. Their past intimacy made her even more alien to his eyes than if she were a stranger sitting in front of him. Perhaps he hadn't just been deluded by the women in his life but, quite literally, out of his fucking mind.

"It was all you, wasn't it?" he said. "Except for Mkeki and Modrescu trying to hijack drug shipments for Cold Moon. You inserted the logic bomb that sabotaged the Drop, killed Cabenza, gave the Taranazuka our exact location on the Whitebone. Even managed to cut open the carrying case so that all the remaining munitions for the Dragon fell out. Then capped it off by faking your own death. Nicely done."

Suslov remained expressionless.

Leyden continued. "The rich girl from Ohzumé who became a freelance soldier. The soldier who became a chaebol mercenary. The mercenary who killed and betrayed us all." Leyden smiled. "I'd say that the Taranazuka got their money's worth. I trust you charged a high enough fee. What do lies and betrayals go for these days?"

"Betrayal," she said. "Don't be so melodramatic, Leyden. And quit taking things so personally. This is business. Chaebol business. I'm hired to provide a service. Which all I'm doing. My client just happens to be the Taranazuka."

"Murder isn't generally recognized as a mercenary function. Even among the chaebols." Leyden paused. "Why was it necessary to kill Cabenza?"

"Does that matter now?"

"I figure that he accidently found something suspicious aboard the *Balliol*. Maybe something that indicated you were planning to sabotage the Drop."

"Close enough," Suslov said. "He found some messages from the Taranazuka. Nothing very specific, but they related to an unauthorized software transfer. I couldn't risk it."

"Why not me? You could have pulled a knife across my throat any number of times."

"You?" Suslov indulged in a small smile. "You didn't have a clue. Cabenza was a problem. You never were, my sweet."

"And if I become a problem now?"

"Don't. Just don't. Agree to our terms and no one else needs to be hurt."

"You mean like Mkeki? The Saar are picking their teeth with her bones even as we speak."

"Hawkwood should have used better judgment. She might have been a bargaining chip — you have so few."

"What? No tears for latest bedmate?"

Suslov gave him a puzzled look. "Want to know if she was better in the sack than you, Leyden? More imaginative, I'll give her that."

"I'll bet. All those piercings."

Suslov laughed. "Oh Leyden, poor baby. You actually think you can bait me the way you did Shinsato?"

"Worth a try."

"Don't waste your energy. I'm a professional here to do a job."

"Which apparently includes drug trafficking."

"Which involves taking a small but invaluable ecosystem through the Illium. Not even unprecedented, as you well know. But we have no interest in Looking Glass. Taranazuka needed outside investors, that's all."

"And those would include Cold Moon."

"We know nothing about triads. Our arrangements are with several individual and corporate investors. What they choose to do with Looking Glass is their business. If they're dealing with the triads, so be it. We are simply providing transportation and research in return for their investment. Straightforward business arrangement. Happens several hundred thousand times a cycle in the Illium."

"Destroying a planet is not business as usual. We learned that from Alnitak. Neither is corrupting the Illium League to get an illegal exploration license — and risking a chaebol war in the process."

"Leyden, just when did you become so conscience-stricken? What is JKH2 — a charity? You're here to exploit the hell out of this place too. Do the Eëlians have any inkling what *your* commercial agreements would have meant to their way of life? Destroyed as thoroughly as anything the Taranazuka plan. We're just more direct about this business."

An image of Sylla seared his mind, not so much erotic as evocative: the setting of the lovemaking. Their pond hung suspended in a fantastic enclosure, amid a bounty of greening, flowering vegetation, in a timeless march to the rhythm of the planet's double suns. That pond existed in the Fourth Zone, designated to be ripped away and transported to survive, in some fashion, perhaps, under an alien sun. It might even survive intact, depending on the boundaries of the excavation.

And yet, confronted with an Illium that always promised to open portals to new worlds, did it really matter? How many theoretical rainforest planets might there be out there? Three? One hundred? Ten thousand?

In such a universe, did the pond in which he swam and made love with Sylla matter at all?

"The question remains," Leyden said. "Why all this effort for an interesting but remote Illium world?"

Suslov stood. "Its been fun but I have no more time for you. The word is that Eëlios is worth the risk. Worth the investment. That's all I know, or care to know. We're running things now and you're not. That's the answer to your question. That's the message for Tirun and Hawkwood."

She started to walk away, hesitated and turned back. "I'm sorry, you know. Perhaps, in another place, things could have been different."

Leyden's turn to laugh. "Different, sure. Let's make a date for the Poseidon resort. You're buying. It'll be fun."

"Joke all you want, Leyden, but time's up. No more talking. Surrender now. That's the message to take back."

"Really? I think the appropriate message is, go fuck yourself."

Suslov ignored him and left.

Leyden lingered to make a few notes before he stood up from the conference table. Enough questions. He needed answers, lots of them. Time to see Hawkwood.

36 RONIN PLANET

In the expedition's main shelter, Hawkwood paced behind Chácon and Holmes as they conducted an inventory of their remaining supplies and weapons.

The expedition's remaining three Multiphase Combat Weapons stood in the corner, battered and with only enough power for a limited number of pulse charges and flechette shots. An algae-like growth infested several ISSUs and other pieces of equipment. The useless Dragon, without pulse charges or kinetics, lay in two sections next to the infantry weapons.

"Time to talk," Leyden said to Hawkwood.

Hawkwood wiped his hands and nodded to Chácon. Leyden followed Hawkwood out of the shelter and along one of the rope bridges running throughout the Guelph settlement. Leaning on the single strand of a twisted vine that served as a railing, they stared into the insect-filled light.

"There's nothing more I can do," Leyden said. "Suslov showed up and issued an ultimatum."

"As expected."

"We're out of time, Hawkwood. Time and options."

"Nothing more in your bag of tricks?"

"Empty. Sorry to disappoint," Leyden said.

"I would have thought the master of Toranga might have a few more moves to hold off the hordes a bit longer. You helped the Toranga Alliance Party run the Illium League in circles long enough."

"Why? Have we got a plan? Reinforcements on the way?"

"No," Hawkwood admitted. "No plan, no reinforcements." He wore a ragged League uniform, the last expedition member to wear Illium clothing.

Even Tirun had abandoned his relatively heavy protective clothes for the standard Eëlian combination of tunic, leggings and caälyx coatings.

"I have another question," Leyden said.

Hawkwood's face held a veneer of fatigue. "Yes?"

"Where the hell are we?" Leyden asked.

Hawkwood didn't seem particularly surprised by the question. "What do you mean?"

"I mean the planet Eëlios never experiences night. This place does. I mean that the planet Eëlios orbits a double-sun system in the Selucid Swarm, which has over five hundred planetary bodies. This place barely has a visible star system in its night sky."

"How would you know something like that?"

"I know."

"You were at the top of the canopy during the night cycle?"

"Something like that." Leyden waited.

"What's your point?" Hawkwood said finally.

"We're not on Eëlios at all, are we?"

Hawkwood continued to stare out at the jungle. "Well, no."

"Okay. Well, shit. Where the fuck are we?"

"A different frontier world outside the Selucid Swarm," Hawkwood said slowly. "One with a cycle that is quickly growing shorter."

"How did you manage that?"

Hawkwood wiped a hand across his face. "Keeping the destination secret was easy enough. Burning through the portal is the same wherever you're going. All we needed was a cover story, a relatively obscure planet with certain characteristics. Double-sun system and high-growth rainforest. Eëlios in the Selucid Swarm fit the bill. It's obscure, barely populated and quite distant in slowtime fusion travel from its portal. Actually, it's an entirely different ecology in many respects — more temperate evergreens — massive firs and spruce-like trees — and the canopy growth is only about half the altitude of here. But close enough for our purposes."

Leyden felt lightheaded, even though Hawkwood's details only confirmed what Leyden had known since he saw the night sky with Sylla. He pushed on the vine railing with all his weight to steady himself, testing its strength.

"But after burning through the portal, during slowtime, I spent time in the viewports like everyone else, watching the Selucid Swarm planets. What did you do? Rig up a digital display?"

Hawkwood shrugged. "Of course. This planet is only a week's travel from the portal. We basically flew an orbit around it for four months so that the slowtime matched that of the real Eëlios."

"And the people here? Calling this place Eëlios?"

Hawkwood smiled. "Have you ever heard their actual pronunciation of this world? We could have named it Raindance if we wanted. We just set up the word equivalents as we did for thousands of other unique or otherwise untranslatable terms. As for the Eëlians knowing where they are in relation to other Illium worlds, how could they? Even now, we don't know of more than a handful who have ever seen a night sky from the top of the canopy. Think of this place as Eëlios II."

"Well, well," Leyden said. "There are ronin worlds after all. Hidden not just by the chaebols but by the Illium League itself. And this is one of them."

"Ronin worlds. Don't get carried away, Leyden. Lots of mythology there."

Hawkwood's answer was not exactly a denial. "This expedition was planned during last cycle's expedition," he said. "Implanting translation chips, negotiating the Guelph deal to collect bio samples."

"Actually, we've sent three expeditions here during the last half century."

"Fifty years?"

"In the Illium League, *ronin* has two meanings," Hawkwood said. "One is for an unclaimed but inhabitable planet. But the original meaning is a planet with a dynamic or unstable cycle. The cycle for this place is closing, from twenty years when we first found it to four standard years between cycles today. Our calculations are that Eëlios II will probably stabilize around three years. Needless to say, a three-year cycle changes everything and makes the commercial possibilities even more favorable."

Leyden leaned over the vine and thought for a moment of what Sylla had done, simply falling over the side into the cushioning vegetation below her. He should have seen all this much sooner. As far back as Musgrave's Dance, when he realized that the buildings seemed far too weathered and deteriorated to have been built a mere eighty years earlier, which was when the forest planet in the Selucid Swarm had been settled. The inhabitants of Eëlios II had lived here far longer than anyone had yet admitted.

"This planet wasn't discovered and settled a century ago, was it?" Leyden said. "Derek Musgrave must have led one original expedition from Earth, through the first Illium portal. Back in Kirov's day. The people of Eëlios II haven't been here for a hundred standard years, they've been here for something closer to a half a millennium, haven't they?"

"Not many records from back then, even in the League's archives," Hawkwood said, "but they indicate that Musgrave was one of the early developers of lightship technology. We're pretty sure he worked with Anton Kirov himself."

"How many on the expedition know all this?"

"Several officers on the *Balliol*. Not the crew. Tirun, Verlaine. Me."

"An San Kee?"

"I think she suspects," Hawkwood said. "Selucid Eëlios, or Eëlios I, has had relatively little in the way of scientific surveys. And when we started this up, we tried to encrypt any of the surveys that had been done. Even so, we couldn't suppress everything — especially in the Quanta — and Kee certainly found some of that material on Eëlios I. But if she knows for sure, she hasn't said."

"I guess that brings us to the heart of the matter." Leyden said. "Why?"

"Look at this place." Hawkwood said with an entrepreneurial gesture that Leyden found more in keeping with Verlaine than a Tribune of the Illium League. "You don't think the potential here is worth the price?"

"Funny. Suslov said the same thing. You know, the biological potential of this place might explain a chaebol investment. Even a series of them. But it doesn't explain why the League has conspired with JKH2 to keep this world secret. It doesn't explain this elaborate fiction that we were going to another location in the Selucid Swarm. And it certainly doesn't explain why a second chaebol, even one as hungry as the Taranazuka, would risk a war to bribe the League and send a mercenary army after us. Much less consider the cost of carving an asteroid-size chunk of the rainforest and transporting it back to the Illium."

Hawkwood was silent. "All right. Why do you think we're here?"

Leyden thought for a moment. "I don't think this is a place that either the League or any chaebol just happened to stash away. I think we're here for something very specific."

"All right."

"One possibility is Looking Glass, that we're just fronting for the Cold Moon Triad."

"You believe that?"

"No," Leyden admitted. "I can see JKH2 conveniently ignoring triad activity. But investing outright in a new narcotic that will be declared illegal as soon as it appears in the Illium? Hardly. The last thing chaebols want are a dozen planetary worlds conducting investigations. Even the Taranazuka."

"This isn't about Looking Glass, you can be sure of that," Hawkwood agreed. "That was Mkeki's and Modrescu's deal. She slipped through JKH2's screening. And she managed to recruit Modrescu because of his personal resentment of An San Kee. We didn't foresee any of that."

"You didn't foresee much."

Hawkwood just shrugged. "It would appear. We misjudged the Eëlians that returned on the last cycle. There were four, all of them became very sick. Ulam survived. Two others died. The fourth disappeared and we assumed he died. Obviously we were wrong."

"I've heard," Leyden said.

Hawkwood looked surprised. "From whom?"

"Verlaine. Who else?"

"That was indiscreet, but I guess it hardly matters now. But yes, we have reports from Guelph sources in the Ghibelline settlement that they do indeed have the fourth individual."

Leyden said, "There's only one possibility left — that we are all after something else. Something growing in the Fourth Zone."

"Presumably."

"Don't play games, Hawkwood. I'm done with my questions. It's time for some answers, from you."

"When the League assigned me to this mission," Hawkwood said, "I was told only that it was of utmost importance. From the League's viewpoint, I had no need to know more. It may well be that no one on the expedition knows why we're here. I do know what our principal assignment is. And you're right, it's very specific. To collect specimens of a certain plant."

"A plant called Eëlios?"

"Yes. Apparently very rare, and very difficult to locate because it grows high in the canopy — up where you did your nighttime viewing. We already have a few cuttings from lower altitudes, but the Guelph tell us that the only place where it grows in any substantial numbers is in the Fourth Zone. Which the Taranazuka and Ghibelline now have under their control."

"Eëlios has lots of remarkable living organisms. What's so special about this one?"

"Wish I knew," Hawkwood said. "Tirun and Verlaine probably don't knew either. Whatever the reason, it's being held extremely tightly by JKH2 and certain elements of the League."

"That was the plan?" Leyden said. "We'd come here and collect our samples of the Eëlios plant, one specimen among hundreds, thousands of others. Go home."

"That's about it."

"Why do *you* think this plant is so important?"

"I'm not in the guessing game, Leyden. I'm here to protect the League's interest. Simple as that."

"That raises an interesting point. What exactly are the League's interests? And why, according to An San Kee, would an Illium officer ask for me, a former rebel from the planet Toranga, to join this expedition?"

Hawkwood straightened. "Let's walk a little. At least as far as we can go without running into any damn Ghibelline."

They continued down the rope bridge and onto a worn anchorwood branch, kicking off shreds of its flaking bark as they walked, its pungent smell filling the air. For a moment, Leyden thought he detected a trace of almonds in the air.

"The answer is perhaps less complicated than you might think," Hawkwood said. "And it has to do with Toranga in a way."

Leyden stopped in surprise. "Toranga?"

Hawkwood turned to face him. "For some time, a number of Illium officers had grown concerned about evidence of corruption in the League. The Toranguin revolt simply brought matters to a head."

Hawkwood hesitated. "When I was assigned to the ground assault against Toranga, I read everything about the place I could get my hands on. So I became pretty familiar with the political arguments on both sides."

"What are you saying? That you were won over?"

"Hardly. Too much of it was overblown nonsense as far as I was concerned. But a number of us felt that the basic argument was sound. The League's absolute control of the portals is corrupting. Suppressing research data on the singularities. Ronin worlds. Evidence that elements of the League are on chaebol payrolls. And at the center of much of it, this place, Eëlios II.

He looked over at Leyden. "The League sent me to monitor this expedition, to see what evidence I could collect. We needed a negotiator. You were experienced, and cheap — and after the mess on Rigel Prime, available. But you had also foreseen what was happening to the League. In the end, I recommended you."

"Those doubts didn't stop you from leading the final assault on Toranga."

"I'm a soldier, Leyden. I follow orders. And my concern about the League didn't mean that I supported the Toranguin revolt itself. Then or now."

"And you intend to go back and save the League from itself," Leyden said.

"As hard as that might be for you to believe, Leyden. The Illium League found me as a child in an Ohzumian ghetto. It's my life. I'm here to save my life."

37 BURNING BRIDGES

Far out on the anchorwood branch with Hawkwood, under the metallic blue light of Nevea Rising, Leyden felt the dull impact of explosions rolling through the wet Eëlian air before he actually heard them, followed by the cries of panic and pain.

Hawkwood was already running back toward the settlement. Leyden followed, but lost sight of him as they were swallowed by the surges of damp smoke from burning huts. In those first moments, he felt himself back during the drone attack on the Whitebone: pillars of water as pulse charges burst in the river, Ehrenberg's dead eyes, the drones as floating executioners.

At least the Taranazuka couldn't deploy drones in the close quarters of Eëlios's rainforest. A great sucking sigh filled the air and a thatched enclosure next to Leyden exploded into flames. Not drones, but Dragons. He could still hear the sabot casings crashing downward through the layers of vegetation. Another Dragon charge knocked him to his knees. In the distance, the dull stutter of flechettes shredded the air. He regained his feet and almost tripped over something. A decapitated body, Guelph, sprawled at his feet, the upper torso still smoking. He pushed himself away, with no idea if the body was male or female, child or adult.

Leyden's disorientation grew as the smoke thickened. In front of him, the rope bridge he had crossed earlier began smoking from the heat of a burning hut. He couldn't tell from what direction the attack was coming, or hear anything that sounded like return fire. In fact, he could see no one from the expedition, only Guelph. Some ran and called out for their families, but many crouched in mute shock. In just a few moments, a people who had mastered the intricacies and dangers of living high in the rainforest canopy were being reduced to total panic and helplessness. None of them had ever been subjected to an attack with flechettes and pulse charges, or even experienced a high-impact explosion of any kind.

Leyden knelt on the rough bark of the anchorwood path as another Dragon charge swallowed the air and exploded behind him. The smoldering rope bridge collapsed in a shower of flames and ignited the dense vegetation around it. Leyden backed away down the anchorwood path. He could see at least three other Guelph structures in flames.

A figure materialized out the smoke — an escaping Guelph — but it resolved into a Ghibelline warrior, his swirls of face paint eerily reminiscent of the markings of the Saar.

"Wait!" he cried out ridiculously, realizing as he spoke that the Ghibelline had no translator implant and understood nothing in Illium Standard.

The Ghibelline carried an Eëlian pike, half thrusting spear, half sword, and with a warbling cry swung it at his head. Leyden dropped and rolled to the side. The Ghibelline's momentum carried him into Leyden, who kicked at his knees and tripped him. Still kneeling, Leyden grappled for the pike and felt the sword edge slice into the palm of his hand. Leyden reached down lower and grabbed the shaft as the Ghibelline tried desperately to regain his footing. Leyden pulled back, hard, then thrust forward even harder; the spear point sank in deep just below the Ghibelline's rib cage. The Eëlian screamed and rolled free when Leyden saw another Ghibelline above him with a two-handed club.

Leyden reached over for the pike and warded off the first blow, but with the second, the Ghibelline knocked the pike out Leyden's blood-slick, wounded hands. The Ghibelline raised his club a third time, but his cry of triumph was cut short as another figure shouldered into him and drove a short sword into his chest.

Hawkwood yanked his sword free and pushed the body off the side. "Time to go," he said calmly.

◆

Kneeling over the arboreal pool, Leyden washed the crusted blood from his arms and soaked the poultice around his throbbing hand. Guelph survivors of the attack, several of them wounded, all of them in shock, clustered around part of the Trans-Illium expedition: Hawkwood, Verlaine, Zia, and Chácon. The others — Tirun, An San Kee, Bertelsmann and Holmes — remained dispersed at several similar sites, hidden from marauding Ghibelline within heavy growths of bamboo and broad-leafed rivertrees. The expedition had suffered only one casualty, Tranner, presumed dead after being hit point blank by flechettes.

Leyden poured several handfuls of water over his head. He could not find Sylla, and none of the Guelph had seen her.

Leyden felt sickened at the thought of how badly he had misjudged Shinsato and his motivations. He had no doubt that Shinsato wanted his victory, which meant domination over the Guelph and his arch rival, Cleanth; in fact he had relied on it. But to savor such a moment of triumph, the adversary must be present and accounted for at the public surrender ceremony. Leyden had played upon Shinsato's vanity, his hunger for recognition by the vanquished. Not this.

He had assumed, wrongly, that Shinsato remained in control. The Taranazuka, however, had no interest in anything as sentimental as revenge: they simply wanted Trans-Illium and the Guelph leadership eliminated so they could deploy all their resources in surveying the bounty of the Fourth Zone in the time remaining before the planetary cycle closed. Up to now, the only constraint on their actions had been possible repercussions back in the Illium. But that argument had obviously been dismissed by the imperative of the present: eliminate the opposition.

Although Shinsato still held authority over his own people, he had been reduced to little more than a proxy for much larger forces. This attack did not arise from the Ghibelline; it was the work of others, of the Taranazuka — Braga and Suslov.

His beard dripping from the moisture, Tirun appeared out of a wall of vegetation, with Cleanth and his ever-present shadow, Nouvé.

As the Guelph leaders moved to the water, Tirun motioned to Hawkwood, Verlaine, and Leyden to join him. "Send Zia and Chácon out with a couple of Nouvé's men. I want to know where their mercs are."

Hawkwood nodded, slipping quickly into the role of the coldly efficient subordinate.

"How are they?" Verlaine asked, nodding toward Cleanth and Nouvé.

Tirun pulled his beard. "They can't believe what's happened. Nothing prepared them for anything like this. The deaths. High-impact weaponry."

For the first time, Tirun seemed diminished from the larger-than-life figure whose sheer presence and will had helped pull them down the Whitebone and up into the rainforest canopy. Leyden looked around at the clusters of Guelph. Before the arrival of the Illium, Leyden knew from his reading, warfare on Eëlios was largely ritual, like an extended jousting tournament. The Guelph and Ghibelline usually didn't fight to kill or take territory, but to capture prisoners, who would then be ransomed back at a healthy price. Deaths certainly occurred, but nothing like this.

After sending off Zia, Chácon, and two Guelph warriors, Hawkwood returned.

"Well," said Verlaine, almost cruelly voicing the thought oppressing them all. "What the hell do we do now?"

Leyden closed his eyes, utterly drained, so weighted down that he wondered if he were capable of ever moving again. He had traveled all this time and distance to arrive at this miserable moment? He felt incapable of thinking ahead to the next hour, must less answering Verlaine's question.

From their burning entry out of space to the burning of the Guelph settlement, they seemed to have traveled in some kind of knotted circle: fire in the sky to fires in the rainforest canopy. Leyden remembered the one moment when he had been freed of the weight of this world: when he had let go and fallen from the anchorwood branch, through the trees to the water below. To Sylla.

"Options?" Tirun spoke in crisp military fashion that seemed to parody their situation.

"Run and hide, or give it up and surrender," Verlaine said. "Both genuinely thrilling prospects."

"Leyden?" Tirun asked, his massive head lowered toward him as though considering a charge. "We were negotiating some kind of deal, when this all happened. What can we expect now?"

"No deals. Braga and the Taranazuka are running the show now. Shinsato wanted our surrender, not our destruction. This attack means he's no longer in charge of anything. The Taranazuka are. And they've decided to go after us, even if it means a chaebol war later on."

Tirun turned to Hawkwood. "You agree?"

"Yes. This was meant to eliminate us from the equation. They destroyed the settlement, but they also aimed the attack at our storage. Most of our remaining supplies — NavComs, lab equipment, weapons — all gone."

"An San Kee?"

"She got away with some of her equipment," Hawkwood said. "The larger packages of bio samples are stored outside the settlement and may still be intact."

"What's their next move?"

"They could continue to try and hunt us down out here and eliminate us completely," Hawkwood said. "But that could be time-consuming and probably unnecessary. All they need to do is keep us scattered and helpless while they finish their survey work in the Fourth Zone and make arrangements for delivery of terra-forming equipment in the next cycle. Our biggest problem is that we've lost the ability to communicate. We've nothing but some personal communicators with a range of a couple hundred meters. All they need to do is make sure we can't communicate with the *Balliol* when it returns — then leave us behind for the next expedition to deal with. The big one that will haul out a chunk of the Eëlios rainforest."

Leyden squirmed; his hand hurt like hell. Where was Sylla? Was she hurt? Dead? "There's another problem," he said.

Tirun looked weary. "Yes?"

"If the Taranazuka are smart, they'll make an offer to the Guelph they can't refuse right now. Turn us in, or at the very least, abandon us, and you can go back and rebuild your settlement. Under Shinsato's authority, of course."

"Cleanth wouldn't agree to that," Tirun said.

"He might not, but what about Nouvé?" Leyden said. "Nouvé might decide this is the time to make his move — eliminate Cleanth, take over Guelph leadership, and win favor with Shinsato at the same time.

"That brings us right back to where we started," Verlaine said. "What now?"

Tirun stood and surveyed the scene. "We stay dispersed in groups of no more than three or four. Far enough away that we don't have to deal with any Taranazuka patrols, at least not on a regular basis. Close enough that we can monitor their activity. For that reason, we should consider allowing, even encouraging the Guelph to return under Shinsato's surrender terms. That way, we can maintain eyes and ears everywhere, including the Fourth Zone."

They all stirred uneasily and eyed each other. Tirun's orders were both logical and unpalatable.

"The critical piece of information we need is the location of the NavComs," Tirun continued. "Without communication, we're dead, or sentenced to remain here for five years or so. Once we locate the NavComs, we can launch a raid to retrieve as many as possible. Weapons, too, if we can find them. But the NavComs are essential. Disperse again, and hang on until the *Balliol* returns. Communication and survival, that's the best option we have now."

"Will the Taranazuka move on the *Balliol* when it shows up?" Verlaine asked.

"I doubt they want to risk a chaebol war right now," Hawkwood answered. "And if we have NavComs with proper encryption, we can warn the *Balliol* as soon as it arrives."

"If we find a way to communicate," Verlaine said. "We can leave Eëlios. A failed expedition. But alive."

Leyden felt a sudden flush of anger. "Yes, and a setback to your once-glorious career with JKH2. Not to mention your coffee chain. How tragic."

Verlaine looked at him calmly. "Important to establish the bottom line here. That's all."

Leyden waved his hand in an half-hearted apology. Verlaine had always been honest with him. Whatever secrets he kept about the expedition had been the official ones. And he had never disguised his corporate ambitions, or even failed to mock them. At the same time, Leyden had no doubt that Verlaine, crouched in the rainforest, was already calculating his next move inside JKH2, despite his ignominious return.

A great boulder of thunder rolled down the invisible sky above them and Leyden knew that he could time, almost to the second, the moment when the rills and drops of the remote rain would descend on them.

"What about weapons?" Tirun was saying.

Hawkwood shook his head. "Two pulse rifles, almost completely depleted. That's it."

"And this," said a voice from behind them. Sylla.

Leyden had to restrain himself from embracing her. She looked tired but unharmed. On her shoulders, she carried the two parts of the Dragon.

Hawkwood and Leyden looked at each other. "Where did you find that?" Leyden asked.

"Hidden," Sylla said. "I hid it away from your other equipment."

"Our thanks," Hawkwood said carefully. "But we have lost all the munitions for the Dragon. Pulse charges and kinetics."

Sylla looked puzzled. "Leyden told me the Dragon could fire almost anything strong enough — any material that could withstand its force field."

Hawkwood sighed. "It can. But there is nothing around here, with the right shape, size and strength.

"But there is."

The all stared at her.

"What?" Leyden asked finally.

"Anchorwood."

Hawkwood shook his head. "Anchorwood is very strong, but it doesn't have the density to be fired from a Dragon. It would simply pulverize it, blast it to dust."

"Not here," Sylla said. "Below. At the base of the anchorwood trees. Where the wood has been compressed for many years. The inside, non-living sections are no longer wood, but more fossilized, like stone or your ceramics. It is a place that those of us who are healers have long traveled to gather medicines."

"Even so," Verlaine asked, "how would we carve it out, shape it?"

Tirun turned to Hawkwood. "How many backpack kits have we got left?"

"Three that are in reasonable shape," Hawkwood said. "All with functioning lasers, as far as I know. If we could carve out even a few kinetics, it would give us something we could use in our raid for NavComs and weapons."

"It would be a complete surprise," Leyden added. "The Taranazuka are confident that we don't have a functioning Dragon at all. Which isn't to say that we actually do, yet."

Hawkwood turned to Sylla. "How long? If we show you how to use the laser, how long to travel to the base of the anchorwood and back?"

Sylla thought for a moment. "We would travel by the swiftest means, from this tree to the base of another. And rise again by a column of floaters vines. Two revolutions of Naryl, I think."

"We only need a couple," Hawkwood said. "Enough for a diversion."

Tirun said, "I will ask Cleanth how many men he can spare."

Sylla shook her head. "I would not. The answer will be none. The word among the Guelph is that he is most bitter."

They all digested this news.

"Who then?" Tirun asked finally.

"The fewer, the faster we travel," Sylla said. "I will go with Leyden."

Tirun looked uncomfortable. "Not Leyden. Cleanth has asked that you and Leyden no longer work as... partners."

"What are you talking about?" Leyden said.

"I think you know."

Sylla handed the Dragon to Tirun. "I go only with Leyden."

38 SPINNERETS

Sylla and Leyden stood at the end of the branch and stared out across a the vast gulf marking the boundary between one Eëlian anchorwood tree and another.

The sound of the wind pouring through the trees was like a vast waterfall. For the first time since the two of them had climbed to the top of the canopy, Leyden could squint into a slice of sky unbroken by leaf or branch, and clearly see the double suns of the Ginn. Nevea burned blue-white, so intensely defined that it seemed more like a polyhedron than a sphere. Naryl, larger but more distant, looked red and pulpy.

In the distance, Leyden could hear the inevitable cough of thunder. Soon the sky would thicken, bringing rain that would take a full Eëlian day to travel more than a kilometer through the canopy to ground level. The rains would cascade into the canopy and cloud forest, filling colonies of bromeliads and a metropolis of orchids and epiphytes. In rills and threads, the waters would flow down stems, drip off leaves, and collect in arboreal pools in their long march into the mottled light of the understory and its dense knots vines and lianas. In perpetual twilight, the waters would snake through accumulations of mosses and fungi where the dead lay and the Saar scavenged. Down the acrid bark of the anchorwood trunk, with its colonies of guillotine ants and flights of sky bees, and into the opaque waters of Blackbone Swamp.

After all his time climbing through a world where every space and every patch of light seemed consumed by a green growing plant, Leyden found this open space between trees an unsettling reminder of their extreme altitude. An San Kee theorized that each primary anchorwood trunk had its own biochemical character, and rejected any outsider plant or growth, much as the body resisted infection. Apparently, even the extraordinary vegetation of Eëlios hadn't solved the problem of crossing several hundred meters of empty space.

Leyden and Sylla had climbed to this spot at an exhausting pace because, as she explained, it offered the fastest possible way to descend from the canopy to the anchorwood base. He still didn't understand quite how, and was reluctant to press the issue since he suspected that the longer he considered the possibilities, the more likely he would resist.

Chewing a koa-koa leaf, he gazed across a heaving, sun-speckled sea of green. Sylla pointed to a cloud-topped mass in the distance, the front edge of the advancing rain storm. The Fourth Zone, she said. Leyden tried to picture the operation the Taranazuka intended: a descending army of terra-forming machinery that would carve out an entire section of their world and transport it inside an artificial torus that would be lifted to orbit and transported to the portal.

Sylla nodded that it was time, and Leyden stood with her on the quaking branch. She gave a quick hand signal and the Iksillas appeared. He couldn't tell the impact of the Taranazuka attack on them, although it seemed certain that a number of those attached to the Guelph settlement had been killed in the explosion and fire.

Twen stuck his tongue in Leyden's ear, climbed on his head, then leapt onto Sylla's shoulder, with Twon on the other. They looked like animated stone carvings from an archeological dig. Reaching into one of her innumerable pouches, Sylla pulled out several dark, irregularly shaped objects. At first, Leyden thought them wooden carvings, but they looked soft and carried an odd odor. Sylla pulled a slender white thread from one of them.

She looked up. "Glands of the spider hawk. Where they produce their webs. What would be called... spinnerets, I think."

Leyden felt uneasy as he began to comprehend what she planned. He tried to remember if he had seen, or heard, of anything larger than a glowbird or lizard getting caught in the web of a spider hawk. "You don't mean one of those could support the weight of a human being?"

"Not a single strand," Sylla said. "But you wouldn't want to get tangled in them. A child, definitely not. Mothers here tell their children that, if they don't sleep, spider hawks will come and take them away to their webs."

"Nice. Wait ...what are you doing now?"

"I'm twisting the strands together. Then they will be strong enough to support the weight of us both."

She caught the expression on his face. "At least I think so."

"Then what? Tie them to a couple of hawks?"

"No. The Iksillas."

Both animals stared at him, unblinking. Exactly how much spoken language the Iksillas actually understood remained a matter of debate. Most believed it was very little — just the words that coupled with hand-signals. Sylla insisted otherwise. With their rich telepathic abilities, in Sylla's view, Iksillas were simply uninterested in human speech, and remained quite capable of following basic conversations if they wished.

"I was not aware that Iksillas could fly."

Sylla smiled at him as her hands continued to pull the milky strands from the spider-hawk gland and twist them rapidly around each other. "They can't. But they fall beautifully. And falling is a more important skill here. As you have already learned."

She looked down quickly and for a moment Leyden thought she might be blushing. Between the shadows and her green skin, he found it impossible to be sure.

Leyden stood and looked out over the gulf between the two anchorwood trees. The wind increased, and the wall of vegetation that fell away beneath them blew in long blue-green waves. A great sighing filled the air, and he suddenly realized that the Saar must be mimicking this sound in their extended cries.

"I don't understand what we're doing," he said. "And it is making me very, very nervous."

Sylla looked up. Her scarlet-and-blue markings blazed in the mixed sunlight. "You have to trust me. Again."

"We don't seem to have much choice, do we?" he said, trying to read her eyes.

"No. And we must return soon." Sylla lifted the Iksillas off her shoulder one by one and swiftly knotted the twisted strands around them. They both scrambled to the end of a branch that hung out over open space and turned back to her. Sylla and the Iksillas exchanged a rapid series of twisted-tongue and hand-signal communications.

Hold tight. Follow. Twen's message bloomed in Leyden's head.

The Iksillas turned, and without hesitation launched themselves into the abyss.

Initially, they seemed completely out of control as they tumbled wildly through the air. But after several seconds, they flattened, revealing webbing that connected their legs to their bodies and stabilized their fall. They glided in a controlled arc, the pale strands trailing behind them, away from their anchorwood tree and toward the quaking continent of the anchorwood on the other side.

Almost unconsciously, Leyden moved to Sylla's side and gripped her hand as the Iksillas dwindled to the size of motes and disappeared into emerald shadows far below. Sylla tied off the ends of the spider-hawk strands to a heavy branch. Looking out, Leyden could see that, in sections, the threads remained twisted around each other; along others, they still blew free and separate.

"How do we know if they made it?"

"Pay attention. They are beyond the normal limits of their ability to reach us." Sylla closed her eyes and became still.

Leyden shut his eyes as well and tried to concentrate. He could feel the trickle of sweat down his left shoulder, the subdued ache of the cut on his hand that Sylla had treated with one of her special compounds, the sound of the constant breeze. Thoughts of the past were too crowded, the future indecipherable. He itched. It seemed unfair: Sylla had had much more practice at this.

Something tickled the back of Leyden's brain, and he felt as though he wanted to scratch the inside of his head.

Here. Ready. Come. Now.

Leyden opened his eyes, and as Sylla turned to him, he embraced her. He could feel the slightness and strength of her back and leaned down to kiss her. Her fingers played along his face and neck, and he felt as though he were already falling into a shadowed abyss.

She pushed him away. "Time to go. You first."

"Why me?"

"If you back off at the last moment, I can push you. If I am on the other side and you do not follow, we will be separated and fail."

"Have a little faith. I thought we trusted each other."

"'Trust but verify.' I read that somewhere in my Illium studies, Leyden."

He shrugged. "An ancient saying. No one knows its origins."

"But wise, I think. Now, time to go."

Leyden tightened the straps on a modified survival kit, which contained little more than caälyx lotion, rations, woven blanket, medications, and a small laser removed from a dismantled Swiss.

Sylla finished tying off her bewildering set of belts and straps; she stepped toward the end of the branch and motioned to Leyden. "Give me your hands."

From one of her pouches, Sylla pulled out a pulley of carved anchorwood with straps on the outside and a deep groove down the center. She inserted the spinnerets into the groove and tied the straps around Leyden's hands.

"That's it?" he asked.

"Yes. Just find a comfortable position for your hands."

"What else?"

"That's all. Just fall."

Leyden looked out over the sun-filled space and down the trail of the long, milky strands billowing in the wind. He could not imagine anything so insubstantial, the secretion of a small bird, supporting his weight, much less both of them. Believe in one impossible thing a day. Had he read that somewhere, sometime, far from here?

"You need a push?" she said from behind him.

"No." Leyden fell.

As he did, head down, eyes shut, he had a momentary flashback to his struggles to regain control of his pod in the first of many falls on Eëlios. The wind tore at his face, and the pulley whined and warmed against his hands. When he finally squinted, he had the sensation of green walls unreeling on either side of him, as though he remained motionless and the world was rushing past him into the sky. He managed to stabilize himself somewhat, legs flared, arms together and stretched overhead, but without the slightest sensation of resistance.

Leyden tried once to look behind him to see Sylla, but he saw only a glimpse of the Eëlian canopy accelerating away from him. As the spinnerets unspooled before him, he plunged into the cloud forest, his face and arms instantly soaked. He lost all sense of speed and direction, as though he were suspended.

The mist began to dissipate and he decelerated. Through the shredding fog, the forest walls began to darken as he slid into the shadow of the understory below the cloud layer. An opening in the foliage appeared before him like a mouth and he made an uncoordinated crash into a clump of williwaw bushes. Motionless, wrapped in vines, he felt Twen land on his chest and lick his face.

Move away. Sylla.

"You're welcome too," Leyden muttered, trying to determine if anything was broken. He rolled through the broken williwaw branches just as Sylla tumbled into their makeshift landing feet first and executed a precise shoulder-over tumbling move.

Sylla stood, laughing, shaking off fragments of vegetation, her face exuberant. She seemed, in that instant, a manifestation of the rainforest itself, a deity of the deep woods who had chosen to reveal herself to him. He wanted to reach out to her but remained tangled in vegetation, Twen excitedly scrambling over him with his sharp claws. He watched her, unconsciously and totally at one with her world, her scarlet markings the slim slashes of desire.

He stood finally, pulling off his pack and checking the laser. "Quite a ride. How many times have you done this?"

"Only a few," she said with a laugh. "When we have to collect medicinal plants from here. Otherwise, our world is so vast — there is almost never a reason to travel to another anchorwood tree."

"A few times? How can you be so sure it will always work?"

"Oh, Leyden. I meditated, prayed to the Ginn for protection, saw a vision in a knot of wood. What does it matter? Besides, there was no other way."

"Sylla. . . I want. . ."

Somewhere in the darkness beyond them came a cough followed by an echoing sigh of profound sadness. It rose to a cry of anger and loss and descended again to a whisper. The Saar.

39 IN THE HEART OF THE WOOD

The air wrapped Leyden and Sylla in a heavy brew of wet wood and the amplified cries of the Saar.

Sylla led the way down into increasing darkness relieved only by the phosphorescence of the mosses and fungi coating the branches. Once again, Leyden felt as though he were swimming deep underwater, where the interlaced branches suspended him as easily as an ocean.

A few invisible birds called out, and a collection of snakes and lizard-like creatures darted in convulsive astonishment at the presence of two blundering creatures from the high canopy. Only once did he get a clear view of one of them: swollen eyes with veins like shattered glass, and a crested head — clearly related to the night caimans the expedition had encountered inside the Mouth of Kronos.

The sobbing cries of the Saar continued to pulsate through the twilight but Sylla seemed strangely oblivious to them, even though the Iksillas themselves remained uncharacteristically close, twitchy, and nervous. They rested for a moment and Sylla sliced open an enlarged seed pod so they could suck out its cool water. Sylla had told him the name of the plant at least twice but he could never remember it.

"The Saar seem close," he said. "Not just close. But everywhere, all around us."

"A trick of theirs. They project their voices. Only two are nearby and aware of us."

"Only two. Sylla, we have no weapons. None. The laser would take five minutes to set up and operate."

In spite of himself, Leyden could see his hand trembling; the scars on his chest itched.

Sylla looked at him in mild surprise. "They are only curious. It's not often that we enter these levels."

"You know this?"

She patted his hand. "I know."

Leyden stopped and held her back. "Back with the bones. On the platform. You were communicating with the Saar, weren't you?"

"Yes. Somewhat. But not like the Iksillas. On and off, like a bad connection with one of your. . . NavComs."

"And now? You're able to reach the minds of the Saar out here?"

Sylla considered. "At times. And only the two that are following us. But enough to know that they are not a danger."

"Why not? We were attacked in Blackbone Swamp, and again in the bone yard. Why not here?"

Sylla spoke carefully; so many of his questions must be like a child's. Clearly, too, she wanted to keep aspects of her telepathic abilities hidden. The Iksillas had similar powers, of course, which enabled him to receive their most direct, uncomplicated thoughts. But he had not really considered the extent of the Eëlians' ability to communicate nonverbally, much less establish links to the great predators of the rainforest.

"Normally the Saar scavenge and hunt in the mid-levels of the cloud forest," Sylla said. "They almost never climb to our settlements. So direct attacks are very rare. But your expedition was a great disruption to the pattern of things. You were alien to them, not Eëlian in smell or appearance. Even more important, you appeared from *below*, which was most unexpected. Any humans they see almost always appear from above. You were seen as a threat and they attacked. In the place of the dead, they are accustomed to us arriving in a slow, ceremonial fashion. When Mkeki and the rest of us appeared so suddenly, it again felt like an attack."

"But you didn't just communicate with the Saar," Leyden said. "You controlled them. You made them turn away from us and the others."

Sylla smothered a laugh. "You don't *make* the Saar do anything. I merely suggested that Mkeki and the rest of them were the enemy, not us."

"Do they always take your suggestions?"

"Not always. But I am somewhat known to them. As I said, sometimes you get through, sometimes not."

Leyden listened; it sounded as though a Saar was breathing into his ear. "And now?"

"Now is not hard. I'm not trying to influence their actions. Only communicate the suggestion that we are not a problem, and remind them that, even if you are strange, they have known and sensed me before."

They continued climbing down into a darkening well. The smell of decay and fetid swamp water rose in the air when Sylla stopped on a section of root tangle as wide as a room, next to a black wall that Leyden knew to be a section of the anchorwood base. She reached out and pulled off a loose piece of pungent bark.

"Shall I paint your face again?"

Leyden sneezed. "Does tradition require it again, like the first time?"

Sylla stepped close and began drawing a careful line around his eye. "Oh, I made that up."

Leyden jerked. "What?"

"Be still," she said. "Not the prayer. But this." She smiled as she drew the line down the side of his head to his neck, licking her fingers and smearing the line to make it thicker. She could have been writing a "Kick Me" sign in Eëlian for all he knew.

"Why?"

"I was curious." They touched noses. "I wanted to get a better look at you. Both you and Kee, but especially you, after those days of watching you as nothing but a lump of bees. See up close the people I had only watched and read about — in the Quanta, or the bone records."

Sylla held him at arms length to inspect her work, then began on the other side of his face.

"Bones?"

She gave him a look. *Clueless*, it said.

"We live at the top of a rainforest, in constant heat and humidity, where anything that is too slow or dead is consumed by a living organism of some kind. We have no materials impervious to dampness for long-term storage except anchorwood and bone."

"I see."

Sylla stepped back to examine her work. "I doubt it. I may be your exotic interest right now. . ."

"Stop it. That's neither true nor fair, you know that."

She pinched his nose. "Just another man. Hungry and curious."

"Is that how you see me?"

"Perhaps. But remember, you are — were — equally exotic to us. . . to me. Our time will come and go."

Leyden grabbed her hands and tossed away her chunk of bark. "Why are you saying these things? Do you already regret our time together?"

With her back to him, she shook her head.

"All right."

She turned to him. "I do not regret knowing you, Leyden."

"Well, that's a start."

She held up a hand. "No more. Time to go."

♦

With its narrow, wedge-shaped entrance, the anchorwood cave felt claustrophobic. Leyden and Sylla, lights attached to their shoulders, had crawled through a twisting passageway for more than twenty meters before reaching the end, a slightly wider space under an oppressively low ceiling. Such caves honeycombed the vast lower sections of the anchorwood, along with splits and fissures and exposed areas where whole sections of bark and wood had torn away. As they pulled themselves and their packs deeper into the trunk, Leyden sensed himself penetrating time, moving through decades, perhaps centuries through which the tree had expanded steadily in circumference as it reached toward the suns, each centimeter a slow, mute contest against the strangler tree that encircled and raced upward with it.

As it grew, its base compacted and fractured under its weight, like the base of a mountain, and the cave wood felt as hard as the ceramic alloys used as basic Illium building materials. The cave was almost lifeless as well, to Leyden's relief. He saw that none of Eëlios's life forms had managed to establish a niche on its unforgiving surfaces.

He detached one of his shoulder lights and scanned the interior space. The wood recorded the steady march of rings marking the tree's growth, much as trees from any other inhabited world. But nothing in the Illium rivaled the anchorwood's size and age.

Leyden turned as Sylla handed the laser through to him. As he set it up, she pointed to carvings along one of the walls, obscure hieroglyphic symbols.

"The marks of those who have come here before," she said.

He looked at them more closely. Some seemed pictographic; in fact, he recognized a stylized image of a Saar and a glowbird. Several were clearly representations of anchorwood itself. But the others appeared more abstract and resembled nothing he had seen in the Guelph settlement.

"Whose are they?"

Sylla pointed. "This one is mine. The others belong to several healers who have also descended here."

"Your names? Just graffiti?"

"Not just that." Sylla traced the columns of markings with her finger. "These are records of the special plants we collect here. See? This shows the location in relation to this section of the tree. The others name the plant and its properties with symbols known only to the healers."

"And this passed down from generation to generation? From your parents and grandparents?"

Sylla looked at him oddly. "From my mother, yes, and other teachers."

He turned back to the laser, already preset to burn out lumpy, roughly cylindrical chunks of compressed wood to be used as non-explosive kinetic charges for the Dragon. As long as they fit inside the goddamn thing, Hawkwood had said, the Dragon's magnetic resonance buildup would blast it out of the tube. But only an actual firing would determine if a projectile made of anchorwood would stay intact, or dissolve into dust.

After he began his first burn, Leyden had little doubt that an anchorwood kinetic would hold: the wood was extraordinarily dense and cutting it proved to be slow tiring work. Even trading places with Sylla, they had carved only four by the deadline Hawkwood had given them. They stayed on, trying to excavate at least two more, the maximum number they could easily carry back up to the canopy. Leyden's shoulders ached and his palm throbbed where the Ghibelline warrior had cut him. He would need Sylla's soothing medication again soon. The bitter smell of burning anchorwood filled the cave.

He took a shallow breath and resumed his cut. Focus and patience, he repeated to himself in what had become a silent mantra. Was there a point to this? Hawkwood had made clear that he, not Leyden, would handle the Dragon this time. When he did, the mercs would slip in and salvage what weapons and equipment they could. All of them would then scatter into the canopy to avoid hunting parties of Taranazuka mercs and Ghibelline warriors. What a pathetic end to the expedition, he thought, even if An San Kee managed to salvage a few of her beloved bio specimens.

As for the future, Leyden tried to erase any thoughts of that troublesome subject, even assuming he survived. He would be fortunate to receive anything, he suspected, much less the fifty thousand talons that Tirun had offered him on Rigel Prime. He had few allies or friends who could afford to be seen with him — much less employ him — and Toranguin and Taranazuka agents would be monitoring his actions. Leyden could see now why the myth of hidden planets, Ronin worlds, whether held by the League or the chaebols, would hold so much appeal.

The portals opened new worlds to the Illium Archipelago; a Ronin world like Eëlios offered a new life.

"Watch your cut," Sylla said.

Leyden shook his head again. Focus. Another minute and their final anchorwood kinetic, hot, darkly marbled and smoking, fell to their feet. It looked as though he had cut out something's heart. When he tried to pick it up, it burned his hands; he cursed and dropped it. Sylla wrapped it in a piece of cloth and placed it in a backpack,.

"I have something for your hands," she said. "We will go now to a place where we can rest."

Leyden held out his palm. "And the cut."

She touched it with her fingertips. "Yes. And your cut."

◆

They climbed to a catch basin that looked like an eroded stone ruin where they washed in the tepid water. It showed signs of long use: a ragged piece of netting for climbing, flattened branches, a neglected hut with vine-woven siding and roof — all items that Leyden recognized instinctively as the modest signatures of a transient Eëlian settlement.

After unrolling their sleeping blankets in the hut, Sylla collected williwaw fruit and several dark-shelled nuts. She reapplied a poultice to Leyden's aching hand, and then ground the nuts into a powder, adding oil and spices from the collection of pouches on her belt. She scooped the resulting paste onto a large leaf with chunks of dried Eëlian flatbread and williwaw. Leyden sliced up the williwaw, a staple he had eaten since his recovery from the Saar attack. The paste, however, held a flavor that reminded him of the island garlics of Arishima.

As they sat outside the entrance, Leyden touched her hair. "When the lightship comes for us," he said, "we will leave together."

Sylla studied him. "That's not possible. You know that."

He leaned over and touched her eyes, nose, mouth, and chin — once, twice.

"Sylla, listen. I may not know Eëlios, but I do know this — you have cared for me, and guided me from the moment I set foot here. Now it's my turn. You were given by the Ghibelline to the Guelph as some sort of consort to Cleanth. He is aware, in some fashion, of us. Tell me, what will he do now?"

She pulled away and bowed her head. "All the Guelph are under attack from these off-worlders. Cleanth's feelings about me are unimportant."

"Are they?" Leyden said. All he could see of her was the top of her tousled hair.

"Let's say that our expedition hides away and manages to leave Eëlios. The Guelph come to terms with Shinsato. What happens to you? Cleanth says that you belong to him — and yet you have disobeyed him. Worse, he loses face with his people. That on top of defeat at the hands of the Ghibelline. On any world I have ever known, this would mean that his position as leader is in great danger. It may already be too late. For all I know Nouvé is already plotting to replace him as headman. So, I ask again, what might happen to you when we leave?"

"Perhaps I will be punished" she said. "It is of no consequence. Besides, you will be gone."

Leyden reached across gripped her shoulders. "No. That's not acceptable. Either that you are harmed or that I should leave without you."

"Acceptable, unacceptable. Quit sounding like a negotiator. I cannot leave Eëlios. There is no point in talking about this."

He reached for her. "But everything has changed now. Come away with me."

"Please stop," she said. "Don't make me break my heart over you."

She turned away, crying silent tears. So was he for that matter. Tears seemed to be universal, on every world, in every culture, as far as he knew.

"I have no wish to break your heart."

"Then leave it where it is," Sylla said. "Let both us be hungry and curious and exotic and strange to each other. And then it will end however it ends. As survivors or not."

"Sylla, you saved. . ."

"Stop." She was sobbing openly now. "I don't need you to save me in return. I didn't come to you to be saved."

He moved toward her again but she scrambled backward, away from the hut entrance and into a bush with trumpet-shaped flowers that hung over the pool.

"Don't," she wailed. "Don't come closer. Don't touch me."

Leyden closed his eyes, listening to the gently falling waters accompany Sylla's tears.

When her crying subsided, he spoke without looking up at her.

"Just take a minute and think about where things are now. I know this is the only home you have known, but now it is disappearing. There is nothing for you here anymore. The Guelph are destroyed, at least for the time being. Even if they were restored somehow, under the control of the Ghibelline, your situation would remain dangerous, with or without Cleanth. You said so yourself. Besides, I couldn't stand the thought of you going back to him."

He could hear Sylla blow her nose and splash water on her face.

"Don't try to be diplomatic and logical with me, Leyden," she said. "Save that for the your chaebol people, or the Ghibelline."

"I'm not, truly. I'm pleading, any way I can, for you to think again. To choose me."

He finally dared to look up at her, the markings on her face smeared as if they had been applied by a child.

"Please stop, please," she said. "I can choose what I want. I can choose you, Leyden. I can choose to fall in love with you. But that doesn't change the world."

He scooted closer to her, but she held up a warning hand to stop him. When he looked upward, into the darkness, he could see glowing red-yellow eyes and bioluminescent shapes moving silently along the overhead branches.

"Stay with me," he said. "Love me. Change the world."

Sylla slapped her legs in frustration. "You think I haven't already turned my world upside down for you? Crossing these lines. Knowing how much I wanted you. Trying to understand where our boundaries were, our responsibilities to each other, to ourselves?"

"I know how difficult — "

"*Difficult?* You are an entire stranger here, Leyden, to me and to this world. And I know that you are in a terrible situation. . ."

"*We* are."

"Yes, we. But you are severed from your past, your home. You told me. I am *here*. This is my home, my family, with the weight of it all still on me — the position I hold with Nausicca in Cleanth's household. . ."

"Which is over now, Sylla, over. Or soon will be."

She dropped her voice to a whisper. "When we were together, in the lagoon in the Fourth Sector, I knew it would be a terrible mistake."

Leyden snatched her hand before she could pull it away. "I'm sorry you feel that way. For me, it was the first time I felt alive in years. I regret nothing."

"You know what I mean."

"I will concede a complication," he said, trying to tease, frantic to give her any kind of comfort. "And I am sorry for that. But a complication is not a mistake. And a mistake is not fate. No matter what happens, knowing you was not a mistake. Never. Not for me."

He stood and reached down to lift her, able to embrace her at last. "Nor for me, either, Leyden," she whispered into his chest. "You know that."

♦

He held her face in his hands, again tracing her scarlet-and-blue markings from eye to cheek to neck and breast. She had cried again and now both of them were calmer as he laid aside the remains of their meal and pulled her to him.

He knotted his hands in her perennially unruly hair and kissed her from mouth to neck. She seemed shy and hesitant in his arms, eyes lowered as he began unlacing her tunic. The top dropped away to her waist. The scent of caälyx lotion combined with a hundred Eëlian fragrances, from the sweetness of Nevea's Nectar to the bite of anchorwood bark. He knelt before her, hands on her hips, his own pale green face against her equally green breasts, her roughened hands stroking his hair.

Sylla's leggings, with her complicated belt, were a problem, and she finally had to help him. The hooks and catches finally fell away, and he held her lightly, as the first time, when she had floated in the pool of white blossoms. He couldn't get enough of her eyes; he wanted to see her up close seeing him, peer into their darkness and tumble in. Yet every time her eyes opened to him, he could only kiss them shut, again and again.

They toppled over from their kneeling position and Sylla wrapped her legs around him and nibbled on his chest.

"Show me," she whispered. "Show me what would please you."

"There is no need," he said. Any other time, with anyone else, he would have accepted such an invitation, both selfishly and reciprocally. But not now, not with her. What would happened in this next passage of time was less important than its link in a chain that led outward, to a real or imagined future of more embraces, play, and passion.

◆

Leyden sat propped against the wall of the hut when Sylla awoke.

She blinked at him. "We should go."

"In a moment," he said, smoothing her hair. She sighed and he could feel her breath against his skin. "When we return, we will find another way, another solution."

She pressed her head into him. "Leave it alone."

"We could sail back up the Whitebone," he said. "Live in a sod hut on the Chaga Sea."

"And do what?"

"Make love and watch the horizon — which would be a novelty for you rainforest types."

"And when you had expended all your hunger and curiosity on me — then what?"

"No idea. Maybe collect several concubines — that's allowed here, right? But by then, I expect to be old and decrepit and irritated at all the little grandchildren underfoot."

Sylla smiled. "You are a sweet silly man. So different from Eëlian men. Sweet and deluded, with your fairy tales. They may be enough to seduce me, but the world isn't going away."

"I do know a little about the world," Leyden answered. "Death and defeat are always out there. If that happens, so be it. But I also know that since I came here, I've lived more of a life than I ever expected, or deserved. And I don't feel like accepting the fact that this world has to break us, and our hearts."

He leaned down to kiss her nose, her mouth, his hands slipping around her hips until she pushed him away.

"Besides," he said, trying to tease, "no one lives forever."

Her eyes flooded with quiet tears again and when she spoke, it was the sound of rain descending, of waters coiling endlessly from stem to trunk in the long march from canopy to Blackbone Swamp.

"We do," she whispered.

40 LEYDEN'S CHOICE

In the vertical distance, wind and rain tore through the upper reaches of the canopy. But at the lower levels of the anchorwood trunk, where light and wind failed, there existed an ancient equipoise of moisture and stillness, a balance of temperature and chemistry that spawned an unchanging ecology. Here, where the light of the double suns was twilight memory, the water-blackened trunks supported a world where, on a thousand-thousand surfaces, life dug, crawled, climbed, fell, nested, mated, procreated, leafed, rooted, ran, flew, hunted, hid, consumed, excreted, spawned, grew, died, and regenerated. But in its own time, to its own rhythm and pulse.

♦

The ancient air, stiff with water, clamped over him like a mask, and Leyden imagined his face melting, the moisture remolding his features. In the stillness, he could still hear the prolonged coughs and sighs of the Saar.

Leyden wiped his face, his hands rich with Sylla's scent. She sat across from him, barely discernable in the deep shadow. He could lean forward and touch her, yet she seemed more distant, more unknowable now than any time since her voice had reached him through the buzzing blue world of the sky bees.

"Well," he said. "Maybe we ought to talk about all this."

Sylla remained silent.

"Sylla?"

"There is nothing to talk about," she said in a tone both indifferent and artificial. "I was making a bad joke."

Leyden ran through the catalog of ideas he had been contemplating for the past few minutes. His thoughts reminded him of a child's connect-the-dots game in which a recognizable shape finally appears.

"I don't think so," he said. "An exaggeration, perhaps. Not a joke."

Sylla stirred, pulling her legs up and resting her chin on her knees. "Perhaps not a joke. Except upon us all."

"You're probably right about that. But first, you need you to help me with some answers. Yes?"

"Perhaps."

Leyden took a deep breath. "It's not that the Guelph and Ghibelline of Eëlios live forever, is it?"

Sylla refused to look at him. "No, of course not."

Leyden thought for a moment. "But in Illium terms, Eëlians do live a very long time. Right? A fact that investigators discovered only after a series of expeditions, when they realized that they were seeing the same individuals after more than half a century. People who were virtually unchanged. And naturally, they wanted to know how you managed such a remarkable trick."

He paused. "Did you just come out and tell them?"

"No," Sylla said. "The translator chips had not been planted then, and communication was very slow and difficult. When we realized what they wanted, we tried to keep it secret."

"But that didn't work."

"They offered us great wealth, enough to travel the Illium at will. And to those who left Eëlios with them. Ulam, and the others."

"But it wasn't that simple," Leyden said. "Away from this world, the Eëlians became sick and died. My guess is that their aging process speeded up as well, to a more typical human standard."

"All those things happened," Sylla said. "And so you have returned. To find the secret of Eëlios again, and destroy us in the process."

"The secret has nothing to do with Mostera and Looking Glass, does it?"

"No. Not Looking Glass."

Leyden remembered another, earlier image of Sylla alone, communing with the rainforest.

"When we first went looking for Mostera, you had a chant, a prayer to Eëlios," Leyden said. "A prayer to many growing things, but also a prayer to one particular plant, to something you called the 'nameless one.' But it's not really nameless is it? It's simply the flower that has the same name as this world."

"My prayer was to the flower of Eëlios," she answered. "The blossom that grows in the highest places, where the canopy meets the sky. Where we saw the night, and you discovered you were not on the planet you thought you were on. That is the flower we celebrate with our sacred tea ceremonies — one that no off-worlder has ever seen."

"The Eëlios flower," Leyden said, "which grows most abundantly in the Fourth Zone. The plant which gives you such long life. Which is why the Taranazuka have sealed off the entire zone."

"So the Illium off-worlders have thought."

Leyden reached forward now for her hand, but she would only allow him her fingers.

"Let me guess," he said. "Last cycle, the Illium took back living and frozen plants, DNA samples, nucleotide sequences, chemical extracts. Everything they possibly could extract from the Eëlios plant to isolate its unique compounds. And what? Nothing. Neither off-worlders nor the Eëlians showed any longevity effect. Plus the Eëlians began to get sick."

"As we warned them."

"You did?"

"Of course," Sylla said. "I don't know your Illium worlds, but I know something of Eëlios and how it functions. The miracle, the blessing of our lives here cannot be separated from this place. We're connected in a thousand ways we know and a thousand more we don't. This isn't magic or faith-based. It isn't even complicated science. Basic ecology, where living things function as part of systems, not isolated organisms."

She lifted his hand. "Look. Look at you now."

"Look at what?"

"Your skin. The color of your skin."

"What about it? It's a bad shade of green, unlike yours."

He reached out to touch her face but she pushed him away. Perhaps she thought he was joking, but he wasn't. The richness of her caälyx-coated skin, its deep multi-hued, emerald color astonished him. When he made love to her earlier, he wanted more light, just a little more light so that he could trace supple shadings of her skin, from neck and breasts to her muscled back and legs.

"What about my skin?" he asked finally.

"Listen to me. Your skin is only the visible sign of the change that has happened to you here. Just as your skin has changed, you and the others are probably aging much more slowly, too. The rains of Eëlios dissolve and carry the essence of the entire rainforest. It penetrates every part of you every day. The Eëlios plant is only the — oh, I don't seem to have the word — the agent of change. . ."

"Catalyst," Leyden said.

"Yes... the catalyst. Take us from Eëlios and we are just another lost human being wandering from place to place."

"Tell me, then," he said. "Exactly how old are you?"

"Exactly?" she said. "I'm not sure I could say. Older than you."

"In years. Approximately."

"In Illium standard years, you mean?"

"Yes, Sylla. Stop it and tell me. Please."

"I am eighty-three years old."

"Well, then."

"In Eëlian terms, I am an adult but still relatively young." She cocked her head to watch his reaction.

Leyden scratched his chin. "I'm either in a relationship with younger or older woman, then — or both."

He listened to the outside silence, punctuated only with the distant huffing of the Saar. Their sounds seemed almost in rhythm with his own breathing, as if he were hearing himself amplified in the distance.

"Who do you think already knows what you have told me?" he asked finally.

"An San Kee, certainly, knows of the Eëlios flower. And the other, the one who was here before."

"The other? Tirun?"

"Yes. With the expedition that took Ulam away. I remember him spending long hours with Cleanth and Shinsato. Cleanth has talked often of the off-world, the Illium. How science will reveal the secret of Eëlios this time. The secret of our long life."

"Cleanth? When did he tell you all this?"

Sylla looked away from him and withdrew her hand. "I am one of his consorts, remember? He talked in those times when he came to me. Before I was sent away to become a healer."

Leyden rubbed his eyes. He had walked right into that bit of information. He had deliberately avoided learning any details about Sylla's relationship with Cleanth. Now at the worst possible moment, when she had transformed from an exotic creature to the woman he desired most, he had received confirmation of her physical relationship with Cleanth. Not to mention she had already lived a entire normal lifetime here, presumably including a lifetime of men. At least it didn't sound like she had been one of his favorites for long.

He wiped his eyes again. Don't go down that road, he thought; no more questions about Cleanth.

The promises that Tirun and the Illium had made on the earlier expeditions clearly explained the ferocity of the Ghibelline attack. Shinsato wanted not only control of Eëlios, but also the vast wealth offered to both him and Cleanth. Even living an undreamed of lifespan, in a place that some might call idyllic, didn't dull the instinct to accumulate more. Hardly surprising: the Illium Archipelago itself stood as a monument to the insatiability of the human appetite.

"But why?" Sylla asked him.

Leyden refocused. "Why what?"

"Why haven't the researchers of the Illium explained the truth? That our lives are just that — ours — and can only belong to those who remain here, breathing our air, living in our waters?"

Leyden looked once into those opaque eyes, understanding a little now of their paradoxical combination of wisdom and naïveté, age and youth. Neither Sylla nor he mistook Eëlios for a paradise, he knew that. For better or worse, Eëlios, with its rich, invasive environment, offered both extraordinary bounty and strict boundaries. If you lived here, you played by Eëlian rules. The Illium, by contrast, opened up universes to be conquered, and led some humans to consider themselves close to being demigods. And now they had discovered, on Eëlios, a possible source of the one godlike attribute that the Illium lacked: near immortality.

"Listen to me, Sylla," Leyden said, "nothing that is happening here has anything to do with logic, or truth. What you don't understand is that the Illium is founded on the idea that there are no limits. Today there are about twenty core worlds and hundreds of frontier planets in the Illium Archipelago. We find the coordinates to a new world capable of supporting life perhaps every decade.

"But the Illium singularities themselves, the phenomena at the center of the portals, don't follow any rules known to us and could just as easily reveal a hundred new worlds tomorrow. A thousand, a million. Reopen the portal back to Earth. Implode next week and leave everyone exactly where they are at this moment. Forever. We simply have no idea. We live by the portals but we don't control them."

"And Eëlios?"

"Those who travel the Illium Archipelago — the League, the chaebols, the explorers and homesteaders — consume planets like meals. Even a place as wondrous and unique as this. If it's worth settling, fine. If it must be sacrificed for something more valuable, so be it. There are probably a thousand thousand more waiting to be revealed by the Illium, aren't there? Sure there are! And, really, who is to argue that, were Eëlios destroyed tomorrow, a dozen rainforest planets wouldn't pop up next year?"

"Destroyed? We don't really know how much the Taranazuka would even be taking."

"No, but you yourself said that the Eëlios plant is only the catalyst for a complicated biological process that confers long life. The Taranazuka know that too, now. And decided what? To transport the *rain*, along with an asteroid-size piece of the planet, back to the Core Worlds. Maybe they will find the happy chemical combination that doubles their lifespan. Maybe not. But whatever happens, Eëlios will change forever — from weather patterns to the nature of life in the canopy — and probably not for the better."

"But they won't succeed. They can't. You cannot separate the living. . . from the source of that life."

"I know, you know, we all know. But it doesn't matter. Anyone controlling even the *promise* of long life will have access to power and wealth on a scale that even the Illium hasn't seen before. They might well dominate the entire Illium Archipelago, even challenge the League itself. I'm sure that's one reason Hawkwood is here."

Finally, Sylla allowed herself to be pulled back into his arms.

"All of this doesn't change anything," she said. "Hide and survive until your lightship returns. What other choice is there?"

Leyden kissed her eyes shut. Good question. Until now, he hadn't thought beyond escaping Eëlios alive and leaving Tirun, Hawkwood, and company as far behind as possible. No one could predict the outcome of the likely chaebol conflict that might break out between JKH2 and the Taranazuka. JKH2 presumably would take every action necessary to protect its investment in Eëlios II, beginning with lawsuits on multiple worlds and in tribunals before the League.

But the League itself appeared to be compromised. If the legal process reached an impasse, JKH2 would face an unpalatable choice: either give up its enormous investment, or launch a war. Without the element of surprise, and with ample time for the Taranazuka to prepare and collect allies, the chance for success would be small. Such wars had often ended inconclusively in the past, with both sides drained of money and resources. Often a third chaebol emerged as the biggest winner.

No, the issue would be decided here on Eëlios: if the Taranazuka left with a treaty and commercial agreement — and were prepared to fight for it — they would almost certainly prevail, and return in the next cycle to carve out their rainforest reward.

But Leyden didn't have to be witness to any part of this. He had come, seen — and failed. Sylla was right. Their vows, their caring and passion couldn't change the world — or a universe of worlds for that matter.

Time to move on. As for Sylla, even as he held her in his arms now, he knew that she belonged to this planet, as much a green hell as a rainforest heaven. He must leave and she must stay.

Sylla put her hand on his face. "Are you all right?" She made a face. "What a stupid thing to say."

"I may not be okay. On the other hand, I'm with you. Things balance out."

"Don't start..."

He grinned at her. "I know, I know — don't break your heart. Well, too late for me, isn't it. What about my broken heart? Don't you hate it when life isn't fair?"

"Don't make fun of me."

"What? I'm making fun of myself. Just think, we'll always have this magic moment... the rain... the smell of anchorwood... the Saar."

Sylla pressed a fragrant palm against his mouth. "Don't, please. Don't be funny and kind. Not now."

When he started to answer, she pressed her hand even harder. "Promise." He nodded and she took her hand away.

The prolonged, melancholy cry of a Saar bubbled in the distance, one that echoed the exploding sadness in his chest so closely that Leyden startled.

Unless he could find another way.

"Tell me more about the Saar," he said.

"What about them?"

"You said you had something like a bad connection with them, telepathically."

"Yes."

"But you could make it better, closer, couldn't you? Close enough to read their thoughts. Or them to read yours."

"Perhaps," she said carefully. "Concepts, maybe images. Not language. You don't talk to the Saar."

"But you could communicate. It could be done."

"It has happened, under Looking Glass," she said.

"And could someone else, an off-worlder, connect with the Saar in the same way?" he continued. "With Looking Glass?"

"No."

Leyden grabbed her shoulders. "No, meaning it can't be done? Or no, you wouldn't think of giving me Looking Glass to do it?"

"You! It would be too dangerous. There must be years of training and discipline to attempt anything as difficult as reaching the mind of another species, much less the Saar."

"Sylla, dangerous?" he said. "Come on. There is no time. No more time for anything else."

Leyden held her painted face, so precious to him now, between his hands.

He had only one choice.

41 EËLIAN EYES

As he had feared, Looking Glass turned out to be a vile brew, a thick green porridge with a clear, yellowish film on the surface. The smell distilled the rot of the rainforest into an overpowering odor.

But that wasn't the worst. Sylla skimmed some of the clear liquid into a grooved piece of bamboo with a tapered end. "This goes in your eyes," she said. "Hence the name."

Leyden recoiled. "You're kidding."

"I don't joke about Looking Glass. But if you've changed your mind, we will stop."

She held the bamboo ladle between two fingers, and looked at him, only a slight tremor on the fluid surface registering her tension. Sylla wanted him to reconsider his decision, of course. They had argued about this endlessly, followed by more hours with Hawkwood, Tirun, and Verlaine. In many ways, those talks had been hardest on Sylla; only she knew, in the most literal sense, what they were talking about.

But Leyden had been insistent, and in the end, convincing. Hawkwood had been the easiest to persuade. Tactically, he recognized that the expedition's best hope for survival lay in hiding and waiting for the return of the *Balliol*. But as a soldier of the Illium, the prospect of returning humiliated and defeated galled him in the extreme. With Leyden's proposal, he could formulate a plan that offered a chance of success, however small.

Tirun, as the expedition's formal leader, presented a more complicated challenge. A mercenary who, in theory, could find himself hired by a chaebol like the Taranazuka in the future, he shared none of Hawkwood's principled outrage over the prospect of a compromised Illium League.

Tirun had fought on a dozen worlds and long ago reconciled himself to the possibility of dying on a remote planet as little more than a hired gun.

Nevertheless, this was his expedition and now it was on the verge of total destruction. The Eëlios Biological Mission, after all, had promised to earn him the dream that haunted millions: enough wealth to explore the entire universe of the Illium Archipelago.

Verlaine proved the most resistant. The Eëlios expedition would be a setback, of course — Trans-Illium, JKH2, and his own career. But presumably all three would recover. A chaebol war back in the Illium might not be inevitable at all, he argued. No one could realistically challenge the validity of Trans-Illium's license; any tribunal would uphold their position. Whether or not the Taranazuka had bought off elements of the League was an internal matter. Besides, Verlaine said, looking at Hawkwood, if the Taranazuka had subverted the League's fabled integrity when it came to the messy politics of chaebols and Illium travel, JKH2 could do the same.

Leyden made essentially the same argument he had given to Sylla before their ascent back to the canopy. This wasn't simply another chaebol dispute over dividing the spoils of a new Illium world. What Eëlios offered, whether contained in a single plant or in some complex biological mix, promised to change human life as fundamentally as when Kirov descended into the first singularity and transformed it into a portal to other galaxies.

Eëlians might not possess immortality, but they sure as hell appeared to have the next best thing: longevity beyond the dreams of any human beings anywhere. The Eëlios elixir, if such a thing could be found, could well mean the establishment of a single chaebol's ascendancy throughout the Illium Archipelago. Its leaders would truly be rulers of the universe.

With that prospect, Leyden asked, did Verlaine seriously think that the Taranazuka would abide by, or even acknowledge, the rulings of any government edict or tribunal? And with their new power would come new allies: other chaebols, other Illium worlds. With an Eëlian connection, they could probably buy or intimidate any authority they wished. Or crush any rival chaebol, most notably his own, Jong Kirov Hathaway Holdings.

Leyden looked at them all. The issue must be decided here, now. On Eëlios.

◆

The first part of Hawkwood's plan unfolded more easily than expected. Guelph spies slipped into the Ghibelline settlement and determined that most of the Taranazuka mercs, and many of the Ghibellines, had climbed out to the Fourth Zone to survey and plant transponders. With that information, Hawkwood led Chácon and Tranner into the Ghibelline village to find weapons and NavComs. They successfully eliminated several Ghibelline guards with knives; only after their escape did the alarm sound.

By then, the rest of the expedition, along with many of the Guelph, had dispersed through the canopy away from the settlement. Everyone remained as separate as possible to avoid detection. With only a few NavComs, the Iksillas became their principal means of communications.

With Twen as his guide, Leyden had climbed alone. Pausing for a breath, one hand on a length of vine, the other grasping a small Eëlian pick, he looked down at himself: a green man with a scarred chest and face paint, climbing to a possible rendezvous with his own demise. Eëlios had transformed him physically, but also clarified his direction.

When he crashed into the soaked tundra of the Chaga Sea, he was seeking an escape from his past. Not now. Now he climbed not toward his death, but toward some kind of resolution to his broken life. He never meant to find such an endpoint here on Eëlios, which he saw only as a detour on the road to personal vindication. But his past life had ended irrevocably. His personal trajectory, his reputation, even his presence in the larger Illium universe had dissipated as completely as a passing cloud. Any measure of peace would only come from letting go — as Sylla had shown — by falling.

The Illium held hundreds of worlds and thousands of choices for living. That was both its wonder and its threat. Leyden hadn't chosen Eëlios. He had blundered into this place and now it had chosen him, transformed his body, and even more astoundingly, offered the prospect of love, however fleeting.

He climbed toward a fate that threatened to take his new-found life away. He climbed for a cause that, at best, would deliver Eëlios into a new world — ambiguous, seductive, unquestionably dangerous — but at least intact.

Twen appeared overhead, and Leyden scrambled to follow him. The canopy thinned, and the light increased in intensity. Now he was coming close to full circle.

◆

Their rendezvous point brought them, according the Guelph's best estimates, about half a kilometer from the temporary encampment the Taranazuka and the Ghibelline had established to harvest the Eëlios plant and explore the Fourth Zone. Unable to move any closer, the Guelph had to rely on the Iksillas and their fluid sense of humans and numbers. It seemed that the camp held between twenty to forty at any one time: Taranazuka mercs, Ghibelline, and a number of Guelph who had apparently been brought along as forced labor.

The hardest thing to pin down from the Iksillas involved the number of armed mercenaries, but it appeared to be almost fifteen, the bulk of the Taranazuka force. Long odds, as they all recognized.

Hawkwood ran through the plan yet again. The main assault group would wait for the rains to cover their attack. It consisted of Cleanth, Nouvé and twenty surviving Guelph, along with the final count of the Eëlios mission: Leyden, Tirun, Hawkwood, Verlaine, An San Kee, Chácon, Holmes, Zia, Bertelsmann, and Chapandagura.

Verlaine sat beside Leyden and pulled out his flask. "Got a couple of hits left," he said. "Might as well kill it. So to speak."

He took a swig and passed it to Leyden, who tilted his head back. Cool and sweet and straight to the heart, like Nevea's Nectar with a kick. How did alcohol mix with Looking Glass?

They began to hear the dull thump of distant thunder and a palpable thickening of the air. Verlaine looked Leyden up and down. "You've really gone native on us, haven't you."

Leyden looked both of them over. "You don't look so corporate yourself."

Verlaine's clothing, in fact, wasn't much different than his — tunic and combination long shorts and leggings, webbed belt and a kind of sandal with modified cleats. Verlaine's skin, however, had only the faintest tinge of green, evidence that, except for his coffee expeditions, he had managed to avoid many more soaking rains than Leyden.

"Not feeling very corporate at the moment," Verlaine said. "But in your case, why do I imagine there's a woman involved?"

"One who talks to the animals."

"Yes, we're so counting on that, aren't we?"

"Indeed."

Verlaine sat back and took a final pull from the flask. "You know, speaking personally, I've long considered the term 'true love' to be an oxymoron."

Leyden shrugged. He was long past any concern for the opinion of others. "What? She broke your heart in the fifth grade?"

"Something like that. Secondary school. I figured that if I became incredibly wealthy I could win her back, or buy her back for that matter."

"Sure. It's all a matter of market prices, isn't it?"

Verlaine looked over at him, his mouth even more thin-lipped than normal. "Mostly."

The thunder announced itself again. Leyden pointed upward to the thinning canopy. "We're just here waiting for the rain. Still time to get the hell out."

"And go where?"

"Warn Braga and the Ghibelline. Save yourself. Win-win all around."

"That's what you think of me, Leyden?"

Leyden slugged Verlaine in the shoulder. "Not now, too late. That's why I suggested it."

"Fuck you too." Verlaine squinted into the treetops. "The problem isn't them. What I'm trying to figure out just what the hell I might be dying for."

"I've seen people die for causes like freedom," Leyden said. "It's overrated."

"Point taken."

They passed the flask back and forth one more time.

♦

Twen led him to an isolated location where Sylla waited with her witch's brew of Looking Glass. The light level continued to drop as the hidden sky filled with clouds. The coming storm would not be a particularly remarkable one, but here, near the upper reaches of the canopy where the Eëlios plant grew, they would be exposed to its full force.

Leyden unenthusiastically stirred the foul porridge one more time. "Does Looking Glass have to smell this bad?"

"No. We add extra ingredients for that."

"Why, for god's sake?"

Sylla scooped up a spoonful and watched him choke it down. "We wouldn't want Looking Glass to become popular, would we?"

"Of course not. But it still tastes like shit."

She ignored him. "When it takes hold, remember your instructions. If you become too disoriented and lose control, you might be lost for a long time. Remember that among all the sights, the visions you experience, there will be one that is you. The image of your mind. You must find and hold to it. Whatever else happens. Hold to that vision. Now keep eating."

Leyden choked down half the foul contents of the bowl, Sylla the other half.

Sylla brought out the bamboo stalk holding the clear liquid. "Head back," she said briskly. "Eyes wide."

As she had warned, the liquid stung. For a moment he could see nothing.

"Count," Sylla's voice said. "Count and breathe."

Leyden breathed, counted, and blinked. "Whatever happens," he said between gasps, "Alive or hanging in the bone yard, I am yours."

Through his blurred, painful eyes, he could barely see her face. He wanted to touch it one more time but by then she was dissolving before him and he was falling into darkness.

His vision cleared suddenly. He blinked. The rainforest became transparent, allowing him to see through it to the horizon. Looking Glass hit, a searing jolt that seemed to melt his body and bones, making him more liquid than solid, his bone marrow transforming to lava.

And then, like the ancient pioneers of the Illium, he burned.

42 DRAGONMASTER

Leyden's mind shattered.

He felt his body fragmenting into thousands of pieces, each retaining sensation and consciousness. He accelerated upward, through layers of the treetop canopy as transparent as mirages, until he floated free in the open sky, underneath the assembling storm clouds. At the same time, he expanded outward like a blanket of air, floating through the riot of rainforest vegetation — bromeliad and blossom, vine and epiphyte, anchorwood and strangler. His consciousness spiraled down as well, along the massive walls of the anchorwood trunks into the permanent twilight and rotting muck of Blackbone Swamp.

Together, these thousands of minute, discrete sensations combined into a single incandescent image of the entire rainforest world of Eëlios itself. Time shifted to the pulse of the plant world, in which days bubbled as an insubstantial flicker, and only the stately pace of Eëlian years and decades registered in his consciousness. The movement of animal life flared like apparitions, little more than background noise to the true business of this place: the unrelenting reach of Eëlian plant life for the sustenance of sun and rain.

This time-out-of-time moment ended abruptly and his mind recoiled — not back to a familiar self, but to a another level of consciousness, of heightened sight and hearing and touch. He seemed to inhabit an enormous space still, filled with multiple images and sounds, all disconnected, without a frame of reference. His vision had become as multifaceted as an insect's. He lost all sense of his own body and its location.

Leyden could see the entire world, but he remained directionless. And utterly lost.

He closed his eyes and tried to concentrate. Sylla's advice had been just that: focus and listen. Don't rely on sight, not at first. The intensity of the visions would be too great to absorb initially. Hone in on sound. Then seek out a single stable image, first to find himself, and then Sylla — or more precisely, her voice and mind.

Something. . . a sound penetrated his consciousness, the clear flow of an arboreal stream. He tried to look, but the multiple images in his head — from the misting canopy to slick, water-blackened tree – confused him as they dissolved and shifted. He felt more disoriented than ever.

The sound of the stream became a river, a rapid, a waterfall, increasing in speed and force. Yet it held no water. He recognized what Sylla had told him to seek: himself as a presence that would enabled his Looking Glass-enhanced consciousness to cohere.

He must create and contain, release and direct this flow of consciousness and river sounds that now constituted his mind and senses. The alternative, he knew, would be the chaos of rain, the descent of a million fragments of a dissipated consciousness — sensation without understanding.

The stream slowed, and the sound of running water resolved into the sound of Sylla's voice. Sound and image, stream and voice became Leyden's guide as he attempted to assemble the broken pieces of his new world. But even as he did, he could sense the stream deepening, running more swiftly into darker zones, paralleling the underlying urgency in Sylla's voice as she sought to guide and steady him.

The deepening waters and the tone of Sylla's voice all held the same message: no more time. They needed to be prepared within less than a quarter of Nevea's passage — the time when Hawkwood, Tirun and the rest of the Illium-Guelph force would advance on the Taranazuka and the Ghibelline.

Are you ready? Sylla's voice emerged from the noise of a river rapid, as though he were back on the Whitebone. Even in the flux of his unmoored mind, Leyden could sense the doubt and fear in her voice; he also knew that her question was a statement. It is time, ready or not.

Yes, he answered. *Ready or not.*

◆

Leyden descended through the living layers of the Eëlios rainforest as both mind and metaphor, vision and visionary. With Sylla somewhere beside him, his enhanced consciousness sought the only other life form on Eëlios that could possibly even their odds and offer hope of victory.

Deep into the understory, Sylla's voice again connected to him. *Now, the hard part*, she communicated. Having barely learned to keep his Looking-Glass consciousness intact, he must deliberately divide it: from his single river-consciousness must come three, four, five streams. . . spreading out, searching for a connection. Hold that thought. Always a stream, always connected, always flowing as one.

He washed up against something. Massive. A great rock of the Whitebone, burnished through eons of flowing water. Not rock at all, alive. Leyden clenched his fists and forced the streams together into a single flow against the submerged rock. He connected, sensing that Sylla had done the same. They had found what they were looking for.

The Saar.

The impact of the connection struck him like a physical object, and high in the canopy, Leyden shuddered, lifting his head and howling to the trees. He felt the Saar's mind as well as the physical sensation of its body: an adult and, he realized with mild surprise, a female.

But the overwhelming sensation was that of the Saar's vast hunger. It wanted food, yes, but much much more. Somehow, the Saar desired more than the bountiful rain of the dead and dying from the canopy above. She wanted to consume the jungle, the planet itself — to extinguish its very world. The Saar, grown and experienced, knew these things to be impossible, and together, Leyden and the Saar gave a twin sigh of infinite sadness and cried out into the dimness. A label, a name emerged as well. *Krell.*

The Krell-Leyden consciousness sensed movement nearby. Another Saar, smaller and younger, quick moving and more angry than sad — not at all convinced that he couldn't possess all that he desired of this or any other world.

Again, Leyden felt the connection, and a name. *Alum.*

They were now three. A triad, yes. A weapon, perhaps.

Sylla's voice penetrated, and Leyden had the sense that, roughly as planned, she had found at least six other Saar. She spoke to them all, not in words but in a succession of images that tried to communicate the evil that the Taranazuka were bringing to their world.

This was the critical moment. Leyden knew that Sylla remained deeply uncertain about the reaction of the Saar to their call. Hawkwood had asked the same question: even if she could communicate with them, would they respond and join in an attack?

No one could answer that, not even me, she said bluntly. Nothing like this had ever been attempted before. The Saar were powerful, driven, independent creatures that, unlike the Iksillas, neither liked nor understood human beings. No one had any idea if they could comprehend the danger, much less be willing to suffer possible injury and death in an alliance with humans.

Leyden felt the stream of imagery pass through him to Krell and Alum, and he could sense their great unease and confusion. The Saar's primary problem was making any kind of meaningful distinctions among humans at all — even if they recognized Sylla.

But Sylla kept repeating one powerful image: that of an entire section of the rainforest being ripped away from Eëlios and taken away into the sky — itself a difficult abstraction for the Saar, who almost never traveled to the heights of the canopy, and could only understand the term as "the place where the rainforest stopped." For the Saar, in other words, the upper canopy marked the boundary of the known universe, and Sylla was suggesting that a portion of their world would be pushed over the edge of the world and destroyed. Literally.

She finished and they all waited. For the first time, Leyden registered the tension, the strain of maintaining his connection with his two Saar. Alum, in particular, was restive and would suddenly try to throw him off as though he were a rider on horseback. The back of Leyden's head started to throb. He had no sense of how much time had passed.

Leyden felt a sudden new sensation, as if he had a terrible itch inside his head, almost more physical than mental. Along with Krell and Alum, he cried out. The Saar were on the move, climbing upward through the canopy toward the Fourth Zone.

Sylla and Leyden had their answer.

♦

In the distance, muffled by layers of jungle, Leyden heard the whining blast as Hawkwood fired the Dragon into the Taranazuka camp. After a pause, he heard the impact; the sounds meant that the first anchorwood shell had remained intact and hit its intended target. Two combat weapons began firing in short bursts: that would be Chácon and Zia firing a pulse charge, moving, firing again, trying both to conserve their ammunition yet create the illusion of a large attacking force.

The firing stopped and the normal sounds of rainforest ceased. An Eëlian horn blew somewhere, undoubtedly Ghibelline, followed by confused shouting. A massive barrage of flechettes and pulse charges reverberated through the canopy as the Taranazuka returned fire. A part of Leyden's mind registered the sound with satisfaction. As planned, the Taranazuka seemed convinced that they had engaged the main attack.

Meanwhile, the Saar began to congregate. Krell and Alum climbed onto the anchorwood branch in front of Leyden; they were terrifying.

Krell was massive, with a scarred head the size of a horse; her physical presence confirmed the sense Leyden had of her solid maturity. She crouched on the platform and regarded him with an unblinking gaze.

Alum was another matter: smaller, snarling, and leaning toward him as though tethered to a leash. In his state of multiple visions, Leyden had a sense of himself through Alum's eyes: strange, threatening, somehow responsible for this massive disruption of the Saar's world. Leyden knew that if he lost contact, Alum, would likely attack him or any other human being within range.

More Saar appeared, five, six, clustered around Sylla, their polished, pebbled hides glinting in the storm's gray light. Alum turned toward Sylla with the Saar's typical sequence of cries, laughs, and clicks — a fusion of the Saar's impulse to devour her physically and Leyden's desire to consume her sexually.

A voice penetrated the noise of the Saar, but not telepathically. Sylla was speaking directly to him.

"Control yourself, and your new friend," she said, "or you'll have to deal with me." She gestured unmistakably toward her six adult Saar, who now loomed up behind her in a disciplined row of hissing, bared teeth and baleful black eyes.

Leyden shrugged. The strain of an actual conversation with her, along with maintaining his connection to Krell and Alum, seemed one task too many.

They dispersed, Saar and humans, and began climbing quickly toward the sounds of combat. The plan was simple enough: distract the Taranazuka with a feint by Hawkwood, Zia, and Chácon, who would employ the Dragon and the expedition's remaining weapons — then close quickly with the Saar, attacking before the Taranazuka could respond and deploy their superior firepower. The Guelph and the rest of the expedition — unarmed except for long utility knives and Eëlian clubs and pikes made of anchorwood — would follow.

Now! Sylla communicated. *Now! Attack with the rain!*

They moved upward through the high thinning canopy, and Leyden heard the storm tear the sky and release its first salvos of heavy rain. The anchorwood trunk shrank in diameter as they climbed, the branches fewer and farther apart. Leyden had to climb vertically with crampons and pick, his progress painfully slow as the rain lashed at him in gusts of wind, blurring his vision and forcing him to turn his head aside to breathe.

Alum had brushed by him and disappeared into the foliage above him. Krell remained just below, but he could sense her impatience at the slowness of his climbing.

On back. On back. For a moment, he thought it was a message from Sylla, then realized it was Krell, who stopped him with the pressure of a massive claw. *Quick now. Back. Join the fight.*

No. Leyden has almost died from his two previous close encounters with the Saar; he had no wish to risk another. *Go. I will follow.*

He looked back down at her. Krell tilted her head and bared a set of yellowed teeth. There didn't seem to be any room for discussion, especially as Krell moved up beside him and practically dropped him onto her back. He dug his hands into the leathery folds of her neck.

Krell bolted upward into the rain and Leyden could feel her massive muscles working like great machines. Moments later they burst into the Taranazuka encampment — a typically Eëlian network of platforms, netting and branch pathways, except that the sky was visible through the thin canopy. The rain fell with full force and the noise muffled the sound of the attacking Saar, and the screams of their first victims.

Leyden slid off Krell's back. Ahead of him, Alum and another Saar chased down a Ghibelline who had been foolish enough to throw a spear.

No! Leyden closed his eyes to try and send the message as powerfully as possible. *Not them. Not Eëlians. The others. The off-worlders.* The Ghibelline ran or huddled in terrified groups; the Guelph could take care of them.

Leyden pulled out his long knife and ran by Alum. *Follow. Follow.* He raced ahead through the pelting rain toward the sound of firing.

They had to reach the Taranazuka and attack them hand-to-hand before they could organize an effective defense.

Out of the corner of his eye, he could see Sylla and the pod of Saar keeping pace with her. Where were the Taranazuka? He couldn't see them, but he suddenly knew that Krell and Alum sensed their presence nearby. Both let out the Saar's signature sobbing wail, followed by a crying laugh and a piercing series of clicks. The rest of the Saar responded in chorus and plunged into the foliage.

Leyden both saw and felt Alum and Krell burst upon the first line of Taranazuka mercs, who were crouched behind branches firing out at Hawkwood and the others. He felt the sensation of Alum's leap, claws scraping at the body armor, biting down on the neck, the crunch of bone, screams cut short by gouts of salt-laden blood.

The sensation, the blood lust of the Saar overwhelmed him, and though twenty meters behind them, Leyden joined in shrieking to the rain and sky as Alum hurled the first body aside and leapt onward, hunting. Leyden wiped his mouth and was astonished not to find blood.

Krell, lacking Alum's frenzy, proved coldly efficient. Leyden had only a flashing vision of a terrified merc, turning to run before her great claws smashed his helmet with one blow, broke his neck with the next.

Onward. Quick, Leyden communicated to Krell as she paced ahead, seeking. They were a hunting pride now.

Two Dragon explosions detonated in front of Leyden, followed by the spatter of flechettes. Outgoing, Leyden thought, toward Hawkwood's location, which meant that the Taranazuka had managed to deploy their own Dragons, but remained unaware of the main Saar attack to their rear.

The firing of multiphase weapons swelled on both sides; Zia, Holmes and Chácon must be advancing, Leyden thought, firing the last of their munitions. An incoming Dragon kinetic smashed through a hut; Hawkwood had maybe one or two anchorwood shots left.

On. On, Leyden urged Alum and Krell. He caught sight of a Taranazuka and for an instant he had no idea whose eyes he was seeing through. Krell's. As she closed on him, the merc turned to fire, but too late, and with a chuckling cry Krell knocked aside the weapon and bit through his neck.

Leyden felt an incredible pain deep into his shoulder and again he looked down in astonishment to see that it was neither broken nor bleeding. Not him, Alum.

A Taranazuka merc had shrewdly positioned herself on the opposite side of a makeshift bamboo bridge and hit Alum in the left flank with a burst of flechettes. Roaring in pain, Alum started to charge the bridge.

No! Leyden commanded. *Stop! Drop down!* Alum howled and rolled off the platform just as the merc fired again. Leyden had no idea where he was in relation to Alum. He tried to look around with Alum's eyes. The merc fired and a flechette round caught Alum in a clawed foot; Leyden felt the impact but registered little pain. The merc was smart to try and conserve her pulse rounds, but misjudged the relatively minor impact of flechettes on a Saar's tough hide. He could also hear the merc shouting into the NavCom: the rest of the surviving Taranazuka now understood what was happening.

Not the bridge, Leyden communicated to Alum. *Up. Up. Cross through the trees.*

Alum crouched and executed a huge leap into overhead anchorwood branches and disappeared as the merc fired again. Leyden located the bridge and crept forward so that he could see it with his own eyes.

He could hear the sound of weapons fire moving upward: the Taranazuka were retreating in the only direction that was open to them, the very top of the canopy. The firing sounded more organized, and for the first time, Leyden could distinguish cries of pain from the Saar: the Taranazuka, too, were finding their targets. An intense light flashed to the side, followed by the heat-blast of a Dragon pulse charge. A section of anchorwood caught fire, and heavy white smoke began to billow through the foliage.

Across the bridge, Leyden saw the merc suddenly stand and whirl around. She guessed wrong. *Now*, Leyden signaled, and Alum, enraged and in pain, dropped from the branches above her. Leyden could feel the sensation as Alum's jaws slashed her neck and ended her screams. Again, he tasted blood.

Leyden ran through the smoke and rain, grabbing the dead merc's weapon, trying to locate Krell. For a moment he couldn't orient himself; she seemed to be staring into a featureless void.

Krell. Where? Krell shifted her focus and Leyden realized that she was climbing up a vertical trunk, into the sky, eyes virtually blinded by heavy rain. She, too, he realized, had been hit at least twice by flechettes fired by a cluster of Taranazuka in the treetop above her.

No farther! You will be hurt, Leyden signaled.

Krell didn't pause. *Hunting*, and continued to climb.

Wait. Leyden gauged the diameter of the tree trunk through Krell's eyes. *Don't climb. Take down the tree branch. Not them. The branch.*

Krell stopped and began to shake the treetop just as one of the three Taranazuka above her fired again and missed. Krell roared and pulled the trunk from side to side until the top was swinging in a wide violent arc. One of the three men fell out and disappeared into the silver-gray rain; the other two threw out his weapon.

Stop. They are finished. Stop. Let the Guelph have them.

Leyden doubted that Alum would have understood or cared about the concept of surrender, but Krell did, or at least comprehended the need for efficiency in eliminating all resistance from the Taranazuka as quickly as possible. She turned and scrambled back down the vibrating trunk. Leyden, distant but visible to the two survivors, raised his weapon and gestured for them to climb down.

With his own eyes, Leyden saw Hawkwood and Chácon climbing toward him, each carrying weapons captured from the Taranazuka. Behind them, he could see Nouvé leading the Guelph forward to take charge of prisoners, both Ghibelline and Taranazuka. Many of the surrendering Taranazuka were armed mercs, but others were non-combatant researchers, many still carrying collection baskets filled with white Eëlios blossoms.

The rain was easing when Leyden felt a stabbing pain in the back of his head that nearly immobilized him. He blinked and looked. Through Alum's eyes, now filling with blood, he saw a group of Taranazuka mercs firing at him. One of them stood, and even at that blurred distance, Leyden recognized Suslov as she hoisted a Dragon. He felt an astonishing flash of heat, then nothing. As though a channel had been switched off. He had just experienced the death of another sentient, living being. Alum had been destroyed.

A great cry tore through his chest, but it came from Krell, not him.

No! he called. *Wait! We have weapons. No need. . .* He found he was talking only to himself as Krell tried to shut off her connection to him. He understood why. Alum was her offspring, her son. He forced himself back into her enraged, grieving mind and this time she didn't resist.

Leyden turned to Hawkwood and Chácon. "Suslov."

He followed Krell as she raced toward Alum's remains. By the time he arrived, Krell had leapt behind a length of anchorwood as it absorbed a succession of laser shots. Suslov stood, sighting a Dragon. In another moment, Krell would be dissolved into the same bloody pulp as her son.

Not there. Down. Down and under. Then up. Now!

Krell snarled in Leyden's general direction and jumped down into the foliage just as Suslov fired and the anchorwood exploded into splinters and flame. Leyden fired a pulse charge and Suslov ducked down behind a pile of branches. He flattened onto the wooden pathway as the two other Taranazuka mercs next to Suslov opened fire in his direction. On his back, unable to sight his weapon, he switched to wide-dispersed flechettes and fired back blindly. The least he could do was try and hold their attention.

He heard a burst of firing and shouts from off to the side and scrambled to his knees. Hawkwood and Chácon had flanked the Taranazuka position and closed on them. They dropped one of the mercs; the other threw down his weapon and fell to his knees

Where was Suslov? Leyden crouched, waiting, then saw her scrambling away from Hawkwood and toward him, empty handed, having abandoned the Dragon.

He stood and fired toward her feet. "It's all over."

Suslov halted, gasping for breath. "It's never over, Leyden. You know that."

"It is for you."

"Listen, I'm going now, so if you want it over, you'll have to be the one." She wiped her face. "But you're not Hawkwood. You're not a killer. I don't think you can do it."

She turned away from him. In the distance he could see Hawkwood and Chácon watching.

"You're right," Leyden said, "I can't." He lowered his weapon. "But she can."

And Krell dropped silently from the trees.

43 CASUALTY COUNT

Leyden stared down at Suslov, dead at his feet, as the slackening rain continued to wash away her blood in a steady pink stream. The rain felt like a violation as it poured on her torn body and unprotected face. He searched until he found a piece of matting that he could use to cover her.

Krell and the rest of the Saar had disappeared, their sobbing cries diminishing as they withdrew into the twilight of the understory. The rain had suffocated most of the fires from the Dragon explosions, but waves of heavy gray smoke still enveloped the wrecked encampment, and figures appeared like apparitions as they moved across the area of battle. A group of captured Taranazuka and Ghibelline stumbled past, led by Chácon and guarded by three Guelph warriors.

Hawkwood loomed out of the smoke, three captured multiphase weapons over his shoulder. "Come on, we've got casualties."

"Who?"

"Tirun, among others."

"How bad?"

"Sucking chest wound. Bad enough." Hawkwood turned back into the smoke.

"You need a healer," Leyden said. "You need Sylla."

Hawkwood stopped. "That won't help, I'm afraid."

"Why not?"

"She's been hit too."

◆

Sylla, Tirun and several wounded Guelph, Taranazuka, and Ghibelline lay on woven mats as An San Kee, Chapandagura, and three Guelph moved among them with medkits. Leyden knelt by Sylla's side. A burst of flechettes had flayed her shoulder and back; the wounds already soaking through her bandages. The air smelled of smoke and blood.

Her eyes, clouded with pain, blinked rapidly, her hand hot and limp.

"I'm here," he said.

She tried to smile. "Leyden."

"I'm here with you," he repeated. An San Kee appeared and handed him a gourd full of water. He took it and lifted Sylla's head. "Here, now. Drink."

She swallowed once and lay back. "You cannot stay. You must promise to leave. . . Cleanth will punish. . . " Sylla closed her eyes, and Leyden could see her body begin to tremble.

He felt a hand on his shoulder and turned to see An San Kee. "She's barely conscious right now. Better not try and talk."

Leyden nodded automatically, and looked over at Tirun, his massive torso swathed in makeshift layers of bandages and anchorwood fronds. His breathing, heavy and labored, rasped in the smoky air.

"How are they?" he asked.

"Both are stable for the moment," Kee said. "Most of the others too. But we've just about run through our medical supplies. Right now, I'm very worried about infection. You have no idea how fast-acting these viral infections can be. We need a healer. We need another Sylla."

"Can't you find one? Where is Cleanth?"

"Right now, I can't find anyone else."

The rain fell as a fine mist and the smoke hung motionless in the still air. "We don't need the Guelph. We need the Iksillas. Where the hell is Twen?" Leyden took a breath. "Twen!" he yelled. "Twen!" No good, he thought, and closed his eyes. *Twen. Iksillas. Now.*

He repeated the thought over and over, like a broadcast signal until he felt a small branch thud down on his head. Leyden looked up into an anchorwood branch that hung down with the weight of Twen and five other Iksillas, all peering at him with unblinking eyes.

Leyden started to sign with his hands but immediately stopped. He didn't know the words or the signs. Besides, there wasn't time. Instead, he stared back at Twen and the others. *Carpal vines. You must take us there now. Quickly.*

No. The message was a collective and emphatic one, followed by an immediate babble that felt as though the Iksillas themselves had just scurried through his head. A moment later he felt Twen's single, clear thought. *Iksillas only. The vines.*

Leyden spoke, signed and sent his thoughts at the same time. *We have many wounded. You need us to carry them back. We must carry back many vines to prepare...*

No. Twen's message rang like a warning bell. Slow. *You are too slow. More Iksillas will bring vines as paste. Quick back.*

The branch creaked under the collective weight of the Iksillas, motionless, waiting for Leyden to respond. Twen had given him no real alternative, yet he and the others waited for his formal word. Iksillas often acted like willful children, ignoring words, suggestions, and commands alike, but Leyden had never felt his connection to Twen more powerfully than he did now. The Iksillas weren't attempting to communicate any reactions directly, either through signing or telepathically, but Leyden sensed Twen's emotional state nonetheless through the focus and intensity of his attention.

Go then. And hurry.

In a scurry of leaves, the Iksillas disappeared. Leyden quickly turned back and knelt again at Sylla's side. When he took her hand, she sighed and twisted restlessly.

"You're disturbing her," An San Kee said. "Go away now. At least until the Iksillas return."

"I want to stay with her."

"I know, but you can't. And you can't do anything for her right now." She pointed off to the side. "Besides, I believe Tribune Hawkwood wishes to speak with you."

◆

Hawkwood handed Leyden an elaborately engraved flask, quite different from Verlaine's, as they walked along a along a partially burned bridge, away from the platform with the wounded. Ahead of them, Leyden could see several Guelph slapping wet branches on one of the last smoldering fires.

The two of them stopped on the bridge, the overhead vegetation dripping water on their head, and Leyden took a drink. He immediately gasped as the liquor burned his mouth and throat.

Leyden cleared his throat with a liquid cough. "What the hell is this?"

"None of your sweet Toranguin crap, I can guarantee you that," Hawkwood said. "Umlivik Four Firewater, I believe it's called."

"Great." He took another hit. "What's the casualty count?"

"Zia is dead," Hawkwood said. "Hit by a pulse charge when he charged a Taranazuka position." Hawkwood contemplated the flask for a moment before taking a quick slug. "If he had learned caution as well as he learned weaponry, he could have been good enough to join the League." He shook his head.

"Who else?"

"Holmes and Bertelsmann missing," Hawkwood said. "Holmes may have been caught in one of the Dragon explosions. Bertelsmann just seems to have disappeared. At least five Guelph dead, nine Taranazuka mercs, and five of the Ghibelline. Three other Taranazuka are missing. Nouvé and a couple Guelph are out chasing down Shinsato."

"Braga?"

"I watched a Saar dismember him. Can't say I minded."

"What about the Saar, then?" Leyden asked.

"As best we can figure, the Taranazuka killed three of them, but more than that were hit. Who knows how badly."

Leyden, wiping water from his head and face, tried to look back at the platform. Still no sign of the Iksillas. "Let's hope the Saar don't have an honor code, equal payment in blood."

Hawkwood grunted.

"What happens now?" Leyden asked. "Seven more cycles and two lightships show up. Ours and theirs."

Hawkwood contemplated the smoking encampment. "Tirun and I talked about this. We thought we might release at least the civilians, the Taranazuka researchers, on parole, and let them go back to their own ship. The surviving mercs will come with us on the Balliol.

"Don't," Leyden said. "Keep everyone. Even if it gets crowded. Send the Taranazuka lightship back with nothing."

Hawkwood looked puzzled. "Why?"

"The Taranazuka come, they sweep the planet with broadcast messages. They send probes, even drop search parties. . . nothing. No responses, no information of any kind — no way of knowing what happened. Which mean they have no way to construct an alternative narrative. The League, and JKH2, on the other hand, not only have the evidence and the captives, but time to get the story out first. Their story. Define the issues. Ensure that the Taranazuka violations and attacks remain the central focus. Avoid giving them the slightest opportunity to push any other version of what happened."

"What kind of story could they possibly tell anyway?"

Leyden took the flask for another drink and coughed again. Firewater wasn't an exaggeration. "That Eëlios II confirms the suspicion that the League has apparently hidden the existence of a Ronin planet from the Illium. All part of some kind of League-JKH2 conspiracy. Of course, they'll try that anyway, but we'll have been there first, with our own story and our own evidence."

Hawkwood pondered. "Fair point."

Leyden looked around for any sign of the Iksillas. Nothing. "And you?"

"Collect whatever evidence we can," he said. "Take it back to the League and find out what happened. Not something that I ever expected to do."

"The League couldn't stay immune to the chaebols forever. Like it or not, you're going to have to learn the political game. You will need allies."

"Such as you?"

"Not me. Verlaine. He could prove to be invaluable, especially in exploring connections between the League and the chaebols."

"Verlaine," Hawkwood repeated skeptically.

Leyden paced back and forth. Where the hell were the Iksillas?

"What about the Eëlios plant?" Leyden asked. "What happens with our secret to a long and happy life?"

Hawkwood shrugged. "Not going to be a secret much longer. Most of the plant and genetic material go to high-security labs on Rigel Prime and New Kirov. Jointly controlled by JKH2 and the League. Kee says it will be many years before we begin to understand the biochemical reactions that translate into extended life spans."

"The Guelph may be right," Leyden said. "You want to live a long time? Stay on Eëlios and don't fall."

Leyden heard a sudden rustling sound in the smoke and mist; he began running back to the platform with the wounded, Hawkwood close behind. The Iksillas had returned, twelve of them, but looking so distorted that at first Leyden thought they had all suffered severe head injuries. A moment later, he realized that they cheek pouches were distended to the maximum with chewed-up carpal vine.

As he watched, An San Kee, Chapandagura and the Guelph unwrapped the bandages and wraps on Sylla, Tirun, and the other wounded. The Iksillas scrambled onto the bodies of the wounded and disgorged their head-full collections of masticated carpal-vine paste. Leyden expected the smell to be foul, but it wasn't; instead, it evoked the memory of his recovery from the first Saar attack with a force that made him stumble to his knees beside Sylla.

"Is that what the Iksillas did to me?" he asked Kee, who was busy smearing the paste into Sylla's shoulder and back with a gauze pad.

"Yes," Kee said, not looking up. "That was the moment when Twen apparently picked you out."

"Here, let me do that," Leyden said. "Go help the others."

"Just work the paste in gently and see that the wound is completely covered." Kee handed him several pads and left.

As he worked, he noticed Sylla's eyes flutter open. "Leyden," she whispered. "You must leave. I. . ."

Leyden stopped and took her hand. "Don't talk. And anyway, I'm not leaving. It's time for you to sleep now, and dream."

A Guelph appeared and together they covered Sylla's eyes with a cloth strip and inserted a short breathing tube in her mouth.

A large blue bee dropped out of the mist and landed on Sylla's ear. It immediately crawled down to her shoulder, smeared in paste. Leyden sat back. A second, third, dozens, then hundreds more appeared.

"I love you," Leyden whispered as Sylla disappeared under a buzzing, blue curtain of sky bees.

♦

Only later, as he stood up, with Sylla's torso coated in bees, did Leyden notice the two Guelph guards standing at Sylla's head and feet.

"What's going on?" he asked before realizing that neither had translator implants. At the edge of the platform, he notice Hawkwood listening to Nouvé, who abruptly turned and left.

Leyden joined him. "What?"

Hawkwood looked grave. "Apparently Sylla is under some kind of arrest."

"You're kidding. For what?"

"Betraying her sacred vows to Headman Cleanth. I believe that was the phrase Nouvé used."

"What the hell does that mean?"

"I think it means she had the bad judgment to sleep with you. And as the Headman's consort, the traditional Eëlian sentence for unfaithfulness is apparently quite clear."

Leyden waited. "Yes?"

"Death."

44 ARAMANTHIAN WINE

Leyden waited out Sylla's recovery on the edge of the Guelph settlement, no longer bothering with his Illium-issue sleeping hutch, but installing his bedding and kit in a mat of musk willow branches. To remain as isolated as possible, he did not visit Sylla as she remained unconscious under her cloud of sky bees. He even refused an invitation to attend the tribunal that heard charges against Shinsato, captured after a long chase. Shinsato had surrendered when two of his Ghibelline followers were picked off by vengeful Saar who seemed to have learned the Guelph-Ghibelline distinction easily enough when it mattered.

On most days, Leyden worked with An San Kee and others to help inventory the extensive collection of bio samples and prepare for the return to the Illium. Avoiding contact with the Guelph proved relatively easy because Cleanth announced publicly that Leyden no longer represented Trans-Illium in its negotiations with Eëlios.

Late in a sleep cycle, Leyden lay on his mat, staring up at a low ceiling of knotted vines, the scented air so evocative of Sylla that he felt as though she might appear. He blinked; not Sylla, but Nausicca, standing before him in tears, accompanied by Chácon, of all people, who came inside with her but stood silently by the entrance.

He took her hand. "What has happened? How is Sylla?"

"She is well," Nausicca whispered. "Her wounds are almost healed. The bees have left."

"The good news," Leyden said. "What else?"

"She has been placed under guard." Nausicca began weeping again; Chácon started toward her but Nausicca shook her head at him and he stopped.

"What happens now?" Leyden asked.

Nausicca wiped her tears. "They say Cleanth will call another tribunal, like the one for Shinsato." She took a deep breath. "They say the verdict will be the same. Death."

"And what of Cleanth himself?"

"He has said that the laws of the Guelph must be obeyed." Nausicca turned away and this time she fell suddenly into Chácon's arms with a violent fit of crying. He glanced at Leyden, then looked down, murmuring and stroking Nausicca's hair.

Chácon had been their ironman throughout the expedition, the consummate veteran, and Leyden recalled him saying, more than once, that this was his last mission. But Nausicca? He had missed that completely.

When she had recovered somewhat, she looked over at Leyden. "We know the guards, and some of us can visit her. You could go and see her."

Leyden thought for a moment. "No. I don't think so. Just tell her that I'm here, that I'm thinking of her every moment of every day."

What he didn't say was that he needed to be removed and rational right now — and very careful in every move and gesture he made.

Chácon finally spoke, still stroking Nausicca's hair. "We are all thinking of her and doing everything to protect her."

◆

During the next sun cycle, Hawkwood stopped Leyden as he walked back after hours of packing Eëlian samples for transport.

"The negotiations with Cleanth have gone well enough?" Leyden said.

"Reasonably. Nothing like victory and the prospect of wealth to encourage agreement." Hawkwood pulled out his flask and offered it to Leyden. "Amber ale this time. Tushangura Gold, I believe it's called, from the Taranazuka's own supplies."

Hawkwood must have just pulled the flask from a stream or pond fed directly from the rain, because it still tasted cool, a rare luxury on Eëlios. He took a second, longer drink.

They walked in silence. Leyden itched; he had only a few more day's supplies of caälyx lotion.

"This question of the woman, Sylla, has become quite difficult," Hawkwood said finally.

"As I'm sure Tirun would attest," Leyden said, "my choice of women is not always prudent."

"I believe he mentioned something to that effect just yesterday. On the other hand, she is as much responsible for our survival as any other single person here."

"Let me guess," Leyden said. "You've tried to bring up the subject of Sylla in the negotiations and Cleanth has refused to hear of it."

"Sylla and Shinsato both," Hawkwood said. "We've tried to suggest that showing magnanimity to Shinsato would help win the loyalty of the Ghibelline."

"And?"

"Not buying," Hawkwood said. "And he won't even let Sylla's name be mentioned."

"I quite understand."

Hawkwood looked puzzled. "I don't think you do. All the signals I'm getting suggest that Cleanth intends to hold tribunals and execute Shinsato and several others. Including Sylla."

"I'm sure you're right," Leyden said. "Remember, Cleanth nearly lost it all. He needs to demonstrate his complete authority — to the Ghibelline and to his own followers, especially Nouvé."

Hawkwood looked at Leyden closely. "What's going on here? Isolating yourself, refusing opportunities to see the woman. You're playing a deeper game here, aren't you?"

Leyden took the flask back from Hawkwood and drank again. Cold beer would definitely improve living conditions around here.

"I would ask one favor of you, Tribune Hawkwood. Tell Headman Cleanth that I request the favor of a private meeting. Nothing official. Strictly an informal business proposition."

◆

Cleanth sat alone on an isolated platform decorated with the carved heads of Iksillas and Saar, and what Leyden now recognized as the stylized leaves of the Eëlios plant. The platform, at the end of a swaying bamboo bridge, hung at the edge of a vertical swath of light and sky that Leyden recognized as the opening for the Floaters to ascend through the canopy to the Eëlian settlements. The view of the rainforest was magnificent. Cleanth's retreat befitted his status as ruler of the high canopy: dramatic, regal, and very private.

"Please sit," Cleanth said, waving him to one of several chairs separated by small woven-bamboo table. His shaved head glistened with lotion, his face paint sharp edged and freshly applied. Although he exuded a new confidence, the narrow-eyed politician's expression remained unchanged from their first meeting.

"You wished to discuss certain business matters?" Cleanth said.

"Yes, Headman. I would like to talk with you of wine."

"Wine." Cleanth contemplated Leyden. "Ours or yours?"

"Both, actually," Leyden said, pushing a small package he had brought with him under his chair.

"Well then, perhaps we can begin with a sample of our poor local vintage."

Cleanth clapped and gave a quick hand gesture to an invisible figure on the other side of the bridge. Moments later, a server appeared with a flask and two anchorwood cups burnished to a high sheen. She poured a rose-colored liquid into the cups and backed away.

Cleanth watched her depart. "One of our better vintages, I've been told, but then I am no expert in these matters."

Cleanth lifted his cup. "So then, let us drink to our future together, Eëlios and the Illium."

Leyden raised his cup and they both drank.

"I appreciate this opportunity, Headman Cleanth," he said. "I know how heavy the burden of leadership must be upon you right now."

"Indeed. I trust you understand why it has not been possible for you to, uh, participate any longer in the talks between the Eëlian people and the Illium expedition."

"Of course. These are matters of state." Leyden noticed that Cleanth no longer spoke of himself as representing only the Guelph, but all of Eëlios. "I myself have had some small experience in such matters. Personal considerations must be put aside at times like these."

Cleanth sipped his wine and stroked the scars along his cheek. "You, perhaps, more than the others, seem to appreciate the nature of my new position. The decision to approve the execution of Shinsato was particularly difficult."

Leyden watched as Cleanth filled both their cups again. Glowbirds and small raptors careened through the open air before them, a combination of aerial ballet and dogfights. From beneath the cloud bank, far below, he heard the distant cough of a Saar.

"The matter of the woman is even more painful to me, on a personal level." Cleanth shifted in his seat. "You may have come here to plead for her. However, I must tell you that these are questions to be settled among the people of Eëlios themselves. Questions that involve the honor and heritage of Guelph and Ghibelline alike, for many generations."

"Of course."

"For this reason, I have chosen not to involve outsiders in such business." Cleanth paused for emphasis. "Such as yourself."

Leyden nodded in agreement. "I do not come because of the woman. I know the burden of high office weighs heavily on your shoulders. I do, however, wish to bring up another subject."

Cleanth looked at the table. "The wine?"

"Yes. In your zeal and commitment to the greater good of your people, perhaps you have forgotten to ensure your personal welfare, and that of your family as well."

Cleanth frowned. "What do you mean?"

"You, more so than anyone else, have remained consistently faithful to the vision of the future with Eëlios as part of the Illium. What was once a largely ignored world is now so much closer to the Illium Core. My understanding is that the Illium League has calculated that your cycle of the Selucid Swarm, and Eëlios, may stabilize at three standard years or less. Whether the Eëlios plant yields long life to off-worlders in the Illium is almost beside the point. You will now become a center of research, travel, and commerce. A thousand different links to the life and work of the Illium Archipelago."

Cleanth leaned back and swirled the wine in his cup. "I am familiar with these facts. I have spent much of the past cycle studying the data from your Quanta — in preparation for the Illium's return."

"Most commendable," Leyden said.

From what Sylla had told him, Cleanth had skimmed a few summaries and headlines over the years, along with a smattering of the feature and celebrity stories that appealed to him. Popular biographies of political leaders and erotic holos were also high on his list.

Leyden leaned forward, as though imparting privileged information. "Headman Cleanth, as you know, this is a time of great wealth and opportunity. But it is also a time of great danger. Even now, here on Eëlios, there are no guarantees in political life, as I'm sure you realize. These uncertainties will only increase with the coming age of the Illium League and the chaebols. We have seen it happen on world after world."

Cleanth refilled their cups. "Indeed. This is so."

"May I speak to you all candor, Headman Cleanth?" Leyden said.

Cleanth opened his arms in an expansive gesture. "Of course."

"Let me suggest, Headman, that to discharge your duties for the people of Eëlios with confidence and strength, you first need to provide for yourself."

"How do you propose to do that?"

Leyden held up his cup. "Aramanthian wine."

Cleanth scratched his scarred cheek. "I recall you yourself saying that our Aramanth berries produce only a . . . a *vin ordinaire*. . . an adequate table wine, at best."

"Doesn't matter," Leyden said, feeling a little dizzy. "The wine may not rival our more celebrated vintages, but almost anything associated with Eëlios will, I predict, shortly become a sensation inside the Illium. Why not wine? The secret is marketing. *Eëlian Rainforest Red. High-Canopy Tropical White.* Made from grapes nourished by greatest rainforest the universe has ever known. And who knows what health and longevity benefits such wine might confer?"

Leyden could feel his own world begin to revolve a bit.

"Just how would this. . . arrangement work?" Cleanth asked.

"I suggest that you form a private company with exclusive rights to market and sell Aramanthian wine in the Illium. You have already, in your wisdom, given all marketing rights for Eëlios teas and coffees to the entire community. The wine, perhaps, should be yours. A small enough reward for the bountiful future you are bringing to this world."

"And you to run this company, for a share of the profits?"

"That was my thought," Leyden said. "Perhaps a share of, say, twenty percent? I have already spoken to Verlaine, and he has agreed that, if you were to authorize such a venture, he would see that JKH2 provides the necessary capital for marketing and distribution. And if you so choose, he would take cuttings to vineyards back in the Illium as well. All owned exclusively by you."

Cleanth regarded Leyden in silence. "Twenty percent seems a little high, especially when we consider the fees and expenses associated with Verlaine and his chaebol. A ninety-ten split might be more appropriate."

"Done." Leyden picked up the package under his chair and pulled out a single slender bottle that had survived the entire Eëlios venture inside his expedition backpack.

"Well, what have we here?" said Cleanth in a tone that marked the first outward sign of the wine's effect on him.

"One of the finest vintages ever produced anywhere in the Illium. A Delium Ghahan Forty-Seven. A small gift to seal our agreement."

"Excellent idea," Cleanth said, and rose, a trifle unsteadily, to signal for fresh cups as Leyden pulled the cork. The wine glowed a deep purple red in the half-light of the Eëlian canopy. Its bouquet — rich with the flavors of soils, tannins, plum and oak — evoked Leyden's exile years on Delium Ghahan, in another time, when he had imagined an entirely different future for himself.

They sat in silence, drinking Leyden's last tangible connection to his old life, contemplating the rainforest vista before them.

"One point puzzles me," Cleanth said finally. "Why have you suggested Verlaine to serve as the agent back in the Illium? Why not yourself?"

"As a member of JKH2, Verlaine has connections and resources far beyond my own." Leyden paused. "There is another reason. I wish to remain here. On Eëlios."

"Indeed?" Cleanth said, clearly surprised. "I have heard nothing of this. Only An San Kee has made such a request."

"I have told no one yet," Leyden said. "I wished to seek your counsel first, and your permission."

"Please continue."

"Let me suggest that, in remaining here, I could serve you, and Eëlios, in future negotiations with the Illium."

"That might well be true," Cleanth said. "But that cannot be your only reason for staying."

"It is not, Headman Cleanth." Leyden set down his wine cup and ran his fingers through his hair. "Let me propose one more step that would help strengthen your leadership position among the people of Eëlios."

"Ah?" Cleanth's voice sounded both wary and intrigued, about the most Leyden could ask for at this critical moment.

Leyden said, "A marriage between a representative of the Illium and one of your people. A tangible, living symbol of the alliance between your world and the Illium."

Cleanth scratched his cheek. "And who would these individuals be?"

"Myself and Sylla."

"Why am I not surprised? A most ill-timed gesture, Leyden, I must say." Leyden said nothing.

"You and Sylla! Ha!" Cleanth glared at him. 'It's better to be feared than loved.' You think I have not read your political thinkers?"

Leyden started to speak but Cleanth held up a hand. "A consort who is unfaithful threatens the authority of the leader. Such matters must be dealt with decisively. It is the Guelph way, the Eëlian way — and not a matter for off-worlders!"

"I understand," Leyden said. "This is a matter of state. But let me suggest that her execution would not necessarily stop the people from talking, and remembering."

Cleanth sneered. "Let them talk. Gossip with the glowbirds. No concern of mine."

"There is another side, however," Leyden said carefully. "One, perhaps to be considered before a final decision."

Cleanth grunted. "Another side."

"Think what would happen if you were to permit our marriage. It would be seen by all as a sign of your forbearance and strength. A sign of your belief in the future of the Eëlios-Illium alliance."

"It would hardly be a sign of strength to change my decision regarding Sylla now."

Leyden wiped his face; for a moment the Eëlian heat felt suffocating. "On the contrary. To change a decision under pressure is one thing. You face no such pressures from any one or any faction. This is your moment of complete triumph. Were you to spare her life and permit this marriage, you would be seen as overlooking a personal injury for the greater good of your people. It would be seen not only as an act of strength, but of statesmanship and vision."

Leyden opened his mouth to continue, then stopped. His throat constricted, and he felt like he was drowning in the humid air.

He had played his final card.

45 TEA FOR THREE

The light, dappled by the breeze-blown vegetation, played across the platform and the two motionless figures facing each other. Leyden idly watched the glint of sunlight off the high sheen of his wine cup and wondered if he should order a selection of glass and stemware for the next Illium expedition. Glowbirds called out, looking almost colorless in the bright air, and he could hear the invisible rustle of Iksillas hunting insects in the foliage. Sylla's image rose unbidden before him, despite his efforts to focus exclusively on Cleanth.

His final gambit had apparently failed. Leyden was not really surprised. At some level, Cleanth may have appreciated the logic of Leyden's argument and seen the advantages of securing an Illium-Eëlios alliance through marriage. Yet clearly the threat to his authority by a publicly unfaithful consort trumped any such calculation.

Leyden closed his eyes; he had come close. He knew that because Cleanth had tolerated hearing him out — and because he had learned much more of Sylla's personal history in the dark hours at the base of the anchorwood tree. Early on, she had become one of Cleanth's many consorts. But once her talent as a healer and herbalist became clear, she was, for all practical purposes, released from his entourage to pursue her medical and biology training. In later years, even discreetly taking an occasional lover had not been a problem, although Sylla gave no further details.

It was, as politics were everywhere, a problem in managing perceptions. Power was the appearance of power — hardly a lesson that Leyden needed to relearn — but one that now appeared to doom Sylla.

He heard a rustling in the overhead branches and looked up to see Twen's familiar head, peering down at him like a small green gargoyle, unfurling his tongue in greeting. A second head popped through the foliage, Twon. Leyden blinked. Twon, Sylla's Iksillia? Two retainers appeared on the swaying bridge with Sylla between them, hands tied in front of her. She looked thin and exhausted, her shoulder and chest still bandaged. Cleanth stood and pointed. "Stay seated and do not speak, Leyden."

"Headman... I..."

"Do not speak," Cleanth repeated. "This is Eëlian business and you have no role in it. It is enough that I am allowing you to be present."

Leyden sat back as Sylla and the guards approached. She gave him only a quick, unreadable glance before Cleanth, still standing, gestured for her to be seated and her hands untied.

Cleanth looked them both over before signaling to the opposite end of the bridge for a procession of servants who cleared away the wine and brought out an elaborate tea service. No one spoke as a woman with tiny features and heavy makeup lifted the pot and poured for all three of them. Another woman, equally painted, took the top off a smaller, intricately carved bowl and sprinkled white Eëlian blossoms in each cup.

He noticed the second server, the flower lady, glance at Sylla and remembered Nausicca pointing her out once: Charisa, or something like that. Cleanth's new favorite. The women bowed and retreated.

Cleanth picked up his cup with the fingertips of both hands and blew across the surface. Leyden started to follow him but Sylla gave him a single, sharp shake of her head and he pulled back.

Cleanth blew again and slurped loudly before slumping down in his chair, his eyes darting from one to the other.

"I recall that I once permitted you and Nausicca the honor of being the Tea Masters," he said. "Despite the fact of your Ghibelline heritage."

"Yes, Headmen, you did."

"Many years ago. When we all were much younger. How the time slips away from us."

He laughed and slapped the table, as if jokes about aging were a novelty among the Eëlians. Tea slopped over the sides of their cups.

Sylla maintained a thin formality, not even pretending to be amused at his witticism. Nor did she cast her eyes modestly downward, but stared straight ahead, past his shoulder.

Leyden's arms twitched as he gripped the arms of the chair, imagining himself lunging across the table and ripping out Cleanth's throat. If he was lucky, all three of them would be dead in minutes; at least he would be relieved of the torture of sitting next to Sylla and being unable to touch or speak to her.

Cleanth, suddenly serious, glared at Sylla. "You are an itch I cannot scratch, woman. The two of you" — he waved in Leyden's direction — "are a question with only unsatisfactory answers."

He sat back, drumming his fingers, waiting for a response. For the first time Leyden wondered if Cleanth was hiding some considerable discomfort of his own.

Sylla said nothing.

"You may speak now."

"I am under sentence of death, Headman. I have no wish to discuss anything further. . . unless you are telling me that these are my last words before execution. Then I will speak."

Cleanth look positively exasperated, as though mention of her impending death were only an irritating distraction. "These were all affairs of state. . . and necessary at the time. You understand."

Leyden straightened up. *What was this?*

"I understanding nothing, Headman."

"Stop! Don't play the innocent with me, Sylla. You know damn well what I'm talking about."

Now Sylla chose to fold her hands in her lap and cast her eyes downward.

Cleanth squirmed in his chair, slurped more tea, stared up into the canopy, and generally behaved like a small boy whose punishment was to sit still. Through the open space, Leyden could see an advance guard of thin clouds that would thicken into a rainstorm within the next two hours.

"I may have released you to become a healer, Sylla, but I did not release you as a member of my household. That is known and understood by all."

Sylla neither moved nor raised her eyes.

Cleanth slapped the table in frustration. "Nevertheless, upon reflection, the situation has proven more complicated than it first appeared. It is possible that certain mistakes were made."

"Sir?" Sylla looked up.

"If we can come to an understanding on several questions, perhaps I can be persuaded to request a reconsideration of my previous decision, which could result in a conditional commutation. . . of some sort."

"Sir?" Sylla's tone remained unyielding.

Cleanth whacked his hard round belly instead of the table. "All right," he growled, looking over at Leyden for the first time. "There will be no execution. All right? You think I am fool enough to execute the one who summoned the Saar to defeat the Taranazuka and the Ghibelline?"

He grimaced. "Besides, we never seem to have enough trained healers." He sounded more like a tired bureaucrat than a triumphant conqueror.

Sylla sagged in her chair and finally permitted herself a glance at Leyden. "Most gracious, Headman."

"Sylla," Leyden said.

"Silence!" Cleanth roared at him. "Neither move nor speak or I may reconsider."

He turned back to Sylla. "This off-worlder, Leyden, has brought me several interesting proposals. I share this with you only because you will undoubtedly learn of them later."

Sylla looked at Leyden with open curiosity. "He has?"

"Among them is the idea that he remain on Eëlios with the title of Interim Illium Consul."

"I. . ."

Cleanth held up his hand, savoring the moment. "That's not all. Along with a private commercial venture — which you will also hear about — he has suggested that a formal union between the two of you, a marriage, would be in the long-term interest of Eëlios as it negotiates its place within the Illium."

"I. . . I know nothing of this. We have not talked. . ."

"You have not accepted his offer of marriage?" Cleanth said in mock surprise. "Perhaps I have been misled on this point."

"I have not talked to Leyden since — "

"Just as well," Cleanth said briskly. "Had you spent more time together, planning this, I might have felt less magnanimous that I do now."

Cleanth squinted at the approaching clouds. "In any event, I remain unconvinced, despite Leyden's shrewd analysis, that your union, formal or not, serves our interests in any way whatsoever. I am more inclined to ship him back with the others."

Leyden rubbed his eyes. All three of them knew full well that Sylla had saved Cleanth's fat ass. Now, from his point of view, he had saved her from his own arbitrary death sentence. All even. God loves politicians.

But there was more going on here. If Cleanth truly found both of them such an inconvenience, he could easily have found a way to commute her sentence and order him to leave Eëlios with little public notice. No, this was something else, as if he wanted to test Sylla further.

Cleanth stroked his hard little belly. "One problem is that this Leyden knows nothing of the realities of life here, despite all that has happened. I suspect he hasn't even heard our best-known saying. *Love is short but life is long.*"

Sylla offered a weak smile. "No, I don't believe he does."

Cleanth grinned. "Well, there it is."

Leyden could see that Sylla, having regained her composure, was fuming at the unilateral proposals he had made to Cleanth, treating her as if she were one of the bargaining points, like wine and coffee concessions. But that was the point, he wanted to scream at her. Make it a package deal. Business and politics. The careful calculations of hard-headed men who understood how the world operates.

What was the alternative? Tell Cleanth, already threatened by the public knowledge of their relationship, how much he was in love with his former consort? For the same reason, he had stayed away from her during her recovery, so that Cleanth would have no cause to believe that they had conspired in making his proposals.

His offer to marry Sylla as a way to secure an Illium-Eëlian alliance had to come as a complete shock to her — and Cleanth had to witness her reaction. That was the theory anyway.

Cleanth seemed in no hurry, happy to prolong the moment. He turned to Leyden. "Despite my heavy responsibilities, I did find time to consider your situation, Leyden. And I asked a friend of yours to assist in a Quanta search for me."

"A friend of mine?" Leyden dared to speak and Cleanth didn't react. Having too much fun.

"Your companion Verlaine—when we were settling the business of the licenses for coffee and juices. I asked if anywhere in the Illium, you had myths of mortals and immortals falling in love, much like ours of the sun god Naryl. Do you know the story?"

Leyden shook his head

Cleanth continued. "He once saw a woman, a mortal, so beautiful that he deserted the sky to make love to her, thereby infuriating Nevea, his twin sister. Nevea proceeded to punish the poor woman in a very special way and. . . well, you'll have to have Sylla tell you about it."

Sylla watched Cleanth like a raptor following its prey.

"I shall. And did Verlaine find such a tale for you?"

Cleanth beamed. "He did. And shared it with Sylla, at my request. From an ancient time on your ancient Earth. Told it to Sylla just the other day. It seems a goddess of the sky or the sunrise, I forget the name. . ."

"Eos," she said.

"Yes, Eos. Anyway she fell for a mortal, a prince named. . . what was it, Sylla?"

"Tithonus."

"Tithonus, that's right. Well, the goddess Eos was so taken with this fellow that she asked the king of the gods. . ."

"Zeus."

"Zeus, yes. She asked Zeus to grant Tithonus immortality." Cleanth chuckled. "But as you might imagine, things didn't work out well, as is often the case with these couplings."

"Fascinating. How does it end?" Leyden asked. He could see Scylla barely able to resist rolling her eyes.

"Well, it seems that Zeus was not pleased at all with Eos's little affair, so he granted Tithonus immortality all right, but not eternal youth. You can imagine the rest. Poor Tithonus grew old, very old indeed, to the point where he was demented and babbling. But still immortal. Eos, out of pity, or because she couldn't stand him anymore, turned him into a grasshopper. Ah, but an immortal grasshopper!"

Cleanth roared with laughter.

"Striking story," Leyden said.

"It is indeed, Leyden. It is indeed."

Sylla looked unamused. "With due respect, Headman, Leyden may be mortal, but I am neither a god nor immortal."

"Perhaps not, my dear. But a story with a lesson that we might all do well to ponder."

Sylla said, "However these fantasy tales may turn out, similar unions have already taken place. Not on ancient Earth, but here. Now."

Cleanth frowned. "What?"

"There have already been several of these unions between off-worlders and Eëlians, Guelph and Ghibelline. Leyden and I are not alone."

"I have not been made aware of any such developments."

"And at least two pregnancies."

"What! I have given no permission — " Cleanth stopped, aware of the ridiculousness of his statement. He cleared his throat. Leyden had the unmistakable sense that their subterranean negotiation was continuing.

"Who are they?"

"One is my sister. Nausicca."

Leyden rubbed his eyes. Chácon hadn't wasted any time.

"The father?"

"One of the soldiers. He is at the end of his tour and wishes to remain, at least through the next cycle."

Cleanth laugh sounded like a bark. "The promises of an off-worlder."

"Either way, there will be a child."

Leyden took the opportunity to scrape his chair closer to Scylla's. "Like it or not," he said finally, "the transformation of Eëlios has begun."

Cleanth ignored him. "My impression is that you have some ideas concerning these children," he said to Scylla.

"The mother or father may be Guelph or Ghibelline, but their children will be neither."

"The mothers will decide."

"Several women have chosen off-worlders — this is true — some of whom are leaving. Others hope to stay. But one Taranazuka researcher, a woman, is pregnant as well and wishes to stay with the father and work with An San Kee."

"We just went through an invasion and civil war," Cleanth said. "When did everyone find time for all this lovemaking?"

Leyden said, "Nothing like the prospect of death to. . ."

Cleanth waved him off. "Why am I asking these questions of you two — of all people."

He turned back to Sylla. "I have granted you your life. Now you're trying to lead me somewhere I don't want to go."

"Headman, I am simply saying that these new mixed families can be neither Guelph nor Ghibelline, but Eëlian only. They could be the beginnings of a new clan that closes old divisions. Such unity will be invaluable when the Illium returns again – as it will. And as Leyden has said, they will return in greater numbers and influence than before."

"Quit parroting each other, it's unbecoming." Cleanth slouched and drummed his fingers, assuming the calculating politician's gaze that Leyden had seen in their first meeting.

Leyden shifted his chair close enough that he could reach for Sylla's hand under the table. She pulled it away.

"You *bargained* for me?" she whispered fiercely.

"For both of us," he muttered back.

"I am not one of your. . . bargaining chips."

"Sylla, of course not. You have to understand—"

Cleanth chuckled. "Oh dear, trouble in paradise already? And so soon."

"Let me explain. . ." Leyden started to say, but he wasn't quite sure if he was trying to explain to Sylla, Cleanth, or himself.

"Silence!" Cleanth ordered. "The matter is decided."

EPILOGUE: RETURN

A great tearing consumed the sky. It had come before and would again. In contrast to the swell and rumble of an Eëlian thunderstorm, the sound vibrated like a massive, invisible tuning fork — the arrival of the Illium's sky hooks.

Twin nanotube cables descended from the clouds, swinging like pendulums in the planet's high winds, glowing blue-red in the light of the Ginn. The assemblage of Eëlians and Illium worlders waited where the rainforest canopy opened to the sky, standing on makeshift rope platforms as the cables writhed downward like eager snakes. Twenty thousand kilometers above them, the Planetary Shuttle Vehicle of the Illium Lightship *Balliol* hovered in geosynchronous orbit.

For frontier worlds without spaceports or lift facilities, sky hooks — magnetic-acceleration vehicles running on high-tensile cables made of carbon nanofibers — proved the most cost-efficient way of retrieving small exploration teams or combat units. In the case of Eëlios, the combination of changeable weather and unstable treetops presented the greatest problem. But after several attempts, expedition members managed to capture and secure the cables to the topmost level of anchorwood branches. The cables hummed in the steady wind as the shuttle energized the cables, and with Nevea setting and Naryl rising, the two first mag cars appeared, skimming down the cables like huge, translucent raindrops.

Hawkwood loaded the first contingent: several mercenaries and a collection of Taranazuka prisoners. All of the mercs turned and looked back to where Chácon and Nausicca stood. With a high-pitched whine, the cable cars accelerated upward. At the same moment, two empty but identical cars dropped from the shuttle hovering invisibly in near space. The process continued for the next two hours.

As Naryl reached its apogee and storm clouds gathered for their daily assault, Tirun, Hawkwood, and Verlaine prepared to board the final car. Leyden stood beside An San Kee, who had been given permission by both Cleanth and Tirun to remain. Leyden slowly shook hands with all three of them in turn.

Tirun looked at Leyden with the same expression that Leyden recalled from their first meeting in the prison on Rigel Prime.

"Your choice in women worked well for us in the end," Tirun said. "Maybe it will work out for you personally too."

"One can hope," Leyden said.

"I will see that you are registered as the official Illium Archipelago consul for Eëlios," Tirun said. "At a minimum, that should help your standing here, with Cleanth and the others."

Leyden nodded.

Verlaine embraced him and pounded his back. "High Canopy Enterprises. Coffee and wine. Unbeatable combination."

"No doubt," Leyden said. In the end, they had decided to divide the wine venture with fifty percent for Cleanth, forty percent for Verlaine, minus marketing costs, and ten percent for Leyden and Sylla.

Hawkwood turned to Leyden. "Toranga to Eëlios. A long, strange journey."

"Indeed," Leyden said.

"One that might not be over, I think, for either of us."

"Perhaps."

Hawkwood paused before entering the capsule. "I wish you success here, Leyden."

"And you too, Tribune Hawkwood, in your work with the Illium League."

Leyden stepped to the end of the platform. The cable lines energized and the mag-lev units spun up their revolutions to a painful, high-pitched whine. The cars leapt upward. Moments later, explosive bolts severed the cables from their anchorwood base, retracting at almost the same speed as the cable cars.

Leyden watched as the clouds enveloped the silver, blister-shaped vehicles and disappeared. A volley of rain spattered on his upturned face.

As the rainfall intensified, he turned away from the sky and looked down along the soaked and swaying rope bridge, down into the shadows of the rainforest, and into the dark, dark eyes of his love.

ACKNOWLEDGMENTS

Special thanks to one early and one late reader: My older son, Kevin, for his careful review of the first draft many years ago. And to good friend Terri Rea, a fine painter and sharp-eyed proofreader. Thanks as well to Brian Prager for saving me from some serious orbital-distance errors. Finally, my deepest appreciation to my wife, Debby, for serving every editorial role one can name: from grammar and substance to book design, page layout, and cover illustration.

ABOUT THE AUTHOR

Howard Cincotta is a freelance writer who served as an editor and writer with the U.S. Information Agency and the State Department for many years. At USIA, he worked on magazines for Africa and the former Soviet Union and directed a special publications unit. He later headed an electronic-media office and wrote speeches for State Department officials.

Cincotta's thirty-two-page booklet *What is Democracy?* has been translated into more than forty languages. His short stories have appeared in a number of literary journals.

Cincotta grew up in California and graduated from the University of California at Berkeley. He lives with his wife, artist Deborah Conn, in Falls Church, Virginia. He has two sons and a daughter.